MIDWINTER
FOLK

MIDWINTER FOLK

REBEKAH CLAYTON

Matador
9 Priory Business Park,
Wistow Road, Kibworth Beauchamp,
Leicestershire. LE8 0RX
Tel: 0116 279 2299
Email: books@troubador.co.uk
Web: www.troubador.co.uk/matador
Twitter: @matadorbooks

ISBN 978 1838590 642

British Library Cataloguing in Publication Data.
A catalogue record for this book is available from the British Library.

Printed and bound by CPI Group (UK) Ltd, Croydon, CR0 4YY
Typeset in 12pt Sabon MT by Troubador Publishing Ltd, Leicester, UK

Matador is an imprint of Troubador Publishing Ltd

MIX
Paper from
responsible sources
FSC
www.fsc.org
FSC® C013604

For Katie and Rohan, my dream children.
May you always chase white rabbits.

In memory of Betty and Ricky:
you taught me to love.

CONTENTS

PART ONE

Unreal City

1

SHADOW

<hr />

IN THE DEEP, WINTER TWILIGHT SNOW WAS falling and, with each silver-soft footstep, Rowan caught her breath. She knew that she was being followed.

A sensation, thin and spiderish, prickled at the back of her neck. She had felt it before. Something was close behind, breathing, watching, its pace slow and deliberate. Sometimes she thought it might be a man, and sometimes a dog. But there was never any sign, or sound, no crunch of feet on snow, no tell-tale footprint.

She paused, her breath misting on the icy air. Whatever it was, it wasn't like the others: the poor grey people, stooped against the bitter cold, who hurried past as if they were invisible. No, this was different. There was a sense, a *scent* of something strange and far away. And, if she was quick, she might just catch it. Heart pounding, she spun on her heel and stared hard through the dancing flakes.

But it had gone.

Before her were the frozen city streets, half buried by drifts; traffic lights standing blind and purposeless; pedestrians trudging through deep snow. London, in its shroud of soft white silence, seemed like a city of ghosts.

Suddenly, powerful headlights dazzled, a grinding engine shattered the stillness and a shower of flakes rained down upon her, making Rowan gasp and splutter. A huge snowplough lurched around the corner, trundling its way past the formless, white humps of abandoned cars.

Rowan shook herself free of the icy particles swirling in its wake and looked again. Did it even exist? This *thing*. Was it all in her mind? She steadied herself against a wall, feeling sick, and closed her eyes.

Now the voices would come.

It happened like this: the peculiar feeling of being followed, then voices. She had tried to ignore them; after all, only mad people heard voices, didn't they? At once soft carillons shivered through her head: strange, unearthly, pure. Where did they come from? Where? She gazed up into the star-flecked sky.

"Look where you're going!"

A man with a big, black dog jostled past, forcing Rowan to one side. The dog snarled, baring yellow teeth.

"I'm s-s-sorry," Rowan stuttered and stumbled into the path of a lady with a walking stick.

"Mind yourself, dearie."

Rowan, mumbling a second apology, crept back to the shelter of the wall. The voices were still inside her head, clearer now, like flowing water. She gazed at the straggling lines of people tramping back and forth, heads down. How could they *not* hear something so sweet, and so sad? For a moment she forgot the bitter cold, the churning fear.

But the voices were fading. A last few silver notes shimmered and then she was plunged back into the dull twilight. Rowan stamped her numbing feet, shifted her school bag to the other shoulder and turned towards home.

On the corner of the high street a newspaper man, half crouching over a brazier of hot coals, bawled out the latest.

"Big freeze set to last 'til April! Country running out of fuel."

His sandwich-boards trumpeted headlines: "Midwinter Madness", "Blizzard Britain", "Snow, Snow, Go Away!"

A small crowd had gathered.

"Worst winter on record. Power cuts threatened," he sang out, brandishing a folded paper at an old lady who seemed to be wrapped from head to toe in woollen scarves. "That'll be fifty-five pence, my darling."

"I reckon it's worse than the winters of 'forty-seven' and 'sixty-three' put together," the old lady said. "Thought we had it bad then, but the past few weeks, oh my Gawd!"

"We're living like Eskimos," chipped in a man with a frosted beard. "Bleedin' government should do something about it!"

"They say another ice age is coming."

"The Gulf Stream has slowed down, that's what it is," responded a bespectacled young man.

This last comment caused a chorus of protest: "What do them bloomin' climate people know anyway!"

Rowan hurried on. Grown-ups always seemed to be arguing. No one could agree why the blizzards had come. She'd seen coverage on the news. The entire country was buried under a thick blanket of snow. Trees groaned after each fresh fall. Telephone lines and electricity cables snapped like guitar strings. Even the sea was beginning to freeze, with ice floes in the Channel.

Suddenly, Rowan stumbled. She felt a nauseating wave of panic. It was there! The thing! She could feel it, watching. And she wanted to get away.

Rowan began to run, as best she could through the snow; past shops, bright with lights and Christmas decorations. She wished she could tell someone about what was happening, about the crazy, scary thoughts in her head – but who? Usually she would have poured her heart out to her best friend, Jashan, or Mum. But this was so out of the ordinary, so *weird*. Jaz would think she was joking. Being followed? Hearing things! "Get a grip, Rowan!" he would say. "Fine if you're a kid of five, but we're Year Sixes now."

Once Rowan would have told Luke. She used to tell him everything. But Luke had changed, turned strange, fallen in with a new crowd of friends. She shivered again. Luke had been the best brother in the world, always there for her, and they'd grown closer since Finn, their dad, had left. But now everything was different. Rowan's heart felt heavy, as if there was a stone in her chest.

The entrance to her flat was on the high street, sandwiched between Mr Rafik's newsagent shop and a dingy off-licence. As she approached the door, it started to snow more heavily. Rowan pulled the key from her coat pocket and, fumbling with gloved fingers, tried to slot it into the lock.

Suddenly, a hand thudded against the door.

"Got the time, sweetheart?" a voice wheezed into her ear.

A man slouched against the doorjamb. His hair was patchy, like moulting fur and she could smell the rotten sweetness of his breath.

Another voice, drawing close, said, "Rather late to be out on a winter's night, for a kid like you."

This one wore a pin-stripe suit and his abundant hair was slicked back with strongly perfumed gel.

"Not safe to be out after dark, is it, Reginald?"

"Oh no, Rafe. Not safe at all."

Their eyes glittered.

Rowan felt a pulse of fear. What did they want? She thrust the key back into her pocket and dug for her wristwatch beneath several cuffs.

"It… it's half past four," she said, her voice small and dry.

"Half four, Rafe, half four," echoed the one with stinking breath.

Rafe gazed into Rowan's eyes, lips glistening in imitation of a smile.

"Shouldn't you be getting in, my dear? It's too cold for standing about on doorsteps."

Rowan's heart began to pound. She didn't want to open the door. The men might barge their way in, try to steal something. They might do anything. And *look* at them – they weren't even wearing coats! Snowflakes dusted their heads and shoulders. They must be frozen; why weren't they shivering?

"I'm waiting for someone," she said.

"But you might as well wait in the warm." Rafe's voice was soft.

"My brother will be here soon." An edge of defiance crept into her voice.

Reginald began to laugh, a snickering, high-pitched sound.

"Your brother, oh *yes*," said Rafe. "So *nice* to have a brother. Isn't it, Reg?"

"He's called Luke," said Rowan, desperate, wondering how on earth she could make these horrible men go away.

"*He's called Luke*," Reg mimicked.

"Shut it, Ragtooth!" growled Rafe; his beady eyes glittered beneath the streetlights. "Now, missy, don't you think you'd better open the door? You'll catch your *death* out here. I saw you put the key away in your pocket."

He looked her in the eye and a quiver ran down into her stomach.

"Just there, if I'm not mistaken."

Sharp-nailed fingers reached towards her. Rowan watched in horror, wanting to knock the hand away. Scream, she told herself. Run away! Do something!

Close up, she could see the cracked, broken nails, the black hairs on the back of his hand. Why couldn't she move? In a moment he would have the key. Sharp teeth flashed behind thin, wet lips. Narrow eyes burned.

She struggled, struggled, but could not raise her hand.

2

WHISPERS

———◆———

THE DIRTY FINGERS SNATCHED AT HER. Rowan stumbled back blindly. There was a cry. She felt a firm hand clasp her shoulder, gently turn her around.

"Rowan!"

It was Mr Rafik, the shopkeeper, panting asthmatically, his long coat flapping about his ankles.

"Ah," he wheezed, pushing his glasses up his nose. "I hoped I might catch you."

Mutterings, hisses of frustration, receded into the darkness.

Mr Rafik pulled a folded newspaper from his pocket and waved it in the air.

"We've had a delivery, at long last," he said. "I'm sure your mother will be pleased. My dear wife said to me, 'Now, if you see little Ro...'"

Rowan barely heard the words. She was peering past Mr Rafik's flapping arm, trying to see where the men had gone, but they had melted into the shadows.

"Rowan?" Mr Rafik's smile had vanished. "Are you quite well? You look so pale."

"It's those men," she said, shivering.

"Men? What men?"

"They were trying to get into our flat."

"Robbers? Thieves? You alarm me!"

A car horn blasted further up the street. For a fleeting moment two shadowy figures were caught in the headlights of a sturdy Land Rover.

"Look, look," she said, clutching at Mr Rafik's sleeve. "It's them!"

The car was braking, skidding violently. Rowan cried out, "They'll be hit!"

But the pair, twisting their bodies, suddenly sprang clear of danger. The Land Rover veered sharply, sounding its horn. Deft as acrobats, the men had landed at the feet of a dark figure with a large snarling dog.

"Look, Mr Rafik!"

"What's all this hubbub? Oh, my poor eyes..." he groaned, squinting into the gloom.

The dog owner grabbed one of the men by the scruff of the neck. The dog barked wildly, straining against its chain. At that moment two huge army trucks trundled by, obscuring Rowan's view, and by the time they had lumbered on all three men and the dog had vanished.

Rowan shuddered.

"You're shivering. You'll catch a chill!" exclaimed Mr Rafik. "Home, child, at once!"

With shaking hands, Rowan found her key and unlocked the front door. It opened onto a stairway, shabby beneath a bare electric bulb.

Mr Rafik tucked the newspaper under her arm.

"Up you go, quick now, and lock the door behind you. Make yourself a hot drink, with lots of sugar. Do you hear? I will phone the police about your robbers."

He slipped his hand into his coat pocket and drew out a paper bag, filled with sweets. He pressed it into Rowan's palm, cradling her small hand with both of his.

"A little something; keep it safe."

Rowan gazed up into Mr Rafik's kind, dark eyes, attempting a smile, and then hurried up the stairs.

She heard the street door click shut safely behind her.

Rowan's hands would not stop shaking. Milk slopped over the worktop as she popped her mug into the microwave.

Was it possible that Luke knew those horrible men? Had they been waiting for him? But why on earth would Luke want to get mixed up with people like that? She remembered Rafe's hot breath on her face, the filthy claw-like hands. If Mr Rafik hadn't come along when he did...

Rowan pressed her palms to her aching temples. No. She must not think like that; must not dwell on what might have happened.

Her thoughts turned back to Luke. Perhaps he was taking drugs? She had read one of those teenage books about what happened if you took drugs. Your personality changed, you had mood swings and you stopped taking care of yourself. Certainly Luke's moods were unbearable these days and he seemed to go for days without having a shower. Perhaps *that* was why the men had come. But drugs cost money. Where would Luke get the money? He had given up his paper round and, last month, he'd blown all his savings on a new computer. Mum had been furious.

But if Luke was mixed up in drugs, wasn't he breaking the law? Wouldn't the police get involved? Wouldn't they take him away?

Rowan froze, an icy lump forming in her throat. She had an image in her head of two burly policemen dragging Luke down the stairs, of Luke pale and dishevelled slumped in a police cell. Rowan gulped. She must not tell Mum about the two strange men. Maybe, just maybe she could speak to Luke alone. Find out what had gone wrong – let him know she was there for him. If *only* he would talk to her like he used to, in that old, easy way.

The microwave pinged. Rowan stirred in heaped teaspoons of chocolate powder and sugar and took the drink into the living room. She switched on the television, buried herself among the cushions on the sofa and gazed at the flickering screen.

It was the wrong channel, a news programme. There was a burning forest, followed by footage of floods, hurricanes and shots of the recent snow storms. A man in the studio was speaking about something called an environmental summit. "This will be the most important meeting of world leaders since…"

Grabbing the remote control, Rowan switched channels but it was more news. There were pictures of dull-looking men in dull-looking suits waving at huge crowds of people. "… the outcome of the presidential election is said to be too close to call. This has shocked supporters of the current and hugely popular president, Washington Armstrong, and there are rumours…"

Rowan jabbed at the remote again. A chat show host was interviewing Doris Threadneedle, an old lady who had been dug out of her snowbound flat and become something of a celebrity, "I lived through the war," she was saying. "I'm a Londoner, my darling.

It'll take more than a few snowflakes to crush my fighting spirit!"

Rowan took a sip of sweet hot chocolate. She could feel the liquid, warm and soothing, slip all the way down to her tummy. She would watch some telly, finish her drink, and that would still leave enough time to peel the potatoes before Mum got home. If only… Rowan bit her lip. No, no, no! She must not think about Luke! Concentrating on the television, she tried to lose herself in the bright colours and crazy music of a silly cartoon.

"Luke should be back by now." Mum's voice sounded weary, anxious.

It was well after eight o'clock. Rowan, holding a delicate paper angel between finger and thumb, sat at the kitchen table surrounded by a mess of glitter and shiny card.

Mum frowned at the kitchen clock, up to her elbows in soapy water.

"The buses aren't running," Rowan said.

Her mother gave an exhausted sigh.

"I thought he was getting a lift. He's going to freeze to death."

As if to punctuate her remark a blast of snow shook the window. Rowan watched the flakes whirl against the glass. Biting her lip, she turned back to the angel and with infinite care painted two eyes, uplifted, mournful.

"Who's this Billy Madden, anyway?" Mum asked, scrubbing at a plate. "I've lost track of Luke's friends. What happened to Chris? I liked him."

"Oh, they fell out."

"Why?"

There was a pause.

"Don't know," Rowan muttered.

But she did know. Luke was so different; his old friends didn't want to be around him anymore.

Rowan had spoken to Jashan about it only days ago. "You know what really upsets me?" she said, shaking her head. "Luke's beginning to *look* like Billy Madden."

"Oh, God, don't!" Jaz shrieked. "He'll be shaving his head next. That lot are totally mental."

"They give me the creeps." Rowan frowned. "I hate the way they look at me, like they're sniffing me out. I hate the way Luke looks at me."

"He'll get over them. He's too smart not to," Jaz said reassuringly.

But Rowan was not comforted.

"So what's this Billy like?" Mum was asking.

Rowan grimaced. "Mean."

"Oh?" said Mum.

"He walks around town with one of those big, ugly dogs. Makes it snarl and bark at people."

"So, you don't think much of him?"

Rowan shook her head.

Another gust rattled the glass.

"Goodness!" Mum snapped, drying her hands furiously. "This snow, it's never-ending!" She snatched up a plate of food scraps and stabbed the pedal bin lever with her toe.

"Blow, it's full." She scraped the plate clean then neatly tied off the bin bag. "I'll have to pop this outside the back door. Can't face those iron steps. Not in this weather."

The skin beneath her mother's eyes was grey and puffy.

"I'll do it, Mum, if you like," said Rowan, jumping up. She pulled her coat from the peg. "I don't mind going down."

"Well, be careful. That fire escape isn't safe."

"It's okay, Mum." Rather that, thought Rowan, than have rats attracted up by the smell. She hated rats and Luke said the bin yard was swarming with them.

Pulling on a woolly hat and gloves Rowan opened the back door. A flurry of snowflakes swept into the room and set the curtains and paper angels flying.

"Oh my goodness!" cried Mum, "Make sure…" but as Rowan stepped out into the night, the slamming door cut off her mother's words.

Rowan gasped for breath. The wind was bitter. She grabbed the handrail and looked down through swirling flakes.

Below was the bin yard, a narrow, poorly lit space hemmed in by the backs of buildings.

Rowan inched her way down, step by precarious step, on the ice-encrusted ironwork. She could see, as she descended, that the nearest bins were full to bursting. Several black sacks had been dumped on the ground and were spilling their insides onto the snow. The stench was sickening, like the decomposing rat they had found last summer behind the boiler.

Only the last bin, topped by an undisturbed crust of snow, looked empty. It stood apart, near the covered alleyway that led to the street.

Rowan picked her way over the mound of rubbish and began to fumble with the lid. But what was that sound, mewling, like a small, frightened animal? She remembered stories of kittens, or even of babies, being abandoned in dustbins.

From the alley came a sudden grating noise, followed by the heavy rolling clank of metal on stone.

Rowan swallowed. A wave of nausea swept over her and there was an icy whispering in her head. "It's com... ing... com... ing... it'sss. Get out... get... it'ssssss. Get out!"

Something lurked in the darkness. She could hear it breathing.

She gulped hard. Was someone playing a trick? "Who's there?"

No answer.

Rowan inched backwards towards the fire escape until the metal rail dug hard against her back. In the darkness of the alley there was a deeper shadow. It was big. Big as an Alsatian dog. Big as a man crouching.

"Who's there?"

She heard a low grunt and then with a shriek it sprang, jaws open, breath rank.

Rowan fell to her knees.

The thing cleared her head with one jump. It was behind her now, clinging to the iron steps, panting, eager. She scrambled to face it; saw the glitter of teeth, a tail coiling from side to side. The creature moved forward – slow, deliberate. She staggered back. Each step was driving her towards the alley.

She tried to call out.

But her voice froze on the air.

Suddenly, a bolt of silver, streaking from above like a shooting star, flew at the slavering, stinking thing. With a snarl of rage the creature leapt past Rowan, knocking her to the ground. It fled into the alleyway. But the bright, spitting comet was on its tail.

Rowan sat up, gulping for breath. There was a terrifying squall of sounds: growls, hisses, screeches – claws scrabbling, glass breaking, a long howl of defiance.

Then nothing but the low moan of the wind.

Rowan got to her feet and stood there shaking, bruised, heart pounding against her ribs; breaths shuddering through her.

She wanted to run.

But she could not drag her eyes away from the gaping passage.

3

LUKE

⸻❖⸻

FROM THE GAPING BLACKNESS CAME A LARGE silver cat. It stalked up to Rowan, tail held proud.

"Oh!" Rowan was breathless.

The animal purred, amber eyes shimmering.

"You chased it away," said Rowan. "That... *thing...*"

She stretched out a trembling hand and the cat took delicate sniffs, then pushed its cheek against her palm. With a growing confidence Rowan ran her fingers along the moon-silver back. The cat arched in pleasure.

"Where have you come from?" she sighed. "You're beautiful."

It gazed up at her, turned and took a few steps into the alley.

"Don't go, not in there!"

The cat waited as if it expected her to follow. Rowan stared into the icy blackness of the tunnel.

"It's very dark, puss. What about that... that creature?"

The cat meowed and padded softly on.

Rowan took a hesitant step forward, then another.

It was suffocatingly dark in the passage, like something alive pressing against her face. Perhaps it was a trick of the light, but the cat's silvery fur seemed to glow, enough for Rowan to edge her way along and see an iron manhole cover flipped back and a stinking black hole plummeting downwards. Something glinted at its edge. Rowan bent down and picked up the object. It was a watch, a silver watch with a leather strap.

The wind whistled down the alley, carrying with it flakes of snow and the far-off sound of dogs barking. The cat stiffened, gave a low hiss and retreated back to the yard. Rowan scrambled after it.

"Hey, puss... wait!"

From above came the sound of a door opening. Light and music flooded the steps and a woman, hitching up her cherry red coat, stepped out heavily onto the icy platform.

"Puss, puss, puss," called the woman, her voice rich and deep. "You out here?"

It was Sophia, their neighbour.

The cat sprang up the steps and pressed itself against Sophia's legs. The large woman crouched down to stroke its handsome head.

"Hey now, where you bin on a cold night like this, puss?"

Rowan followed. "He's your cat then?"

Sophia smiled, her cheeks as shiny as new-shelled conkers. Sophia had come to Britain from the Caribbean, many years ago. "To seek my fortune in London," she had once said to Rowan, with a sly wink.

"What, like Dick Whittington?"

Sophia had laughed at that, eyes dancing. Then her expression had become thoughtful. "But, you know, I think I left the real treasure behind me." Rowan always imagined a pirate's chest brimming with gold and pearls, half-buried in the sand, but perhaps Sophia hadn't meant that kind of treasure.

"My cat? Oh no, darlin', that's not my cat. We're just good friends, cat and I. I've a dish of peach pie and cream to share."

"Oh, I wonder who he belongs to, then?"

"I'm not sure he belong to anyone." Sophia smiled.

"But he looks... special."

"Well, yes now, he is special," Sophia tickled him under the chin. "But perhaps that's because he *belong* to himself."

Rowan gazed at her, curious.

"Do you think, maybe, if he's homeless, we should call someone, the RSPCA?"

Sophia began to roar with laughter, her cheeks flushing deep rose.

"Does that cat look like it need help?"

The cat leapt gracefully onto Sophia's shoulder, curled its tail around her neck and sat watching Rowan. Sophia was right: the cat knew how to take care of itself.

"Perhaps he's after something?"

"Ah, could be, could be." Sophia nodded.

Rowan took a deep breath and then in a rush said, "He nearly caught something, just now."

"Is that right?"

"Something was in the alley. Something horrible, there was a fight. The cat chased it away."

"Well now." Sophia had been listening intently, her eyes like candles, soft and bright. "Perhaps there's your answer."

"What do you mean?"

"That cat, no doubt, has got business of his own."

A dog barked again, nearer now.

The old woman suddenly turned.

"Well, child, it's too cold to stand out here. You best get off home."

Rowan gave the cat a last stroke and made her way up the fire escape. All the time she was aware of Sophia's eyes on her.

Rowan pushed the back door open, closed it firmly behind her and turned the key in the lock. The kitchen was empty. She began to pull off her outdoor things, but there was something still clasped in her left hand. It was the watch. She frowned, turning it over. There were initials engraved on the back: *To L.P.M. love Dad.*

She swallowed hard.

It was Luke's watch, a present from Finn.

"Rowan!"

Rowan gave a start and thrust the watch into her pocket.

"Rowan!"

"Coming."

Mum was in the bathroom, hair tumbling in untidy strands about her pale face. She was separating the dirty laundry into piles.

She held up a pair of jeans.

"Are you sure these need washing, love?"

"I've been wearing them for a couple of weeks, Mum." Rowan tried to make her voice sound ordinary.

"Your clothes never look that dirty to me."

"There's some red paint on the knee, look."

"Oh, yes, I suppose so. It's just, if I can keep the wash to one load, it saves money."

"Well, I guess I can use my old pair."

Her mum smiled.

"Are you seeing Jashan tomorrow?"

"Yes."

"Skating as usual?"

"Yes, but not at the rink. He wants to go to the Thames."

"The Thames?"

"Haven't you seen the news, all the people down on the ice?"

"Skating? Are you sure it's safe? I thought they'd put barriers across the river steps."

"Jaz says a couple are still open. They wouldn't let us on if it was dangerous."

"Hmmm."

"Please, Mum."

"Well, I suppose if…"

There was a sudden crash as the front door banged open and then slammed shut again.

"That'll be your brother," said Mum, getting to her feet, her mouth a grim line.

Rowan took the watch from her pocket and slipped it into a pair of Luke's grubby tracksuit trousers, then followed her mother into the hall. Luke stood on the doormat, clothes thick with snow.

He shrugged off his coat and let it fall, along with a shower of flakes, to the floor.

Her mother's face was like thunder. "Luke, where have you been?"

"Out." His look was challenging.

"In this weather?"

Luke just glared.

"Why weren't you back for tea?"

"I told you I didn't want any. Is there any Coke? I *so* need a drink." He began to move towards the kitchen.

"Luke, you *told* me you'd be back by seven!"

"No I didn't."

"Boots please, Luke. The carpet!"

"Oh forgodsake, Mum. The carpets are wasted. Tell that bloody landlord of yours to get you some decent ones fitted!"

"Luke!"

Luke kicked off his boots, sullen, ungracious.

"And hang your coat up."

Rowan sensed danger and began to back away. She hated it when Mum and Luke argued. It happened all the time now. Luke had altered so much. He used to make Mum laugh, take her mind off things. Now he seemed to go out of his way to upset her.

Rowan retreated into her bedroom. She gazed out of the window at the swirling snow. She wished she could block out the sound of raised voices. Mum must have followed Luke into his bedroom.

"Aren't you even capable of picking your dirty clothes off the floor?" Mum was saying. "It smells in here, Luke. No, actually it stinks. You used to be so good about keeping your room tidy. What's happened, Luke?"

Luke couldn't stand it when Mum went off like this. He would turn his back on her, feigning indifference, but his lips would be white. He'd begin hunting for nothing in particular, banging drawers and cupboards as he went. "Are you listening, Luke?" she would cry. Sometimes, in a sudden explosion of anger, he would storm out of the room, screaming, "You're doing my head in. No wonder Finn dumped you!" Mum would be left framed in the doorway, startled and helpless.

Rowan glanced around her bedroom. She wished it was a mess, then she could tidy it up, occupy her mind, but it was perfect. Her school books lay in a neat pile on the desk. Her pencils were sharpened; eraser, ruler and colouring pens arranged with care. The bookcase was organised alphabetically. Her few ornaments were set out on a shelf above her bed. Mum laughed sometimes, wondering where Rowan had got the 'tidy gene' from. Luke called her a freak.

The argument was in full swing now. Luke was shouting vile things.

Rowan clenched her hands over and over.

What shall I do, what shall I do?

4

THE FÀINNE DUILLEOGA

R OWAN'S EYES FIXED ON THE SHELF ABOVE
her bed.

The Box of Treasures, yes of course!

She dropped to her knees and searched the narrow
gap beneath her wardrobe, drawing out a small silver
key. Jumping onto the bed she took down a wooden
box from the shelf and ran her hands over the lid. It
contained nothing valuable in the ordinary sense, but
each item was precious to her.

The box had been a gift from Finn, a present for
her ninth birthday.

She could remember unwrapping the fragile tissue
paper and gasping with delight. How grown-up and
beautiful it was, a box made of yew wood and carved
with a swirling, spiral pattern.

"It's Celtic," her father had explained. "It's the
Tree of Life."

"What's the Tree of Life?"

"Well, the Celts believed that a magical tree stood
at the centre of the universe."

Looking more closely, Rowan had seen flowers,
fruit, even animals hidden amongst the strange
branches.

"Open it. Go on!"

She did so, and there upon the dark velvet lining lay a piece of silver jewellery, a delicate circle of leaves hung on a slender chain. Finn had taken it in his fingers and with a gentle touch, fastened it around Rowan's neck.

"It's called the 'Fàinne Duilleoga'.

"The what?"

He spoke slowly. "Fawn-yuh Dill-og-ah. It's Irish; it means Ring of Leaves. See, there's holly and oak, just like the real thing, but tiny."

"It's lovely," she half whispered.

"It belonged to your great-grandmother. And she had it from her great-grandmother. You remember the story I used to tell you, about Glas Sidhe, the fairy woman?"

Rowan nodded, looking up at him. "Tell me again."

"Well, it's a long tale."

"Please."

And so he had. She heard once more of Col Maloney, Finn's forefather, who was beguiled by a flame-haired, green-eyed fairy woman. She had promised to marry him if he did her will, then set him an impossible, elvish task: to dance with her, all night long from dusk to dawn, and though he nearly died in the attempt, it was done.

"And that, Rowan, is why you–"

"Why I've got green eyes?"

"But, of course."

"Only they're hazel really and my hair's boring, just brown." She ruffled her bob.

"Not brown: rich auburn!" With a smile Finn smoothed her hair. You've got fairy blood in your veins, all right."

"But I—"

"Oh, you have. And this necklace —" he touched the Ring of Leaves, "— is a fairy amulet. My old Gran gave it to me, long before you were born and made me promise that I would give it to my little girl. She knew, you see."

"Knew what?"

"About you, of course." He was smiling, a wicked wonderful smile, and Rowan couldn't tell if he was teasing or not.

Now with the little key, Rowan unlocked the Box of Treasures and gazed at the contents. There were bright feathers, pressed flowers, skeleton leaves, locks of baby hair, seashells and white sand. But her favourite things were the small watercolour of a mermaid painted by Mum, the creased photo of herself as a baby being cradled by Finn, and of course the Fàinne Duilleoga, safe in its soft leather pouch.

Rowan took everything out and dusted the objects carefully. An old sprig of heather with its fragile, papery flowers reminded her of their last holiday with Grandma and Grandpa, in Yorkshire: picnics on the moor, paddling in the beck, building dams in the shallow water. That was the last time that Luke… She stopped herself, rubbed her head fiercely. That was before everything had changed. What was happening to him? If *only* he'd let her in. She sighed, and with great care put the treasures back.

There was another outbreak of shouting from Luke's room. Rowan heard her name mentioned.

She closed and locked the box, slipped it under the bedcovers and replaced the key in its hiding place.

Opening the door she peeped out and then tiptoed across the narrow hall to the kitchen.

Rowan sat down at the table. It was still covered with a jumble of paper angels, glitter and glue. She took a pair of scissors and a new sheet of silver paper and began to cut out a cat shape. She pasted the figure onto a piece of pale blue card and applied some sparkles.

She could hear Mum saying, "... because *some* of us have to work, Luke!"

And Luke's outraged response, "Oh, forgodsake, fine!"

He came into the kitchen a few minutes later and slouched over to the fridge.

"Where's the bloody Coke?"

"There isn't any," said Rowan, looking up at him. "Mum got that cheap orange juice instead."

Luke stood there, with the door open, staring at the half-empty shelves. Swearing beneath his breath, he closed the fridge with a bang and tipped a plastic bottle of milk to his lips. When it was empty he crushed it in his fist.

"Out of milk," he declared. "So what you doing, weirdo?"

"Christmas cards." She ignored the insult.

Luke picked up one of the silver angels, twirled it around in his fingers and put it down again without comment. His fingernails were filthy.

"Give us some paper," he said, pulling up a chair.

Rowan pushed a clean sheet towards him.

Luke took a drawing pen from the pocket of his combats and began to sketch. He was good at drawing. Watching him, Rowan felt a kind of tingle. It was just like old times.

Luke leant back in his chair and threw the drawing down in front of her.

"There, finished!"

It was a pen and ink sketch of Father Christmas being devoured by a giant spider.

"It's... great," Rowan said hesitantly. "Although..."

"What?" Luke demanded.

"A bit... gruesome."

"Why do I bother?" he mumbled and picked up the glue pot.

"But it is good, really," she insisted.

"Yeah, yeah."

Luke, it seemed, no longer cared. He was transfixed, watching slow milky globules of latex-gum drip from brush to table.

Rowan gazed at him, then, swallowing hard, said, "Luke, you are okay, aren't you?"

"Yeah!" The tone was hard, belligerent.

Rowan tried again.

"You're not... worried... about anything?"

"What you going on about, freak?"

Rowan sighed and got up to get some cotton wool from the kitchen cupboard. She sat back down.

"Can I have the glue, Luke?"

No response.

"Luke, please, I want to do snow."

He grunted.

Mum came into the kitchen with an armful of dirty washing.

"Hey, Mum, look," said Rowan, holding the card up.

Mum glanced over, her face darkened. "Luke, what *do* you think you're doing? Get a cloth and clear that mess up, now!"

Luke shrugged and lurched to his feet.

Rowan grabbed the pot.

"Oh, it's empty," she said.

"Luke!" snapped Mum.

"Yeah, yeah, yeah," he drawled.

"That stuff costs money!"

Luke picked up a tea towel and carelessly began smearing glue over the table top.

"You're making it worse," Mum cried.

Rowan began to scrape the remains of the glue out of the pot with her forefinger. She focused hard on her picture.

"I don't know why you do it, Luke." Mum was throwing things into the washing machine.

"The cotton wool keeps sticking to everything," Rowan babbled.

"Is that good enough for you, *Mother*?" Luke's scowl was fierce.

"No, use a damp dishcloth!"

"Oh forgodsake!"

"It doesn't really look like snow; it's all gone grey and lumpy." Rowan knew that no one was listening.

"Do it properly, Luke."

"I'm doing it properly!"

Suddenly, Rowan pressed her fingers into the table top and said in a loud, deliberate voice, "At least it *will* snow this Christmas."

Her mother stopped and gazed at her, perplexed.

Rowan went on. "Cos it doesn't usually, does it? It's stupid, Christmas cards with snow on."

Luke laughed and began to sing in his cracked tones, "I'm dreaming of a White Christmas..."

"They always play that song in shops and stuff," Rowan added, "and then what do we get? Same old wind and rain."

"Global warming," Luke said.

"What?" asked Rowan.

"Glo – bal war – ming," said Luke with exaggerated slowness, as if he were talking to an idiot. You know, climate change, like on the news!"

"I know what global warming is; we've done it at school. But you mean that's why…?"

"That's why *everything's* gone so mental."

Mum frowned. "Yes, thank you, Luke, enough of the geography lesson."

"Environmental studies, *actually*," he retorted.

"Yes, well." She was looking at Rowan thoughtfully. "It's a depressing subject; let's drop it, please."

"Mr Tyler, at school, reckons this cold weather is just the flip side of the coin. Climate's going crazy."

"I said drop it, Luke."

But Rowan felt a kind of defiance rise up in her. She didn't want the talking to stop. If *only* they could keep on talking. Talk about things that really mattered. She took a deep breath.

"I saw something weird down by the bins just now!" she blurted out.

Luke and Mum stared at her.

"It went for me."

"What was it?" Luke was curious, an odd, half-expectant look on his face.

"I… I don't know. It had a tail and claws."

"Rats," Luke pronounced in a sinister tone.

"But it was big, like a dog."

"I've seen them down there," he insisted. "Huge rats, black rats, carrying the plague probably."

"Don't be stupid, Luke," snapped Mum. "There aren't any black rats anymore."

"Their fur's black, forchrisake! And they're big enough, whatever. Not bloody normal," Luke insisted.

"Look, Luke, will you just stop this?"

"What?"

"Just stop it, okay!"

The phone rang.

"That's mine!" said Luke, leaping up.

"You stay put," said Mum, "*I'm* expecting a call. I don't want you hogging the phone all evening. Do something useful, put the kettle on."

"Wouldn't have this problem if you got me a *proper* mobile," Luke sulked.

"You've got a mobile."

"What? That piece of… It's broken, anyway."

But she was gone.

Luke slouched over to the cupboard and took out a packet of teabags.

"Last bloody one," he muttered, throwing it into a mug.

"Mum didn't have enough money to get any more," Rowan said.

Luke sighed irritably.

"They're all mad."

Rowan stared at him.

"Who?"

"People, adults, whatever. They're messing everything up, the whole bloody world and they couldn't give a —!" The word hung, ugly and defiant, on the air.

"I suppose they're not that bothered about snow."

Luke snorted, flung out his hand and grabbed her by the neck. He dug his dirty nails in, hard.

"Ow!" She tried to pull away, could feel the tears welling in her eyes.

"You're such a *little girl*, aren't you, Ro?"

Releasing his grip, he turned his back and said no more, but switched on the radio and, fiddling with the tuner, flooded the kitchen with a discordant, crackling stream of noise.

5

FINN

As Luke switched between stations the radio gave out a crackle of static, snatches of pop music, a sober news report "... *and next week world leaders are meeting in London for a landmark environmental summit...*"

Luke jerked the dial and found a weird oscillating wail. Rowan stared at her brother. Perhaps she should try one last time.

"Luke."

He scowled. "What?"

"Is anything wrong?"

Luke glared at her.

"Some men were looking for you today."

There was the slightest flicker of reaction, something in his eyes.

"You're not in trouble, are you?"

He looked up, his face narrow, suspicious. "I'll tell you a secret," he hissed.

Rowan hesitated then drew close. Luke put his hand on her shoulder. "I didn't want to tell you this, before..."

"What?" she whispered.

He brought his lips to her ear.

"You stink!" he bellowed and gripped her throat with his hand, squeezing hard.

"Get off!" she gasped, wrenching herself away. She ran from the room. She didn't want Luke to see the tears. What use was it, trying to talk to him about those men, about anything? He was crazy. He would only turn on her again.

She could hear Mum, in the living room, speaking on the phone. Rowan lingered in the doorway, half listening.

Mum looked up. "It's Finn," she mouthed.

Rowan's heart gave a lurch. She pressed her hand to her chest. Had it stopped? No, it was there all right, doing somersaults.

Mum was checking her diary and nodding.

"Yes, in the New Year, the end of January? Right, so you'll drop in here first?"

It sounded as if Mum was making arrangements. Rowan's heart leap-frogged.

"Yes," Mum continued. "That's fine."

Rowan chewed at her finger nails. Please let him have time to talk.

"Okay then. And you'll give us a call if…"

The conversation seemed to be winding to a close. Surely Mum wouldn't just put the phone down.

"Okay, Finn."

Rowan began to shift from one foot to the other. Should she ask to speak to him? But Finn could be anywhere, on a train, at an airport, on the other side of the world. It wasn't always convenient.

"Okay. Bye then."

Rowan's heart sank.

But Mum was holding out the handpiece, smiling.

"He wants to have a word. I'll go and get Luke."

Rowan took the telephone as if it were made of glass and placed it tentatively to her ear.

"Hello?" she half whispered.

"Rowan, sweetheart, it's me," came the soft Irish accent, unmistakably Finn's. "You've not gone all shy on me, have you? You know who it is now, don't you?"

At the sound of his voice, Rowan's face flowered into a smile.

"Yes, Dad."

"Now that's better... so how are you, anyway?"

"Okay."

"You keeping well?"

"Yes. Where... where are you?"

"At home, darlin'."

"In Ireland?" Rowan's voice rose hopefully.

"No, no, Baden-Baden. You know, my home in Germany."

Rowan had sent cards and letters to that address many times, but she had never been there. Finn said it was a beautiful town and that Rowan must visit one day, but he never made any definite plans.

"Oh, I see." She couldn't disguise the disappointment.

"But I'm coming to England soon. We've got some gigs all around the country. I'll be able to come and see you. I've arranged it with your mam."

"Could you..." Rowan knew she should not be asking this. "Could you come over for Christmas?"

"Oh, darlin', I'm sorry, I can't. I'm really busy with the band and everything." There was a pause. "I'm sorry, darlin', perhaps next time?"

Rowan couldn't speak. That's what he'd said last year.

"But, sweetheart, it's not that long now, is it? I'll make it up to you. We'll go out to some great places. Do loads of wild t'ings. The zoo, the Eye, the Tower." His accent was getting stronger and he was rushing the words, as if trying to fill up the empty spaces.

"Hey, d'you remember that time on Tower Hill when you pretended to chop me head off?" Finn forced out a laugh. Rowan knew there would be a crease of tension forming between his eyebrows.

"Yeah," she managed to croak out. But inside there was a dull ache.

"I bet you're really tall now, aren't you? I won't recognise you when I see you. You'll be a proper young lady. It's been a long time, hey?"

"Almost six months." She tried to keep her voice level.

"No, not that long. Really?"

"It was the summer holidays."

"Oh yes, of course. There was that crazy heatwave, wasn't there? We ate loads of ice cream. How many did Luke have? Six was it?"

"Four," said Rowan.

"Yes, that's it, four. Hah. And how is Luke? Your Mam said he got caught in the snow, coming home?"

"Yeah, it's been snowing like mad."

"Same here, piles of the stuff. Snowed in, we were. It's the same all over. You seen the news?"

"Yeah," said Rowan, trying not to sound as miserable as she felt. She knew that afterwards she would be furious with herself. Why couldn't she just enjoy this conversation? How often did she get the chance to talk to her dad?

"Nic was saying that the South of France looks like Svalbard, or something," continued Finn.

"Oh. How… how is Nic?" she asked, not knowing what else to say.

"Oh, she's fine. You know she'd like to meet you, some time."

Rowan found that difficult to believe. Nicole had only ever spoken to her once, when Rowan had phoned to wish Finn a happy birthday. Nicole had hardly seemed to know who she was. *"Rowan? Who?"* she had asked in her clipped voice. Then a businesslike, *"Right. I will get him."* No warmth, no friendliness, not even a goodbye.

Rowan had seen a photograph of Nicole though. It had come in one of Finn's rare letters: a glossy print of the pair standing outside an exotic temple in some far-off land, Finn looking predictably handsome and dishevelled, with long dark hair and a wide, roguish smile. Their arms were flung around each other's shoulders. Mum let out a short laugh when she saw it and described Nicole as 'Finn's type': tall, blonde and leggy. "But you're not like that," was Rowan's response. Mum had smiled wryly. "No, no, I suppose not. I met Finn long before he made it."

The phone line crackled with static.

"You and Luke doing well at school, then?"

Finn was trying hard to keep the conversation going.

"Yes. At least, I… I don't know about Luke."

"What d'you mean?"

"Oh, he's got in with a funny crowd."

"What d'you mean *funny*? Red noses and big shoes?"

Rowan smiled despite herself. "No, just… not very," she knew she sounded clumsy and finished lamely, "… not his sort."

"You mean troublemakers?"

A sudden burst of sound pounded through the flat: Luke's music. Mum came back into the living room, her face set into a frown.

"Well…" Rowan wished she hadn't started this.

"You tell your big brother to steer clear of that kind of thing. He's a clever boy, got a lot of talent and he shouldn't waste it. He'll listen to you, darlin'. He thinks the world of you. Will you do that for me?"

Rowan sighed. If Luke was going to listen to anyone it would be Finn.

"Okay." Her voice sounded very small.

"Now listen, darlin', I've got to go soon. You go and get Luke for me, and, Rowan, remember I love you… and I'll see you soon, I promise…"

"Bye, Finn. Bye, Dad."

She held the phone out to her mother.

"He wants to speak to Luke."

Mum shook her head.

"Luke's not coming."

"What?"

"Here, let me have the phone. I'll explain to your dad."

Rowan passed the handset over reluctantly. She wished she could tell Finn that she loved him and that she thought he was the best dad in the world, even if… even if… He'd think she was so moody, sulking like that. But she hadn't been sulking. Not really. It was just she wanted Finn to be here, now, warm and real, talking and laughing with her. Not hundreds and hundreds of miles away, at the end of some stupid phone line.

"What is it, love?" asked Mum, after putting the phone down.

Rowan sighed and slumped down onto the sofa. "I just wish Finn…" But she didn't know how to continue.

"Oh, darling, I know," Mum said, sitting down and slipping her arm around Rowan's shoulder. Rowan snuggled up close. Her mum's baggy jumper was warm and soft.

"He wasn't really cut out to be a dad."

"But I think he's a lovely dad!"

"He's a lovely *guy*. Even I think he's lovely, after everything we went through. But he has no sense of responsibility. Life's just a game to him. And when the fun stops he just moves on. He's like a kid, really, a big kid."

"Like Peter Pan?" Rowan said.

Mum laughed. "Yes, *just* like Peter Pan."

Rowan stared at Mum's fingers. The nails were painted a pearly grey.

"Mum?"

"Yes, love?"

"Do you think he will come, after Christmas?"

"I hope so, darling." But Rowan could hear the sigh in her mother's voice.

Suddenly, Mum became brisk. She tousled Rowan's hair and stood up. "I *must* get on with these designs or Mrs Flint, the head teacher, will have a fit. Do you have any homework that needs doing?"

"No, I did it yesterday."

"Well, I'll be working in my bedroom. Don't stay up too late, darling, it's almost nine."

Mum left the room and Rowan could hear her thumping on Luke's bedroom door. The loud music abated, slightly.

Rowan shivered. It felt cold, even though the radiators were on, clunking and gurgling in the background. Since the snows had come, Mum had not turned off the heating. "If I do the pipes will freeze, not to mention us. It's madness. I'm not even going to start thinking about how much the bills will be."

Rowan thrust her hands deep into her thick cardigan pockets. Something rustled against her fingers. It was the bag of sweets that Mr Rafik had given to her. Curious, she drew it out, opened up the neck and dipped her hand inside. The sweets felt hard, sugary, like pear drops or cough candy. Good, she thought, I'll have one now and take the rest with me tomorrow, when I meet Jaz.

"Ow!" There was a searing, scorching pain at her fingertips and in an instant she had pulled her hand free of the paper bag.

6

RIVER OF ICE

———◆———

"LOOK AT THAT!" JAZ BREATHED.

The two children stood gazing out over the Thames, gripping the railings. It was the first time since the blizzard that Rowan had seen the river, a vast ribbon of pale green ice, reaching away to the east and south of the city.

"Oh my God," Jaz said. "How cool!"

Everyone seemed to be having fun: lads shrieking with laughter, parents pulling children along on sledges. Further out, people were skating, some wobbling nervously, others skimming over the ice with skill.

"I suppose it's safe?" said Rowan.

"Of course, dahling, it's frozen solid," said Jashan. "There's been a Victorian fair up near the Tower for absolutely days, with people in costumes and bonfires and everything. The ice is so hard even the flames can't melt it. It said so on the news. Come on, let's go and hire some skates for you. There's a guy over there on the river steps."

The children went over to his makeshift stall.

Jaz took a pair of smart white ice-skating boots out of his rucksack. The hire man shook his head, frowning.

"Them fancy skates is no good. They'll be shot to pieces in no time, mate. You need something solid." He held up two pairs of hire skates. "Look, you strap these on over your boots. They're bomb-proof, right? Nice strong blades. Only five quid an hour. Can't say fairer."

It was Jaz's turn to scowl now.

"Mine will be all right. Ice is ice!"

"The ice out there is as rough as a badger's arse. Do yourself a favour." The man thrust the skates at them.

The children paid their money and crouched down to strap on the blades. Once ready, they clumped and wobbled down the snowy steps to the river. They had to pick their way over the flotsam and jetsam at the river's edge: water weeds, twigs, plastic bags, poking up through the frosted-green ice, all caught in a wintry stillness.

When the way was clear the pair thrust their bodies forward, gliding smoothly, matching each other stride for stride. They overtook the large group of stragglers who kept near the shore and soon caught up with those swooping, with easy confidence, up and down the middle of the river.

On each bank of the Thames tall, elegant buildings glittered in the winter sunlight. They could see the snow-topped dome of St Paul's away to the east and the Shard sparkling like a huge upside-down icicle. Behind them, where the river made a sharp curve south, was the great Ferris wheel of the London Eye and beyond that the Houses of Parliament, looking like a Christmas matchbox souvenir.

The river stretched on before them greenish-pale and sparkling with frost. Here and there patches of transparent ice formed clear-black windows into the frozen depths. The friends shivered as they gazed downwards. There seemed to be things below, moving, coiling, uncoiling. Or was it a trick of the light?

"I keep thinking of faces, peering up," said Rowan. "White and not alive."

"Suicides," Jaz murmured. "Long drowned."

"Let's not," said Rowan and pushed away on her blades. "Come on!"

Jaz darted after Rowan and caught hold of her hand.

"Okay then, but you've got to tell me about this big mystery of yours. You sounded very enigmatic on the phone last night. Mum wondered why you were calling so late."

Rowan glanced over her shoulder then nodded ahead.

"Let's keep going, away from the others. Most people aren't skating further than Waterloo Bridge."

"Well, how about going to the fair? We're skating in the right direction."

"To the Tower? It's a bit far."

"Not by river. Look, you can see it in the distance, and we'll go fast on the ice. Come on, it'll be a giggle. There'll be stuff to eat, hot dogs and toffee apples, and fires! We *have* to see the fires."

Jaz squeezed Rowan's hand.

Rowan attempted to smile. "Okay."

They began to pick up speed. On either side they passed spectacular icicle formations, where water outlets spouting into the Thames had frozen, mid-flow, creating vast, twisted, gothic shapes, sparkling with hoar frost. They saw barges and large boats trapped in the ice, gulls circling above crying out in chorus. Ahead, spanning the river, were the gaudy arches of Blackfriars' twin bridges.

"So?" Jaz cried at last. "Are you going to tell me this amazing secret?"

"Well…" Rowan began. "There were these men."

"What men? Where?" Jaz's voice was eager.

"They were hanging around, yesterday, outside the flat."

"And…?"

"They…" She shivered again.

"What?"

"They gave me the creeps."

"The creeps! Oh, Rowan, is that it? Just say 'push off or I'm calling 999'!"

"But I can't do that kind of thing, Jaz, I'm not like you. Anyway, my mobile phone's broken."

"Yes, dahling, but they didn't know that, did they? Give them some attitude. It freaks them out."

"I don't know. These men were weird."

They skated on beneath the deep shadow of the bridge.

"Weird? How?" Jaz's voice made an eerie echo below the huge iron arches.

"Like…" Rowan's forehead creased. "Like they knew something."

"Knew something?"

"Yes. At first I thought they wanted to rob the flat. But I think it was Luke they were after."

"Luke? Why Luke?"

"He could be in trouble."

There was a pause and their pace slowed.

"Don't stop here," Rowan said quickly, looking up at the great blood-coloured pillars. She could hear something scratching around in the girders above, felt the shivery sensation of being spied on.

They came out into the sunshine on the far side.

"This is really getting to you, isn't it?" Jaz said, looking at his friend with genuine concern.

Rowan kept her eyes fixed ahead. "Yes."

"So, what sort of trouble is he in?"

"I don't know. Something's changed. Luke's changed."

"D'you think it's the Invertebrates?"

Rowan's lips twitched at the word. Jaz had coined it during last year's nature project. It suited Billy Madden and his gang down to the ground, spineless lot. They were always hanging around the primary school, bullying the younger children.

"Yes, it's always them, but…" Rowan came to a halt, her blades spitting out a shower of ice. Jaz made a dashing stop beside her. "I think it's something else too."

"Like what?"

Rowan stared into her friend's eyes and looked away.

"Jaz, do you ever hear voices?"

"Voices?"

"Shhh… I mean like music, or, or singing."

Jaz's eyebrows were raised high.

"Rowan, you are *not* hearing voices."

"Do you ever feel that you're being followed?"

Jaz's mouth had dropped open.

"Well," Rowan sighed and looked down at her shabby boots. "Perhaps I'm imagining things."

"Honey," Jaz exclaimed in mock drawl, putting his hand on Rowan's shoulder, "You are startin' to worry me!"

Rowan shook her head.

"It's just things have been happening. Things I can't explain."

She reached into the pocket of her parka and withdrew an object, keeping it concealed in the centre of her gloved fist.

"What do you make of this? Last night, when those creepy men were around, Mr Rafik turned up. He gave me a bag of sweets. I didn't think much about it at the time, but then, later, I found this."

She uncurled her fingers. Nestling in her palm was a dull black pebble, about the size of a fifty pence piece, but thicker, heavier. A pattern was engraved on its surface, sinuous lines fanning out from a central stem.

"It's a tree, or plant, isn't it?" said Jaz, altering the angle of his head, to see better.

"But what is it?" Rowan insisted.

"It's just a trinket, isn't it? Some old jewellery he didn't want. Perhaps it dropped into the bag by accident. Oh, Rowan, come on!"

"Jaz." There was a tremor in Rowan's voice. "Feel it. Go on. Take your glove off."

"But…"

"Just feel it!"

Jaz's eyes sparked black and fierce. With a gesture of defiance he whipped off his glove and grabbed the stone.

"There, you see, it's just – ow!" Jaz flung his hand up into the air. The pebble flew in a high arc and descended, rattling across the ice.

"See?" Rowan cried, skating after the stone and scooping it up into her gloved palm. She wheeled around. "How can that be right? How can it be hot?"

Jaz was shaking his head, visibly agitated.

"I don't know. This isn't a trick, is it? Swear it's not a trick."

"I'm as freaked out as you."

Jaz held out his hand. "Look, it's red."

The two friends gazed at the pinkish mark across Jaz's fingers.

"Could it be magnetic or radioactive? It's got to have a scientific explanation."

"No. Something's not right. It's just too–"

Suddenly, they were startled by a dog barking. The sound, deep and threatening, seemed to boom out across the ice.

"Look!" said Rowan.

On the south bank of the river stood a huge, black hound, barking wildly and baring its teeth. Rowan stiffened and clutched at her friend's fingers. A short, burly man had hold of the dog's collar and was unclipping a strong chain.

"Oh God, it's him!" Rowan hissed.

"Who?"

"The man with the dog. He was with them, yesterday. Oh God Jaz, we've got to go!"

"Ro, what...?"

Rowan's every muscle was straining towards flight but something held her there. Behind the dog handler was another figure, tall, thin and dressed in furs, spider-web grey. His face was as pale as the frozen river. She had never set eyes on him before, but she knew him.

He stood, still as stone, looking straight at them.

"Oh, Jaz! Now! Go!"

They flew like small birds before a hawk, their flashing blades sending up a spray of ice. They skated so fast the air seemed to pierce their throats. On and on they went. Seagulls screamed and circled overhead. Glancing back, Rowan could see the men were in pursuit, moving swiftly along the snowy riverbank. The black dog bounded ahead, scattering passers-by, barking like something possessed. The noise pounded through Rowan's head.

On they skated, hands clasped, under the silver arc of the Millennium Footbridge towards the great expanse of Southwark Bridge. The dog, now loping along the embankment wall, was drawing level, had overtaken them, doubled back.

"It's looking for a way onto the river!" Jaz panted.

"Oh God," whispered Rowan.

"Look, it's trying to get through that barbed wire."

"Keep going!" Rowan cried.

They sped onwards. Rowan could feel her chest burning with the effort, her legs growing weak. The barks were hammer blows inside her skull.

"I can't go on..." Jaz gasped, slowing.

"We must!" Rowan pulled at her friend's arm.

"Need... to catch... breath."

"Jaz, just a little further!"

Rowan bit her lip. It was her fault Jaz was mixed up in all this. What if he got hurt?

"I can't."

Frantic now, Rowan gripped her friend's hand and began to increase the pace of their strides.

"Yes, you can!"

The hound was a shadow at the edge of their vision. They would not be able to outdistance it. Any moment it would find a way down onto the river.

"Rowan, please..." Jaz gasped. "I've got to stop."

7

THE ICE FAIR

ROWAN'S CONCENTRATION WAS SLIPPING. The skates felt like lead weights. Desperate, she scanned the north bank of the river for some means of escape: open steps, perhaps, or a causeway. Perhaps they could lose their pursuers in the streets of the City?

Jaz cried out, gesturing to the right, "Look! Look!"

Rowan swung around. The dog had stopped, its way blocked by buildings. The riverside path had come to an end. The hound stood on the wall, threw up its head and howled.

"Yes!" said Rowan, clenching her fist. "It'll give us time. Can you go on, Jaz?"

Jaz bent over, resting hands on knees, gulping great lungfuls of air.

"I'll – be – fine."

The howling dog had attracted attention. People were trying to grab hold of its collar. It turned on them, snarling, snapping.

"We need to go, Jaz, now."

Jashan stood upright, panting and reached for Rowan's hand. Half pulling, half supporting her friend, Rowan pushed off.

It was some moments before Jaz could speak.

"So wh… what was that about?" he gasped.

Rowan shook her head.

She couldn't stop thinking about the Grey Man. He haunted her. She knew him, but how? How? "Oh, Jaz, I just don't know. It's Luke…"

"You say he's mixed up in all this?"

"I think so."

"Have you asked him?"

"Yes, I've got the bruise on my neck to prove it!"

"Perhaps he owes them money. Could be a gang, drugs, that sort of thing?"

"But what about all the, you know, the stuff we can't explain?"

Suddenly, Jaz turned his head. "Listen, can you hear music?"

For a fleeting second Rowan thought it was 'the voices'. She felt a surge of relief. So Jaz could hear them too. But then she realised it was real music, a spiralling carousel of sound coming upriver. In the distance they could see the bright banners and marquees of a fairground and the blue-white shimmer of rising smoke.

"Hey, it's the Ice Fair," Jaz cried in delight. "Come on!"

A dazzling kaleidoscope of stalls and old-fashioned carnival attractions stretched from bank to bank. Straw had been piled onto the ice to construct makeshift walkways between the stalls, and crowds of people jostled along the aisles.

"Wow, fantastic!" Jaz said, his eyes sparkling. "It's like a theme park on ice."

Rowan frowned. "But we can't stop."

"What?"

"We have to get off the Thames." Rowan glanced over her shoulder.

"Come off it," Jaz protested. "They'll never find us in this crowd."

"No, Jaz, we need to go."

Obstinate, Jaz put his hands on his hips. "We're surrounded by people, Ro. What could be safer? Better here than being tracked down on the open ice, or in some backstreet, blocked by drifts."

Rowan felt her throat tighten.

"Look," said Jaz, more gently, "we've got a better chance of losing them in the middle of this lot. Would they set a dog on us in front of everyone?"

Rowan's fingers clenched.

"Okay, then," she relented. "But we can't hang around."

They sat down on a straw bale to remove the hired skates, strung them around their necks and slipped into the swarming crowd.

The fair sparkled like a glitter ball and swirled with fairground music. The merry-go-round horses were a blur of colour, striped swing boats see-sawed high into the sky and the big wheel shrieked with laughter. Striding through the crowds on stilts ("How on earth?" exclaimed Jaz) was a red devil carrying a long trident. He poked at passers-by and hollered through a megaphone.

"Roll up, roll up, come and see Cobrus the Boneless, the Incredible Snake Man! And witness 'Pearl of the Ocean', the only remaining mermaid in captivity. At Mr Montefiore's Magickal Monsterium!"

"Oh, Rowan, a mermaid," Jaz sighed.

"It'll only be a woman in a costume. Or some poor fish in a tank."

"But, Ro…"

Rowan took Jaz's hand and led him further into the crowd.

Jaz was captivated. His head swivelled from side to side, eyes shining.

"Oh, look, Rowan."

They were passing a magnificent display of coloured bottles with fancy labels. There was everything from frankincense to the elixir of life. Jaz picked up a particularly ornate, unmarked flask, covered with jewels.

"What's this, then?"

The stallholder, an old man with a face like a raisin and wearing an extravagant gold turban, smiled widely, revealing brilliant white teeth. "Ah, most special, young sir, it contains an efreet, a genie."

Jaz stared, eyes wide, "You mean it's a genie in a bottle? Oh, that's *so* cool!"

"Come on, Jaz," said Rowan, pulling her friend away.

Hot steam drifted up from food stalls, filling their nostrils with a confusion of scent: mulled wine, chow mein, tikka masala and deep-fried Mars bars. It made their mouths water, their heads spin.

Best of all were the bonfires. Raised onto huge iron braziers, they burned with a dazzling heat, white-orange flames sending showers of sparks high into the sky. People watched, mouths open.

A man, with the word 'Steward' printed across his fluorescent tabard, was adjusting some railings, which encircled the blaze.

"Why aren't they roasting ox then?" Jaz asked him with a cheeky grin.

"Health and safety regulations," the man answered, with a wry laugh. "Didn't have *them* in the olden days, did they?"

There was something hypnotic about the great leaping flames and the warmth was comforting. It seemed to Rowan that within its circle they were safe.

Then a firecracker exploded nearby. Unnerved, the children spun around.

"Ladies and gentlemen, for your delight, the Midwinter Mummers present 'Sir Gawain and the Green Knight'!"

A troupe of players dressed in masks and outlandish costumes leapt and somersaulted into a roped-off area near the fires.

Rowan shook herself. "Jaz, we need to go."

"Oh, can't we watch these…"

"We need to go."

"But I'm starving." Jaz pulled a dramatic face. "I need hot dogs or I'll *die* of hunger."

Rowan smiled grimly.

"I thought you'd be sick of dogs by now."

"Not if they're covered with ketchup."

They searched amongst the crowds and at last found a hot dog stand, close to the north bank. Along this stretch of the embankment the Tower of London rose up, majestic, against the sky.

"Look, Rowan, there are some steps over there."

Rowan stared at them, thoughtfully. "And they're open. Tower Hill Tube must be that way."

"But first some good old-fashioned nosh," Jaz insisted, eyeing the sausages. "What are you having: mustard or ketchup?"

"No thanks."

"Come on, Ro. We've got to keep our strength up."

Rowan noticed a sign farther along, which read, 'Mother Meg's Spiced Apple Pastries'.

"I quite like the look of those."

Behind the stall was an old lady, barely taller than Rowan, just taking a batch of baking from her quaint stove. With her voluminous fur-lined red cloak, frilly mob cap and half-moon spectacles she looked like an illustration from a children's book.

She met Rowan's eye, spectacles glinting.

"Like a nice pie, dearie?" she called in a soft, reedy voice. "They're piping hot."

Rowan moved nearer. The pies looked mouth-watering, a light golden crust, topped with a delicate pastry decoration in the shape of a tree.

"Apple trees, my sweet, so pretty," the old lady crooned.

"They look nice. How much?"

"A pound each, dear. They are worth every penny, I assure you."

Rowan glanced at her. The edge of the red hood had fallen forward to shade the top half of the lady's face. Rowan felt a sudden urge to walk away, but thought it would be rude.

"I'll have two, p-please," she said.

The lady put two pies into a paper bag and popped in a third.

"Oh no, I..." Rowan exclaimed.

With a curt nod Mother Meg offered the bag but, as Rowan reached to take it out, the old lady grabbed her hand.

"Take care not to burn your mouth, my dear."

Rowan was startled. The old lady's grip was like steel.

"I... I'll be careful," she spluttered and pulling back, hurried away.

At the hot dog stand Jaz was waiting for his second order.

"Was'sat'en?" he asked, pointing to the paper bag, his mouth crammed full of food.

"Oh Jaz! You've got ketchup all around your mouth."

Jaz licked the sauce away with greedy jabs of his tongue.

"Mmmm. Dee-licious! Is that pudding?"

"They're apple pies." Rowan drew one out of the bag. "Aren't they pretty?"

"Let's see." Jaz took the pie and studied it. "Wow, that *is* weird..."

Suddenly, a dog's bark boomed out.

The friends turned.

"Oh my God!" Jaz cried in terror.

It was the black hound, charging at them across the ice. It did not lose its footing. The huge paws remained swift and steady on the frozen river. Rowan could feel her heart hammering.

"Jaz, drop everything and run!" she yelped.

If they could make it to the river steps, perhaps they had a chance. She flung the skates and the paper bag to the ground and sprinted ahead towards the north bank, her boots slipping on the straw path. She staggered, almost fell, but glancing back saw Jaz had not even moved.

"Jaz!" she screamed.

Jaz was rigid. Rowan ran back, grabbing his sleeve. "Come on! Move!"

Jaz's eyes were glassy. The dog was less than fifty feet away, fangs bared, slaver dripping from its jaws.

"Jaz, please," begged Rowan, tugging at him.

But her friend was rigid. Bound by bound the dog drew near, eyes wild, deep-throated barks rending the air.

"Oh, Jaz," Rowan whimpered. "Oh, Jaz."

Her fingers pulled ineffectually at Jashan's arm.

What hope was there?

What could she do?

The dog was almost upon them.

Without hope she stepped forward in front of the boy and threw up her hands in a weak, defensive arc.

"No. No," she cried. But the words were barely a whisper.

The great beast leapt, lips curling back from yellow teeth. She felt its hot, stinking breath. With hammer force the massive jaws clamped down onto her arm. Rowan cried out: half defiance, half terror. The pain was unbearable. Around her there were shouts, voices.

"It's gone mad!"

"Where's it come from?"

"Get it off her!"

"Hit it!"

"Something hard."

"She'll lose her arm."

"Oh my God!"

She felt sick. The faces around her were swimming, looming, melting into the silver-whiteness of the sky.

"It'll kill her!"

"Do something!"

As the powerful fangs gripped tighter, there was the cracking of bones. Rowan screamed. She had never known such pain. Her spine jerked, twisting away from the beast's mouth. A nauseating, swirling darkness swallowed her.

Suddenly, there was a voice, strong, commanding and speaking words she could not understand. Rowan felt a pulse of power surge through her arm, saw a flash of bright light and the dreadful pain was receding.

The great dog cowered. The voice came again. Turning, Rowan saw the pie lady, tall now, her red hood thrown back, one hand raised high.

"Back!" she cried. "Go back! Return to your master, creature of the Foul Folk!"

The creature snarled, snapped. The woman's eyes blazed a furious green. The dog whimpered.

"Away!"

The hound gave one last yelp and ran off, its tail between its legs.

Rowan was aware of kindly voices, helping hands.

"Sit down here on this bale, sweetheart."

"You too, my lad." Jaz was placed next to her.

"Careful now."

"Get the first aid."

"But… there's no blood."

"Would you like a cup of tea?"

Rowan found Jaz's hand and held it tightly. All she really wanted was to be left alone. The crowd broke out afresh.

"Dog just went for them."

"Huge great thing it was."

"No sign of the owner."

"Should be destroyed."

"Danger to the public."

"Almost had her arm off."

A voice rang out, clear and strong.

"The child needs some air. Move away now."

It was the old lady. There was something compelling in her tone. Rowan could hear it, could see it. The tiny woman managed the crowd as effectively as she had managed the dog, dispersing them with a wave of the hand. The two children were invited to warm themselves by Mother Meg's stove.

The old lady gave Jaz a cup of steaming liquid, ruby-red in colour and smelling of cinnamon.

"What's this?" Jaz asked, sniffing it.

"Something that will make you feel better. Now drink."

Rowan stared in astonishment. For once Jaz did as he was told. The greenish pallor of his skin soon disappeared and returned to its usual creamy-caramel glow.

"You too." Mother Meg held out a second cup.

Rowan caught the full power of her gaze. When looked at directly the woman's eyes were a startling green. The green of spring leaves, of crab apples, of gem stones. Against the scarlet of her hood they seemed to shimmer. Rowan looked away.

"There now, Rowan. Drink up. It will give you heart."

Rowan took a small sip. The drink was delicious, sweet and spicy. It flooded her head with memories: mince pies and Christmas songs, hot punch and pine trees, parcels around the tree and candles flickering in the night.

Rowan looked up.

"You stopped that dog."

"Yes, Rowan."

"How did you do it?"

"I suppose I have a way with creatures."

"But it wasn't just an ordinary dog, was it?"

"Its desires were base, dog desires."

Rowan frowned.

"You mean it wanted to attack me, like any mad dog? But why?"

"It was driven by its animal nature, partly."

"You called it something: 'Fal Fawk'. What's that?"

"It was of the Foul Folk."

"Foul Folk?"

"There are many races. Things come in many guises."

"So it wasn't a dog?"

"Its nature is dog-like. Its fangs crush like any dog's."

"It broke my arm! I felt it. But look."

She wriggled her limb back and forth. "The pain just went! How? It's impossible."

"Look in your pocket."

Rowan glanced at her.

"Your coat pocket."

With a sense of apprehension, Rowan undid the zip and pulled out the engraved pebble. It was no longer black, but pale grey, like an empty shell. Rowan pulled off her glove and held it in her palm. It was cold.

"You carry an Earthstone," the old lady said. "It has powers of protection."

This was too weird. Rowan began to shake her head.

"But I don't understand."

"Rowan, sometimes *understanding* is like a garment that is too large. One must grow into it."

"But…"

"Hush; time is short." With a sudden urgency she scanned the far river bank. "You must go."

"But the men, who are they?"

"They are the Hunters. For a brief moment you will be hidden from their eyes. You must return home. You are safe there, at present."

"But what do they want?"

The old lady looked long into Rowan's eyes. In the green depths Rowan thought she could see faces amongst leaves, human-like, creature-like, deer running in the shadows of a great forest.

"They are in for the kill, Rowan. Remember, you have allies. But take care, for '*they*' have many spies. Now off with you!"

Rowan stood up at once. Jaz, she noticed, was still staring into his empty cup, as if in a day-dream.

"One more thing," Mother Meg murmured. From inside her cloak she withdrew a small package, wrapped in crumpled brown paper. She handed it to Rowan.

"W… What's this?" asked Rowan, startled.

"Open it."

Rowan unwrapped the parcel. Inside was a small, rusted key.

"To unlock many secrets."

"But…"

"You must leave. Now!"

The old woman made a flourish in the air and Jaz seemed to wake.

"Come on, Jaz," Rowan said, taking his hand. "We're going home."

"Did you notice something," Jaz began, as they reached the river steps. "About those apple pies?"

"What?"

"And that spooky stone of yours."

"No, what?"

"The pattern was exactly the same."

8

STOLEN

THE SCHOOL CLOAKROOM THRUMMED WITH the sound of many feet upon linoleum floors. Children jostled and pushed, dragging on thick coats, laughing, shouting, shrugging away the cobwebs of the long school day.

"Hey, get off my bag!"

"Anyone seen my gloves?"

"What's tonight's homework?"

"Someone's nicked my chewing gum."

Rowan slipped an arm into the sleeve of a shabby duffle coat and glanced out of the window. All afternoon a snowstorm had been brewing: overhead ominous yellow clouds gathered.

"Hey, Rowan, that's mine."

Rowan gave a start and looked up. Chanel Cook was standing there.

"What?"

"You got my scarf."

Rowan glanced down at the length of Burberry check.

Her mind seemed to have built up a soft layer about itself, a kind of insulation that filtered out the ordinary world.

"Oh, sorry, must have picked it up by mistake."

"Well, I didn't think you was nicking it, did I? What you wearing that old thing for?" Chanel tugged at Rowan's coat. "Where's your new parka?"

"I..."

"Well?"

"It got torn. By a dog."

"A dog? Cor, how?"

"Ripped it, got hold of... my arm."

"What, it went for you?" Chanel seemed impressed.

"Yeah, kind of." Rowan shrugged, trying to show it wasn't a big deal.

"Cool!"

"My mum didn't think so."

Chanel laughed. "That is so like mums, right?"

Rowan smiled, "You should have seen Jaz's mum: she went crazy."

"So where is Jaz, then?"

"Off sick."

"Wicked! Was he hurt?"

"No, delayed shock, his dad said."

There had been quite a scene at Jashan's house the night before. Jaz's mum, concerned about the torn coat sleeve, had asked too many questions and Jaz, in a fine fit of temper, had said too much and broken down in tears. This was so unlike their self-assured son that Jaz's mum and dad had bundled him off to bed with a hot drink and some paracetamol and insisted on driving Rowan home, though it was only a ten-minute walk.

Now, without Jaz, she would have to walk home alone and the weather was getting worse by the moment. Rowan watched the first few snowflakes and shivered.

Chanel laughed again.

"Cheer up, Ro. Why don't you come with me and Jade to the Big Grill, for a burger and chips?"

Rowan smiled. It would have been a great relief to share the company of these boisterous, easy-going girls. But it was impossible. She thought of the old woman's warning. She might be putting others in some kind of danger.

"Thanks, but I really need to get home."

"Fair 'nuff," said Chanel, shrugging amiably. "See you then."

Rowan groped for her own scarf, which had fallen into the dust beneath the bench, then swung her school bag onto her shoulder and hurried through the cloakroom door.

Outside, in the playground, snow was falling fast. The flakes settled like dandelion fluff on the heads and shoulders of waiting parents. They stamped their feet and rubbed their hands to ward off the bitter cold. Rowan felt a tug of regret as she watched the infants gathered up into bear hugs, faces beaming, little hands holding wobbly cereal-box models. Luke had long since stopped coming to collect her from school. When she had finally gathered up the courage to ask why, he had snapped, "For God's sake, Rowan! Isn't it about time you grew up?"

Now for the first time in ages she wished her mum was there. An eerie twilight had fallen. People were hurrying away. Soon the playground would be deserted.

Pulling up her hood, she hastened out of the school gates. The trick was to stay near other people.

She glanced over her shoulder. There was plump little Sadie Blythe skipping along beside her mum. Ahead, Christian, Oliver and Trafford, boys from her class, were swapping retro trading cards.

"Woah, look, I've got Nu-loth. He's an arch mage of Krulak. He's well rare!"

"Not! My brother's got three of him. How about Fiest? She's a Shi-ian deity, and a right babe."

"Okay, I'll swop you Va-Vi for Fiest."

"No way!"

Rowan half listened to their chatter. It helped to lull her mind, keep fears at bay. She let her eyes follow the course of snowflakes, spiralling down from the sky. They drifted through the air, light as swan's feathers.

At the road junction Sadie and her mum turned left and the boys paused, debating whether to visit the Co-op on the high street or turn towards home.

"They might have got the latest edition in."

"I'm dying to get the Ghol Warrior. They've only printed about nine."

"It's getting late though."

"Yeah, but what if they sell out?"

"Oh, go on then."

Rowan felt a wave of relief. She could trail after the boys. Her flat wasn't that far from the Co-op.

An outbreak of shouting close behind made her jump. It was a group of teenagers from the comprehensive school, whooping and jostling. Rowan shrank back and drew her scarf round her face, praying that Billy Madden and Luke weren't with them. But it was only a bunch of girls and boys too absorbed in horseplay to notice little kids.

"Give him a kiss, go on," one squealed.

"Stuff a snowball down her neck!" cried another.

"Don't you bloody dare!"

The snow was coming down fast now. People braced themselves, heads lowered, hats pulled down.

The three boys crossed over a side road and passed by a row of shabby shops. Rowan followed. The last shop was a greasy-spoon cafe which, before the snow, had been frequented by lorry drivers and taxi-cab men. The snow-cleared forecourt was a patchwork of oil-stained ice and dog ends.

A biker sat astride his machine, revving the engine. With each thrust of his leather-clad wrist, clouds of exhaust gas billowed into the air. Rowan felt herself gag on the stench of petrol fumes.

The shop door burst open and several youths tumbled out, laughing and cursing. They greeted the biker, circling his machine, touching the paintwork and chrome almost reverently, like starstruck fans.

Suddenly, Rowan's heart gave a lurch. One of the lads was Luke. His hood was pulled tight, obscuring his face, and his back was turned towards her, but she recognised the heavy jacket, the one he had painted with a death's head motif.

Then two things happened at once. Out of the cafe strutted Billy Madden, gripping the chain of a large, black, snarling dog. In the same instant the man on the bike removed his helmet.

It was the dog handler.

Rowan's stomach heaved up into her throat and the ground lurched from under her feet. It was as if she could feel the bone in her arm cracking. She had to force herself to keep walking. Walk slowly, she told herself. If you run you will attract attention. If you run you will become prey. *"They are the Hunters."* The dogs would be summoned. The Hunters would sound the call and give chase.

Her heart hammered in her chest, tight little punches. The lump in her throat felt bruise-raw. She focused on each step, boots crunching through snow. Running was impossible, anyway.

Any moment she expected to hear a frenzy of barking. But there was only the staccato roar of the motorcycle. Again and again the accelerator was thrust forwards and eventually the angry growl of the machine diminished. She had reached the high street.

As she turned the corner, her breath escaped in a moan. She steadied herself against a wall. They had not seen her; she couldn't believe it. A few minutes more and she would be home, safe.

As Rowan stepped through into the door-well she heard a familiar meow of welcome and something leapt in off the street. It was the silver cat. He weaved his slender body in and out of her legs, tail high in greeting.

"Oh, puss, it's you," she cried, crouching down at the bottom of the stairs, gathering the cat in her arms. It began to purr, its body vibrating against her cheek.

"I am so glad to see you," she said, stroking his ears. "So glad... so glad."

She shivered and glanced behind her, certain she had seen something, something pale, out of the corner of her eye.

"Come on," she said, jumping to her feet, and slammed the street door shut behind her.

How still and dark the flat seemed, with its faint scent of incense. Rowan reached for the light switch, then paused and shivered. Some half whisper in her head was warning, "*Don't turn the light on. Don't give yourself away.*" For a moment her hand hovered uncertainly in mid-air then she drew it back and slumped back against the front door. It closed with a click. The world was spinning, like it used to when she was little and Luke pushed her too fast on the roundabout. She slid to the floor and shut her eyes tight, but it was no use. Urgent questions were tumbling in her mind, falling into confusion.

Billy Madden with that man! Was Billy one of the Hunters? And Luke, oh God, *Luke*, did that make him one too? "*In for the kill*": that's what the old woman had said. She shivered again. Luke might not be in trouble. He might be in *danger*.

The cat jumped into her lap and pushed his head against her face.

"Oh, puss," she sighed, cradling him to her chest. "I wish I knew what to do."

The hallway shifted beneath a pattern of shadow and light. Beams from a vehicle headlamp spilled out through the living room door, skimming across the walls and ceiling, like a searchlight.

"Luke will be home soon."

Rowan took a deep breath and pulled herself up. She double-locked the door, attached the security chain and with a sense of apprehension moved forward into the front room, the cat beside her silent as a shadow.

Pulling back the net, she looked out onto the frozen city. The 'authorities', whoever they were, had just about managed to get London working again. Most main roads were clear and the Underground was open. The majority of people could move between home and work. But it was a strange, white sculpted landscape, barely recognisable. Snowdrifts and icicles had reshaped the city.

Below, people trudged through the snow, some with umbrellas raised, others pulling down hats against the dizzying swirl of flakes.

There was no sign of Luke.

Rowan knew she didn't have much time. Luke might be home any minute and she had to find out. She could feel the prickle of sweat on her palms.

She returned to the hallway and paused outside Luke's bedroom. There was a sign on the door, 'THE PIT, NO ENTRY!', illustrated with zombie faces, cobwebs and dripping blood.

"Luke hates anyone snooping about in his room," she whispered to the cat. "He'll kill me if he finds out."

Rowan gave the door a push. It opened. The cat mewed in protest at the waft of stale air. It was the rank odour of school changing rooms, but beneath there was a hint of something more sinister. And the mess! Even in the darkness Rowan was aware of the impossible jumble of things, strewn across the floor. There was a torch on the bedside table, Luke's old Batman torch. Rowan picked it up and clicked the button. A strong yellow beam shone out.

It revealed more evidence of Luke's untidiness: piles of dirty clothes, Manga magazines and mouldering coffee cups. Every surface was cluttered, every drawer filled to overflowing. The only sign of order was a row of empty drink cans arranged along the windowsill.

"What are we looking for, puss? There must be something."

Rowan began her search. She directed the beam along bookshelves, in drawers and cupboards, over the desk top, behind chairs. There were some grisly pictures stuck on the wall by Luke's bed: insects, spiders, rats and reptiles. She shuddered at a particularly large and hairy tarantula, its front legs curling around a small bird.

There was a pile of games stacked in front of Luke's console. Rowan knew that he swapped a lot of things with his mates. Billy Madden had all the latest stuff, or so Luke was always boasting.

"Nothing obvious," she murmured. "Where would he hide things?"

The cat disappeared beneath the bed. Rowan, craning her head low, peered into the shadows. A variety of things were crammed under here: old shoes, a shabby suitcase, a punctured football, more magazines and a great deal of dust. The cat was sniffing at the suitcase. Rowan grabbed at the handle, gave a tug and it slid out, trailing grey fluff. She had expected it to be heavy, full of junk, but it seemed empty. She was about to push it back, when something caught her eye. From beneath the loose flap came a glint. Rowan pulled back the top and gasped.

The glint had come from some gold price labels, stuck to several unopened PlayStation games. Rowan swallowed hard. Underneath, she found a couple of pairs of unworn Levis and a brand-new phone, still in its box. These were things Luke had wanted for ages, had begged Mum to buy for him. She had said *maybe*, for Christmas, but that they were so *expensive*.

"Where did Luke get them from?"

The cat's eyes gleamed like lanterns in the gloom.

"Luke doesn't have money."

And what was this? There was something wrapped up very securely with tape, in a black bin liner. Rowan tried to peel back the strips of clear tape, but it was stuck fast. She would have to cut it. She paused, listening, straining to hear the sound of a key in the lock, or the thump of the downstairs door closing. But there was only the click and whirr of the gas central heating.

Rowan jumped to her feet. She had seen a red craft knife on Luke's shelf; yes, there it was. She grabbed it, pushed up the triangle of blade and sliced the plastic through.

Her heart felt like a clockwork toy that had been wound too tight. She put her hand inside the bag. As soon as her fingers closed upon the object, she knew what it was: the Box of Treasures, her present from Finn.

When had he taken it? It had been in her bedroom on Saturday night. She had hidden Mother Meg's old key in there and the Earthstone.

What was Luke after?

She drew the box out, inspected it and ground her teeth. All along the edge of the lid were deep, ugly score marks. Rowan's fingers gripped the wood until her fingers hurt.

He had tried to wrench the box open! Luke had taken something, a knife or a screwdriver, and tried to lever off the lid. He had not been able to. Rowan was perplexed. Why had he not been able to force the box open? He wasn't worried about damaging it. The brutal gouges in the delicately carved wood made that clear enough. No, the lock must be far stronger than it looked. Rowan felt a big angry lump forming in her throat.

There was a sudden rattle and a bang from below, a sound Rowan knew only too well. It was the sound of the street door opening and closing.

9

A LETTER

H ANDS SHAKING, ROWAN PUSHED everything under the bed, scrambled to her feet and flicked off the torch.

She stepped out into the dark hall, the cat at her heels. She could hear scuffles, then the slow, hesitant tread of feet upon the stairs, someone treading softly, someone trying *not* to be heard.

Rowan crouched low, gathered the cat in her arms and shrank back into the shadows. The footsteps drew nearer. There was a pause on the first landing, a strange panting sound. The steps (more than one set of feet, surely) continued up the second flight to the upper floor. Rowan felt a desperate urge to crawl to the telephone, call Mum, or Finn, or the police, but she could not move. The same thought spun in her head: the Hunters know where I live; they know I am alone.

Through the thick, patterned glass of the door Rowan could see shadows moving, could hear a low slavering breath. She inched backwards, pressing herself against the wall, wishing she could melt into darkness.

A key rattled in the lock, the handle turned, the door pushed forward; it met the deadlock.

A hoarse whisper of voices.

"S'up?"

"It's locked, from the inside."

A low growl.

"Shut it, mutt!"

Rowan gulped. It was Luke, she was sure: Luke and Billy Madden and Billy's brute of a dog.

There was a stiff squeak as the letter box was prised open.

Rowan pressed herself against the wall, her right arm throbbing with sudden pain.

"She's in there, must be."

A voice called softly, "Rowan, Rowan."

Rowan closed her eyes, held her breath.

"We know you're in there."

A menacing rumble issued from the dog's throat.

"Smash the bloody glass!" The letter box snapped shut and someone gave the door a hefty kick. Suddenly, downstairs, the street door crashed open. The dog went mad; its barks shook the walls. There were shouts, curses, and then a husky voice bellowed up the stairwell.

"What you think you doing? Luke, is that you? For shame, boy. Get that vicious animal out'a here! An' that no-good friend of yours!"

Sophia!

Footsteps pounded down the stairs.

"I'll tell your mother, Luke Maloney!"

The street door slammed shut.

The silver cat gave a loud mew and Rowan, scrambling to her feet, unlocked the front door and flung it open.

There was Sophia standing below on the first-floor landing.

"Oh my word, chile!" She clutched her chest. "You near scared me to death. I thought no one was home."

"And I thought *you* were at work."

"No, it's my day off, I been Christmas shopping. But, child, what are you doing all alone in the dark? Were them naughty boys bothering you?"

"I wasn't alone; the cat was with me."

"Ah!" exclaimed Sophia, as if this explained everything. "Well, honey, if you could do my poor creaking knees a favour and go collect my bags. I dropped them when I saw those rascals, thought we had burglars. Thank the Lord I didn't buy anything fragile."

Rowan hurried down to the entrance lobby, quickly gathered up the shopping bags and several letters scattered on the door mat and just as swiftly returned to Sophia.

"Thank you, child. Ah, the post."

"Yes. One for you," she handed the letter over. "The rest are for Mum."

"Well now, honey, you get yourself back indoors, an..."

Sophia paused, her eyes gleaming bright as a cat's.

"A... and?" Rowan half whispered, shivering.

"Don't open the door to no one but your mother, you understand?"

Rowan nodded, made her way up to the flat and, closing the door, reset the deadlock.

She stared at the letters blankly. It was some time before she registered what she was holding. There were three official-looking envelopes, with crinkly windows and printed addresses. The fourth, she noted, was good-quality paper, handwritten in black ink. She shook herself: what was she doing? OMG, the box! Leaning in through the kitchen door she flung the letters onto the work surface, then dashed to her own bedroom.

Luke must not find out that she had been snooping around, or that she had discovered his secret. What had the old lady said, something about spies? What else could Luke be? *They* had got to him. Billy Madden, the dog handler, the Grey Man.

"They've changed him, puss. He's not my brother anymore. But what's he become?"

The question sent a tremor to the pit of her stomach. With wild motions she groped beneath her wardrobe for the key to Finn's box. She must hurry.

Rowan returned to Luke's room, pulled the Box of Treasures from underneath Luke's bed and ran her hands over the damaged lid. Again sparks of anger flared. How dare he? She turned the key in the lock, paused to draw a steady breath and opened it. The contents, usually arranged with such care, were a terrible muddle. Feathers tangled with dried petals, skeleton leaves with locks of hair, broken seashells caught in nets of sheep's wool. The unicorn picture was creased and Finn's photograph had a nasty tear down the middle.

Rowan's eyebrows drew together, a hard line across her forehead.

"There's something here Luke wants, but what?"

She stared hard at the cat, who was watching her closely.

Rowan picked up a soft leather pouch, strung on a thin cord. Inside was the silver Fàinne Duilleoga – the ring of tiny leaves. It seemed to glimmer with a light all its own. This necklace, of all her possessions, was the only thing of value, the only thing Luke could hope to sell. Was that it? Was he after money? Yet somehow she doubted it. His new friends seemed rich enough. Wouldn't they provide him with what he wanted, for 'favours' of some kind?

Her fingers brushed over acorns and shells and stopped at the Earthstone. Its colour had deepened since Saturday. There was perceptible warmth radiating from its surface. Rowan rubbed her arm, the memory of the dog's bite still vivid. This stone seemed to possess real magic. The Hunters *must* want it, either for their own nasty purposes or to stop her using it. She pondered for a moment, gazing into the box and then took the old key, small and dull, between her finger and thumb. How could this have any worth? Yet it was a gift from the old lady at the fair. There was no denying that Mother Meg was a person of extraordinary power: "*To open many secrets*" were her *very* words; it must be important.

"What should I do? Hide them?"

The cat, watching with glimmering eyes, mewed.

Rowan stared at him, hard.

"I suppose *you're* to be trusted?"

The cat gazed back, unblinking.

Rowan took a paper tissue from her pocket and, with great care, wrapped each of the three precious objects and put them in the leather pouch. She loosened her collar, hung the leather cord about her neck and tucked the pouch inside her shirt. There it would stay, safe, hidden, next to her heart. Luke could go mad searching, but neither he nor the Hunters would find what they were looking for.

Five silvery chimes rang out, the living room clock marking the hour. Just before she closed the lid, Rowan took out Finn's photo and stuffed it in her pocket. Then with fumbling fingers she relocked the Box of Treasures and hurried to the kitchen for a roll of tape and a black bin liner. Wrapping the box, she returned it to the suitcase and pushed it beneath Luke's bed. The torn plastic scraps were tidied away and Luke's torch put back on the bedside table. She gave the room one last searching look. It was such a mess he wouldn't notice a thing. She shut the door behind her.

As Rowan entered the kitchen the cat padded over to the back door, letting out a thin wail.

"Need to go out, hmmm, puss?"

The cat brushed again and again against her legs. Rowan unlocked the back door but hesitated, unwilling to let in the bitter chill of night and just as unwilling to let the cat go. She crouched down, tickling his chin.

"You will come back?"

The silver cat pushed his head close to her face, purring.

"Please come back."

Rowan stood up and opened the door no more than a hand's breadth. The cat slipped through and was gone.

———◦———

"Oh, the Tube!" Rowan's mother exclaimed, collapsing into a chair. "I feel as if I've been vacuum packed. It's more crowded than ever since the snow."

Rowan handed her a cup of tea and attempted a smile.

"Oh, darling, thank you, and could you get me a digestive? I think there are some in the tin."

Her mother clasped the hot mug between both hands. "My fingers are frozen!"

Rowan prised open the lid of the biscuit tin.

"Two left," she said, placing them on the table.

"But that was a *new* packet!" said Mum.

"Perhaps we've got mice?"

"Yes, very big mice, the two-legged, teenage kind!" Mum put her feet up and sighed. "I'm exhausted!"

"Never mind, Christmas holidays soon," said Rowan, pouring herself some tea.

Mum smiled. "Bliss. No more Mrs Flint, no more frazzled teachers, no more horrible schoolkids!"

"I'm a schoolkid, Mum!"

"You're at junior school, darling. You haven't drunk the Jekyll and Hyde potion yet."

Mum took another sip of tea. "So what are you and Jaz planning for Christmas?"

Rowan rested her chin on her hands and thought about all the things they loved doing: Christmas shopping, the youth centre disco, skating at the rink, making decorations, putting up the tree. Yet, this year everything was different. Rowan wished she could shrug away the weight pressing down on her shoulders.

She tried to sound breezy. "Oh, same old stuff."

"By the way," said Mum, reaching for the last biscuit. "Have you seen Luke?"

"No. He... he..." Rowan had a sudden, overwhelming urge to tell Mum everything.

"He what?"

But the words would not come. What could she say? Who would believe her? And if Mum knew then *she* might be in danger! It was no good. Mum mustn't be dragged into all of this.

"You okay, love?"

"Oh… he… I… I think he's out with his friends."

Mum was looking at her with concern.

Rowan turned her eyes away then, seeing the letters on the side, grabbed them and thrust them into her mother's lap.

"You've got some post!"

"Bills, I suppose?" Mum took them with a sigh of resignation. "Well, that's water, that's gas, that's broadband," she said, casting them wearily onto the table. "And this? Oh, it's from Helena! Christmas card, I should think. Goodness, I wish I were that organised."

She put the last piece of biscuit into her mouth and opened the letter. Rowan sat down and began to spoon sugar into her cup, stirring, lost in thought.

Rowan's mother gave a gasp, almost choking on the biscuit crumbs. She was staring at the sheet of paper in her hand.

"What is it?" Rowan asked, looking up.

"Oh no…!" Her mother's mouth had dropped open.

"What?"

"It's Helena." She was scanning the letter urgently.

"Is anything the matter?"

After what seemed like a very long time, her mother looked up, dark circles beneath her eyes.

"Helena's very ill." There was a long pause. "She's got cancer."

After that there were lots of phone calls: to Helena, briefly, and to Tom, Helena's husband. Her mother spoke very little during this call but her face became pale and her eyes seemed to grow darker. Rowan busied herself with the preparations for tea: grating cheese and mixing tuna mayonnaise for the jacket potatoes. Meanwhile, her mother made lengthy calls to two close friends. Rowan could not hear very much of these conversations, just the occasional word, but once she thought she heard her mother crying. Later, Mum phoned Grandma and Rowan knew she was making arrangements for a visit.

When her mother came back into the kitchen she looked washed out, as if a migraine were threatening. Her mum sat down heavily and leant against the table.

"Dinner's almost ready, Mum. Do you want some?"

"What? Oh, thank you, darling. You've been very helpful." But Mum was miles away.

Rowan set the table and brought over the baked potatoes and a bowl of steamed broccoli.

"How is Helena?" she asked.

Her mother sighed.

"She's really very ill. She didn't want anyone to know, until things... Tom said she wouldn't let him tell anyone."

"But she has told you, now."

"Yes." For a brief moment her mother put her head in her hands then sitting upright said "yes" again, louder this time.

There was a pause, her mother seemed to gather herself.

"Rowan, I've got to go down to Brighton. It'll only be for a few days, just at the beginning of the holiday. I feel bad about leaving you and Luke, but Helena's asked me to go. She needs me to be there."

Rowan gulped, feeling suddenly sick. She would be alone with Luke for days. Anything might happen.

"That's fine, Mum." Her voice was a mousy whisper.

Mum put out a hand and squeezed Rowan's arm.

"I've asked Grandma if you can stay with her. It'll be a bit cramped in the cottage – they're pretty much snowed in up there – but you'll manage, won't you, darling?"

"We'll be fine. I'll help Gran with the cooking and decorations and everything."

"And I promise you, Rowan…" her mother leant over and kissed her, "I *promise* I'll be there for Christmas."

Rowan gave a weak smile, her heart sinking. Without Mum everything would be unbearable. Luke would be out of control. Poor Grandma wouldn't be able to cope. And yet… and yet… if Mum went away… Suddenly, it was as if the sun had come out from behind thunder clouds. If Mum went to Brighton then she would be *safe*, out of harm's way. And if the two of them, she and Luke, had to stay in Yorkshire, far away from London, from Billy Madden, from the Grey Man and the Foul Folk, wouldn't things return to normal? Wouldn't the real Luke come back?

Rowan sat up and gave her mother a big smile.

"It's fine, Mum. Honest, we'll be fine."

Her hand went to the outline of the leather pouch hidden beneath her shirt. She remembered the words of the old lady: "*You have many allies.*" That meant she wasn't alone; she must not forget that. Perhaps the silver cat was an ally, or Sophia, or even Mr Rafik? After all, he had given her the Earthstone. Maybe she should pay him a visit, ask for his advice.

"You're looking very thoughtful, Rowan," said her mother.

"Sorry? Oh, yes, I've just remembered something."

Tomorrow, she thought, I'll go and see Mr Rafik. Tomorrow, after school. He'll know what to do.

10

GALLOWS YARD

———◆———

"Ro! Rowan! Slow down a bit," Jaz cried, half skidding across the playground. It was a clear night. The moon rose, hard and bright, casting a bluish light over the crusted snow.

Jaz grabbed at Rowan's arm.

"What's the hurry? I thought we were walking home together. Look, I've got ginger beer to share; mind you, it's a bit shaken up. Vic went and dropped it." He pulled a can from his school bag.

Rowan stared down at her boots and nudged at a lump of sparkling snow. She had planned to slip away quietly after the last bell. She couldn't risk Jaz getting mixed up in all of this. Not again. Not after what had happened on the river.

"I... I..." she could feel herself blushing. "My mum... she wanted..." Her breath coiled away on the frozen air.

Jaz stuck his chin out, obstinate as ever. "You were trying to give me the slip, weren't you? For goodness' sake, Ro! Something's happened hasn't it, and you're not telling me."

Rowan's shoulders sank, but she forced herself to look Jashan in the eye. "Look, it's... things could get so... risky."

Jaz snorted. "Your brother's gone insane hanging around with a gang of criminals. Of course it's bloody risky! So what are you planning to do, dahling, *all by yourself*? Make a citizen's arrest?"

Sparks of electricity crackled in Jaz's eyes.

Rowan looked around at the emptying playground. Something pale seemed to lurk in the deep shadow of the school building. Or were her eyes playing tricks?

"It's late," she said and began to hurry towards the school gates. She hoped Jaz would just give up and go, but, stubborn as ever, the boy followed.

"So, that's it, is it?"

"Look, Jaz, people could get hurt, really hurt."

"And does *people* include you, Ro? Come on, you'd think I'd let you face those psychopaths alone?"

Rowan couldn't help smiling at the thought of Jashan taking on a gang of crazed thugs. That's what she had always loved about Jaz: he was so 'out there', so fearless. But these weren't just thugs, these creepy men with their killer dogs. She remembered the eyes of the Grey Man: dead, and yet as insatiable as a black hole, dragging all into nothingness.

She shivered and turned to face her friend.

"Okay, Jaz, you're right. I can't do it alone. I'm going to talk to Mr Rafik. I think he'll know what to do."

But as soon as they passed through the school gates Rowan knew something was wrong. A trickle of ice seemed to pool in the pit of her stomach. Through the straggling groups of parents and children she saw the scrawny, moth-eaten form of Reginald, slouched against the school railings.

"Jaz," she hissed. "Turn, now! It's *them*."

The two children pivoted abruptly, but there, perched on the bonnet of a snowbound car, fiddling with a length of slender rope, was Rafe, his mouth a wide, hungry leer.

"Well now," he said, licking his lips. "If it isn't Luke's *adorable* little sister."

Rowan swallowed hard. "What do you want?"

Rafe jumped lightly to the ground. Reginald was edging his way along the railings.

"We want you to come quietly. Like good little children. Not too much to ask, is it?" He wrapped the cord around his fists and took a step closer.

"And what if we scream our heads off, you creep?" said Jaz, waving his can in Rafe's face.

Ignoring him, Rafe fixed his narrow eyes on Rowan.

"Your mother gets home about six, doesn't she, sweetheart?" With a snap he pulled the cord tight, and moved closer still.

"Please don't..." Rowan began, but in an instant Jaz had thrust the drink can further forward and ripped off the metal ring. Ginger beer exploded into Rafe's face.

Jashan grabbed Rowan's hand. "Run," he cried. "Run!" He flung the can at Rafe and pulled Rowan across the road.

"After them!" Rafe spluttered, hands pressed blindly to his eyes.

The hard crust of frozen snow gave a firm footing. The two friends flew on breathlessly, pursued by the desperate scurry of footsteps. They turned a corner into a snowbound labyrinth: street after street, a maze of terraced houses, twisting this way and that. On they went, through gates and along alleyways, across back gardens and over fences. Then, at last, gasping for breath, they found themselves in a dimly lit, unsavoury area, full of old garages and storage units, overshadowed by the towering arches of a railway viaduct.

They had reached a dead end.

Rowan glanced back, gasping for breath, but there was no sign of Reginald.

Jaz stared at the cracked windows of the shabby buildings, illuminated by the desultory flicker of a single working street lamp. "This place gives me the shivers," he said. "I can feel eyes, watching."

"Perhaps we can hide under the bridge," Rowan suggested. Still holding hands, they approached the gloomy shadows of the railway arches.

"Except," whispered Jaz, "*those creeps* will probably be able to smell us out."

"Look!" said Rowan.

Sandwiched between the last garage and the bridge was an alley.

Jaz peered in. "Urgh, it smells. Can't see a thing. Could be anything lurking down there."

Rowan glanced over her shoulder. She was sure she had heard something behind them, the scratching of claws, a probing sniff.

"Have you got any matches, Jaz?"

"No, but I've got this." Jaz handed over a fluorescent pink lighter. Rowan sparked a flame. It cast a dull glow, enough to illuminate the frozen puddles and rivulets of dirty ice streaking the walls.

"Come on, Jaz. I'll go first."

Rowan began to make her way down the tunnel. Old patches of graffiti showed through the ice and, despite the cold, it smelt dank and unpleasant.

"I bet people do things down here," Jaz muttered. "God knows what we're walking through, but it reeks."

The passageway seemed to go on for ages, shadows loomed in the guttering light, but at last Rowan saw a dim gleam ahead and eventually the children emerged into a bleak yard of crumbling walls and dark corners, illuminated only by the rising moon.

To their left was a vast derelict building half buried in snow, to their right a high brick wall, hung with massive wrought iron gates. Somewhere beyond loomed scaffolding and cranes and, gleaming in the reflection of the blue-white snow, new hoardings proclaimed 'Bullingdon Construction'.

The far end of the street was blocked by a great drift. And yet this end, which seemed to lead nowhere, had recently been cleared. The road was coated in a thin layer of fresh snow. Rowan could see footprints and tracks leading back and forth from the mouth of the alley to a point in the middle of the road, just level with the huge gates.

"Where is this?" Jaz moved forward, his head turning from side to side.

"Here's a street name," said Rowan, brushing snow from a rusty metal sign. "Gallows Yard."

Rowan felt the same odd prickling sensation in her guts. She didn't like the way the moonlight glinted in the shards of broken glass on top of the high wall. She didn't like the silence.

"There's no way through," she half whispered.

But Jaz was already walking towards the double gates. "I wonder what this old place used to be?"

"Jaz, don't," Rowan said urgently. "We need to get out."

Jaz's feet crunched through the shallow crust of snow. The shadow of the gates fell across the smooth white surface. *Like prison bars*, Rowan thought.

She tried to call Jaz back, but her voice failed. It was as if, behind every shattered window and every broken doorway, eyes followed.

Caught in the snare of shadows, Jaz gazed up at the tall iron gates. "Look at this, I can see letters at the top, some missing. There's a B, an L, then a big space where it's all broken, then a K. Black! Could be black. There's a space and an O and a G. Black... og. And then the word Brewery. Og, Log? Bog? It must have been here for a hundred years. The building is enormous!"

"Dog," said Rowan.

"What?"

"Dog. It says 'Black Dog Brewery'." She shivered.

Suddenly, like a cork from a bottle, a large object burst upwards from the middle of the road, and fell back to earth with a thundering clang. It was as if a church bell had hit the ground. The vibrations hit Rowan in the solar plexus, punched against her ears. She staggered backwards, head swimming, ears ringing.

Jaz crumpled like a rag doll.

A figure emerged from a gaping hole in the road.

Something with claws and a thrashing tail.

11

UNDERGROUND

"**N**o!" ROWAN SCREAMED.

But in a moment the creature was on top of Jaz. It dragged his limp body towards the manhole. Rowan lurched forwards, reaching out towards her friend, but something grabbed her, a stinking palm clamped hard across her mouth. She felt her arm wrenched painfully behind her back.

"Don't make a sound, missy," hissed a voice.

Rafe!

Rowan could see the creature pulling Jaz to the rim of the hole. Reviving, Jaz had started to kick and struggle. Inspired, Rowan aimed a boot heel at Rafe's shin.

"You little bitch!" he cried and slammed her so hard on the side of the head that the world started spinning.

There was a gurgling scream in her ear, a horrible, agonised sound. Rowan fell, face down. The next thing she recalled was a soft, silvery cheek pushing itself against hers.

She groaned, spat out snow.

A cat's wet nose nudged her cheek, its meow insistent. Rowan sat up, head splitting. "It's okay, puss, I'm fine," she mumbled in confusion. Through the haze of pain she sensed something large and pale dragging a squealing Rafe into the stinking alleyway.

Puss meowed again and bounded towards the manhole in the road. Oh God: Jaz! Rowan got to her feet and staggered after the cat.

Iron rungs led down from the mouth of the hole into blackness. The cat balanced for a moment on the edge, then gave a sudden leap and was gone. "No!" cried Rowan. "Wait!" Trembling, she grabbed the handrail, placed her foot unsteadily on the metal bar and began to descend.

The shaft was black as... Rowan didn't want to think it, but the word 'death' loomed at her, pale and ghost-like, out of the darkness. It was so dark that it didn't matter if she closed her eyes or not. She felt as if she was breathing the blackness in. She had to feel her way down, bit by bit, boots slipping on metal treads. Only the thought of Jaz being dragged away for some unthinkable purpose kept her moving.

Suddenly, Rowan's foot struck the ground and she almost overbalanced. The place stank, worse than the alley! And *where* was the cat?

"Puss," she called, her voice a croak of fear.

There was the faintest echoing mew... far away.

Rowan remembered the lighter, took it out of her pocket and struck a flame. It guttered alarmingly, throwing shadows all around. She was in a man-high tunnel; the walls and roof were encrusted with countless glittering icicles, and a thick, stinking, luminous sludge flowed in a gully below. Alongside the reeking channel ran a narrow footway. Must be the sewers under London, thought Rowan.

"Puss!" she called again. "Puss!" She could hear the desperate edge in her tone. Holding the lighter in a shaking hand she began to make her way along the edge.

Now and then water would gush from a side sluice, throwing up a fug of foul-smelling vapour. The tunnel branched. Rowan paused, head still throbbing, and decided to take the left-hand turn. "If I keep to the left it will stop me from getting lost, at least I read that somewhere, once. I think." Trouble is, she already felt more than lost and there was no sign anyone had ever been this way. There was no dropped glove, no revealing footprint, no sign of a struggle. The passage divided again. Where was puss? She strained her ears to listen. Was that a meow? No, it sounded more like music; how odd. Was she hearing things again? Music in the sewers? "It sounds like one of those old-fashioned barrel organs," she murmured. "And there are voices echoing down the tunnels. And, up ahead, isn't that a shaft of light?"

Thrusting the lighter into her pocket, Rowan hurried towards the yellowish gleam. Yes, there was another ladder leading upwards, rather rusted in places, and up above she could see a broken grate.

She climbed up and thrust her head through the hole. After the silence of the tunnels the noise seemed overwhelming. She was looking out at a crowded marketplace, its tattered, faded awnings fluttering in the night air. The market stalls occupied a paved square, lit by old-fashioned street lamps and edged by dilapidated buildings. People swarmed back and forth, jostling one another, impatient to see the goods on display.

"Taters, genetically modified, one hundred per cent guaranteed!"

"Freshly baked bread, no brick dust, no chalk!"

"Kensington chicken, get your delicious Kensington chicken!"

Rowan hauled herself through the hole and slipped into the crowd. The clamour of street criers and pounding, discordant music filled her head. Hurdy-gurdies rivalled fiddles, trumpets shrieked over lutes, strolling drummers drowned out everyone with their flamboyant rhythms. And people were dressed in such an odd assortment of clothes: patched velvet crinolines here, an old biker jacket there, a top hat, a grubby pair of green fluorescent leggings, a corset, red stiletto shoes, studded boots. Everyone seemed ready to barge and elbow their way through the throng, snarling obscenities. The street lamps hissed, casting an uncanny, jaundiced gleam. And, strangest of all, there was no snow. It was warm, so warm that Rowan was beginning to sweat.

"'Ere, miss, fancy a crispy hopper? Only one token." A snotty little kid held up a kebab stick. Something many-legged and burnt to a crisp was skewered on the end.

"What is it?" Rowan couldn't help asking.

"S'a hopper, o' course. Only a token."

"Where are we? What part of London?"

"Wot?"

"Where are we?" Rowan repeated. "And it's so hot. What's happened to the snow?"

The grubby faced boy stared at her askance.

"You from Summerland then, miss, from the Palace?"

"What?"

Suddenly, a woman pushed the little boy aside. "Is he bothering you, missy? Get off wiv you, Charlie! Can't you see this nice lady don't want no nasty hoppers. No, a nice slice of Kensington chicken would be the thing, the very thing. You're looking a bit rosy, miss. Must be that lovely greatcoat you're wearing. Don't see much o' these nowadays. Antique, is it?"

She fingered the sleeve of Rowan's duffle coat.

"You'd feel a deal more comfortable if you took it off, miss. Come from the Crystal Palace, do you?"

"No. Is this Crystal Palace?"

"What? Is *this* the Crystal Palace?" the woman began to laugh. "Oy, Gazza, you'll never believe it. Our little lady 'ere; she's asking if *this* is the Crystal Palace? Oh my eyes!"

A bearded man with acned cheeks came forward, grinning. "That's a good 'un! Yeah, a right royal sense of humour, she's got, coming from the bleeding glass dome. Pah! So, Nelly, is she buying or wot? Looks loaded."

The woman turned and stared Rowan straight in the eye. "You're buying, ain't you, darlin'? We'll be disappointed if you don't buy nothin'. Come to our stall. Gazza does the best Kensington chicken, outside Kensington, o' course!"

She began to laugh again, and Gazza joined in with stomach-heaving mirth.

On the stall, portions of fried chicken were laid out on old newspaper. Only, thought Rowan, it didn't look like chicken, not really. And hanging from the back of the awning she could see fur pelts, tabby-striped.

Nelly picked up a piece of meat and smiled. "How about a nice thigh? Only five tokens. That's nothin', is it, for a little lady like you."

"I… I'm not really hungry, I'm looking…"

"I *said*, only five tokens, miss. *Nothin'* for a little lady like you!" The woman's voice had turned dangerous.

"I don't have any tokens. I've only got…"

Rowan scrabbled around in her pocket and pulled out a coin and the pink lighter. "A pound. Is that enough?"

"What's this?" sneered Gazza, grabbing the coin. "Some kind of funny money!" He bit it. "Hmmm. Metal, though. Copper, I reckon, an' some nickel. Worth a bit."

"And this!" Nelly cried snatching up the lighter. "It's one o' them flamers. Pretty! How's it work? Show me!"

She thrust it back at Rowan. Rowan swallowed, her mouth feeling dry, and sparked the flint. A flame leapt up.

"Woah! That is spanking!" The woman grabbed the lighter and, absorbed, started flicking the wheel with her thumb. She carelessly flung the fried meat in Rowan's direction. It tumbled into the dust and several rats darted forwards to grab it.

Seeing her chance, Rowan melted back into the crowd and headed for the manhole. She slithered down the ladder so hastily her knees were grazed against the rusted iron.

Now, without the lighter, the sewer seemed darker than ever. What was she going to do? A luminous mist was rising up from the sludge. She must find Jaz, she must! If only puss was with her. If only... She felt the sting of hot tears in her eyes, a burning at the back of her throat. What good was crying? It wouldn't help anyone. She wiped her nose on her sleeve and stumbled a few steps further along the tunnel, but the greenish cloud engulfed her. All she could see was the brick wall where her shaking hand rested.

Something echoed around the walls. Was it the drip of water? A rat swimming? The patter of footsteps? Nelly and her cronies following? She tried to press herself against the wall of the tunnel. Surely no one could see her here in the deep shadows and swirling fog?

A rough hand seized her throat, squeezing hard.

She gave a hoarse yelp.

"Got you, you little bitch!" His wet mouth pressed roughly against her ear. "Thought your big, scary friends had saved you, hmmm? Hurting Rafe like that. My poor, poor leg. Well, let me tell you, sweetness, *you* are going to be locked away with that vile friend of yours. The one who bites and scratches like a cat. Locked away in the deepest dark."

"Puss!" she shrieked. "Help! Puss, help!" Her voice rebounded up and down the tunnel.

"Scream as much as you like, darling. There's no one to hear. No one." He gave an unsettling snicker. "The dogs have dealt with *them*."

Rafe leapt into the stinking sludge, dragging Rowan after him. She struggled and fought but his grip was like iron. "Such a prize," he muttered to himself. "A lovely tender morsel for His Magnificence. And, oh, what won't they do for Rafe then? Every luxury, every advantage! Sir Rafe. Lord Rafe. Your Grace. At last they'll recognise my worth, my entitlement!"

He continued to witter as he limped along, dragging her further and further into the darkness. Rowan could see nothing, only hear the occasional gush of water and the splash of their footsteps. After a while even this sound faded and once again she could feel the cold seep beneath her thick coat.

Then there was a faint glow of light. A flaming torch guttered on the wall ahead, illuminating a place where the passageway branched off in several directions. Rafe put his nose into the air and sniffed.

"Don't like the smell of that, oh no."

He pulled Rowan roughly towards the right-hand passage. She made a futile attempt to grab at the torch.

"We'll have none of that!" Rafe bellowed, and swinging her around to face him he slapped Rowan full across the mouth. Then he grabbed her hair and shook her. "Your repulsive furry friend hurt poor Rafe. Do you hear? He HURT poor Rafe!"

"Please, please," she begged.

"He HURT POOR RAFE!"

Suddenly, Rafe shrieked and froze.

A knife glinted at his throat.

12

THE VEILED WOMAN

---·◆·---

"**D**ROP HER!"

The light from the torch ran like liquid off the razor-sharp blade.

Rafe gulped and released his grip. Rowan staggered back. There was a heavy crunch, a groan, Rafe's eyes rolled up into their sockets and he fell forward to the floor.

"Are you injured?"

A tall, veiled figure, clad in furs, long dark hair spilling out from beneath a thick cap, bent over her.

"N... no," Rowan stammered. "I... I'm..."

"Then come."

The voice was low, but mellow in timbre, like that of a woman. The figure drew a small glass object, shaped like a teardrop, from beneath her tunic. It shimmered with light.

"Quick. There may be others, and they have dogs."

The tall woman strode ahead. Rowan had to run to keep up. As she followed, Rowan realised they were no longer in the sewers. The floor here, like the walls, was hewn from bare rock that sparkled with some kind of crystal. Where were they? And how far from Jaz?

"Wait, please. I need to find my—" Rowan panted.

The woman held up a hand. "It's too dangerous to talk. Come."

They hurried on, down tunnel after tunnel, and eventually ascended a sloping pathway. A bluish mist glittered before them. Plunging through the swirling cloud, Rowan was struck by bitter cold. She gasped in shock.

"Wait," said the woman, and once again reached into her tunic. She pulled out a thin silver-grey cloak. "Wrap your head and shoulders in this."

The woman took her arm and they moved forward into what seemed, to Rowan, to be the blank howl of nothingness. Yet, as the wind hit her, she realised they had emerged into a snowstorm. They must be outside, yet the world, utterly featureless, was a blur of white. Where had London gone?

They seemed to walk through that blizzard-swept landscape for a long time, but perhaps, thought Rowan, it wasn't far at all. Perhaps the wailing maelstrom of snow that blinded and choked also swallowed one's sense of time and space.

Suddenly, the woman was gesturing and pushing Rowan down. A narrow opening had appeared at their feet, a low tunnel of ice. Rowan stooped and scrambled through on hands and knees. It opened out into an oval chamber, some kind of igloo, carpeted with leather hides. After the snow storm the hush was astonishing.

"Sit," said the figure, motioning towards a pile of furs. "You need a hot drink and some balm."

The veiled figure hung the glass light from a filigree cradle fixed into the ceiling. She gathered handfuls of dry bark and twigs from a wood stack by the wall and set a fire going. A tripod and pot were positioned, fresh snow collected and soon water was boiling over the flames. The figure added a sprinkling of herbs from a pouch, honey from a flask.

"So, what were the Foul Folk wanting with you?" the woman asked at last, handing Rowan a cup of hot liquid.

"They've got my friend. I need to find him. That, that… man, Rafe, said they would lock him up in the dark. I've got to go back and find him."

"Yes," murmured the veiled woman, her brilliant blue eyes searching Rowan's face. "They have a penchant for locking up children."

"I've got to go and find my friend," said Rowan, half rising. She could feel panic inside. "We've got to get back… to London. Everyone will be worried."

"Drink first." The woman took a small ornate jar from a bag, removed the lid and placed it by the fire. It was filled with a greenish, mint-scented salve. "Tell me," she said, as she applied the warmed ointment to the side of Rowan's face, "did they bring you by sea? Many of the children forget. They put something in the food."

Rowan stared at the cup in her hands and put it down hurriedly. "No, I… we… we came through the tunnels, the sewers."

"The tunnels?" The blue eyes fixed on Rowan. "You're quite sure? You came through the tunnels?"

"Yes. From London."

"That's new. Lord Medick will find this interesting. They've been digging, and we suspect…"

The figure stared into the flames for a moment then glanced back at Rowan.

"Drink. It's not drugged, don't worry. I'm here to help you."

Rowan blushed, picked up the cup and sipped. It tasted sweet and potent, like Mother Meg's spiced punch. And the salve had eased the throbbing ache in her head. She gazed at the veiled figure. "You called them the Foul Folk."

"Yes, that is what they are, *foul*."

"Do... do you know Mother Meg?"

"No, I've never heard the name."

"If you want to help... why... why don't you...?" She made a gesture, then lowered her gaze. She couldn't meet the woman's ice-blue eyes.

"Why do I wear the veil?" The woman laughed softly. "Concealment. Anything to disconcert the Foul Folk. And to protect those we help. If *you* know nothing they will not be able..." She paused suddenly. The look in her eyes was grave.

"You should rest, child."

"I can't. Please, I need to find my friend. Please." She could hear the sobs in her own voice.

"Hush, drink. You must calm yourself. We can do nothing until the blizzard passes. I shall prepare a bowl."

Rowan sipped more of the herb drink. She could feel the knotted feeling in her chest and stomach loosen and her headache had almost gone. She watched the woman take out a beautiful silver bowl from a leather bag and fill it with clear water.

Passing her hand over the glass light, it dimmed and the woman set the bowl before Rowan.

"Gaze, little one. It will help."

Rowan looked into the water. The interlaced markings on the inside of the bowl reminded her of the Box of Treasures. She thought she could make out a tree shape, branches and leaves and berries, or was it just a spiralling pattern, going round and round and round and… Her head drooped forwards.

"I feel… strange…"

Suddenly, there on the surface of the water something glimmered: light dissolved, rippled, coiled… and she could see, she could see…!

A flickering, waving picture formed, grew clearer… a snowscape, viewed from above, high above, as if from the eye of an eagle; a fixed point in the sky, surveying the world below.

White lands lie vast and formless beneath a bitter, night sky. To the east the barren landscape begins to alter. Hills rise up in gradual, swelling curves, skirted with thickets of pine.

A waxing moon shines down so brightly it turns the deep, hard snow to silver and over its frozen stillness two shadows race.

Shoulder to shoulder and pace for pace they run, heading for the uncertain cover of the trees; two great white wolves, large of stature, lean of limb, their shaggy pelts rendering them almost invisible against the snowfield.

"Take heart, Sage. We are almost there," the female says. "Amongst the trees we shall have the advantage."

The second wolf is silent. Every sinew and fibre of his exhausted body is straining to cross this last stretch of open ground and reach the lower thickets.

The female glances back. In the far distance 'they' can be seen: a pack of dogs, large and muscular, moving along at a constant, loping pace. As she looks, two hounds, with a sudden burst of speed, break away from the group.

"They are strong," she cries. "I have never known them to match our kind in stamina before!"

She tosses her maned head.

"But we shall outwit them!"

The two wolves, driven by desperation, sprint onwards. Their strength is failing. The chase has lasted many hours; the wasteland of ice and snow offers no haven, no respite. But at last the land begins to slope upwards and here and there conifers grow, bearing the sharp scent of resin.

The tree cover becomes thicker the higher they climb. It is familiar territory to them and, with a skill born of instinct, they weave their way past the low lying, prickly branches; up and onwards, deep into the night-shadow of the trees. Eventually the woodland ends, revealing a moon-white dome of snow, the crown of the hill, topped by a dense grove.

They study the scene for a moment and then the female murmurs a few words into her mate's ear. The two wolves part, one moving left and the other right along the dark line of forest from which they have just emerged. Encircling the hilltop, they meet on the far side, then, turning sharply, make for the summit, where they crawl in amongst the thickly matted boughs. Here, on a high vantage point looking down over the hillside, they can see without being seen.

They sink to the ground, panting. The male rests his weary head upon his paws and closes his eyes. With great tenderness, the female licks his muzzle. She knows his strength is almost gone.

"We have gained a little time. The woods will slow them. They'll have to work hard to pick up our scent."

She lowers her head, but her ears are pricked high. She can hear sounds, far below, at the bottom of the hill. It will be some time before the first dogs break through the line of trees. By then she and her mate will be ready.

She thinks of home, of her last litter of cubs – fine, strong children all, with the exception of Grey Paw. He was a frail creature, mistaken for stillborn, until somehow he had struggled into life. Even now at six months he is thin and weak, though smarter than any of his brothers or sisters. She remembers how he had gazed up at her just before the parting, his yellow eyes enormous in his small face.

"Why do you stare so, little Grey Paw?" she had asked, holding her head close to his.

"To drink you up, like sweet water from a clear spring."

"And why should you wish to drink me up, funny pup?"

"Then I won't feel so empty when you are gone, Mother."

And when they had come to the final leaving, she had not been able to look back.

She raises her head, alert. Something draws near. She turns to her mate and finds that his breathing has settled into an even rhythm. He is asleep.

"Sage," she murmurs softly. "They are coming. We must prepare ourselves."

Her mate opens his eyes and lifts his head, ears cocked.

"How many, Swift?" he asks.

"No more than two, at present."

Both wolves stand up and move to the edge of the copse.

106

"As soon as they break cover we must attack," she says.

Sage nods and reaches over to lick the tip of her nose.

For a moment she holds her cheek against his. Then they turn, looking out over the sloping expanse of moonlit snow to the line of trees below.

They can hear the sounds of crashing, flailing branches. Swift feels the hackles rise. Suddenly, out of the woods bounds a large black dog, panting with exertion. Moments later another follows. The creatures hesitate, thrown into a state of confusion by the diverging trail. One bounds to the right then doubles back. The other has its nose close to the ground.

"Now!" cries Swift.

The two wolves fly forward, covering the open ground with immense speed. By the time the hounds have seen them, it is too late.

Swift launches herself into the air. Stricken with fear, the dog staggers backwards, falling beneath the assault. Swift seizes the advantage, sinking her sharp teeth into its throat. Moments later she is up. Sage and his foe are rolling over and over on the ground, snarling. The black dog is powerful, but Sage is big, even amongst his own kind. At the final turn Sage is on top, pinning the hound beneath him. Swift sprints to his side. Amongst the trees she can hear more dogs approaching. As she reaches her mate, Sage deals the death bite. Another dog crashes out of the wood, barking loudly. Both wolves turn to face it. It leaps forwards, jaws dripping. Sage counters and both animals struggle for a moment, attempting to seize *the soft flesh of his opponent's throat. Swift, seeing her chance, ducks low and bites deep into the hound's flank, then makes a deft turn as another dog emerges from the trees.*

This is bigger than any dog she had yet encountered, black as night, with eyes that glow like a dying sun. Her heart quails, but she stands her ground.

A growl, low and menacing as thunder, rumbles from the hound's throat. It makes a leap, a great darkness over the white. The full force of its massive body bears down upon Swift, slamming into her chest. At the last moment she twists away, scrabbling and sliding backwards over the snow. She is badly winded and there is a sharp pain in her ribs. The beast comes at her again, snarling with menace. She rears up, their jaws meeting in a terrible clash. The dog manages to shake her off, but as she falls she turns sharply and clamps her teeth upon its shoulder. The strike drives the creature into a frenzy. With a snap of its huge head, it lunges.

Sage, raising his eyes, sees the danger and races towards his mate.

The mighty hound picks Swift up by the neck and shakes her like a pup. Sage springs; smashing into the dog's right flank, he hears the crack of bones. The force carries both animals some way across the frozen ground. Sage leaps to his feet. The great black beast seems to be moaning in pain. Swift is lying, still, upon the snow.

13

THE PARTING

⸺⸺⸺◆⸺⸺⸺

KEEPING A WARY EYE ON THE HOUND, SAGE
approaches his mate. Her eyes are closed.

"Swift, oh my dear heart, Swift."

Her eyes open.

"Swift! Are you all right?"

"Yes," she murmurs weakly and attempts to get to
her feet.

"You are hurt?"

"Yes, a little."

She manages to rise and takes a few hobbling steps
forward.

"You're limping!"

"Yes, but we must go on. The others will come soon."

Sage gazes at her with deep concern. Swift
remembers the look in their young son's eyes.

"Come, Sage. We must go."

"Swift...?"

"There is no time... Come!"

She begins to lope away up the hill, wincing with
every stride.

Sage takes one last look at the injured hound, then,
hearing the remaining pack members approaching
through the trees, follows.

It is some time before Sage realises they are no longer being pursued. With three pack members dead and their leader badly wounded, the few remaining dogs must be rethinking their strategy, making new plans.

Sage glances at Swift, his heart heavy. Her front right paw can bear no weight and with every step her pace grows slower. But far worse, he realises, the blood staining Swift's fur is not that of the enemy but her own and dark beads spring up on the snow as she passes.

They cross a narrow, fast-flowing stream, of which they drink long and deep, then once more begin to climb up a steep hillside covered in pine forest. Ahead, he can see a rocky outcrop that forms a series of shallow caves.

"Let's stop and rest," Sage says, fearful that his mate might protest. "We are not being followed."

"I know," says Swift.

"How about here?" He bounds up to a dark crevice in the rocks. "This is dry and I smell no danger."

Swift limps after him and, with no word of protest, sinks down upon the cave floor. Sage lies beside her and begins to lick her wounds. She whimpers beneath his touch, but says nothing and soon she is sleeping. For a while Sage watches her, a pale shadow in the darkness, and thinks of the many litters they have raised together, thinks of the first time he saw her at the Summerland Wolf Meet, a young she-wolf, slender, strong and swift. Ah, Swift – well named indeed! He remembers how they would lie in the rich green meadows, the scent of summer blossom on their fur.

He places his muzzle next to hers, and he too sleeps.

He is woken by the baying of hounds. At once Sage is on his feet, ears pricked, nostrils scenting the air. They are far distant yet, but moving closer. They must have picked up the trail. The clear night has given way to leaden clouds, driven in by a chill morning breeze. The first flakes of snow are beginning to fall.

They must flee. Yet is Swift able? She is sleeping still, deep and heavy. He licks her ear.

"Swift, we must go."

She opens her eyes, blinks against the light of day and stares at him, dazed.

"Swift, they are coming."

She heaves herself up and hobbles forward on three legs, then collapses.

"Swift, my spring-mate, my true heart, you must try!"

She makes another attempt, but her legs have no strength.

"It is no good, Sage. You must go on alone."

"I will not leave you!"

"You have a duty."

"I will rip their throats out!"

"No, you must go on, Sage. Find the child."

"Do not ask this of me, Swift."

"But, Sage, we gave our word. We knew this journey would be dangerous. If we fail then peril will come to all. Find the child, protect her. There is no other way."

Trembling, he pushes his face close to hers and she licks his eyes, his cheeks, his muzzle, like a mother washing her pup.

"Flee now, my darling; all hope lies with you."

He leaps up and suddenly is gone, bounding away through the forest.

With a sense of relief Swift watches the falling snow settling over his tracks. She knows it will help to throw the enemy off the scent. For a long time she lies there, listening. The sound of baying draws ever closer until it seems to echo throughout the forest and eventually the dogs come into view. They race through the trees, towards the outcrop of rocks, three vigorous creatures, with lolling, red tongues. Swift knows she must draw their attention.

She struggles to her feet, moves slowly out of the cave, raises her head to the sky and howls.

Rowan woke and gazed at the curved whiteness above. There were sounds: a chink of metal, the soft crackle of burning wood, someone moving with care.

She sat up. The woman, still masked, was placing various objects beneath her tunic, strapping a second dagger to her leg, buckling on a short bow and sheaf of arrows. Then, kneeling, she stirred something in a pot suspended over the fire.

"Broth," she said. "You will need something before we go."

"Are we going back?"

"We are going to find your friend."

She passed a bowl of thick soup to Rowan. Rowan lifted the spoon, then put it back down.

"Mother Meg said *they*, the Hunters, the Foul Folk, were in for the kill."

"Yes," said the woman.

"Will they kill my...?"

"Your friend? Only when his purpose, his usefulness, is at an end."

"What are they? What do they want?"

"What do they always want, the *Foul* Folk? Power. Power over all."

Rowan gulped and tried to eat the broth. But something seemed to stick in her throat.

14

SMOKE

———◆———

THE BLIZZARD HAD PASSED AND A FULL
moon painted the snow with diamond light.
Rowan could see that the ice shelter was located on a
mountain plateau, bordered by sharp peaks. London
had vanished. She couldn't understand it. This was
like nowhere she had ever seen before. It didn't even
look like England.

"Where's London?" she half whispered. The
woman put her gloved hand on Rowan's shoulder.

"Don't worry. I'll get you back," she said gently,
then strode forward.

If she had not been with her tall companion
Rowan would never have dared take a step into the
smooth, white landscape for fear of being buried up
to her neck. But the fur-clad woman made her way
effortlessly through the snow, feet never sinking more
than a few inches into the drift. "Tread where I tread,"
she said. "You will be safe."

Soon they came to a sheer rock face rising upwards
and the woman, glancing up into the skies, drew close
to the dark shadows beneath. They skirted the foot
of the cliff and then, without warning, the woman
pulled Rowan into a hidden cleft. The tapered opening
gave onto a narrow tunnel, sloping downwards. The

woman pulled a piece of cloth from her tunic and tied it over Rowan's mouth and nose. "You will need this." She withdrew the tear-shaped glass and resting her hand on Rowan's shoulder said in a low voice, "Quiet as the hunting owl." She took Rowan's hand and led her once again into the darkness.

For a long time they descended.

Despite the labyrinth of passageways, the woman seemed to know exactly where she was going. Every now and then she would pause and listen. Rowan strained her ears but could hear nothing, just an endless silence.

Deeper they went, and Rowan could feel the weight of the mountain above. But the silver light gave her comfort; it made her feel certain that they would find Jaz and, somehow, make their way back to London.

The woman stopped, signalled for caution. Rowan heard a low harmony, like the bass notes in a choir, deep and clear. A shimmering blue mist swirled suddenly about them and Rowan felt dizzy, as if the world had shifted.

"Come."

The woman took her hand and they walked on through the haze.

Emerging on the other side, they heard a dripping sound and saw moisture running down the rock walls.

On into the darkness they went and at last came to a place where the tunnel divided into three.

The woman held her finger to her lips and listened. "We are being followed," she said. She reached into her pocket and threw something to the ground, which erupted with a thick, green, evil-smelling smoke. Rowan was thankful for the face mask.

"To cover our scent," said the woman and drew Rowan into the middle passage.

The path twisted back and forth like the elaborate patterning on the silver gazing bowl, spiralling into countless side tunnels, and grew so narrow they could no longer walk side by side. Indeed, thought Rowan, it felt as if the walls were closing in on them; the pathway must be less than a foot wide now, more like a fissure in the rock than a proper passageway. The woman hid the light beneath her tunic and for a moment Rowan groped blindly.

She felt the woman's hand on her shoulder, guiding her forward. They came out onto another, wider passage, lit with flaming torches. The relative brightness made Rowan blink, but the fusty, smoke-filled air pricked the back of her throat. She swallowed hard in an effort not to cough. The woman crept forwards, like a stalking leopard, and motioned Rowan to follow. Ahead, Rowan could see a tunnel lined with heavy wooden doors, each with an iron grille.

The woman looked through the first grille and indicated that Rowan do the same. Rowan peered into the gloom. The stench hit her first, even through the fug of smoke. She could just make out a bare, straw-strewn cell. Then the grainy darkness resolved into numerous small figures huddled together. The woman held up the glimmering teardrop and its silver light spilled out onto their poor wasted faces. They were children, not a single one older than twelve and some much younger. The woman shook her head and drew Rowan on to the next cell. Sometimes there were several children occupying the same grim chamber, sometimes a lone figure. Worst of all were the ones who didn't stir when the light shone in, who lay stiff and expressionless, eyes wide and glazed, like dead things.

Only one child spoke when the light appeared, his face ashen and bruised, but alive with anger.

"What now, you creep? You bloody wait 'til I–!"

"Jaz!" Rowan exclaimed, beneath her breath. "It's me."

"Rowan, oh my God!" Jaz thrust his hand through the bars, entwining Rowan's fingers in his own. "Oh God, Rowan, I knew you'd come."

"Silence," whispered the woman. "The dogs will hear. We must get hold of the keys."

It was obvious that Jaz didn't want to let go, despite his show of bravado.

"I'll come back," Rowan promised.

"There are other children," said Jaz, his voice growing hoarse.

"Yes, we know," said Rowan. She tore her hand away.

The woman bent down, her lips close to Rowan's ear. "I will attack, disorientate them. You must take the keys and unlock the cells. Do nothing else, understand?"

Rowan nodded, but a thousand questions flooded into her head. The woman was already moving forwards, past the cell doors, along a curving passage and to some roughly hewn stone steps. The flight ended in a solid door with a small wooden shutter. The woman indicated that Rowan should wait at the bottom, and leaping up, two at a time, pounded on the heavy wood. Rowan almost cried out in fear. The woman was mad!

There was a pause, then an outburst of voices, the barking of dogs. The shutter slammed back and a grimacing, vulpine countenance appeared, but the woman was ready. A searing bright light burst in the guard's face, knocking him backwards. The woman threw two small devices in through the opening and stuck an object to the door. Jumping down she forced Rowan's head to the ground. Moments later there was a shuddering explosion and thick purple smoke came pouring out of the shutter and from the gap under the door. There were sounds of spluttering and lung-racking coughs, the whimpering of dogs.

The woman counted to nine then leapt up. "Come," she said, racing up the steps. "Look for the keys! I'll hold them off!"

There was a gaping hole in the door where the lock should have been. With a powerful movement the woman kicked the door open. The last wisps of smoke curled upwards to the ceiling. Two guards lay on the floor, and three great black hounds paced in circles trembling and retching. But the far door was open, as if someone had made a hasty exit, and echoing down the corridor was a terrible baying that seemed to make the walls shudder.

"We don't have long!" cried the woman, slamming the door shut, lowering the bar and nocking an arrow to her bow. "Check the belts!"

Rowan's hands shook uncontrollably; she could feel the hot slavering breath of the three huge dogs and her arm began to throb.

She tried to focus on her task. "The keys, the keys," she whispered, her teeth chattering. Both guards lay face down, snoring hard, and she realised that she would have to turn them over. She tugged as hard as she could on a leather tunic and at last the guard flopped backwards. Rowan gasped. His face was elongated and hairy, with sharp, protruding teeth, barely human, the hands long, claw-like. He looked like a rat.

The far door shuddered as something lunged against it. Rowan searched for the keys but could not see them. She would have to turn the other guard. Thankfully, they were thin and small, not as large as full-grown men, but still great weights for someone of Rowan's size and strength. She tugged and tugged.

Suddenly, the door burst open and two snarling black hounds flew through. But the bow sang out and the creatures fell at once, arrows quivering in their throats. Rowan gave a last desperate tug and the second guard flipped over onto his back.

Something more rat than man leapt through the open doorway, its sinuous tail thrashing from side to side, teeth bared. The woman shouldered her bow and, pulling out a dagger, met it head on. There was a terrible cry and the thing crumpled.

"Child, the keys!" cried the woman.

Rowan looked down. There it was: a heavy iron ring holding a single key, looped over the guard's belt. She scrabbled with the buckle. Her fingers felt numb, as if they belonged to someone else. Why wouldn't they do what she wanted? At long last, after a final yank, she released the leather strap and the metal ring came free.

Two more dogs, fangs bared, crashed into the room. The blood-soaked dagger flew through the air and caught one beast full in the chest. But the other animal bore down upon the woman, slamming her to the floor.

"Go, child," she gasped. "Run!"

Rowan jumped up, ran to the steps, but could not help looking back. The dog pinned the woman to the ground, its wide, slavering jaws inches from her throat. Rowan barely had time to think. Grabbing a wine jug from a nearby table, she dashed the contents in the creature's eyes. The moment of disorientation, as the dog threw up its head, gave the woman her chance. She whipped the second dagger from its sheath and thrust it deep in the dog's side. It stuck there, quivering. The dog yelped and staggered backwards and in an instant the woman was up. She grabbed Rowan's hand and they ran down the steps towards the cells.

But still they were pursued; thunderous barks echoed all around.

The woman turned, nocking her bow. "Go," she cried. "Unlock the cells. Get the children out."

Behind her, Rowan could hear sounds like the soft thud of flour-bags hitting the floor. Green smoke snaked around her ankles. "Jaz, Jaz," she called, ripping off the face mask. Her hands shook so much the heavy iron key rattled in the lock. "They've got dogs," she said. Jaz, bruised and white, emerged. "We have to get the others." One by one Rowan unlocked the wooden doors. Some prisoners came out shivering and bewildered, but some drew back in fear or simply did not move. Rowan wrenched a flaming torch from the walls and thrust it into the hands of an older child, then took one for herself and Jashan. The sound of barking pounded through her head. "Look out," Jaz screamed. In the tail of her eye Rowan glimpsed a great black body launching itself through the air. But a spitting fury of silver met it halfway, sank claws deep into its eyes. The dog howled in agony, shaking its head in a spray of blood, yet could not dislodge the cat.

"Come, quick," cried Rowan. A straggle of wide-eyed children hurried after her. "Here, here. Jaz, you go first, I'll follow." She ushered them through the narrow fissure. Glancing back, she saw that the silver cat had released its grip and jumped free. The dog staggered about blindly, then stumbled and fell, an arrow shivering in its back. Out of the green mist flew the masked woman. "We must run. There are more. Many more. The brute leading them is huge!"

"But what about the other children?" asked Rowan. "We can't–"

"There's no time!" cried the woman. "Go!"

As they squeezed into the cleft the woman tossed one last device behind her and everything was lost in a billowing purple haze.

───◆───

At first, Rowan thought it must be sheer blind luck that led the frightened, whimpering children in the right direction through the impossible, snaking maze of narrow tunnels. But, when they arrived at the three-way forked passage, she saw the silver cat at the head of the procession, its amber eyes gleaming.

"Puss, puss," she cried, falling to her knees. "Where have you been?"

The masked woman knelt down and gazed deep into the cat's eyes.

"Yes," she said with a half chuckle. "Follow him: he will take you back to Lun Dun. I must get these poor creatures away from the tunnels, to Lord Medick and safety. Go quickly. The Foul Folk have many means and devices at their disposal, and may bring these tunnels down around our ears."

The silver cat gave a loud meow and bounded ahead. For a brief moment Rowan looked back. The pale, sunken-eyed children gazed up at the masked woman in bewilderment, but at the first sound of her firm, clear voice followed meekly, as if they had long been drilled to obey.

"What are we going to tell everyone?" said Jaz as they followed the silver cat. "My mum and dad will have gone completely insane. They've probably got the police searching for us." He pulled out his mobile phone. "I can't get any signal down here."

"I think we're further away than you…" Rowan began, then paused.

The cat meowed and disappeared into the darkness ahead.

"Hurry," said Rowan. "We mustn't lose him."

At times, Rowan thought, it seemed as if the trek through the dark, cold tunnels would never end. Then suddenly before them was the shifting miasma of bluish mist, and passing through they found themselves back in the icy, foul-smelling sewers of London. The cat led them to an iron ladder, where a circle of moonlight glimmered above. Ascending, they emerged onto Gallows Yard. The derelict buildings loomed stark against the snow.

The silver cat padded ahead, then paused and turned to look back. A church bell sounded. Rowan counted four sombre chimes.

"Jaz, check your phone," she said urgently.

Jaz reached into his pocket, brought out the mobile phone and swiped the screen. "That's weird. I haven't got any messages. You'd have thought…"

"What's the time?"

"Four o'clock."

"And the date?"

"It's the… no, that must be wrong. It says the fourteenth. It must be the fifteenth. We've been away for a day, at least."

"Have we?"

"Of course we have. Those creeps kept me locked up for hours and hours. A whole bloody night."

"I think it's the same day, almost the same hour."

"But that's impossible!"

"Yes."

"Psychos are one thing, but this… I mean, for goodness' sake, Rowan. What's going on?"

"We need to get back, talk to Mr Rafik. I think he'll know."

15

FEVER

———————◆———————

THE SILVER CAT ACCOMPANIED THEM TO MR
Rafik's newsagent's shop, deftly slipping past the
many feet crunching through snow. A gritting lorry
thundered by. In its wake followed a snake of slow-
moving vehicles. As the children pushed open the
shop door, an old-fashioned bell jangled and the cat
disappeared into the back of the shop.

The air smelt of chocolate and spice. A man
with a chesty cough was buying cigarettes and a
newspaper. As he tucked the paper under his arm,
Rowan caught a glimpse of the headline: 'Get a
Load of Bull!'. An unflattering picture of the new
American president was slapped across the front
page, jowls blown out, mouth pulled into a clownish
smirk. Behind him, in the background of the
photograph, just out of focus, was... Rowan froze.
Surely she was seeing things? She stared hard at the
grainy photo, mouth open. The customer frowned
at Rowan, shifted the newspaper to his other arm
and hurried out of the shop.

Rowan gulped. The figure in the background had
been the Grey Man.

"Did you see the date on his paper?" Jaz hissed. "It
said the fourteenth. And look!" He held up another

newspaper, and another. They were all dated 14 December. That's impossible!"

"We've been away for no more than half an hour."

"Can I help?"

Rowan turned. Standing behind the counter was a young woman, cradling a baby in her arms. Strands of long hair escaped from a white headscarf.

Rowan moved forward, shy and hesitant.

"I... I was wondering if I could see Mr Rafik?"

A slight shadow seemed to pass over the woman's face. The baby gave a weak cry and she repositioned the infant, cradling it tenderly against her other shoulder.

"I'm... afraid he's not here at the moment."

"Oh." Rowan paused. There was something about the expression in the woman's eyes. "When will he be back?"

The young woman began rocking the baby back and forth.

Then she said, "You're Rowan, aren't you, from next door? I thought I recognised you. Last time I saw you, you were this high." She indicated with her hand. "I'm Afshan. Do you remember?"

Rowan stared at the woman then smiled. "Mr Rafik's granddaughter? You used to share your sweets with me."

"That's right." The woman smiled back. "I'm married now and this little lady is called Kalila. Do you want to see her?" She pulled back the blanket. Rowan saw a crumpled red face with puckered, angry lips. The baby mewled in protest and Afshan recommenced the rocking motion.

Rowan attempted a smile.

"Will your grandfather be back this afternoon? I want... I *need* to talk to him."

Afshan went very still.

"Ah... I'm afraid he won't be back at all. He... he's in hospital."

Rowan stared at the young woman.

"What's wrong with him?" asked Jashan.

"He collapsed."

"What?"

"Last night," Afshan continued. "He collapsed down by the bins, when he was taking the rubbish out."

"Did he slip?" Rowan's heart was beginning to pound.

"They don't think so. We thought it might be a heart attack, but the doctors said no. Sophia found him. She heard a cat fight, and went to investigate, and there was Grandfather lying in the snow, unconscious, covered in bites and scratches, as if something had attacked him. The paramedics didn't know what to make of it."

All of a sudden Rowan felt very peculiar.

"H-h-he's not going to...?" She couldn't say it. Her fingertips were pressing rhythmically against the counter top. One, two, three...

"Oh no, of course not, he's not badly hurt. It's just, he's old, you know. Oh, don't cry, it's okay, the doctors are keeping him in for observation, that's all. Are you all right?"

Rowan felt the floor rising up beneath her feet. Overhead the lights shifted alarmingly and she heard Jashan's voice – "Ro, are you okay?" – and someone cry, "Ammee, quick...!"

Rowan's head seemed to be full of dreams. The rats were swarming over her, biting hands, fingers, ears. No, not rats but dogs: great black dogs with eyes like burning coals and mouths of fire; they sank their teeth into her body and she felt her blood sear with flames. Then her mother's voice pierced clouds of swirling smoke.

"Her temperature's 105. How on earth can we keep it down?"

"Ice baths. If it goes any higher she'll have to be admitted."

Mum's face looming over her.

"I can't leave her. Not now. I'll have to call Tom."

Trying to speak, wanting to warn her mother of the danger, but her voice had been transformed into a raven's croak. There was Mother Meg, face hidden in the folds of a red cloak.

"Hush now, child. The deer are fleet-footed."

The old lady was smiling down at her, yet beneath the red hood was a cat's face, no, a man's face, with silver hair and amber eyes.

Then, a pale shadow following her in the darkness; wolves running through the forest; vision shifting like mist over water. Now a hand reached out, slender and white; a woman of startling beauty: hair gold as buttercups, eyes like young apples.

In the blink of an eye, the closing of one scene, another revealed.

Afshan was skating along the frozen river, not Afshan but Jaz, no, not Jaz at all. It was a girl, someone she did not know, with long, wild hair, black eyes, red lips. They were running over icy wastes, which lay still and blue beneath the great moon, stretching out to a far horizon.

An urgent cry: "Rowan, c'mon! Run! They're coming!"

Throat burning with thirst.

"I can't. Let me rest."

A hazy light filtering through the gloom.

"Come on, Rowan. You must drink this."

Mum tilting a cup to her lips. Ah, cool refreshing water!

"Drink this, there's a good girl."

Swallowing it down and falling back into sleep.

When she woke, Rowan found she was in her own bed. There was a glass of water, a bottle of medicine and a thermometer on the bedside table. The clock showed half past ten in the morning. What happened? thought Rowan. Did I faint? They must have brought me home to bed. I can't believe it; I've been asleep for over eighteen hours. She sat up and reached for her dressing gown, which was hanging on the bedpost. Suddenly, there was the sound of footsteps and the bedroom door opened.

"Rowan, what are you doing, darling? Get back into bed at once! It was her mother, face taut with worry.

"I'm fine, Mum, honestly."

"You've been very poorly. Where's that thermometer? Into bed now. I want to check your temperature."

Mum took the slender tube out of its casing and popped it into Rowan's mouth.

"Bud I ong…!" Rowan tried to speak, her tongue fighting the cold glass.

"Ssssh! Don't talk. You need to keep your mouth closed."

Rowan pulled a face. Her mother smiled.

"Well, you certainly seem well enough. But you're to stay in bed until the doctor comes. You gave us quite a fright, you know."

Rowan repeated the grimace and suddenly was gathered up in a great bear hug.

"I was really worried about you, darling."

At last Mum removed the thermometer and read it, frowning.

"Well that's strange."

"What is?"

"It's perfectly normal!"

Rowan began to giggle. "It's strange that I'm normal?"

"For the past three days you've been burning up."

"Past three days? What do you mean?" The smile had gone from Rowan's face.

"You've been ill for three days. You had some kind of fever."

"Three days?"

"Yes, darling. It was Tuesday when you fell ill and this is Thursday. Do you remember fainting in Mr Rafik's shop?"

"Yes, of course. But I thought it happened yesterday. I didn't realise… Three days!"

"You were almost rushed off to hospital. The doctor was reluctant to move you at first, thought it might be pneumonia. But he said if there was no improvement by tonight he'd send for an ambulance.

I think he's going to be amazed at this sudden recovery."

She tousled Rowan's hair. Rowan gave a half smile, but then she sighed.

"How is Mr Rafik?"

Her mother gazed at her with great tenderness.

"Oh, sweetheart, he's absolutely fine! You mustn't worry. Afshan says he's coming out of hospital this weekend. In fact, Mrs Rafik brought over a get-well card when she found out how poorly you were. It's here."

Her mother got up and pulled opened the top drawer of Rowan's homework desk. She drew out two sealed envelopes.

Rowan took the first and ripped open the flap. Inside was a card illustrated with a blue beribboned bunny rabbit. The scrawl of handwriting read,

Sorry BIG TIME about the revolting pic – Dad chose it! GET WELL and I mean it. See you soon. JAZ. xxx

The other card was of a tree, tall and slender with red berries. Inside someone had written,

The roots of the tree are strong.

Fear not, dear Rowan.

Rowan sank her head back upon the pillow and let out another sigh.

Her mother reached out, laying her palm against Rowan's forehead.

"You need to rest, sweetheart."

Rowan gazed at her mother thoughtfully.

"Promise me you'll still go to Brighton."

Her mother looked startled.

"Brighton?"

Rowan felt something urgent and fierce rise in her heart.

"Promise me."

"Oh, Rowan, you've been so ill. It won't be fair on Grandma."

"You *have* to go, Mum."

"I'll talk to the doctor, darling."

"But you don't mean it. Promise me!"

Her mother was silent for a long time, staring hard at Rowan, as if she were a difficult puzzle that needed working out. At last, she took both of Rowan's hands in her own.

"If the doctor gives you the all clear, if he's *one hundred per cent* sure that you're better, then I'll go. But, Rowan, it's a *big* if."

———◆———

Rowan stared at the stone in her hand. It was growing warmer, darker and Jaz had been right: the engraving did look like a tree. In fact, it reminded her of the Tree of Life pattern on her Box of Treasures: it had the same curving form. She heard the front door bell ring and stuffed the stone back in its pouch, tucking it beneath her pyjamas. There were voices, a soft tap at her bedroom door.

"Come in."

A grinning face appeared.

"Jaz! Thank goodness. I'm going loopy. Mum won't let me get out of bed."

Jaz entered, sat down on the duvet and hugged her.

"I got you these," he said handing her a huge packet of chocolate buttons.

"Great, I'm starving." She tore open the packet. "Mum's got me on invalid rations, you know. Boiled eggs and soldiers, that sort of thing. Here, you have some."

Jaz stuck his hand in the bag, pulled out a fistful of chocolates and stuffed them in his mouth.

"I was so worried about you," Jaz said, munching away. "I went into a complete panic at the shop."

"Did you find out any more about Mr Rafik? Mum keeps telling me he's all right."

"He seems to be. I only know what Afshan told us, that they found him down by the bins, covered in scratches and blood."

"Like he was attacked."

"Oh God, you think it was *them*?"

"I think he was protecting me, Jaz."

Jaz frowned and dug his hand in his pocket. He pulled out his phone and leant forward.

"I've got something to show you." His voice was low and anxious. He scrolled through a series of screens then angled the phone towards Rowan.

"I don't suppose you've seen the news today?"

Rowan shook her head.

"Look at this."

It was a BBC news programme. A group of important-looking people were gathered on the snowy steps of a grand building. At the front stood a man with a wide smile, and by his side was a fat, hearty-looking fellow whose smart camelhair coat clashed with the large white cowboy hat on his head.

Behind them stood the Grey Man, tall and thin with dead white skin.

Cameras flashed, microphones were thrust in faces. A reporter stood talking to camera.

"As you can see, the new American president, Josiah J. Bull, is behind me right now, with the prime minister and various heads of state, on the steps of Wexford House."

A cut to the studio showed an elegant female newsreader smiling up at a screen.

"Shouldn't this be seen as something of a public relations exercise, Andrew? Hasn't there been evidence of trouble today?"

The picture cut back to the reporter.

"You're absolutely right, of course. For weeks now this London meeting of world leaders has been touted as the environmental summit to end all summits. The word from behind the scenes was that groundbreaking agreements had been reached, covering everything from reduction of carbon emissions to worldwide protection of tropical rainforests. Everyone seemed to be on board: Russia, China, India and of course, most importantly, America. Tonight we were expecting an announcement of landmark proportions."

"So, Andrew, what went wrong?"

"Well, rifts have been increasingly apparent throughout the course of the day. One by one nations have backed down. It's difficult to say why, exactly. Suspicion and distrust seem to have spread like wildfire. At this juncture things are very far from being resolved."

"And where does that leave the all-important treaty?"

"To be honest, there no longer seems to be a treaty."

The elegant woman continued. "I understand there have been large protests in the city."

The camera cut to a crowd scene: a carnival of protestors wearing fancy dress. One girl with bright green hair was dressed as an Eskimo and someone in a clown mask was skiing up and down at the head of the demonstration. Their hurriedly scrawled banners bore slogans such as 'Permafrost not Petroleum!', 'Forests under Fire!', 'Climate Change Crisis!'

"*Yes,*" nodded the reporter with a wry smile. "*Police estimates say that hundreds of thousands of people have gathered in London today. The original intention, it seems, was to celebrate the outcome of this summit, but over the past few hours the mood has grown very dark indeed.*"

Suddenly, a scuffle broke out behind the television reporter. A photographer was being manhandled, rather roughly, out of the president's path, by several dark-suited men. The reporter swung round and found himself, somehow, face to face with Joe J. Bull. With professional instinct, he raised his microphone.

"*Mr President what do you have to say to those members of the British public who are angry at this sudden U-turn in policy?*"

The president frowned for a moment, as if thrown by the question, but then snapping his smile back into place directed his gaze straight to camera; his voice was a thick drawl. "*Well, from what I can see these folks are worried about climate change, ain't that right? For years now we've all been worried about how the world is turning into one almighty green house and hows we're all gonna shrivel up and burn. Well, all I can say is: look around you. The good Lord knows that the Northern Hem-eye-sphere is in the grip of the worst cold spell on record.*"

Temperatures have fair plummeted. We're freezing our butts off here. Doncha think a little warming, on a global scale, is kinda what we need right now? My new advisors are telling me…"

The Grey Man stepped smartly in front of the president and said in a chilling, precise voice, *"The president and, indeed, all the world leaders are aware that there are people who are opposed to their policies, and of course they recognise their right to protest. No more questions."*

He held up his hand in a commanding gesture.

In a moment the fat president had been whisked away into a waiting limousine.

Rowan lay back on her pillows. Her mind was racing and yet at the very core was a terrible blankness, a murky place in which she seemed to flounder. Who was this man, this grey stranger? Like a spider, he lurked in the dark recesses of her memory: an enemy, a foe, a hunter; something not merely dangerous, but deadly. *They are in for the kill*: she could hear the words echoing, magnified, as if spoken in a great hall or cavern. There came a bitter cold, a dread, a deathliness, and the Grey Man stood before her, cloaked in silver, glittering like frost in the moonlight…

She jerked upright; a sudden intake of breath, heart racing. What had she seen? What was it? It was slipping away from her, shrivelling like flamed cobwebs. It would not, would not come.

"Rowan, are you okay?" Jashan's voice was urgent. "Rowan!"

"It's okay. I'm… okay…"

"It's him, isn't it?" said Jaz. Rowan nodded.

"But how?" Jaz exclaimed. "I mean, how can he be there, on television, with the most powerful men and women in the world? How?"

"I don't know, Jaz, but I know what I've got to do."

"What?"

"Get Mum away, get her out of London, safe. And Luke too, if I can."

Jaz, silent for a moment, took Rowan's hand and squeezed it.

"Is there anything I can do to help?"

Rowan felt a rush of gratitude and held her friend's hand tight. "Yes, have a word with my mum. Tell her I'm desperate to go to Grandma's. Tell her you think it'll do me good."

"When would you go?"

"As soon as possible. This Saturday, I suppose."

Jaz pulled a face, half comic, half sad. "I won't have time to get you a Christmas present or anything."

"I know. I'm sorry, Jaz, but I've got to protect them. Or try, at least."

Jaz sighed. "All right. I'll miss you though, dahling, like crazy."

Rowan smiled and gave her friend a sudden hug. "Thank you so much!" Then drawing back she looked into Jaz's dark eyes. "Thing is, Jaz, I think you'll be safer, a lot safer, if I'm not around."

16

On the Scent

———◆———

ROWAN GAZED UPWARDS, HER HEAD REELING.
The roof of the railway station arched overhead
like a cathedral. All that space. Such a contrast to the
tight-packed crowds below, where elbows bristled and
tempers flared.

"This is absurd!"

"Six-hour delay, man!"

"The bleedin' timetable keeps changing!"

"It's utter chaos!"

Every few minutes an echoing tannoy would
announce,

*"We wish to inform passengers that railway
services to and from this station are experiencing
a high level of disruption. This is due to adverse
weather conditions, with blizzards affecting northern
areas. We apologise for any inconvenience this may
cause."*

"Oh no!" Mum exclaimed. "The 14.15 to York has
been cancelled." She scanned the display board. "The
next one's due at... Oh blow! There doesn't seem to
be a next one."

"Hah!" Luke barked.

Mum's face registered irritation, but she kept her
lips pressed tight.

"Does that mean we can't go?" Rowan asked, with a stab of fear.

Mum sighed.

"I'll have to check at the information desk." She glanced over towards the ticket office. "Look at the queue!"

She took a ten-pound note from her purse and thrust it into Luke's hand.

"You two wait in the shop, buy yourselves a comic or something and make sure you stay there until I come back. Okay?"

Rowan nodded.

"Luke?"

Luke grunted, pocketed the money and gave a terse "Come on then!" He set off towards the shop, rough-shouldering his way through the crowd.

Rowan hurried after.

"Luke. Luke!"

He charged ahead, not bothering to check whether or not she was following. Determined not to lose him, Rowan fixed her gaze on his death's-head jacket and pushed her way into the swarm of people.

Then all at once she stopped, frozen, heart pounding, head swimming.

She could hear them!

Voices.

Angel voices.

A choir of angels, a spiralling melody of sound, rising up into the spaces beyond.

She looked around wildly. Luke had disappeared from view, swallowed by the crush of grown-ups. Bodies pressed in on every side. Rowan felt panic rise in her throat. She was suffocating! But, to her left, the weight of people seemed to lessen. From that direction, like the rippling of water, came the unearthly sound, drawing her on. The crowd separated. A fat man moved to one side and she was outside in the open air.

She must have passed through the station entrance. An early dusk had fallen and a great Christmas tree sparkled with coloured lights. At its base was a low stage. Here stood a group of carol singers: girls dressed in white gowns and cloaks, each wearing a crown of holly and holding a flickering candle. In the dim gloom of the winter's afternoon, the little flames shone out like circles of gold.

It was not a song they sang; rather, their voices blended together in pure harmony, sweet and melancholy. Rowan, feeling tears rise, swallowed them down.

Firecrackers exploded with a loud, sulphurous bang. A clownish face loomed out of the crowd.

"Ladies and gentlemen, let me present to you the Midwinter Mummers!"

Leaping out from behind the Christmas tree came a band of curious figures. Rowan recognised them as the entertainers from the Ice Fair. There were two characters, covered from head to foot in green leaves performing a kind of wild dance. A third figure, sporting a suit of rags and wielding a long sword, wove back and forth between them, in a figure of eight. One player wore a leering mask and a jester's hat. He frolicked up to bystanders, making provocative gestures and hitting them with an odd-looking balloon on a stick. Next came two animal figures, a stag and a white fox (or perhaps it was a wolf) with heads made of papier-mâché. They were pursued by a character riding a hobby horse and blowing a horn.

The song changed to a merry folk tune. The company started turning cartwheels, juggling balls and standing on each other's shoulders. The jester continued to play the fool, falling over his own feet, attempting to steal kisses from pretty girls in the crowd. The onlookers, who only minutes before had been fuming with indignation and frustration, began to laugh and clap and cheer.

Rowan was laughing too. The music seemed to be playing right inside her head. She had forgotten all about Luke and Mum. She squealed with delight when the hobby horse man started breathing fire. Then, somehow, his horse was snorting fire too, hot bursts of orange flame shooting from the nostrils. The fox and stag mimed fear and began to run to and fro. The horse gave chase, snapping at their heels. Rowan shivered. The hobby horse had turned sinister, its head no longer a mere pantomime prop but skull-like, threatening. She turned away. The jester was there, at her shoulder, his mask a broad, mocking grin. He bent down, his red mouth level with her ear.

"Who will win?" he hissed. "The hunter or the hunted?"

She swung around to confront him, stung by his words. He gave a sudden, bold cry, made a wild somersault, and a series of effortless cartwheels carried him away.

The crowd broke into applause.

Rowan wanted to run. Her thoughts scattered, rebounded, in all directions.

Then she saw the man with the dog.

He stood in the crowd, watching her.

Heart thumping, she turned wildly, but there, to her right, was the Grey Man, a great brute straining at the end of his lead.

She gulped, backing away.

Mum, she thought. Mum would be at the shop. But where was the shop?

Urgently, Rowan pushed her way back through the crowd and into the station. It was difficult to see anything. Everyone was so much taller than her. She craned her head upwards and saw the signs for the platforms. Weaving a path between the press of bodies and suitcases, she heard a dog barking, a deep resounding bass echoing above the clamour of the crowd.

Squeezing her way through, Rowan emerged by the temporary barriers. A few trains were waiting, but the guards didn't seem to be letting anyone past. She hovered by the railings. Perhaps she should ask a guard for help? However, none of the staff looked approachable; most of them were too busy fending off disgruntled customers.

Rowan stood on tiptoe, trying to catch a glimpse of a brightly lit shop sign, but the mass of people pushed in around her.

She turned back to the railings and felt the hot smart of tears. Mum would be frantic, she thought, rubbing her sleeve across her eyes; and, worse, with no trains running, they could be stuck in London, all escape routes blocked! Rowan shuddered. Perhaps it was all part of *their* horrible plan?

Perhaps Luke had tipped them off.

Suddenly, a cry intruded upon her thoughts.

"Special northbound service leaving platform three in five minutes!"

Her head snapped up. A guard, in a smart green uniform with shiny brass buttons, was walking along the railings, making the announcement.

Northbound? Did that mean York? Rowan wondered. They had to change at York.

"Excuse me!" she called out. "Does the train stop at York?"

"Yes, it does, missy. Is that where you're going then?"

"We're going to Gillkirk, but we have to change."

"Well, you're in luck then, miss. This service takes you straight through to Gillkirk."

"Oh! That must be our train then!" Rowan cried out. "But I don't know where my mum is, or my brother. We've only got five minutes before it goes…" To her shame she found she was sobbing.

"Never you mind about that, missy. Here you are." The guard punched a few keys on an old-fashioned contraption that hung around his neck, cranked a handle and out popped a pale yellow ticket.

"Take this and they'll let you onto the platform. No doubt you'll see your mother there and your little brother. Here, my tuppence." He handed her a large, spotted handkerchief. "You give that nose a good wipe. I'll be along in a jiffy, to blow the whistle." He continued on his way, hollering "Special northbound service…!"

Rowan hurried along the line of metal barriers until she reached platform three. The train waiting there looked grand and antiquated, its green doors inscribed with curly, gold lettering.

She gazed into the crowd, searching for her mother's face. The sound of barking was getting closer. "Out the way, out the bloody way!" a guttural voice cried. The crowd was parting, moving back in fear as something approached. It was a black hound, straining against its chain and at its side was the dog handler. He gave Rowan an ugly grin.

"No!" she cried. "No!"

"I think you want to be coming this way, miss."

A young man in a handsome, green uniform stood at the gate. His blond hair curled out from beneath a peaked cap. He smiled and gave Rowan a friendly wink.

"Quick now, run along through. Train departs in… let me see." Out of his pocket he drew a golden fob watch. "Oh, my giddy aunt, less than two minutes."

Rowan stared at him in dismay, clutching furiously at the handkerchief. "B-but my mum, and L-Luke. The other man said they'd be…"

There was a cry.

"Rowan!"

She spun around. Bursting through the crowd were her mother and Luke, cheeks red, hair flying.

"Oh, Rowan, we thought we'd lost you!"

The next moment she was enveloped in a breathtaking hug.

"Where on earth were you, darling? I was going spare! Thank goodness we found you."

Over her mother's shoulder she could see the Grey Man and his blood-eyed hound. He was reaching for something inside his coat.

The old guard with the shiny buttons reappeared.

"No time, no time!" he cried. "Curtail all kisses and sighs and long goodbyes. Train is due to leave in precisely... fifty-nine seconds." He pulled a brass whistle from his breast pocket.

"I'd advise all those wishing to travel to board immediately."

The Grey Man held up a black, curved object. Was it some kind of weapon? He put it to his lips. Rowan felt a shiver of dread. There was a sound, low and hollow and deathly; it seemed to Rowan like a thread of poison running in her veins. It was a horn: the Grey Man was sounding some kind of hunting horn.

"Oh!" Mum exclaimed, stumbling. "I suddenly feel..."

"No time to waste!" cried the old guard. He raised his brass whistle high and it seemed to catch the light. There was a sudden golden flash, a silvery carillon and the horn shattered in the Grey Man's hand. At that the brutish dogs gave a wild howl, turned tail and fled, pulling their masters after them.

"Board immediately!"

"Oh goodness, let's hurry!" said Mum. "Luke, have you got the bag?"

They sprinted along the platform.

"Just get into the first carriage. Not that one: it's the guard's van. The next one," Mum panted out.

Rowan fumbled with the ornate handle and managed to pull the door open. She leapt up and Luke followed, pulling the bag after him. The door clunked shut. They leant out of the window.

Mum grabbed their hands, one in each of hers, and reached up to kiss them.

"Oh Mum, forgodsake!" Luke protested, wiping his cheek.

The two men in green uniforms were moving at a smart pace up the platform.

"Now, remember, the money for Grandma is in an envelope at the bottom of the bag. The train should be getting in about eight o'clock and she'll be there to meet you. I couldn't get through this morning – gremlins on the line – but I'll try and give her another call before I get my train. Be good and have a wonderful time and..."

A sharp whistle blast sounded.

"... remember I love you very much. Luke, look after Rowan for me and don't have too many squabbles, please. Think of Grandma and Grandpa and..."

The whistle sounded again. Mum stepped back from the train. The two guards stepped up into the adjacent carriage.

"I love you, Mum," Rowan called. "Please take care."

"Of course I will, darling. Don't worry about me."

"Bye, Mum," said Luke, voice gruff.

Slowly, the train began to pull away.

Mum blew a kiss and waved.

Rowan blew half a dozen, but it seemed to her that they were caught in the updraught from the moving train and lost on the wind.

PART TWO

Unquiet Slumbers

17

TEA FOR TWO

⌖

"GOD!" LUKE SNEERED, GIVING THE DOOR A kick. "This is a bit of an old rust bucket, innit?"

"Oh, it's lovely," said Rowan.

They stood in the train corridor, which gave access to several compartments.

"This first one's empty," said Luke, yanking back the sliding door. "May as well dump ourselves here."

Rowan exclaimed with delight. "It's like something out of a museum!"

The compartment was upholstered in faded green velvet. There was real wood panelling, ornate light fittings fashioned in brass and even a fold-down table.

"Ready for the scrap heap, if you ask me," Luke grumbled. "Why can't we have something cool and modern, forgodsake, like the Bullet or TGV. They can reach speeds of over 350 mph. We'll be lucky if this pile of junk makes fifteen."

"But old things can be nice too," Rowan protested.

"Old things bore me to death," Luke pronounced, flinging himself down in a corner and propping his scruffy boots up on the seat. "Now shut up. I want to read my comic."

Rowan sat down with care on the plush material and looked out of the window at the deepening twilight.

The train was moving slowly, past buildings. She could see brick walls half hidden by drifts; roofs and chimney stacks thick with snow; window ledges overhung with icicles. Perched upon a length of guttering were scores of pigeons, feathers fluffed out like pom-poms. In the grey distance, tall snow-topped towers of concrete, glass and steel rose up in the midst of scaffolding and cranes.

Grim old London, Rowan thought; it would sprawl onwards for many miles, reaching its tentacle arms out into the northern suburbs, but at last, at last, they would leave it far behind.

Rowan hugged her knees.

It was dark outside. Pressing her nose against the glass, Rowan felt her stomach rumbling. Luke was buried deep in his magazine. Every now and then, the lightbulbs above their heads flickered alarmingly, raising a loud tut from her brother.

"Bloody things," he growled. "You wouldn't think this was the twenty-first century."

Rowan took her chance.

"Luke, Mum gave us some money, didn't she, for food?"

"Might've done," he said, eyes fixed to the page.

"I thought I'd go to the buffet car and get something to eat."

"Hah! If they've *got* a buffet car!"

"Well, shall I go and look? And, if they do, what do you want?"

Luke stuck out his lower lip. He seemed to be considering her proposal. After a long pause he stuffed his hand into his jacket pocket and drew out a five-pound note.

"Burger, fries, Coke," he reeled off, then, still holding the fiver in mid-air, stuck his nose back between the pages of his comic.

Rowan got up, took the money and, with a half-shrug, slid back the door on its squeaky track.

She stepped out into the corridor. The lights glowed a soft yellow, making dim reflections in the polished wood. To her left the corridor formed an 'L' shape, where the carriage came to an end. Here was a plain, windowless door marked with the word 'PRIVATE'.

In the other direction the corridor stretched out ahead. Rowan could see the carriages swaying as they trundled over the track. She began to move up the train, steadying herself as she went.

Passing by the other compartments, she could not resist peeping in, but they were all empty. The last compartment of the carriage proved to be a toilet. The porcelain bowl and washbasin were fluted and decorated with small blue flowers; the taps were golden, a china dish held a fresh bar of soap, and there was a real towel hanging on the brass rail, monogrammed with curly lettering. Rowan gazed in wonder. What kind of train was this, anyway?

She continued through the adjoining door into the next carriage. Here the compartments were occupied. In one an elderly couple played chess, with pieces carved like little Elizabethan courtiers. The pair looked up as she passed, and smiled. In the next, a mother and father were tending to their young family – several small children, overdressed in frills of lace. In a third a rather rowdy group were singing along to a piano accordion and, now and then, erupting into riotous laughter. How strange, thought Rowan; she had never been on a train like this before. Everyone seemed odd, somehow, like the train itself: old-fashioned and a little faded.

The buffet car was near the front end of the train. Rowan gasped, her eyes wide with astonishment. It was very grand, with a polished wood floor and a counter of smooth grey marble. The aroma was irresistible, like freshly baked hot cross buns. Display shelves, made of sparkling glass and shiny brass, were filled with the most delicious array of cakes and pastries. There were iced fingers and apple turnovers, fruit tarts and chocolate choux, little cakes with coloured icing and big cakes covered in cream and cherries. There were sausage rolls, cheese slices, Cornish pasties and pork pies, all with a pastry so light and golden it seemed as if it would melt before your eyes. Behind the counter stood the young guard with the curly yellow hair, his hat pushed back at a jaunty angle. He gave Rowan a wink.

"Were you wanting a spot of tea then, duck? Come and have a good look round."

Rowan edged closer. She felt rather young and silly, and worst of all began to worry that her money might not go very far. After all, these lovely things were bound to cost a fortune!

"I, erh…" she half whispered, thinking of Luke's curt request. This didn't look like the kind of place that would sell fast food.

"Um, do you do burgers?"

The young man looked at her and scratched his head.

"Burgers?" he repeated quizzically.

"And, um, fries?"

"Fries?" There was a perplexed expression on his face.

"You know, chips."

"Oh chips." He seemed to brighten, but then shook his head. "No, we don't do chips. But we've got some lovely pasties, fill you up a treat. Now, *Albert*, the head guard, he swears by our pasties. Or we can do sausage and mash, or shepherd's pie, or vegetable hot pot."

They sounded lovely, but expensive.

"How... how much?"

"Well now." He looked down at her knowingly. "We have our special tea-for-two menu at the moment. That comprises a full high tea for two persons, drinks included, and, you know," he searched her eyes for a moment, "you strike me as someone who would be particularly partial to jam roly-poly served with creamy custard. Am I right?"

Rowan's jaw dropped.

"It's my favourite."

"Ah ha!"

"But I don't..."

"Ah... worried it'll break the bank, hey? Well now, how much have you got."

Rowan placed the crumpled note onto the counter.

"Five whole pounds? Well, I should think, let me see. Oh yes, here it is." He picked up a gilt-edged card, covered with fancy writing. "It says here that the tea-for-two menu is, well I never, five pounds exactly! However, we mustn't forget that today's Saturday and the month has got an R in it and of course it's snowing, so that's twenty per cent discount, makes four pounds in total. Is that all right?"

Rowan nodded eagerly.

"Very well, duck. There's your pound change. Now hurry back to your seat and 'Oscar the Fabulous Waiter', namely yours truly, will bring your food in two shakes of a lamb's tail."

Staring at the coin in her hand, Rowan made her way back out into the corridor. She could not stop thinking about rich suet pastry and hot strawberry jam. Her empty stomach was making the most alarming noises. And even Luke couldn't grumble about...

A sudden sound made her look up. In a compartment to her left were two men, snoring loudly. They were slouched against their seats, legs sticking out, revealing battered old boots. They wore identical coats; long, grey and shabby, with collars pulled up and caps pulled low. Every now and then one would mutter and squeak and sigh.

Rowan peered in through the partition window. Why did they seem familiar? They looked shabby, grubby almost. But, with the exception of a glimpse of a whiskery moustache, or elf locks, curling around their collars, the faces were completely hidden.

Rowan frowned and rubbed her forehead. The people on this train really were very strange. She frowned and moved on.

Luke received the news of their impending meal with a dirty scowl.

"Forgodsake! All I want is a burger. What's their bloody problem?"

But when Oscar arrived ten minutes later pushing a trolley piled high with steaming hot dishes, even Luke was speechless. His eyebrows rose skywards as Oscar arranged the plates on the fold-down table. He didn't object to the creamy tomato soup, or the sausage and mash with onion gravy, or the treacle tart with clotted cream. Rowan received her cheesy potato pie with a glorious smile, and almost kissed Oscar when she saw the golden roly-poly topped with custard. Oscar set down a large teapot and teacups, then slipped two iced fairy cakes onto Rowan's plate with a wink.

"Bon appa'teet, chick. And, remember, don't leave a crumb or I shall be deeply offended."

There was no danger of that, thought Rowan. Luke was already halfway through his bowl of soup and even he mumbled a crumby thank you through a mouthful of bread, as Oscar departed.

When Luke had finished, he stretched his legs across the plush seat.

"I am stuffed," he said, yawning. "Think I'll get some kip."

Rowan, licking the last traces of icing from her fingers, could feel her own eyes beginning to close. She folded her coat to make a pillow and curled up in one corner.

Her tummy was full and she felt deliciously warm and cosy. She gave a yawn and a sigh.

"I suppose we'll wake up in time for Gillkirk. They're bound to call us…"

Her head dropped onto the coat, she drew her arms around her knees and with her next breath she was asleep.

18

SNARL

WHEN ROWAN WOKE, THE TRAIN WAS IN darkness and creeping along at a snail's pace.

She sat up. "Luke, what's happening?"

But the seat opposite was empty. Luke had gone.

Rowan frowned and moved nearer to the window. Outside white fields gleamed beneath a silver moon. Black trees were thrown into sharp relief against the wintry landscape. She could see shapes, dark and sinuous, loping through the snow, following the train.

Suddenly, a howl split the silence. It chilled Rowan to the bone and her arm began to throb.

"Foul Folk!" she cried.

The compartment door was drawn back with a thud. There stood the guard with the brass whistle, the one called Albert, holding a brightly lit oil lamp.

"Just making sure you're all right, lass. Electrics are playing up. We're sorting them out. Shouldn't be long."

"Where are we? I fell asleep."

"About halfway. It'll be another two hours, I reckon, as long as we hit median speed. It's all a bit *too* slow for my liking."

"Why *are* we going so slow?"

"Drifts on the line. Blizzard again last night. When the snowbanks get top-heavy they cave in and there they go, a-tumbling down onto the track, just like ole London Bridge. We're pushing our way through now. Specially fitted, see, with the snow plough. Have to take it easy, don't want to come off the rails. Oh no, indeed." He gave a nod towards the vacant seat. "I see your brother has gone prowlin'."

"Perhaps he needed to stretch his legs."

"Should be lookin' after you. That's what your mother said, and in my opinion she's quite right. Not the thing, going off like that."

"I'm okay, really."

"Well, lass, he could have left you a note. Simple courtesy, that's what I call it."

Again came the sound of howling.

Albert moved to the window and muttered something under his breath.

"What is that?" Rowan asked, shuddering. "I saw something out there, chasing the train."

"Dogs. There's been trouble with dogs. Driven mad by the cold, people say. They don't come too close, not unless we stop. Don't like the noise, see. But don't you worry, my dear, you're perfectly safe. Dogs can't get through doors, can they? Not unless some idiot lets them in. Last week a foolish young man leant out of the window to throw a meat pie and 'crunch!': almost had his hand off."

Rowan shuddered.

"No need to fret, lass, you'll be as safe as houses, providing you keeps that door and window shut tight. Now I must be off, attend to the other passengers. If I see that rascal brother of yours, I'll send him back with a flea in his ear."

After Albert had gone, the darkness seemed to flood back. Rowan curled up beneath her duffle coat, shivering, not with cold but fear. She slid her hand beneath her collar and closed her fingers around the concealed leather pouch.

Outside, the howls were growing louder. She wished Luke would come back. Even his sullen presence was better than this horrible sense of isolation. And then there was a sickening jolt as the train lurched to a halt.

The howling of the dogs stopped.

The silence was so complete it seemed she must be the only passenger left on board.

Rowan edged her way to the window and peered out. She soon wished she hadn't. Below, gathered on a low embankment, was a pack of huge, black dogs: twelve or thirteen in number. They began to bark, baring great, yellow fangs. It was not hunger she saw, blazing in their eyes, but raw malice. Rowan shrank back. The door between her and these creatures seemed the flimsiest of barriers. She turned. Should she move to another compartment? Find Luke? Find anyone? But surely it was as safe here as anywhere? The guard had said the dogs would never get through.

With frantic barks the dogs began to run back and forth along the length of the train, as if looking for a way in.

And then a different sound. Rowan caught her breath. It echoed across the fields; a solitary howl, but, in nature, so unlike that of the Foul Folk. It was eerie, true, but melodic, almost beautiful and seemed older, much older than the voices of these growling brutes.

The pack froze, tails stiff, heads held high to scent the air. The largest, most powerful dog drew its lips back and snarled. At that moment, Rowan heard someone whistle: a sharp, beckoning signal. The pack of dogs, setting up a monstrous baying, turned tail and flew towards the head of the train.

Rowan heard shouts, screams, then a frenzy of barking. She scrambled to her feet in horror. The sounds were inside the train. Someone had opened the doors. But who would have done such a dreadful thing? Then a terrible thought occurred to her, perhaps there were Hunters aboard? She must get out of here: escape over the fields, hide in the hedgerows, find an old barn. But one glance through the window revealed two red-eyed creatures standing guard outside her carriage. Rowan retreated. She knew then, with utter certainty, that the hounds were after her and her alone. They would not hurt the other passengers, unless their way was blocked. It was not blood they were after, but conquest.

With caution, she pulled back the sliding partition into the corridor and looked out. The sounds were drawing near: doors slamming, thumps, cries of terror and a volley of deafening barks. There must be somewhere to hide. At the far end of the carriage was a toilet with a lockable door, but would she have time to reach it? The compartments next to her own were empty, but offered no real hiding place. To her left was a dead end, the plain door to the guard's van, the last carriage of the train. Yes, that's it, she thought. If nothing else it might delay them.

Rowan made for the van, jerked the handle downwards and pushed. It opened and beyond was a great, dark space, smelling of oil and dust. She stepped forward and let the heavy door swing shut. For a moment blackness engulfed her. As her eyes adjusted to the gloom, she made out two small windows, flat squares of murky grey.

In one corner of the van lay a formless mound, which, she realised, consisted of a great jumble of crates, sacks and parcels; in the other corner leant two old bicycles. Beneath one of the windows stood a wooden chair and a packing case upon which were laid out a number of objects. Moving nearer she recognised a spirit stove, a kettle, a tin mug and a pipe. Must belong to the head guard, Albert, she thought, biting her lip. She hoped he hadn't tried to stop the hounds; after all, it was her they were after. But, knowing Albert and Oscar, they would have defended their passengers to the bitter end.

She grabbed hold of the little stove, unscrewed the cap and sloshed the contents onto the floor. It would help mask her scent.

A cry rang out. The voice of the pack altered and became a frenzied baying. In horror, Rowan threw the stove aside, sank to her knees and scuttled into a space between two bulging sacks. But it was no use: in her heart she knew. The hounds would sniff her out like a fox in the undergrowth.

She pressed her hands against her eyes, trying to block out the pictures that flickered inside her head: animal pelts torn to pieces, matted fur, muzzles red with blood.

Then she heard voices in the corridor, high-pitched shrieks of victory.

"Yes, yes. This is it! We saw her sleeping here. Oh yes, with our very own eyes."

Chattering cries of delight.

"And the scent is strong. Yes, you have it in your nostrils, my Lord, fresh and sweet!"

A howl of triumph.

"This is the place. In here!"

There was the sound of a sliding door crashing back on its rails. They must be entering the compartment where she and Luke had been sitting. There was a madness of snarling, ripping, smashing.

Then a silence, which seemed to go on forever.

It was broken at last by a growl so resonant the whole train shuddered.

Rowan felt sick.

"But she was here!" came a frantic cry. "You can smell her. You saw through the window!"

Again the terrible growl.

"Please, no, Master. She is hiding somewhere. That's it! We will hunt her out. She cannot have gone far. Oh no. Who can hide from *you*, Lord of the Black Hunt? Ragtooth and Redclaw will make their change and join the chase!"

Ragtooth! Redclaw! Those voices! She knew them. Reginald, Rafe! They must have been on the train all along.

Rowan could hear the blood pounding in her head.

"Ah, here, look. This is not the last carriage. Yes, behind this door. The scent lies here."

The handle to the guard's van rattled and the door creaked open.

Rowan whimpered and pressed her fingers, one by one, against the soft leather pouch about her neck.

There were low snarls, squeaks, scufflings.

"Oh foul! Treachery. The stench scorches our nostrils! But still the girl-scent is there, beneath. Oh yes."

"*Yes, yes, yes…*"

"Come out, little girl. We shan't hurt you."

A chuckling echo. "*Hurt you, hurt you, hurt you…*"

Rowan willed herself not to move, tried to hold her breath, but little rags of air rasped at her windpipe. She clasped the pouch so tightly it dug into the flesh of her palms.

Please, come now, please, something was her silent prayer.

But there was nothing.

"No use hiding, little girl. We know you are in here. We can smell you!"

The boxes, the sacks, the very darkness, seemed to bear down upon her. Like quarry she was cornered. There was nowhere left to run.

"Behind those boxes, my prince. There, there! You can almost taste her!"

Lunging forwards, the great hound let out a volley of thunderous barks and the pack followed his lead. Rowan clasped her hands to her ears and squeezed herself into a tight ball.

There was a howl.

It pierced the darkness like moonlight.

Plaintive, enthralling, it called to the deepest part of her. She must answer.

Hardly knowing what she was doing Rowan jumped up from her hiding place and saw the side of the van open up and a large sliding door roll aside. Two bright shapes leapt through the opening and turned to face her attackers.

It was a great white wolf and a silver cat.

The pack of hounds was thrown into confusion. Many streaked away back along the train, howling in despair. The remaining dogs growled, edging backwards. But the pack leader stood his ground, fixing the wolf with a dreadful stare. By his side cowered two animals. Or were they men? Rowan could hardly tell. They were rat-like, yet man-like, with long limbs, pointed snouts and twitching whiskers. A shudder ran through her – Ragtooth and Redclaw: the scabby pair from the sewers!

One began to twitter, "Take care, my Lord. We don't want to harm our lovely fur."

"*L-l-lovely fur…*" the other echoed.

"The cat creature is more dangerous than it looks."

"*Oh, very dangerous…*"

The Lord of the Foul Folk gave one low, guttural bark and the rat-men fell to their knees, whimpering.

"Silence!"

Rowan shuddered with horror. The black dog was speaking!

"Give we human child, old one. Else we rip your throat. Like we rip the throat of your she-wolf!" Each word was the grating of millstones.

For a moment, a dark fire of despair flared up in the white wolf's eyes.

"No." The wolf's voice was as deep and soft as snow. "Go back. She is under the Lady's protection."

"Give we child!"

The remaining hounds broke out afresh, like rolling thunder.

The leader lowered his head, hackles raised, fangs bared.

The white wolf stood proud, unflinching.

"Go back, Foul Folk. Tell your grey master you have failed."

At this, the hound gave a howl of fury and sprang at the wolf's throat. The wolf rose to meet it and they collided in mid-air, twisting and flailing, falling to the floor with a crash.

At once they were on their feet, circling each other warily. The onlookers pushed themselves back against the carriage walls, clearing a space. Rowan could see that the animals were well-matched in size and strength. The wolf was taller and the dog more powerful about the shoulders.

Suddenly, the dog lunged towards the wolf's underbelly. The wolf swerved and sprang away, then doubled back to face his aggressor. Again, the dog made a leap and this time its teeth bit deep into the wolf's shaggy mane. The wolf staggered backwards. There was the scrambling and skidding of claws, but then he was up, standing his ground. The black hound moved forward slowly, jaws drooling, its eyes blazing with unnatural light. For a moment, it stood quite still, then lunged and lunged again, its great bulk driving the wolf into a corner.

The wolf isn't fighting back, thought Rowan. What's wrong? Is he badly hurt? Something dark and wet was streaking his fur. She caught her breath and made a movement towards him. But the cat was by her side.

"Hold, child."

For a moment the Lord of the Foul Folk was distracted, and swung his massive head towards Rowan. He growled and the full force of his fiery gaze struck her. It was like looking into a pit of flames. She gave a small cry of horror.

The dog turned back to his cornered prey.

The white wolf crouched low, pressing himself into the floor, as if he were crushed beneath the dog's commanding presence. The hound drew himself up, bared his fangs and made one last victorious leap, to finish the fight. But, as the dog flew through the air, the wolf twisted forward, reared up beneath him and clamped his jaws around the exposed throat.

"Now, child!" an urgent voice cried. "The Fàinne Duilleoga!"

Rowan's fingers scrambled for her leather pouch and drew out the circle of silver. Rays of brilliant white light pierced the darkness. Howls of misery rang out. She heard squeals of pain. "My eyes! My eyes!" Then the remnants of the dog pack fled, with two scabby creatures scuttling in their wake.

19

THE CAT SPEAKS

———◆———

THE GREAT BULK OF THE DEAD DOG LAY slumped on the floor of the train, dark blood oozing from its throat.

The wolf stood over it, panting. He staggered backwards a pace or two, sank down and rolled onto his side.

"Sage!" cried the silver cat, springing forward.

"Is he hurt?" Rowan asked. She knelt and took the wolf's head onto her lap.

Rowan parted the red-streaked fur at the wolf's neck, revealing a deep wound. Fresh blood soaked her fingers. She could feel it wetting her jeans.

"We need something to stop the bleeding," she said. "Some wadding. My T-shirt might do it."

"Child." The cat's voice was low.

"What? What is it?"

"It's too late for that," said the cat.

"But…" She wiped a bloody hand across her forehead. "We have to try."

With trembling fingers she began to unbutton her cardigan, slip it from her shoulders.

"He has lost too much blood."

"No…"

"His heart grows weak. I sense it."

Rowan paused, staring at the cat, and let her hand rest on the white wolf's ears.

"He's going to die," she gulped.

It was not a question.

The cat's eyes were brilliant amber.

"Use the Earthstone, child."

Trembling, Rowan reached for the leather pouch and drew out the black pebble.

It was hot, almost too hot to hold. She could feel the energy, more than heat, a tingling, crackling sensation, surging through her fingers and up into her arm.

She looked at the wolf. He lay so still. Had he stopped breathing?

"What shall I do?"

"Press it against his throat," said the cat. "Quick or it will be too late."

Rowan held the stone against the thick fur.

Nothing happened. She could feel her heart pounding in the darkness. The silver cat brought his head close to Sage's muzzle. Perhaps he's dead after all, Rowan thought. Like the she-wolf, like Swift. *They* had ripped open *her* throat. She had seen the pain in the white wolf's eyes. Perhaps he wanted to die?

With a dazzling flash of light that seemed to course through her body, Rowan felt the heat disappear from the Earthstone. In one bound Sage was on his feet, shaking himself as if he had just scrambled out of a river.

The cat leapt back with a mew of protest.

"By our Lady, brother, next time give warning of your recovery!"

"Why, Ash, did I startle you?" Sage shook himself again. "I'm so pleased to be out of that dark place. Did you not call me?"

"No, brother. *The child* brought you back."

Sage turned to Rowan and bent his head low.

"Dur'ae, I greet you. I owe you my life."

Sage lifted his head and moved forward, resting his muzzle against Rowan's palm.

Rowan didn't know what to do. She wanted to bury her hands and face in the wolf's thick white fur; wanted to hug Sage the way she might hug any big friendly dog. But she knew in her heart that he was a wild creature.

She placed her hand on the top of his noble head.

"I should thank *you*, Sage. You've been with me for a long time, I think."

His eyes were the deepest gold.

"Longer than you know, child."

Suddenly, Sage's ears pricked high.

"I must go. There are Foul Folk abroad!"

He bounded towards the large opening on the broad side of the guard's van and leapt down onto a bank of deep snow.

"Farewell, Dur'ae; farewell, Ash. May the Lady's blessings go with you." He held their gaze briefly, then, swift and silent, raced over the fields, a silver shadow against the white.

Shivering, Rowan slid the van door back into position.

The electric lights flickered on and she blinked in the sudden glare. There were footsteps approaching, voices calling out. The cat slipped into the shadows.

Albert and Oscar appeared in the doorway, at the head of a group of passengers. They were brandishing an assortment of implements: walking sticks, coal shovels, umbrellas.

"Oh, bless my giddy aunt, the kid's all right," cried Oscar.

The cry was taken up by the passengers.

"She's all right."

"Thank goodness."

"The child is safe."

"What's that you say?"

"The young girl, she's safe!"

Albert was as white as paper. He stared down at the massive body of the dog, lying in a pool of blood.

"I'll be blest, young lady. I thought you were a goner. Are you quite sure you're not hurt?"

Oscar stepped forward, palm clasped to his cheek. "What happened? You're covered in blood!"

"They... they..." Rowan stammered, searching for a convincing explanation. "The dogs were fighting each other. There was so much blood... I slipped... fell."

"Turned on themselves, hey?" the guard said, his face grim.

Oscar prodded the dead animal with his toe.

"A good thing they did. Just look at the size of this brute!"

The old guard shuddered.

"'Orrible sight. Not for the likes of a little girl. Come away, everyone; the adventure is over. We'd best get on our way as soon as possible and clean this mess up. Oscar, the young lady needs a cup of strong tea."

"Right away, Albert," Oscar said. "Come with me, duck. You'll be right as rain in a twinkling, though it'll take more than elbow grease to get the blood out of those trousers."

As Oscar ushered Rowan through the crowd Luke appeared in the doorway. His face was pale and he would not meet Rowan's gaze.

"Now then, young man," said Albert. "I've a bone to pick with you. What were you thinking of, abandoning your post? Your mother entrusted you with the care of this young lady!"

Luke hung his head, dark hair flopping into his eyes.

"Look at this great brute. Where was you when those giant fangs were inches from your sister's throat? Yes, that's what I'd like to know."

Luke murmured something.

"What was that? Speak up, lad."

"I'm sorry," Luke said. He glanced at Rowan with a strange, wild look in his eyes. "I... I went to the loo."

Rowan gave a weak smile. "It's okay."

"All's well that ends well, that's what I always say," Oscar chimed in. "You both need a huge pot of tea and some of my flapjacks. Oh, I tell you, you will never, *ever* find flapjacks as moist as mine. I'm famous for my flapjacks. I've won prizes."

Oscar placed a friendly arm around both Luke and Rowan, and guided them to a new compartment. The old compartment, they saw in passing, was mauled and shredded beyond recognition, the wood gnawed and splintered and scraps of velvet upholstery and goose-feather stuffing scattered about like snow.

"Now, you settle down in here, nice and cosy like," said Oscar, ushering them into the new seats. "I'll go and get the necessary, including some soap and water for you, my girl. Back in two shakes."

Luke threw himself down on a seat. Rowan sat opposite.

It seemed very quiet once Oscar had gone.

Again, Rowan tried smiling at Luke. Luke gave a sigh and looked at the floor.

"You okay?" he asked. There was a stiff, awkward edge to his voice.

"I'm fine."

Luke glanced up. His eyes were drawn to the bloodstains on her hands and clothes. His face was a funny colour.

"Don't worry, Luke. That Albert, he didn't mean..."

"Yeah, whatever."

Luke turned away and pressed his forehead against the window. The moon was high in the sky, shining down on the white hills. The train gave a lurch and began to move slowly forward.

"It wasn't your fault."

"Just leave it, Ro!" Then, quietly, "Just leave it."

He refused to say any more. Rowan stared at the backs of her hands, red from Sage's wound.

Oscar returned, balancing the tray of refreshments in one hand and a jug of warm water, plus towel, in the other, cleverly countering the jolting rhythm of the carriages.

"You clean yourself up, duck," he said. "Don't want your grandmother having a turn, do we?"

Luke drank two cups of tea straight down, then started a third. Rowan, having washed her hands and face, was only halfway through her first cup when Luke fell fast asleep. He curled up like a small child, his dark hair falling over his face. Oscar put his hands on his hips.

"Oh bless! The poor lad, he's had a nasty shock. Looks a bit peaky. Needs a nice warm blanket, that's the thing." Off he went again.

"I found your travelling bag," he said on his return, two woollen rugs tucked under his arm. "Saved it from the chaos next door. It was up in the high rack, out of their reach. What a blessing. You'll not be short of stockings and petticoats."

Oscar spread a blanket over Luke.

"There, he'll sleep like a baby. And here, duck, you wrap yourself up. Always the risk of a delayed reaction. Shock is like that, you know; you must take care."

Suddenly, Rowan felt safe. Safer, in fact, than she had felt for a long time. It was not simply the knowledge that Sage and Ash were there to protect her. No, there was something else.

The Hunters are not invulnerable.

This thought went through her mind, time and again. It gave her a sense of hope.

With a last tweak of Luke's blanket and a hearty "toodle-oo", Oscar departed. Rowan smiled a grateful farewell then started devouring slabs of warm, chewy flapjack, quite as delicious as the young guard had promised. Yawning, she considered following Luke's example. I do feel *so* sleepy, she thought.

She looked up at the moon, a bright disc above the sparkling fields. How odd, the way it seemed to race over the treetops, keeping pace with the rattling train. She knew, of course, it was the moon that remained still, a fixed point in the vast black sky, whilst *they* moved through the snowy landscape. But she could not shake off the idea that the moon was following, silent, watchful. How it shimmered, almost too bright to look at. Rowan blinked; her eyelids felt heavy. The sphere of light had developed a halo, had softened, blurred. Far off she heard angel voices, singing. Then a different voice.

"Rowan."

The silvery light dimmed, took shape. There was something leaning over her.

"Child."

Rowan blinked again, rubbed her eyes and sat upright. Had she fallen asleep?

"Child. There are things we must speak of."

Next to her sat the silver cat.

"Ash?"

"We must talk."

Rowan glanced at Luke, curled up, snoring slightly through parted lips.

"Is it safe?"

"Quite safe. He is in a deep sleep."

Rowan leant forwards. "Then, he is one of *them*?"

The cat's eyes sparked fire.

"No. He is not one of *them*. Never believe that. But they will use him, if they can."

"But why?" Rowan asked breathlessly. "What do they want? Why do they want to hurt me?"

"They fear you, child."

"Fear me? Why?"

"You are one of the Dur'ae."

"Dur'ae? That's what Sage called me. I don't even know what it means."

"Your memory of such things is… like a clouded mirror. At present you cannot remember, but time and experience will clear the glass."

"You mean I've… I've been a… a *Dur'ae* before?" The word felt awkward on her tongue.

"You have always been what you are. With each cycle it takes a little time for the memories to return. This time our need was urgent. We had to find you, perhaps before you were ready. The Hunters were on your trail. We could not risk them getting to you first."

Rowan thought of the attack at the Ice Fair, the crushing jaws of the dog. She felt a wave of nausea rise in her tummy. *"In for the kill."*

"But how can they fear… me?" Her voice had dropped to a whisper.

"Because, child, you can stop them."

Rowan shook her head. "I don't understand."

The silver cat gazed at her with a kind of solemn tenderness.

"Do not doubt yourself. Soon you will be called."

"Called?"

"Called to duty."

"But…?"

"You must prepare yourself."

Rowan sighed. Things seemed to be making less sense than ever.

"How will…?"

"Hush!"

The cat raised its head, ears alert. "Someone is coming." He leapt down from the seat and padded over to the door. Rising up on his hind legs, he pushed against the sliding partition and it opened.

"I must go."

Moving forwards, Rowan knelt down by his side and stroked the broad silver back.

"Ash, will I see you again?"

He held her gaze for a moment, his eyes soft as candlelight.

"By our Lady's grace."

"I wish you could stay."

The cat rubbed his cheek against her palm.

"Ash, thank you."

With a sudden bound Ash was gone. All she could hear was his voice, low and clear and urgent, echoing down the corridor.

"Be ready for the Calling."

The Calling?

Rowan stood up, turned and looked down at Luke. With an absent-minded gesture she brushed the long fringe out of his eyes. He stirred, shifting position. Mum had told Luke to look after her, but in truth he was the one who needed taking care of. Sighing, Rowan sat down, wrapped the blanket about her shoulders, curled up in the corner of the plush seat and closed her eyes. She could feel the train swaying from side to side as it clattered over the railway tracks, a rattling, hypnotic rhythm which seemed to fill her head. *Clat-ter clat-ter clat-ter. He's not one of them. Nev-er be-lieve that. Soon you will be called. By the Lady's grace. You must be pre-pared. Clat-ter clat-ter clat—*

Rowan woke with a start. Someone had called her. A loud voice, breaking through sleep.

"Luke?" she mumbled. "Luke?"

Then it came again. Albert's voice.

"Gillkirk! Gillkirk Station! All those wishing to alight at Gillkirk!"

"Luke!" she cried. "Luke, wake up. We're here!"

20

HOLLY AND IVY

$$\sim\!\!-\!\!\longrightarrow\!\!\!\longleftarrow\!\!-\!\!\sim$$

ROWAN AND LUKE WERE THE ONLY passengers to alight. They stood in the thick snow, shivering. Steam hissed and curled about the engine wheels and the great bulk of the train pulled away. Albert and Oscar were leaning out of a window waving their caps.

"G'bye, lass," called Albert. "It's been an honour."

"Toodle-oo, duck. Wrap up warm and remember, whatever you do, don't…"

Oscar's last words were lost beneath a long, melancholy whistle. Rowan raised her hand in farewell.

A few flakes of snow drifted down from the black sky, settling on their hair. Rowan turned and looked around. It was a small country station with a single platform and a stone-built cottage. This served as the station master's house, ticket office and waiting room, all rolled into one. Rowan remembered what it had been like in the summer, bright with flowers and sunshine and day trippers. But now, in the depths of winter, it looked so different: so dark, so silent.

"Where's *Grandmother* got to, then?" Luke said, his voice dangerous. "I'm freezing." He pulled his combat jacket collar high and stomped his feet.

"Well, the train was on time," Rowan answered, nodding at the station clock. "It's just past eight. Gran should be here."

Luke cursed under his breath, his mouth an ugly curl. Grabbing the handle of the travel bag, he stalked off towards the cottage. Rowan hurried after him, as best she could in the deep snow.

Lights shone out from behind lace-curtained windows and Luke rapped on the front door, knuckles loud against the shiny red paint.

"Come on, come on," he muttered.

The door was opened by a portly man pulling on a uniform jacket and peaked cap.

"Aw raight, aw raight, canna tha see ahm come?"

The man's face was flushed red and he wore thick, tartan slippers.

"What can I do for thee?" he asked, fumbling with the brass buttons on his jacket.

"We were expecting to be picked up," Luke said.

"Come again, lad?"

"Our grandmother was meant to collect us from the station. We've just arrived, on the train."

"Oh aye, thy grandmother?"

"Yes. She's not here."

The station master poked his head out of the door, peering left and right.

"Tha's raight enough theer."

"Well, can we phone her?"

"Phone her?"

"Yes. Is there a telephone?" Luke was pale with anger.

"A telephone? Oh no, lad. Line's bin down for two day nah."

"Well, have you got a mobile?"

"A mo-bile? No, no lad. No mo-bile."

Luke's jaw clenched and unclenched.

Rowan stepped forward.

"Has our gran left a message? She's Mrs Beckthwaite of Dale View, Gillkirk."

"Oh aye." The man's expression softened and he tousled Rowan's hair. "Betty Beckthwaite. Of course, I know Betty. So you're her grandchilder, hey? I can see tha teks after her. Well now, well now." He chuckled to himself, rubbing his fat chin.

"So, there *is* a message?"

"A message? Ah. I'm afeared not. But I'll tell thee what I'll do. I'll send young Bob wi' a note up t'village. We'll soon have it sorted. Never fear, lass. Now then, you two best come and sit in't wetting room. It's cosy as toast in theer."

He showed them into the adjoining building, which could be accessed both via his hallway and from the station platform. It was a long, low room with open fires burning at either end. Mismatched armchairs were arranged in intimate groupings and on the walls hung old-fashioned oil paintings of farm animals.

"Just settle dahn. I'll go put kettle on."

Luke threw the bag to the floor. With an angry lunge he grabbed an armchair and half dragged it to the fire, but as he pulled it over a threadbare rug it snagged and overbalanced and the wooden claw-foot slammed hard against his ankle.

"Jeez!" he gasped, kicking the fallen chair. "Bloody-stupid-thing!" With each word he threw another kick.

"Luke," Rowan protested. "You'll break it!"

"Don't talk to me!" Luke snarled. He heaved the chair upright, manhandled it into position and slumped down into the seat. Rubbing his ankle, he leant forwards towards the fire.

Rowan sighed and turned away. It was no use. In this kind of mood Luke was impossible.

She walked around the room looking at the pictures. The animals were strange, long-bodied creatures with spindly legs. The men holding them looked out of place in a farmyard, with their fine wide-cuffed coats and knee-length britches and three-cornered hats. Over the far mantlepiece was an old mirror, speckled with age. Drawing near, Rowan gazed at her reflection. What an odd little person stared back: a white face with a bob of brownish hair and great dark eyes like smudges of charcoal.

Behind her, in the looking glass, she could see Luke, or, rather, one of his arms lolling over the side of the chair and his dark hair falling against his shoulders. He looked different: small, lost, far away. Rowan got the sudden, horrible feeling that, when she turned to look, Luke would be gone. The fear was so real it made her catch her breath.

She spun around, heart pounding.

"Luke!"

"What the hell do you want?" His voice was a lazy sneer.

Rowan gritted her teeth. She wanted to slap him.

How dare he? How dare he! After what he had...

She closed her eyes and reached for the leather pouch beneath her clothes. She could feel its outline, safe, reassuring.

She took a deep breath. I must get away, she thought. Just for a moment. I have to be alone.

She moved towards the door.

"I'm going out," she said.

As she yanked the handle and pushed the door, he drawled, "And you think I'm bothered?"

Clenching her jaw, she banged the door shut behind her. In the darkness the sudden noise seemed dreadful and alien. Out here it was like another world: still and white and bitterly cold.

Rowan held her breath, listening. There were no sounds: no solitary car engine, no far-off radio music, no dog barking, no human voice. She could hear nothing but the crunch of her own feet through the deep snow. With slow, careful steps she made her way along the platform, past the wooden gate that, she remembered now, led out onto a country lane. She wandered past the bare flower beds and wooden benches, buried beneath the weight of winter, all the way to the platform's end. Here, on the rising slopes of the embankment, grew fir trees, their thick branches heavy with snow. Above the pointed treetops the moon shone silver-bright, casting deep shadows below. An owl hooted and in the distance came an answering call. Then something emerged from the trees, gliding, a shadow caught against moonlight. There was a swoop, a struggle, a thin, defenceless squeal.

Rowan shivered and turned back. But as she retraced her steps something made her pause.

What was that?

She listened intently. All was silent.

But, wait! There it was again; the sound of sleigh bells!

Rowan began to hurry, striding through the snow. The jingle of bells was drawing closer. It must be coming down the lane. What could it be? Whoever used sleigh bells nowadays? It was the sound of Santa's grottos, of toddlers' Christmas parties, of pantomimes, a sound considered childish after the age of six, though secretly it still made one's heart thrill. But it was not something to be heard on a dark winter's night, in the middle of nowhere. Rowan reached the gate and leant over.

Coming down the snowy lane was a sleigh drawn by a sturdy white pony. Two people sat in front, well wrapped against the cold.

"Whoa there, Ivy, lass," said the driver, his voice, steady and low. Giving the slightest touch on the reins he drew up, level with the gate.

"Why," cried the other figure, pulling the woollen rug aside and clambering down, "you must be the young girl. Rowan. Yes, yes, *Rowan*. Awfully sorry we're late."

It was a lady. Not young, but not quite old. She was plump, with a broad, rosy face and bright eyes. She wore a thick tweed cap with flaps that came down over her ears and a voluminous tartan cape.

"There's a boy too, isn't there? Older. Now, what *was* his name? Something from the Gospels. Rather French. Marc? No? What was it?"

"Luke," said Rowan.

"Yes. That was it. Luke. Must try and remember. Awfully bad manners not to."

"Have you come about Grandma?" Rowan asked opening the gate.

"Bless you, my dear, yes. Should introduce myself." The lady thrust out a gloved hand and shook Rowan's vigorously. "How do you do? May Sloethorn's the name. Your grandma is a good friend of mine, in a spot of bother, with poor Alf, your grandfather. So we've come to the rescue. A friend in need and all that. Now, where's that William got to?"

May Sloethorn strode through the gate, up to the station cottage, and rapped on the cottage door.

Rowan, following after, heard the waiting room door creak ajar. Luke peered out, curious but sullen. Moments later, the station master, his hat slipping sideways, opened the front door.

"What is it now?" he grumbled.

"Good evening, William," May trumpeted.

"Oh, erh, now then, Miss Sloethorn. An' to what do I owe this pleasure?" He attempted to set his cap straight.

"I've come for the children. They're Elizabeth Beckthwaite's two."

"Oh aye, I know, I know. Sent young Bob off a while since."

"Alfred has been taken ill, you know."

"Oh. Ah. I can't say I…"

She turned to Rowan.

"Your grandfather's bronchitis has flared up again, I'm afraid. Nothing serious, but he's rather poorly. He needs peace and quiet and rest, that sort of thing. Your grandma's cottage is on the small side. She asked if you could lodge with me. Plenty of room, you see, just until things look up."

Rowan nodded.

"Ah! Hallo there!" cried May, turning and catching sight of Luke. "You must be Marc!"

Luke half-drew back, then thought better of it. He mumbled a response.

"Well, there we are. All present and correct. Come on then, best be on our way. Get your things together," beamed May.

Luke disappeared, then re-emerged carrying the travel bag. Rowan ran forwards to help him, resting her hand on his arm. Luke scowled and roughly shrugged her away. She paused for a moment, sighed and trailed after him.

"Why didn't Gran come to meet us?" Luke demanded, glaring at May's back. May Sloethorn turned and fixed Luke with a firm gaze.

"She's nursing your grandfather. Wants to be on hand, just in case. I'm sure you understand. Now then, pass your luggage up here," she said as they reached the sleigh. "You two jump in the back. Plenty of rugs to keep you warm. Wrap up well. Wind's pretty keen when we're on the move."

Rowan scrambled up eagerly, exclaiming in delight. Luke, reluctant, came after and threw himself down in the far corner of the seat. As if to put as much distance as possible between the two of us, thought Rowan. Gritting her teeth, she turned away. If Luke wanted to be difficult let him. It wasn't going to spoil her fun. She snuggled down into the soft, thick blankets, half smiling. Imagine what Jaz, or Mum, would say about this, a real sleigh ride in the snow!

"Now," said May. "Must do introductions. Rowan, Luke, this is Mr Holly."

The driver turned around and gave them a nod.

Rowan caught a glimpse of an old, whiskery, weather-beaten face beneath a shapeless hat.

"'Ow do."

"Mr Holly is a marvel, can turn his hand to anything, from shoeing a horse to growing an orange. Do you know, he made this sleigh out of an old pony trap. Simply perfect for this weather. Knocks spots off the Land Rover.

"And this is Ivy. Welsh mountain, wise as the hills and gentle as a lamb. She'll take a saddle too, if either of you ride."

Luke made a scornful noise, but May didn't seem to hear.

Mr Holly gathered the reins and made a low clicking noise in his throat.

"Here we go!" May whooped.

The pony set off, bells jingling, the sleigh gliding smoothly over the snow. The lane ran beside a frozen river, and shortly they came to a wider road. Here they turned right onto a pretty stone bridge.

Mr Holly murmured, "Hwisha hwisha" and the pony, gathering speed, encountered the incline with confidence and skill, her hooves steady on the firm snow. On the other side they passed into a tunnel of trees, the overhanging boughs glittering with frost. Through the branches shone the moon, casting its spell upon the world, deepening the pearly bloom on a bank of snow, the shadows of a dark hollow. It seemed to Rowan that she could see things moving through the trees, but, as she blinked, the forms would dissolve into odd-shaped rocks and branches and stumps.

When they emerged from the woods, Rowan caught her breath in wonder. Great hills rose up ahead: an expanse of white, sparkling in the moonlight. Here and there the tops of stone walls or stunted thorns could be seen, marking out field boundaries, but for the most part the scene was simply a uniform stretch of snow, rising and dipping with the land.

Feeling the cold air on her face, hearing the jingle of the harness, breathing in the fresh scents of winter, Rowan hugged herself with delight. It seemed as if some enchantment was at work. Had the world ever been so beautiful, or so mysterious?

At a fork in the road the pony slowed. A quaint signpost read 'Gillkirk 1 Mile'.

"Up ahead is the village," said May. "But Sloethorn is this way."

Mr Holly guided Ivy to the right and the pony set off at a spanking trot down a country lane.

Suddenly, Luke leant over, his breath hot against Rowan's cheek.

"They could be taking us anywhere," he whispered.

"What?" Rowan stared at him.

His face was a knot of suspicion.

"We've got no idea where they're taking us," he hissed.

"But we're going to—"

"That's what they *say*."

Beneath the sneer of scepticism, he looked genuinely worried.

Rowan shrugged and turned away. But her lovely vision was gone. If Luke had intended to frighten her he had succeeded. She could feel her heart leap in her chest. What if Luke was right? After all, there was no real proof that May Sloethorn was Gran's friend. Just because some stranger turns up and claims... Rowan shook herself. How ridiculous. Just look at May: she was so friendly and straightforward, what Gran would have called 'jolly'. Rowan stuck her chin up in the air, defiant. She would not let Luke ruin this for her. She wouldn't! But she could feel the doubts seep back in. What if it *was* all a deception, what if the intention was to *kidnap* the two of them? What if May and Mr Holly were Hunters?

For a long time Rowan stared out at the white landscape: cold, bleak, isolated. There was a lump of ice in her stomach. Again, she heard the hoot of an owl, the distant bark of a dog. The moon appeared sinister, a pale, malicious eye. Why did Luke always have to spoil things?

"Well, and here we are at last!" cried May. "Soon be cosy and warm."

The sleigh swung through an impressive yet crumbling gateway into a long drive that wound its way between tall trees and bushes. Rounding a bend they saw the house and Rowan gasped. It was a large, rambling, snow-topped building, half buried in ivy. Golden light shone from the myriad windows.

"This is your house?" she squeaked.

"Yes indeed. Sloethorn Manor, acquired by my great-grandfather, Thaddeus Arthur Sloethorn. Known as 'Artie' to his friends."

They drove over a small bridge which straddled an icy beck and swept round onto the expanse of white snow in front of the house.

"Down we get, chaps. Mrs Croft will be here in a moment to… ah, and here she is."

The front door opened and there stood a plump woman wrapped in a thick woollen shawl.

"Theer's hot cocoa and shortbread and a roaring fire waiting for thee. Be quick abaht it."

Rowan scrambled down from the sleigh and trotted up the steps. Luke slouched behind, jollied along by May.

"Don't want to get on the bad side of Lily Croft, young fellow. Look sharp there."

They were shown into a large hallway. The walls were panelled with dark wood and a fine oak staircase swept upwards to the floor above. To one side of this stood a tall, undressed Christmas tree, filling the air with the scent of pine needles.

At once a volley of barks broke forth. From somewhere at the back of the house, three silky-haired dogs emerged, racing and sliding over the polished floor.

Rowan stepped backwards, straight into May Sloethorn.

"Ah ha!" May chortled, placing her hand on Rowan's shoulder. Meet Mustard, Clove and Mace. Daft as brushes, really they are."

The dogs gathered around May, panting, their tails thumping the floor.

"Oh. I…" Rowan began.

"Not afraid, are you?" said May. "No need. Well, apart from getting licked to death. We've had Cocker Spaniels in the family ever since Artie Sloethorn's day."

Seeing Luke adopt his usual sneering expression, Rowan crouched down, holding out her hand. The russet-haired dogs pushed their wet noses and warm tongues into her palm.

Rowan couldn't help smiling. They were so silly and friendly and floppy.

"There, made friends already; they don't hang about, these three. Watch out, though: they'll have your Christmas dinner from you in a trice."

Getting to her feet, Rowan looked up at the large fir tree.

May followed her gaze and gave a hearty chuckle.

"I'm counting on you two to help out with the decorating, you know. Lots of silver stars and baubles and gingerbread men to make. Jolly good fun."

"Them mun 'ave a hot drink fust," said Mrs Croft dryly.

May laughed again.

"Absolutely right. All that can wait for another day. I'll leave you in Lily's capable hands. Must go and take some of that cocoa to Mr Holly and check on my Queen Mab. Goodnight, chaps, sleep tight."

She strode off, the dogs at her heels and disappeared into the shadows at the far end of the hall.

Queen Mab? What a curious name, thought Rowan. Was it another dog, or pony, perhaps? Somehow she wouldn't be surprised if there was a real queen, with wide skirts, ruff and jewelled slippers, hidden away in the depths of this strange old house.

Lily Croft ushered them through a door into a grand living room, filled with heavy furniture. There were old-fashioned sofas, wing chairs, writing desks, spindly tables, footstools and numerous cabinets displaying an array of ornaments. To Rowan, it seemed like something out of one of those costume dramas you saw on telly. Yet, passing her hand over the fine upholstery, she saw that it was faded and shabby, and the Oriental rug beneath her feet threadbare.

Mrs Croft directed them to a pair of armchairs drawn up before a blazing fire. Here, on a low table, stood two mugs, a jug of steaming cocoa and a plate piled high with golden shortbread.

"Drink up while it's hot," she commanded. "We don't want thee catching thy death. Then it's up t'bed wi' thee. I mun go see if the hot-water bottles are done."

Rowan sat down on the edge of the chair, gazing around in disbelief. Luke stood, glassy-eyed.

"It's... just... incredible," Rowan sighed.

Luke said nothing.

"It's like..." But she couldn't find the words.

She turned and looked at the great stone fireplace, carved into a scene of oak leaves and running deer.

"It's wonderful!"

Luke came to life. He flung himself down into the armchair and grabbed a handful of biscuits.

"*It's wonderful*," he mimicked. "Forgodsake, Rowan, you are so..." He clenched his mouth shut, breathing heavily. Then burst out, "Have you got a brain in there? Why haven't they let us see Gran, or phone her at least? Do you think Mum would be happy with this? Do you? This is... so..." He kicked out at a basket of logs on the hearth.

Rowan leant forwards and poured herself a cup of cocoa. "May's okay. She's not a kidnapper, Luke. She's just Gran's friend."

Luke made an ugly noise in his throat.

"Oh and you *know* that do you?"

"No, I don't know it, but you've got to admit it's more likely. Do you want cocoa?"

"Chu! Probably drugged, or poisoned."

Rowan filled his cup anyway and sat back sipping her own drink.

"Anyway, Luke, the station master said all the phone lines were down, remember."

"Conspiracy!"

Yet, despite these accusations he crammed a whole biscuit into his mouth and took several gulps of cocoa.

Rowan stared into the fire, nibbling on the warm shortbread. She could feel a smile rising up from her belly and, for Luke's sake, fought against it.

"Luke, don't you think this could be... fun?"

"Erh, no!"

"Oh Luke."

"You're in denial," he said, frowning, and then the frown turned into a yawn.

"But this house and the garden, and the po..." Her sentence finished in a copycat yawn.

"See," quipped Luke. "They've drugged us."

"We're just tired."

Mrs Croft returned, carrying two hot-water bottles.

"Come on then, the pair of you, off t'bed."

Luke sprang up. "I want to use the phone."

Lily Croft gave him a sharp look. "Theer's no phone here, young man."

"But..."

"Miss Sloethorn's never 'ad need of one," she snapped. "Now, follow me."

Luke pulled a grotesque face behind her back.

Rowan, shaking her head furiously at Luke, smothered the urge to laugh.

21

A Winter Garden

At the top of a stairway stands the white wolf. Its fur is matted with thorns and blood. The girl is panting. Are the breaths her own, or the beast's?

"You want me to follow?" she says, heart pounding, feeling the prick of sweat in her palms. The creature fixes her with its stare.

All is silent but for the heavy tick of the grandfather clock. Her pulse races, four beats to the bar of its slow wooden heart. The girl begins to climb the stairs, yet before she is halfway up the beast turns and lopes off into the darkness.

"Wait, wait...!"

She stumbles up the remaining steps, in pursuit: a frightened foal, a maimed hare, a blind girl.

Darkness.

She falters, stops. The fear she feels is a live thing, coiling at her centre. She has lost all sense of space or direction. Sightlessly, she gropes the air in front of her, trying to find a firm surface, an object, a reference point. Her thoughts catch as they rise, like trapped bubbles. "This is what it is like to drown."

Something is beneath her fingertips, yielding, soft. Not a wall, nor a door. Is it a curtain? She pushes the heavy material to one side, light razors into the gloom. She can see the thick tapestry concealing an archway and beyond a spiral staircase. At the foot of the stairs, the wolf is waiting, eyes like yellow moons.

How familiar those eyes seem.

"Sage?" she gasps.

The wolf turns and bounds up the steps.

"Sage, please!"

She can feel tears burning in her throat.

———◆———

Rowan woke up, crying.

She turned, sobbing into her pillow. It had a strange new scent, mingled with the salty taste of her tears.

"I'm at Sloethorn!" she cried, sitting up, blinking in the sunlight.

The white curtains were half open and daylight poured in through a tall window. Last night, by glowing firelight and guttering candlelight, the room had seemed strange and full of shadows. Exhausted, she had fallen asleep at once. Now, in the morning sun, it was bright, if a little bare. The furniture, child-sized, was painted white. There was a bed with a quilted coverlet, a bedside cabinet and a dainty wardrobe. Hung on the wall was a painting of a bay pony. On the cabinet stood a china bowl and jug, a candlestick and several leather-bound books.

Rowan glanced at the titles: *Arabian Nights*, *The Wonder of Natural History*, *Lamb's Tales* and *Robinson Crusoe*. They seemed to have been chosen with a child in mind, but a child from the long-distant past. Rowan picked up a copy of *Lamb's Tales from*

Shakespeare and flicked through the musty pages. There were elaborate illustrations of heavy-lidded maidens and rosebud-lipped youths, the kind that Luke would mock mercilessly.

Rowan replaced the book with care and pulled back the bedcovers. The air was chilly, despite a fire burning in the grate. Slipping her feet into a pair of waiting slippers and reaching for a thick dressing gown she moved over to the window seat. She leant forward, drawing the curtain back.

"Oh!" she murmured with an odd catch in her voice.

What a symphony of white and blue!

The scene was dazzling.

Below, a great patchwork of gardens was laid out. A white expanse stretched from the back of the house, and at its centre sat a large fountain. To the right were walled gardens and beds and glasshouses, to the left stables, paddocks and a long yew walk, and at the far edges she could see a frosted tangle of trees and brush and bramble. Beyond this, snow-covered hills rose up, curve upon curve, to the clear sky.

"Am I dreaming?" she whispered to herself. It was as if time had stopped, as if she were gazing down upon a world long past. Was it quite real? Rowan felt she wouldn't know until she was out there, treading the snow-covered walkways, feeling the cold, cold air on her face.

Eagerly, she began to search for her clothes. These she discovered in the wardrobe, neatly put away by unseen hands. Shivering, she pulled on several layers, dragged a brush through her hair and splashed a little warm water from the jug onto her face.

Her bedroom door opened onto a wood-panelled corridor which led to a gloomy landing. She remembered coming up the great stairs the night before, with nothing but a candle to light the way and feeling rather nervous in the darkness. The walls were hung with old-fashioned portraits: haughty ladies in voluminous silk dresses and stony-faced men. What light there was came in through two stained-glass windows set high up in the wall. Each depicted a branching tree, fashioned in emerald greens, amber golds, ruby reds and lapis lazuli blues.

From somewhere below came the smell of sizzling bacon and the yapping of dogs. Leaning over the banisters Rowan looked down onto the entrance hall.

May was striding towards one of the lower rooms, the three russet-haired spaniels dancing around her ankles.

"Come on then, you scallywags," May boomed. "Ready for your breakfast, hey? What about a lovely piece of bacon?"

At the word "bacon" the dogs set up a frenzy of barking.

"Now, now, patience!" cried May.

"Uummgh," groaned a voice at Rowan's shoulder. "What's the bloody row?"

It was Luke, his dressing gown cord trailing on the floor, yawning and blinking the sleep out of his eyes.

"Breakfast's ready, I think," said Rowan.

Luke grunted. "Did you sleep much? Took me *forever.*"

"What was the problem?"

"Weird bloody house, *that's* the problem."

"I like it."

"You would. Where'd they get the creaky floorboards? 'Amityville Interiors Ltd'?"

"It's called 'character', Luke."

"*Yeah*, along with the lack of electric lights and hot showers. You'll be telling me there's no loo next. And that reminds me: where is the bloody loo?"

"It's down the corridor on the right, first door to your left. Didn't Mrs Croft show you?"

"Probably wasn't listening," he shrugged, slouching off.

"Careful when you pull the handle though," Rowan called after him. "It's a bit cronky."

Luke raised a cynical eyebrow. "Why doesn't that surprise me?"

Half smiling, Rowan began to make her way downstairs. Her footsteps seemed too loud against the polished oak. Just like... *what was it like?* Then, in a rush, it came back: *the dream*. There below stood the grandfather clock, with its sonorous tick; here was the banister, and the wolf would have stood at the very top. A prickle of fear brushed the back of her neck. It would be standing at the very edge of the top step. What if? Heart racing, she turned. Sunlight streamed through the stained-glass window, a bright shaft of gold pooled and dazzled. For a moment, it seemed as if a shape was moving just beyond the glare.

She heard footsteps below. A bustle of activity came from a door at the back of the hall. A pretty girl with bright eyes hastened through, carrying a large tray of breakfast things.

She grinned up at Rowan.

"Ready for a bite to eat? May's sat down already in the morning room, with the dogs. If you want bacon you'd better be a bit sharpish: *they* usually get the lion's share. Spoils them rotten, she does."

Rowan hurried down the last few steps and followed the girl. The morning room was a large bright space, with tall windows, through which the sunlight flooded. It was decorated in whites and pale yellows and possessed a kind of faded grandeur. A table, covered in a crisp, white cloth, was set for breakfast and here, with her back to a blazing fire, sat May, feeding strips of grilled bacon to each of the spaniels in turn.

"Now, Clove, you wait your turn." One eager muzzle had pushed itself into May's lap. "This is for your brother. Mustard, here, boy, here. Need to be quicker than that to beat your sister. She's as keen as, keen as... oh, I say, ha ha. Keener than Mustard, she is!" May seemed delighted with her joke. Beaming she looked up at Rowan.

"Good morning, my dear. Slept well, I trust? Now, you sit down and have a bit of breakfast. There's porridge and eggs and bacon and toast and some kippers here somewhere." She lifted the covers on various dishes, as if she had lost something.

Rowan slipped into a chair. "Oh, porridge will be fine, Mrs..."

"Just call me May, my dear. Aunty May, if you wish. Ah, yes! Here's the porridge." She passed a steaming silver tureen to Rowan. "And there's the cream and brown sugar, or honey if you prefer."

"Sugar, please," Rowan half whispered, wishing she didn't feel quite so shy.

"Do you fancy a cup of tea? Poppy's just brought in a fresh pot."

"Yes, please."

May poured the tea into a delicate china cup. "Milk or lemon?"

"Oh, milk, please."

"Right ho. Oh, Poppy, my dear, could you bring one or two crumpets, and a pot of that delicious damson jam?"

"Certainly," Poppy replied as she moved towards the door, "and I'll bring some of the crab apple jelly, the young 'uns might like to try something new."

"Excellent idea. Clove! I say! You rascal!"

The spaniel had jumped up, taken the last piece of bacon from May's plate and fled to the far end of the room.

"Goodness, she's a wicked elf. Wouldn't be without her for the world, though. D'you have pets, me dear?"

"Oh no. The… the landlord won't let us."

"Oh, what a shame, what a shame. Difficult in London, I suppose. All those streets, tarmac, traffic. Not much space to breathe. Goodness knows where I'd be without my animals. Always had animals around, since I was a nipper. Father adored them. He was an amateur naturalist, you know. Great regard for old Mother Nature." She beamed at Rowan.

"What sort of pet would you choose, my dear?"

Rowan thought of Ash. "I… I think I would quite like a cat."

"Ah, jolly useful, cats, especially if you've got a rat problem."

At the word "rat" the dogs' ears pricked up and they gave a low growl.

May chuckled, ruffling the silky fur on their heads.

"Yes, I know, ruffians, you can give the rats a good old run for their money, too. Cats are wondrous creatures, but I grew up with dogs, you see. Not these ones, of course, their forebears rather: great-great-great-grandparents. First pup slept in the pram with me. I've got a photograph, somewhere."

"Did... did you ever have a p-pony?" Rowan stammered, thinking of the painting in her bedroom.

"Oh yes, indeed. How I loved my ponies, Bonny and Chieftain and Moth and Lady. Had a whole stable full of horses. And, of course, there were the wild creatures. Father had a way with them; they came to us injured. People brought them, you see: hawks, deer, hedgehogs. Had an owl once, would you believe? Blodeuedd was her name (Welsh, you know). She had a broken wing, beautiful creature, devilish sharp bite. And, of course, there was Wat Tyler, the fox cub."

"A fox!" Rowan exclaimed in spite of herself.

"Oh yes, saved him from a gamekeeper's trap when I was no more than eight or nine. Nursed him back to health. He used to follow me everywhere, just like a puppy dog. Darned clever too."

"I... I didn't know you could train foxes."

"Wouldn't obey anyone else, mind, but we were inseparable. He was with me for almost two years. Then one spring he was off and I thought he had gone for good, but he came back. Oh yes. A night in June, it was, just waiting for me in the orchard, like old times. I followed him all the way up to the high moor and there, well, by Juno, I saw a vixen and her cubs playing in the moonlight. Never forget that sight, Wat's own little family..."

She paused and sighed.

"That winter the hunt came through, over our lands. Father was furious, couldn't bear the idea of creatures being maimed and killed. Can still remember the way he challenged the MFH, waving his walking stick. 'How dare you, how dare you!' But the damage had been done. They caught the fox in the upper pasture; oh, the dreadful baying of the hounds as they tore it to pieces. Nothing left but the tail. And I knew as soon as I saw it."

Rowan gave a little gasp.

"The markings, you see. Not just a white tip: the colour stretched right down, almost halfway down the tail. Terrible thing, terrible, but, you know, even today you can see foxes hereabouts with the same distinctive markings. His spirit lives on, as it were."

May stooped down to make a fuss of the spaniels. Clove had come creeping back, still licking her lips.

"Ah ha," May said, chuckling. "You expect to be brought back into the fold, hey?"

But she didn't scold when the dog laid its auburn head in her lap and gazed up with adoring eyes.

"Oh goodness, mustn't forget," May said, spearing a kipper. "You're visiting your grandmother after lunch. She's longing to see you. Mr Holly will take you over in the sleigh. But what d'you fancy doing this morning? Glorious day, you know."

"Could I, perhaps, explore?"

"Explore the grounds? Capital idea. Never run out of things to do in the great outdoors. Used to *live* outdoors when I was a…"

The door opened and Luke stood there looking uncomfortable.

"Ah ha, young Marc!" May exclaimed. "Good morning. Do find a pew. Hungry as a hound, no doubt, eh? What'll you have?"

"I, erh, I'm not that bothered." He had an odd, guilty look on his face, as he dropped into the nearest chair.

"What?" May chortled. "Never keep your strength up that way. Ah, look, Poppy's arrived with the crumpets. I'm sure she'll be able to tempt you with something."

"I'm not hungry," Luke said, looking down at the tablecloth.

"Not hungry?" Poppy echoed, laughing.

Luke looked up at her, black sparks of anger flying.

"Hah! We'll soon see about that." Poppy lifted the lid on various dishes and began to shovel crispy bacon, fried eggs and fat brown sausages onto his plate. The savoury smell was enticing. "From our own pigs, these are," she said determinedly. "None of that supermarket rubbish. Go on, tuck in."

Luke sat there, staring at the food.

"I..."

"Think it's poisoned, do you?" Poppy laughed, hands on hips.

"Now, now, Poppy," May murmured. "The wise traveller is ever cautious, lest he wends his way to the Land of Fairy. Young Marc is simply being practical."

"He's being daft, if you ask me."

Luke clenched his jaw, grabbed hold of a fork and shovelled a plump sausage into his mouth.

"That's more like it!" Poppy cried with a slight thrust of the hips. "And don't forget," she said, uncovering a dish piled high, "for afters there's hot crumpets and jam." She turned on her heel and swept out of the room.

Luke, his mouth full, nodded in her wake.

"Ah, all's well, as they say," May chuckled reaching for a buttered crumpet and getting to her feet. "Must get back to work. Finding the crown a little tricky: all those roses, you know. I say, you should both come up to the studio some time and look around. I've an idea for a figurine called 'Girl with Fairies'; could use you as a model, my dear."

With that, she strode from the room, munching on the crumpet, the spaniels scampering hopefully behind.

"She's one pill short of a packet, she is," said Luke.

"Huh?"

"Bloody mad woman in the attic!"

"She's all right."

"And where did the 'Marc' thing come from? Why can't she remember my name?"

"It's just, she's probably…"

"Yeah, mental."

"Ssssh. They'll hear."

"And that bloody Poppy," he continued, filling his mouth with bacon.

"Well, you *are* hungry."

He pulled a face and mumbled something in reply.

Sighing, Rowan stood up. "I'm going out. May said we could look around. You coming?"

Luke shrugged. The shutters had come down behind his eyes.

She moved towards the door and looked back. "Oh, by the way, May says we're visiting Grandma after lunch."

Luke reached for a crumpet, his face blank. It was as if he hadn't heard, as if she didn't exist.

Rowan turned on her heel and stepped out into the hall, straight into the arms of Mrs Croft.

"Watch thyseln, lass."

"Sorry, I... I..."

"Now, now, don't fret. I suppose you're rushing out to play in the snow?"

"Yes."

"Then you'll be wanting thy clouts?"

"Wanting...?"

"Your coat and all."

"Oh, yes, please."

Mrs Croft went over to the oaken wall, pressed one of the panels and, with a click, a door opened. Inside was a large, dark, rather musty cupboard filled with boots and shoes, coats and cloaks, walking sticks, lacrosse sticks, tennis racquets, riding crops, bridles, dog leads, riding hats, indeed hats of all shapes and sizes and oddly a large stuffed owl. With a shiver, Rowan remembered Blodeuedd.

"There you go," said Mrs Croft, handing Rowan an armful of clothes. "Thy coat's not up to much. Try one of these on for size. It's a lovely day, but keen as knives. Now I mun get on." Pulling a large dishcloth from her apron pocket she disappeared into the morning room.

Rowan searched through the pile of old coats and found a thick sheepskin jacket that was only slightly too large. She buttoned herself securely in, turned up the cuffs, pulled on hat, scarf and gloves and approached the great front door. It looked very heavy. Tugging with both hands, Rowan pulled it opened and, with a sudden intake of breath, stepped out into a cold, white world.

She brought her hand up, shielding her eyes against the glare. Sunlight glanced off of every surface. Here and there, deeper tones and textures gave shape and form to the scene before her: the dark tangle of ivy beneath frost, the reddish-brown bricks of a partly sheltered wall, sprays of holly berries, scarlet beads against bright leaves.

Somewhere a bird was singing, filling the morning air with a shiver of notes.

"I thought I was used to snow," she whispered, breath freezing on the air. "But, oh…"

For *this*, away from the roads and buildings and traffic and noise of the city, with its peace and space and dazzling light, *this* was like a world made new.

With a happy sigh, Rowan closed the great door and made her way down the steps, boots crunching through deep snow. She surveyed the flat, white expanse that stretched down to the frozen stream. There was the bridge they had driven over last night and to the right and left grew tall evergreen trees. Beyond, there were open fields, and moorland, reaching up to the pure blue sky. From somewhere she could hear the rhythmic ring of metal on metal and a soft chugging sound, and in the far distance came the mournful bleating of sheep.

A sudden bang shattered the peace. The front door slammed open and Luke launched himself into the snow.

"SORTED!"

Behind him, Mrs Croft shook her head disapprovingly and shut the door.

"Luke, I don't think Mrs Croft…"

"Oh, she's an old bat," he said with a toss of his head, pulling his combat jacket close.

"Still, Gran would want…"

"Oh, *whatever*!" He squatted down and scooped up a handful of snow. "Hey, fancy making a snowman?"

Rowan eyed him cautiously. "Erh, okay, I suppose…"

"I'll scrape a mound together, a big one for the body, *God it's cold*, and you can roll a massive snowball for the mid—"

Luke was staring into the distance. He had gone rigid.

Rowan turned and followed the line of his gaze but could see nothing. Out of the corner of her eye she glimpsed a sudden movement, then felt the hard, icy shock of compacted snow against her face.

"Ouch! Luke!"

Luke was laughing and dancing around like a baboon.

"Fooled yah!"

Rowan rubbed the melting snowflakes out of her eye. "That hurt."

"*That hurt*," he mimicked. "God, it's only a bit of fun."

"Fun for who?" she muttered under her breath.

"God, you are *so* boring. Can't even have a laugh with you anymore."

Tears began to prick behind Rowan's eyes. She turned away.

"Oh forgodsake," Luke jeered. "If you're going to have one of your moods, then I'm off."

Rowan watched his hunched form stump away, down towards the stream and over the bridge. Sighing, she turned and trudged in the other direction.

22

GYPSY

———◆———

THE PATH LED AROUND THE SIDE OF THE house to a row of stables. Through a large arched doorway came the sound of ringing metal and, drawing closer, Rowan could see Mr Holly hammering a piece of red-hot iron against an old-fashioned anvil. With great tongs he thrust the metal back into the heart of a brilliant fire.

"'Ow do?" he said, looking up.

Rowan crept nearer still. The heat of the fire was delicious. It cast a strange light onto Mr Holly's face, making him look ancient and goblin-like.

"What are you doing?" she whispered.

"Mekking runners," he smiled.

"Oh. What's that?"

"Runners," he repeated and after a moment added, "for a sledge."

"Oh."

Mr Holly seemed to be a man of few words, but his eyes glittered in the firelight. She watched as he took the metal, white hot now, out of the coals and started to pound it once more, raising a shower of sparks.

The scent of the burning coals, mingling with the warm animal smell of horses, felt heady and new. Rowan shivered.

"Can you make horseshoes?"

"Oh aye," he grunted, between heavy blows of the hammer.

"Do you make them for Ivy?"

"Indeed I do." He was sweating. Rowan could see droplets forming on his wrinkled brow.

Now, with a rapid, light tapping motion, he shaped the metal into a fine curve.

"Not long nah," he said, thrusting the iron back into the fire. "Has tha' come to see Ivy? She likes a bit o' company." He lifted his chin to make an odd snickering noise and was greeted at once by an answering neigh.

Peering outside, Rowan saw the pony's head appearing over a stall door.

"Tek her a treat," Mr Holly said, indicating a string net full of apples, hanging against the wall. Rowan reached in and picked one out. Mr Holly sliced it in two with a sharp knife from his belt. "You'll not find a rosier apple in't'ole of Yorkshire. From our own orchards a' these."

The pony watched Rowan approach, eyes soft and dark, steamy breath curling from its nostrils.

"Keep tha palm flat, like," called Mr Holly, holding out a broad, weathered hand.

Rowan felt the pony's warm, velvety lips snuffling against her glove. "It tickles," she breathed, hardly daring to move. Ivy crunched both pieces of apple and lowered her head to Rowan's pockets.

"I think she wants some more."

"Ah," said Mr Holly. "Apples is her favourite. An' she likes thee, I can tell."

"How can you tell?"

"It's in her eyes, and that odd little sound she meks. You'll have to tek her out for a ride."

"But," Rowan began, feeling shy. "I don't know how to ride."

"Ivy'll teach thee. Best teacher there is. She'll tek thee round paddock, this afternoon perhaps."

"Oh!" Rowan exclaimed, with sudden disappointment. "We're visiting Gran after lunch."

"Never mind. Tomorrow then, if weather suits."

Rowan stroked the pony's arched neck and smoothed down the flowing golden mane.

A sudden clanking sound came from the direction of the house. There was Poppy, clumping along in big boots, wrapped in a red woollen scarf and long tweed coat, carrying two galvanised buckets.

"Aye up, Mr Holly," Poppy called, smiling broadly.

"Aye up, lass."

"Hi, Rowan."

"Hi."

Poppy strode on over snowy paths, past the stables, past the great lawn with the ornate stone fountain and disappeared through an archway in a tall, dark hedge.

"She's off to feed t'animals," said Mr Holly.

"Animals?"

"Aye, go tek a look."

Giving him a sudden shy smile Rowan danced off after Poppy. The older girl had gone through a gate to the left, which led into a field. From a collection of pens and stone outbuildings came a cacophony of bleating, clucking and grunting. Rowan could smell the hot-sweet stink of manure.

Poppy stumped over to a pen and let out two great orange pigs that snuffled and grunted and let themselves be scratched behind the ears. She crooned to the pigs the way a mother might sing to her child.

"Come and say hello to Tristan and Isolde," Poppy called. Rowan drew close. "They're my babies, gentle as kittens. Go on, give them a scratch."

Rowan took off her glove and leant over the stone wall. The pig's back felt like an old scrubbing brush.

"What do they eat?"

"Nothing but the best. Pass that bucket over."

Rowan groaned with effort as she lifted the metal pail. Poppy chuckled, and grasping hold of the handle swung it down with ease.

"We'll soon build thee up."

She strode over to the trough. The pigs, each the size of a small sofa, followed at Poppy's heels, grunting.

"Theer you go," said Poppy, pouring out a slop of cold porridge, bread crusts, left-over stew and stale cake. "Mrs Croft's finest cooking. Fit for a queen and her courtly lover."

Rowan watched as the shiny snouts pushed their way into the swill, and gave a small sigh.

"Will these pigs be...?"

"What? Turned into bacon, you mean?" Poppy laughed. "No. They're our breeders. But there'll be a litter in the spring and it's those as ends up on t'table. Some get sold, of course."

"It must be sad, if you've looked after them."

"That's why we don't name 'em. Don't get attached. But they have a good life: space and fresh air and proper food. Not like some."

Poppy came back through the gate grinning.

"Come on, let's get eggs."

Suddenly, a streak of russet-red caught Rowan's eye. "What's that? There, up ahead?"

Something loped across the snowy field towards the evergreen hedge and vanished.

"Old Mr Fox, I bet, caught the scent of our hens."

"A fox? Could it be one of May's foxes?"

"Ah, you've heard of Wat Tyler, then. Could well be. Why don't you track it? You can see his prints, in the snow. He's gone up the yew walk."

The fox tracks followed the hedge for a few feet then disappeared beneath it.

"You'd better hurry; he'll not wait around."

Rowan ran back through the gate to the narrow hedged pathway. The paw prints continued for some distance in the snow and then the trail diverged. One set of tracks led through a leafy archway into a formal garden, the other continued straight ahead. She slowed down, breathing hard. Which way should she go? She peered into the garden, where clipped trees stood in formation, like toy soldiers.

A sudden flash of red on the path ahead made her turn. Black-pointed ears and bright eyes were peeping up out of the snow. Suddenly, the fox vanished through the hedge, and reappeared, like a little magician, on the other side, darting here and there. It bounded back through the leaves and scampered up the path. It's almost as if he's playing a game, leading me on, thought Rowan, following.

At last the yew path opened out into a large field, bounded by wild hedgerows.

But the fox was nowhere to be seen.

Here several immense trees stretched their bare branches against the sky. A well-trodden footpath crossed the snowy field leading to a stile and beyond that were snow-clad hills, covered by dense winter woodland.

"There he is!" Rowan exclaimed.

The fox was at the far edge of the field, looking back at Rowan, its white-tipped tail held proud. Then, darting into a tangle of thorns, it was gone.

Rowan waited, but the fox did not reappear. So she retraced her steps back to the topiary garden. Here, in leafy alcoves, strange figures stood. They were wrought from greenish metal and wood and glass, human-like, yet not quite human, with thin metal leaves twining about their limbs. Perhaps May had sculpted them? They seemed to fit this silent, frozen landscape. They were like winter spirits, the whole world in thrall to their spell.

Rowan trudged through the snow, passed through a second archway and came to a series of walled gardens. Many beds were buried beneath the snow, but here and there the soil had been partially cleared and she could recognise the tops of vegetables: Brussels sprouts, kale, leeks and parsnips. There were climbing plants, too: espaliered fruit trees (long bare), thick curtains of ivy, twiggy stumps, and a walkway of twining roses, naked and thorny now, but in summer how beautiful they would be. She passed the glasshouses, many empty, but one or two were heated by a complicated system of hot water pipes connected to what must be an old steam engine, puffing and rattling away. These were lush with green, growing things, a summer oasis in a desert of ice and snow.

Rowan saw she had come full circle. She once again found herself at the wide, white lawn. It sloped gently to a stone terrace at the back of the house. The sun glancing off the snow was reflected in countless windows, and there was Mrs Croft coming out of a back door, carrying a large, steaming black kettle, which she proceeded to pour down an icy drain.

The path now continued round the east side of the building. Rowan was surprised to discover a round tower, built into the wall of the house. There were no doors, only small slit-like windows.

"So it can only be reached from inside," she mused. "At least it will be something to tell Luke." It could be exciting, searching the house for secret rooms and hidden passageways.

A rustle in the nearby laurel bushes made her turn. Was it the fox? More rustling, then a dog bounded out. She stepped back suddenly. It was of medium build, with a short brindled coat, and its tongue was lolling out of its open mouth in a grin.

The dog padded up to Rowan, tail wagging, sniffing at her hands, then, pricking its ears, bounded away. Rowan felt curious and started to follow. It had disappeared into the tall shrubbery that edged the sweeping driveway. From somewhere beyond she could hear a voice calling, a child's voice.

May hadn't mentioned any other children. Perhaps whoever it was lived on a nearby farm. It would be nice, she thought, to have a friend here, someone who'd like to build snowmen or go pony riding.

Rowan made her way through the bushes to a thick, tangled boundary hedge. The dog, still directed by the child's call, had disappeared through a hole at the bottom. Crouching down and scraping at the snow, Rowan managed to squeeze her head and shoulders through.

At the far side of an orchard, beneath a canopy of apple branches, amid thin spires of bluish wood smoke, stood a group of caravans. Most were shiny and modern with large windows and chrome fittings, but one was a traditional gypsy wagon painted green, yellow and red.

On the steps of the wagon stood a child, a girl, close to Rowan's age. It was she who, in a firm, clear voice, was calling the dog.

The animal jumped up to lick the child's face. But at one simple command from the girl he lay down at her feet, still as stone, ears pricked high, waiting for the order of release. It was given and the girl, black hair flying, jumped down from the wooden steps and flung her arms around the dog's neck. His tail began to pound the ground and she rewarded him with titbits from the deep pockets of her oversized red coat.

Jumping up, the girl moved close to the fire. Here an old woman, wrapped in a coloured blanket, was sitting, stirring a pot, which hung suspended from a three-legged fire iron. Some words passed between them and the old woman filled a mug with steaming brew and passed it to the girl. Within moments, more children had appeared, little kids, bundled up in several layers of clothing, clamouring in a language which Rowan could not understand. Now adults were joining the group, bringing their own mugs, seating themselves around the fire on logs and wooden crates. One man proceeded to dip chunks of bread into his newly filled beaker and feed it to various infants.

As the young girl sipped her drink, she looked over in Rowan's direction and their eyes met. Blushing, Rowan backed up through the hole and ran down towards the frozen stream. They would think she was spying, poking her nose in where it wasn't wanted. Travellers were very private people, kept themselves to themselves. She remembered there had been a family of gypsies at her school last summer, but they hadn't stayed long.

Rowan bit her lip. It was a pity. She had liked the look of that girl, had liked the look in the girl's dark eyes, bright and fearless.

Feet trailing, Rowan made her way along the stream of ice to the stone bridge at the bottom of the drive. This was the way Luke had gone. She could see his footprints in the snow, large crenulated soles. He had crossed the small bridge and continued down the drive to the road. Here Luke had been undecided, turning first this way, then that, then crossing the road to gaze over the drystone wall opposite. A stile gave access to a field where sheep were scraping at the snowy ground with cloven hooves to reach green sprigs beneath.

Finally, Luke had turned left and continued along the road, keeping to the verges where softer snow gave a firmer footing. Rowan decided to follow. The lane was quiet. The only sound was birdsong and the bleating of sheep.

Suddenly, the peace was shattered by thunderous barks.

She saw black shapes at the far edge of the sheep field, where a plantation of dark conifers formed stark spears against the sky. Emerging from the trees were two tall figures, a man and a woman dressed in black, each preceded by a pair of massive dogs. Behind them came Luke, hunched up against the cold, looking miserable.

Instinctively Rowan dropped to the ground and crept behind a bramble thicket, into the shelter of the drystone wall. Luke with strangers! Who were they? Questions pounded through her head. Where had they come from? Had they seen her? Daring a glimpse, she saw that they were talking to Luke.

"You must learn to take the hounds, boy," the man was saying.

"Oh yes," the woman crooned, her two dogs straining against their chains. "There's nothing like it. All that power beneath one's grip."

"Teaches one mastery and control."

"You would adore it, I'm sure." With a flourish the woman ran her hand along the back of one of the animals. It snapped its head back, growling.

"Such a healthy pursuit."

"The thrill of the hunt."

Luke murmured a reply but it was drowned out by the frantic bleating of sheep, fleeing this way and that from the barely restrained dogs.

The woman laughed in delight.

"What sport! I would love to let Guzzle off the chain, just for a moment."

Rowan shuddered at the tone of her voice.

"Not worth it, jewel. The farmer makes such a damned fuss."

"Fool!" she cried licking her red lips. "We'll make him suff—" She stopped and stared in Rowan's direction.

"What is it, treasure?"

Rowan ducked down further, heart pounding. It seemed an eternity before the woman spoke again.

"I thought..." the woman began, then, altering her tone, "Probably one of those filthy little gypsies. *Why* that Sloethorn woman lets them camp on her land I simply *can't* understand. Complete eyesore, lowers the property prices. Should be ex…"

But her sentiments were lost as the four hounds let loose another barrage of ear-splitting sound.

"Maw! Rip! Hunger!" The man roared.

Rowan pressed herself against the stone wall. Had they got scent of her? There was no chance of escape. If she moved she would be seen at once. Perhaps, crouched low and still, she would go unnoticed.

Brandishing a slender steel-tipped cane, the man roared threats and abuse at the dogs.

"I hate to see my babies treated like that," hissed the woman, her eyes narrow.

"Well let's get them into the lane, Nyche, my *diamond*," said the man, breathing heavily, "before they're quite beyond command."

He gave a hollow laugh but the woman snarled and strode ahead. The man and Luke were left to stumble after.

The woman leapt the stile with ease, ordering the dogs to follow.

Then she stood, as if scenting the air.

Rowan held her breath, wishing herself as grey and invisible as stone.

At last, the two stragglers caught up, clambering up the steps and over onto the other side.

The man was going on and on about something and laughing inanely. The woman ignored him, hands on hips, her skin white as ice.

"I… I guess I should be going," Luke mumbled.

The woman turned to Luke, suddenly all guile and charm. Speaking low, she slipped something into his pocket, then stroked his hair as if he was one of her dogs. She brought her palm to rest against his cheek. Luke, gazing into the woman's eyes, seemed to be carved out of stone. The man gave Luke a hearty slap on the back, and pushed him in the direction of Sloethorn. Then the couple were waving their goodbyes, voices too loud, smiles too wide, watching Luke disappear down the drive. When he had gone they turned in the other direction, towards the village.

Rowan stayed crouched against the hard stones of the wall until the man and woman had rounded a sharp bend in the road; even then she did not rise, not until the ferocious outbursts of barking were far distant. At last, stiff and cold, she got to her feet and found they had gone numb.

23

A Visit to Grandma's

——◦——

THE GRANDFATHER CLOCK WAS CHIMING the quarter-hour as Rowan entered through the front door.

Mrs Croft, wearing oven gloves and carrying a large, steaming soup tureen, hurried across the hall.

"You're late, child. Everyone's sat down. Get out o' them things and be quick abaht it."

Rowan dragged off her outdoor clothes, threw them in the musty panelled cupboard and followed Mrs Croft into the morning room.

It seemed full of people.

At one end of the table sat May deep in conversation with Mr Holly. Luke, feigning indifference, sat opposite Poppy, who was laughing under her breath. Mrs Croft positioned herself at the head of the table and proceeded to dish out bowls of steaming stew. Rowan slipped in besides Poppy.

"No doubt those hands are mucky," Poppy whispered, winking.

Rowan smiled and hid them beneath the table.

"Pass round the bread please, Poppy," Mrs Croft said.

Poppy winked at Luke when she offered him the basket of rolls. Luke blushed, gritted his teeth and hung his head over his plate.

"And the cider, lass." Mrs Croft's tone was curt.

Grinning, Poppy began to fill everyone's glass from a stone jug.

"Ah, capital!" May exclaimed, looking up as jug clinked against glass. "Gillkirk Gold. Memories of a fine summer. I propose a toast. To our guests, Rowan and Marc, erh, Matthew, no, no, what is it now? *Luke*, yes that's it! Welcome to Sloethorn."

Everyone echoed her sentiments and raised their glasses.

Rowan, half smiling, felt the blood rush to her cheeks.

Luke stared at the tablecloth.

It was a pleasant meal, nevertheless. The adults were jolly and talked about curious things. Mr Holly had seen badgers again up in the top pasture and was planning to take mistletoe from the King Oak. May had completed Queen Mab's crown and declared she would brew her festive punch to celebrate. Mrs Croft was delighted with her crop of hot-house potatoes, and Poppy recounted some horror story about a headless opera singer who was said to haunt the upper corridors of Sloethorn.

"Why would anyone want to behead an opera singer?" Luke scoffed, the first words he had spoken during lunch.

"You obviously never heard her sing," answered Poppy, rolling her eyes. There was a general guffaw of laughter, but Luke's ears burned.

"So," cried May. "Hope you young 'uns had a good old explore this morning, eh?"

"Y-yes," stammered Rowan. "The garden's so big."

May beamed. "It's our pride and joy. You ought to see it in summer, all the borders in bloom, roses and honeysuckle, hollyhocks, foxglove, meadowsweet, hemlock and the fruit: raspberries, strawberries, apricots, cherries and plums, quite delicious. Mind you, one can't move for artists then, you know. We run courses from spring to autumn, a school, a retreat. A kind of family of creative souls."

Mrs Croft muttered something about creative souls being all very well, but creative bodies needed feeding.

May chuckled. "And talking of food, Lily, my dear, is that apple pie and cream I spy on the side board?"

Luke cleared his throat. He looked pale and, though he tried to speak in a casual tone, his voice was strained.

"That big wood up on the hill, what's it called?"

Everyone turned to look at him.

It was Mr Holly who spoke first. "You mean Fray's Wood?"

"Ah, Fray's Wood," echoed May. "Known originally as Freya's Wood, Freya, or Freo, being the Anglo-Saxon goddess of love and fertility, identified with the Roman deity Venus. There's evidence of an Iron Age settlement there, you know, which of course predates the Saxon period by half a millennium or more. However, the barrow mound at the very centre is thought to be Neolithic in origin."

Luke stared at May, mouth open.

"You'll have to forgive me, dear boy. Like an encyclopaedia when I get going."

"Hag's Knoll," Poppy chimed in. "That's what we used to call it. When we were kids we would dare each other to stand in the circle of trees on the barrow top." She lowered her voice dramatically. "People have *seen things* up there. Mr Bragg, the farmer what owns the land, was scared witless once. Swears he saw a pale woman, all in white, wandering through the trees after sundown. He was just about to call out when she disappeared, into the hillside. Ghosts, he said, but my mam says it was more likely too much Old Weasel."

May smiled. "Well, it can't be denied that Mr Bragg is fond of his ale."

"So," said Luke, clenching his jaw. "How d'you get there?"

"Ah ha!" cried Poppy. "A ghost hunter. We can't dissuade him with our humble fears and superstitions."

"Poppy, that will do," said Mrs Croft.

"Just tek the footpath from the top pasture, lad," said Mr Holly, pouring cream onto his apple pie.

"Yes, yes," May added. "It's quite straightforward. Can't get lost. Often take the dogs up there myself, for a run." The clock chimed the hour. "Goodness, one o'clock already. Well now, eat up. Your grandmother will be waiting."

Between mouthfuls of pie, Rowan watched Luke. His face was as white and stony as ever and his eyes (Finn's eyes) were empty, as if he had retreated a long way back, so far back he was barely there at all.

The sleigh bells jingled as Ivy trotted along the lane. The landscape they had passed through last night was transformed by day. What had seemed so unearthly and mysterious in the darkness now sparkled with snow and light. Each fir tree wore a silver-white mantle and bare branches glittered with frost.

Rowan opened her mouth to say something, but the sight of Luke hunched in the opposite corner, tugging his cap down over his eyes, made her press her lips together.

She wrapped the blanket close about her shoulders and stared at a crooked line of large, black birds flapping across the sky towards some tall trees. Something with a bushy tail loped across a white field, dark against the dazzle. High in the sky, a hawk circled and hovered.

Even Luke's attention was caught now. He gazed upwards, mesmerised by the impossible stillness of the bird, balancing on its wing tips, suspended above the frozen land.

As they approached the village of Gillkirk, rooftops appeared: sturdy stone cottages, squat beneath the square church tower. There were shouts as children threw snowballs and careered along on sledges. Some ran by the side of the sleigh as it passed, waving and calling out.

"Gis a lift, mister."

"Gis a tow."

There were grown-ups about, too, some shovelling snow to clear pathways, others attempting to dig out their cars. A red-faced group had congregated outside the village pub, leaning on their shovels, sipping beer. They looked up as the sleigh went by, raising their mugs to Mr Holly.

"You've got the raight idea theer," called one old man. "Ah thee tekking passengers?"

Mr Holly gave out a reply in such thick dialect Rowan could not understand it, but it brought forth a roar of merriment.

At last, the sleigh drew up outside their grandparent's cottage. Rowan saw the front door open and out came Grandma buried in a thick, tartan coat.

"Hello, my dears, it's so lovely to see you. Come in, quick, out of this dreadful cold."

Then it was powdery kisses of welcome and the familiar smell of Grandmother's perfume and Mr Holly saying he would be back at five.

Grandma bundled them into the living room and sat them down before a coal fire. Rowan saw that nothing had changed since their last visit. Large, framed photographs of Luke and herself as babies still took pride of place on the mantelpiece. The walls were decorated with horse brasses and some of Mum's watercolour landscapes. The carpet was the same swirling pattern of flowers that made Rowan feel slightly dizzy and the room was filled with the overpowering scent of a plug-in air freshener. The only obvious difference was the small plastic Christmas tree decorated with flashing lights that stood in the bow window and some lengths of golden tinsel draped over ornaments.

Luke sank back into his armchair with a glazed expression. Rowan fidgeted with a small hole in the knee of her tights. After the spacious rooms at Sloethorn the cottage felt almost cramped. A coal on the fire hissed, sending out a greenish flame. Grandma, who had disappeared into the kitchen, came back carrying a tray of tea and biscuits.

"Can I help?" said Rowan, jumping to her feet and ignoring the sudden sneer on Luke's face.

"Well, if you could just clear the magazines and things from the coffee table, I can pop it down there."

"How's Grandad?" Rowan asked.

Grandma spooned two sugars into a cup and began to stir.

"As well as can be expected. When we've finished our tea we'll pop our head around the door and say hello. He'll be pleased to see you, I expect. Now, Luke, would you like a bourbon or a custard cream?"

Luke took a bourbon, but it remained on the side of his saucer, uneaten. Rowan struggled through a custard cream.

"So," said Grandma, settling back in her chair. "Tell me *all about* school."

The afternoon dragged on. Grandma's conversation rambled around Grandpa's illness, the terrible weather, Mrs Higginbottom's lost cat, crossword puzzles and soap operas. Rowan smiled and nodded, all the while feeling guilty at her own creeping boredom and angry at Luke, who barely grunted in response to Gran's questions. Rowan couldn't understand it. Last summer it hadn't been like this. But then they had been out so much, playing and picnicking and paddling in the beck, and anyway Luke had been his old self.

"Oh my goodness, I almost forgot," Grandma said as she brought in yet another pot of tea. "My memory is dreadful nowadays. There was a telephone call this morning; the lines are up again, thank goodness. It certainly has been a nuisance."

"From Mum?" asked Rowan, hopefully.

"No, dear. No, it was from your father."

Luke sat up in his chair.

"From Finn!" Rowan exclaimed.

"Oh yes, now, what was it he said? The line was very crackly, you know. I suppose the telephone engineers are all working flat-out in this weather. It was something about a… a *gig*? Is that right? About a *gig* being cancelled?"

"Cancelled?" Luke's voice was an echo, his face white.

"Yes, he wanted to know where you were staying. Thought you were staying here; couldn't get hold of your mother, of course. I explained about her being in Brighton with that sick friend of hers, but he said, at least *I think* he said, that he wanted to see you, to come and visit you here, I suppose. The line was very bad and then we got cut off."

"Finn's coming for Christmas?"

"Well, it's difficult to say."

"We could phone him," said Luke. He looked ill.

"I don't think I've got his phone number, dear."

Luke reeled off the Baden-Baden number, followed by Finn's mobile.

"We could phone him," he repeated.

"Well, yes, by all means." Grandma gave a nervous, coquettish laugh. "I'll just pop into the pantry and get some sponge fingers."

Luke jumped out of his chair, grabbed the phone and dialled, clenching his jaw as the old-fashioned dial telephone whirred its way slowly through the numbers. Watching him, Rowan held her breath. She would know at once if Finn was there because of the alteration, the softening in Luke's expression. But the seconds ticked by; another coal on the fire fell and settled. Luke pressed the receiver with white fingers.

"No answer," he said, and turned his back on her.

He dialled again, a different number. But almost immediately put the phone down.

"It's switched off," he said, without turning around.

"Perhaps he's travelling? You know, on a plane or something."

Luke shrugged. "He's let us down before."

He looked as if he was going to be sick. Rowan couldn't bear it and stared at her feet.

"Well, now," said Grandma, bustling back into the room, beaming. "Grandad is awake. Who'd like to help me make him a cup of tea?"

Rowan jumped up, her voice hard and bright and overloud. "Yes, I will, Gran!"

She prayed Grandma had not seen the expression on Luke's face or heard the cruel words muttered from dead, white lips.

On the way home, Rowan gazed out into the darkness, watching heavy clouds roll across the full moon. A bitter wind was driving down over the moors, sending before it flurries of snow. She couldn't bear to look at Luke, who sat stiff and pale beside her. If only he would let her say something, but he turned away when she tried to speak.

Yet Finn might come. Just because they couldn't reach him didn't mean a thing. You could never get hold of Finn, everyone knew that. Unreliable, that's what Mum said. "Should have been your dad's middle name."

Rowan clutched the blanket tight. Whatever Luke thought or believed, she couldn't let go of that hope; she couldn't.

Suddenly, they were surrounded by barking, snarling dogs. The pony shied and stumbled. Dogs leapt up, threatening, fangs bared. Ivy let out a terrified neigh and half reared in the traces.

"Down, girl, steady now." Mr Holly's voice was calm. In one hand he held the reins firm and the pony was soon under control, with the other he grabbed the long-handled horse whip and lashed out at one of the dogs. There was a sharp crack of leather, a searing yelp, and the brute shot off into the night.

Shouts came from ahead. Two tall figures emerged from the blackness.

"Maw! Rip! Guzzle! To heel! To heel!"

"What do you think you're doing, you vicious little man?"

It was that woman, Nyche! She strode forward. Rowan shrank behind her blanket.

"How dare you threaten my hounds?" she hissed.

"You call off your dogs and there'll be no need for this," Mr Holly answered.

"These animals are priceless! Priceless! Do you hear?"

"The lowest cur that heeds his master's call has more value," returned Mr Holly.

"How dare you!" she spat, lips drawing back in fury.

Rowan could see sharp teeth glinting. One of the dogs lunged forwards and Mr Holly lashed out.

The woman shrieked a single word.

"Attack!"

But Mr Holly was too fast. With a mighty thundercrack of the whip, another dog turned tail and fled.

"I'll ask one last time. Call off yorn beasts."

"Oh, really, this is absurd," the tall man exclaimed, coming forward. "Let's get the dogs and go, my precious. And *you* –" he shot a haughty look at Mr Holly, but could not meet the old man's gaze. "– *You* will be hearing from our solicitors!"

In an undignified manner the couple dragged the remaining hounds away and began to call for the missing animals.

Mr Holly put the whip in its holder, reassured Ivy with a few gentle words then, clicking his tongue, set the sleigh moving.

"Is all well wi' thee?" Mr Holly asked, over his shoulder.

"Yes, we're fine," Rowan squeaked.

"No need to fret. That *theer* were Maister Mint and his delightful missus. They moved in t'big house dahn road just a couple of month back. Heard of Mint's Supermarkets? That's him. That's how he made his money. Billions, they say. Stores all over the country. Don't mention him to Mrs Hamble as owns the village shop. Don't hold wi' supermarkets, she don't. Tekken all her business. Mr Aran Mint, ha! Name suits. He's a cool customer, aye, indeed."

But Rowan was barely listening. With a stolen, sideways glance at Luke's ice-cold face, she wondered what terrible hold they had over him.

24

THE SPIRAL STAIRCASE

---

*T*HE SNOW IS FALLING UPON HER UPTURNED *face, feather-soft. She feels warm and comfortable, as if she were wrapped in a thick eiderdown.*

She turns around and around, feeling the cold flakes against her lips.

A movement to the left makes her stop.

Something lopes over the frozen ground towards the house.

It is a wolf.

The creature pads up the stone steps and stands in the open doorway, looking back.

"Sage?"

The creature turns, bounds into the house.

"Sage, wait!"

Rowan tries to run, but her feet sink into the deep snow. She scrambles through the front entrance. The beast crosses the hall and mounts the stairs.

Rowan follows the wolf, up the stairs, along a dark corridor. Here a tapestry hangs, richly embroidered with a hunt scene; deer fleeing, hounds in pursuit. Drawing back the heavy drapes she sees it conceals a spiral staircase. Rowan follows the concentric windings of the stairway and emerges into a gloomy passageway. At the far end a pale shape melts away into shadows.

"Sage, Sage!"

She is running, running, running, into the darkness.

"Wait, please wait!"

She must make herself wake up.

A door swings open.

At her side stands the wolf. She feels warm breath on her cheek. In a voice deep as trembling earth it speaks,

"You are called."

⊰•—•⊱

Rowan woke with a cry.

"Sage!"

The room was filled not with the brilliant sunshine of yesterday but a soft, pearly light. Jumping out of bed, running to the window and pulling back the curtains, she saw it was snowing. White flecks danced down from the sky and the gardens were lost in a misty haze. She caught her breath as she watched a snowflake settle on the window pane. There was a strange lump in her throat. She told herself it was because the snowfall would postpone her ride on Ivy. But deep down inside she knew it was something else. She had an image in her head of a car trying to push its way through a snowstorm. People didn't travel in this kind of weather. Finn would not come today.

Shivering, she crouched down before the flames of the fire. Once again, unseen hands had been at work: new logs on the fire, hot water filling the china jug, clean clothes laid out on the chair. She felt spoilt, undeservedly so, and saw Mum's disapproving face.

She had promised to make herself useful. "Don't expect to be waited on hand and foot. Do your share. That goes for you too, Luke."

At breakfast, Rowan was surprised to see Luke downstairs already, seated at the table, shovelling scrambled eggs and toast into his mouth.

"Snow's set to clear by mid-morning," May was saying, spreading her crumpet with a thick layer of blackberry jam. "But we're pretty holed up until then. Ah, Rowan, good morning. Pleasant dreams, I trust?"

Rowan sat down with a shy smile.

"I keep dreaming about this house," she said and took the cup of tea May offered.

"Ho ho, Sloethorn has that effect on guests, you know," May beamed. "Gets right inside one."

Luke stood up suddenly, fingers white against the table top.

"Can I use the library? There are some things I want to look up."

"Certainly, young fellow. '*Knowledge is power*' and all that."

Luke turned on his heel and left.

"Need to keep an eye on that one," said May, nodding after him. "Sickening for something, I shouldn't wonder. White as a sheet."

Rowan bit her lip, fighting the urge to pour her heart out. Luke would never forgive her. He was walking along some perilous ridge and 'telling' might push him over the edge.

"Is there," she began, eager to change the subject, "a spiral staircase at Sloethorn?"

May swigged some tea and took a hearty bite out of her crumpet.

"Umm, yed, umph, a spigal stirky," she said through buttery lips. "Goed from the grud floor, near the –" she munched and swallowed, "– kitchen, all the way up to the attics."

"I saw a tower yesterday, when I was in the garden. It doesn't have a secret room or anything, does it?"

"'Fraid not. Just lots of steps, all the way up and all the way down. Great fun for playing King Arthur and loathly ladies and dragons and stuff."

"And what's up in the attics?"

"Well, in the summer we open up some of the rooms as accommodation for the artists, but now they're pretty much left to dust and cobwebs."

"What were they before? I mean, when your grandfather was alive."

"Bedrooms for the servants; grander ones for the housekeeper and the butler, smaller ones for the maids. And there's the nursery, of course. Father and his siblings spent many a rainy day keeping themselves amused under the rafters, and I also, in my turn."

"Could I go and explore?" Rowan asked.

"By all means, dear girl. Come to think of it, there may still be some games and toys left up there. You can't get out until this snow stops anyhow, and there's nothing like exploring draughty old attics and shadowy corners to while away a morning."

The hall clock struck half past nine.

"By Juno, is that the time?" May cried, getting to her feet. "Must get on. It's mince pies and mistletoe today."

By the time Mrs Croft came to clear the table Rowan had finished her second boiled egg.

"Let me help," Rowan said, reddening and jumping up.

Mrs Croft gazed at her, one eyebrow raised.

"Well, if you like. You can carry that tray o' dishes t'kitchen, while I wipe round."

Picking up the tray Rowan struggled out of the room and Mrs Croft called after her.

"Through back o' hall, fust door on raight."

The door at the back of the hall swung freely on its hinges and led out into a corridor. Directly opposite was a grand doorway leading into a large room hung with paintings. To the right and left a corridor ran, each ending in a green baize door. Rowan turned right and passed through the door into another long passageway. Halfway down was a door from behind which Rowan could hear the sounds of clanking pots and a hearty duet rising above the clatter. Rowan, her arms feeling like putty, shouldered her way in, through to a large old-fashioned kitchen smelling of cinnamon and oranges. Poppy stood at a steaming stone sink, waving the pan brush in front of her like a conductor's baton. In soprano she sang the melody:

O, the rising of the sun
And the running of the deer,
The playing of the merry organ...

May, who was stirring something in a large pan on an ancient range, added her harmony in a mellow tenor.

Sweet singing in the choir.

"Rowan, hi!" Poppy called. "You come to join us?"

"Oh, I... I..."

"Put that lot on't'table. Are your arms still in their sockets?"

"Well, they're a bit..."

"Oh, I say, Rowan," called May, "I can't leave this pan for a single moment. Could you nip into the larder and get me a pinch of nutmeg?" She took a sip from the spoon. "Just the thing for my mulled wine."

Rowan followed directions and found herself in an enormous store cupboard, filled from floor to ceiling with labelled bottles and jars and things wrapped in brown paper. There were ingredients she recognised: honeycomb, dried apple rings, pickled beetroot, chutney, parsley, and those she did not: ash keys, truffles, cob nuts, tansy buttons, eyebright, and then there were things that she *knew* should never be included in any recipe: nightshade, hemlock, monkshood, yew, and fly agaric. Perplexed, she found the nutmeg and took it to May.

"Ah, splendid! You can run along now and play, dear girl. Leave us to the baking. There'll be mince pies and gingerbread and cinnamon buns, but later on we'll need your help to decorate the tree. So be prepared!"

Rowan trailed back to the hall feeling rather forlorn. The kitchen had been warm and cosy and fragrant with the scents of Christmas. The prospect of the cold and dusty attic rooms, the haunt of forgotten ghosts, suddenly seemed much less appealing. Outside, flurries of snow rattled the windows.

She climbed the wooden staircase listening to the wooden tick of the grandfather clock. The tall fir tree, its uppermost branches level with the top of the stairs, stood in the hall waiting for its adornment. Leaning over the banisters, Rowan could touch the pine needles and release their pungent, oily scent.

"You are called."

Rowan turned.

Had she imagined the voice?

She looked up at the landing, half expecting to see a white wolf. But there was nothing, only the solemn portraits staring down at her with stony disapproval. The stained-glass windows alone seemed welcoming: finely patterned trees, their colours glowing vivid, even in the strange wintry light.

How like the dream, thought Rowan. A nervous thrill pulsed through her. She moved up onto the landing and, catching her breath, began to hurry. Along the corridor she went, past her bedroom, past the turning on the right that led to the grand bathroom, past Luke's room and further still. The passageway was dark, with many doors and seemed to grow more shadowy with each step. At last she came to the corridor's end and here a great tapestry hung.

Had she been sleepwalking? For, indeed, there it was, a stag leaping through the forest, men and hounds on its tail. She reached out to feel the silken threads, the antique wool. She could almost hear the dogs baying, the shouts, the heaving breath of the hunted deer.

Pulling aside the curtain, she saw the spiral curve of steps, going up and down. She began to ascend. It seemed to Rowan that this, too, must be a dream and yet the fact that she could reflect on this point, question its truth, proved, somehow, it was not. Dreams did not allow that kind of logic; they shimmered and changed and shifted, like flames in a fire.

The archway at the top of the stairs opened out into a narrow, chilly passage.

It was lined with doors and, opening one, Rowan saw a small bare room with a sloping ceiling, its window covered with a thick layer of snow. Rowan shivered, not altogether from the cold. In the summer she could imagine playing 'hide and seek' or 'secret dens' up here, but now, with an icy wind whistling under the tiles and the smell of damp, it felt desolate.

Down the corridor she tiptoed, wondering about the people who had lived behind these doors: the servant girls and parlour maids, the cook, the butler, the valet, the nurse; so many people to serve just one family. It must have been a busy place, ringing with voices, and yet now so silent. She brushed aside a cobweb. She almost hoped she might see something: the shadow of young girl, hurrying along, tying her apron strings, or a smart-suited valet combing his oiled hair. But they were memories now, or ghosts, or less than ghosts. She opened a second door and a third. These rooms were larger and one contained a brass bedstead and a wardrobe. All had been left to time and dust.

At the end of the passage, standing slightly ajar, was the last door. Rowan took a breath to steady herself and pushed it open.

The room beyond looked like a picture in an old-fashioned children's book, and it gave Rowan that same mournful sensation, the realisation that the children for whom it was originally intended were long since grown up, and dead and buried.

This was a nursery, faded, threadbare and dim beneath a shroud of cobwebs. There was a rocking horse and seated below the dormer window on a cushioned seat was a collection of white faced, wax dolls. To the left stood a trunk on which rested the antlered head of a stag; to the right was a doll's

236

house. Shelves held scores of old books, boxed games, clockwork toys, wooden soldiers and a painted fort. In one corner rested a hoop and some skittles; in another was a child-sized chair.

Rowan entered and ran a finger through the dust, marvelling at the polished wood beneath. Picking up a clockwork Pierrot she wound the key and the sudden whirring of the mechanism filled the room, followed by chimes; a musical refrain. She watched, hardly daring to breath, as the toy whirled and danced on its pedestal, its face a painted mask of tears.

The silvery tones seemed to hang in the air long after the toy had come to a stop and in that hushed, suspended moment light flooded through the window and made the eyes of the trophy stag glint green.

The eyes, of course, were made of glass, Rowan reasoned with herself. The glass had caught the light. Yet still her heart beat fast. There was something uncanny in the effect – the glitter of sunlight on deep forest pools. It reminded her of Mother Meg.

She crouched down by the trunk and with some effort lifted the antlered head to the floor. Pushing up the banded lid she peered inside. It was full of old clothes, dressing up clothes: lace petticoats, jewelled slippers, fake beards, velvet capes, a cutlass, long silk gloves and curling feathers that made her sneeze. At the bottom was a book. It was big, bound in green leather and secured by a wide band of silver metal and a silver padlock. It looked like an old-fashioned Bible, but the title, embossed in silver letters was *The Book of Green Magick*.

Rowan sat back on her haunches and stared.

It was beautiful.

And yet...

She traced her fingers over the silver lettering.

It looked old, much older than the nursery, or the house, or the other antiques downstairs.

And yet...

"Rowan." A faint cry, somewhere below.

Someone was calling her name.

With a thumping heart she put the book back in the trunk and closed the lid.

"Rowan!"

She hurried out of the room, flew along the corridor and reached the top of the spiral staircase.

"I'm coming!"

Jumping down the steps two at a time, she almost collided with Mrs Croft at the bottom.

"Goodness child. You'll break your neck on those stairs! May's wanting to see thee, sharpish. There's a letter. And don't run!"

Rowan continued at a sedate stroll until Mrs Croft had disappeared into one of the bedrooms and then she ran like the wind.

May was in the hallway sorting through huge piles of greenery. She smiled broadly as Rowan approached and from her apron pocket fished out an envelope.

"For you. Germany, special delivery."

Rowan drew a sharp, involuntary breath. It was Finn's handwriting, addressed to herself and Luke. Hands shaking, she ripped it opened and out came a Christmas card and a scribbled note.

"Tracked you down at last! Gig cancelled. Am coming for Christmas!! Will get flight early tomorrow. Should be with you late same day. Much Love. Finn."

So he *was* coming! Grandma was right.

Checking the postmark, Rowan saw it had been sent by special courier yesterday morning, dated Sunday, 20 December. How on earth had it got through? she wondered.

"It's from Finn."

"What's that, dear girl?" asked May, her hands full of ivy.

"My dad's coming to see us. He'll be here tonight, the twenty-first." Even saying the words, Rowan could not believe them.

"Ah, splendid! Midwinter's Eve and all that!"

"Yes." She stared at the crumpled note. Her dad would be here in half a day, a few hours.

"Oh goodness. Luke! I must tell Luke."

"He's studying in the library," May said in a low voice, nodding towards a fourth grand doorway leading off the entrance hall. "Didn't like to disturb him."

"Oh, he won't mind," Rowan gasped, flying towards the door. "Not for this."

She turned the brass knob and went through into an enormous book-lined room at the centre of which stood a long table of polished wood. Luke was not there but one of the elegant chairs was pushed back as if vacated in a hurry and several books lay open on the table.

Great French windows at the far end of the room looked out onto the snowbound garden, and there a dark-coated figure could be seen making its way across the white lawn.

Rowan ran back into the hall, unlatched the panelled cupboard and began to drag on her sheepskin coat.

"He's just gone out. I'll catch up with him," she cried. "He'll want to know."

"Jolly good," said May, arms full of mistletoe and ivy. "But do remember lunch is at one."

25

FREYA'S WOOD

L UKE WAS WALKING FAST. ALREADY HE HAD disappeared from view. The air was full of lightly falling flakes, partly obscuring her vision; only Luke's footsteps could be seen, fresh in the snow. Rowan followed the newly made tracks – long, determined strides – and found that they entered the tall shadows of the yew walk. The great evergreens towered above her, menacing in the cold, flat light. It was like a maze. She hesitated, thinking of the labyrinth, of its hidden horrors, and wondering if... But how silly; she must hurry or she would never catch up.

The footsteps ploughed straight ahead, past the archway to the topiary garden and up to the wide field, or the 'upper pasture' as Mr Holly had called it. Luke had crossed the field and climbed over the stile. Rowan screwed up her eyes against the falling snow. Yes, she could see him, a small figure on the hillside, black against white.

Rowan hurried on. Luke would be so happy when he heard the news. It would all come back: the old smile, the light in his eyes, the kind voice. And then they would be together, the three of them, with so much to do and see and explore. It would be like a proper holiday, the kind that real families had.

She was panting. The steep footpath kept within the shelter of a stone wall, yet still the snow was halfway up her shins. Occasionally, a startled sheep would stumble out of the way, then turn and gaze back, reproachfully, with its long mournful face. High in the sky a hawk wheeled and hovered, wheeled, hovered.

Luke, much higher up, had veered to the right, heading towards a broad stretch of woodland. Rowan remembered that he had been curious about that old wood, had asked questions. Poppy had spoken of ghosts and hauntings. 'Freya's Wood', May had called it, and for a moment Rowan faltered, watching the circling hawk, then giving herself a shake she continued her pursuit. Finn was coming. She must tell Luke. She *must* tell Luke.

She stumbled along in Luke's tracks and eventually reached the edge of the wood. The tangle of winter branches was unexpectedly dark. Overhead, the bare boughs had grown into a dense canopy. Beards of lichen and trailing stems of ivy hung down like long curtains. Occasional breaks in the canopy let shafts of light pierce the gloom and here the undergrowth flourished: bramble, dog rose (a winter tangle of thorns) and holly bushes. The thick scrub made it difficult to see more than a few feet ahead, but a narrow path wound its way through the trees, now rising over rocks and boulders, now dipping down into mossy hollows, but always climbing higher.

Rowan could feel the sweat beneath her clothes, but dared not stop to rest. Here, in the shelter of the trees, the snow had almost disappeared. She could no longer rely on following Luke's trail. He might decide to leave the footpath altogether and then she would lose him.

She strained her ears for any sound that might betray his presence, but the wood was silent. No leaf rustled, no bird sang, no branch creaked.

But, passing a particularly gnarled and ugly tree trunk, Rowan was startled by a wild shout.

There was an answering cry.

She could hear angry voices ahead. One belonged to Luke.

Heart racing, Rowan hurried forward and, rounding a large, moss-covered rock, saw Luke face to face with a young girl. It was the girl from the gypsy encampment, with her red coat and wild, black hair. She held aloft a fat pine cone, a second was ready in her other hand, and her coat pockets bulged.

"You dirty little pikey," Luke hissed, rubbing his cheek. "I'll get you for that!"

"Have to catch me first," said the girl, chin in the air.

"Your lot should be..." He spat on the ground. "Why don't you just get lost!"

"Why should I? Not doing no harm."

"You stupid little... This is private property. You shouldn't be here."

"Ha!" The girl's laugh was from the belly. "So, what're you up to, then?"

Luke lunged forward, fist clenched, but the girl darted to one side and sent the cone flying. It caught Luke smartly on the forehead. He clapped his hand to his face.

"You little bitch!"

He made another lunge. Rowan leapt after him and grabbed his sleeve.

"Luke, stop it! Stop!"

Luke spun around, face hard with fury, and shook her off.

"Keep out of it, you," he snarled.

Rowan tried to grab him again but he was already lurching towards the gypsy girl. The third cone missed and Luke managed to throw himself forwards and grab the girl's coat.

"Oh!" she exclaimed, as Luke's weight slammed her against a tree trunk.

"Luke, no!" cried Rowan.

But Luke was shaking the girl like a dog with a hare.

"Luke, stop!"

His face was so white, so rigid, it was no longer a face, but a mask. There was blood trickling down the gypsy girl's temple.

"Luke!"

Desperate, Rowan grabbed a handful of old wiry nettles from the undergrowth and pushed them into Luke's face. Gasping, Luke jerked his head backwards. He dropped the girl and staggered away, blinking, shaking his head.

The girl, half moaning, sank to the ground. Rowan, scraping some snow out of a hollow in the ground, pressed it to the girl's forehead.

Her eyes opened. She smiled.

"That's a handy trick. Nettles, ha! Must remember that one."

"Are you okay?"

"I think so. Knocked me head a bit."

"There's blood," said Rowan.

"S'only a scrape. Just need to catch me breath."

The girl gazed at Rowan with her dark, dark eyes. "He's your friend, then?"

Rowan looked around, but Luke was gone.

"My brother."

"Ah. Got a bit of a temper."

"He's not... he's not himself at the moment."

"I seen him before. With them."

"With...?"

"Them Mints, what sets their dogs on people. Always going on about trespassers, they are."

She paused and narrowed her eyes. "Your brother shouldn't want to go making friends with them, you know. There's something *weird* about them."

"What were they doing, with Luke?"

"Dunno. They were all over 'im though. Specially her. Kind of gave me the creeps."

Rowan frowned.

"So, is he in trouble, then, your brother?"

Rowan looked hard at the ground, then up at the girl's face. The black eyes stared back at her, steady and bright.

"Yes, yes he is."

"You know, that's probably where he's gone, to the Mints' place. Have you seen it?"

Rowan shook her head.

"Big white house, with high, high walls."

Rowan's hands were shaking.

"Will you take me there?"

"It's not safe, you know."

Rowan nodded.

The gypsy girl grinned, her mouth wide and red.

"Well, I s'pose I do owe you a favour." She held out her hand.

"Help me up then. So... wot's your name?"

"Rowan."

"Rowan. Like the tree. I'm Charli."

"Charli?"

"Well, it's Shuri really, that's Rom. But I like Charli."

Rowan didn't understand what she meant, but the girl had already turned to scan the woodland.

"Right. This way."

Leaving the footpath the girl plunged into the gloomy heart of the wood, scrambling over thick roots, fallen branches and jutting rocks. Rowan wondered how she knew her way in this endless twilight tangle of bush, bough and bramble. She herself had lost all sense of direction, but Charli was scampering on ahead, darting under branches, weaving through undergrowth, leaping from boulder to boulder. After many minutes, they came to another path, little more than an animal track. To the left it rose sharply; to the right it fell away in a steep decline.

"We got to go down."

They half walked, half skidded down the slope, Charli laughing, throwing her arms wide like a skateboarder, Rowan, more cautiously, catching at twigs and exposed roots for support.

At last they emerged from the wood onto sloping farmland bordered by hedgerows. Downhill, to the right, Rowan could see the apple orchard and the gypsy encampment and beyond that Sloethorn House. Ahead, on the far side of a lane, was the dense, black, fir plantation she had seen yesterday, skirted by a stone wall.

"The Mints live in the middle of that," Charli hissed. "S'like a prison."

"How do we get in?"

"Well, they got a proper posh entrance off the lane, with 'lectric gates and everything, but I know another way. First we got to follow this hedge an' get down to the road."

The girls kept to the ploughed edge of the field, where the snow was not so deep.

"Luke's not been this way," Charli pointed out. "No footprints."

But on reaching the road Rowan saw the crenulated prints from Luke's boots, crisp in the new snow.

"He's come from further up the lane," Charli said. "Must have legged it. An' he's heading for the main gates, see."

The footprints led on down the lane, over a stone bridge, and they could see that after a distance of a hundred feet or so the tracks turned into a driveway.

"Are you sure we can get in?" Rowan asked in a low voice, gazing at the dark thicket of evergreen trees, behind the high walls.

Charli winked, "Look," she said, patting the rough stones of the bridge. Some five feet below, a frozen stream ran on through the wood, under the prickly boughs of the trees.

"Here, the wall of the bridge is wobbly. If we pull hard enough we can..." Charli prised several stones loose to form a gap, then squeezed through and jumped down onto a floor of pine needles. Rowan scrambled after. They crouched for a moment beneath the dark and silent trees. Charli put her finger to her lips.

"We must be quiet; there's guards 'n' things."

Charli set off into the gloom, following the course of the frozen stream. They stooped low beneath the branches, dropping at times to their hands and knees.

A bird, startled by their presence, took flight and flapped wildly through foliage overhead.

Charli froze, hand stretched out in warning.

Rowan could feel her heart pressing against her throat.

But the silence returned, deeper than before.

Charli veered right, crossing the stream, and a moment later Rowan saw a high wall looming up between the trees. The perimeter walls were smooth, white and modern, like tombstones, impossible to climb. Charli pointed out a solid wooden door in the wall with a notice that read 'KEEP OUT. PRIVATE PROPERTY. CCTV OPERATING ON THESE PREMISES' in bold red letters.

She pulled on Rowan's arm, leading her to a tree which grew close to the wall. It was a yew tree, with sweeping, evenly spaced branches. Charli clambered up first, swinging easily from one bough to the next. Gulping, Rowan followed.

The top of the wall was set with shards of broken glass, but perched on the overhanging branches the girls were able to see into the garden below. Rowan saw a wide snow-covered lawn, edged by laurel and rhododendron bushes, which sloped downwards from an elegant white-pillared house. Dark-coated men with sunglasses and sleek black dogs patrolled the grounds. She drew back quickly, almost losing balance.

Charli clutched her arm.

"Look!" she hissed, pointing.

Through the tall French windows they could see three figures. There was Mr and Mrs Mint, both drinking wine and wearing cruel, triumphant smiles; between them stood Luke. Most horrible of all, Mrs

Mint was wrapping her long arms around Luke's neck and showering his white forehead with kisses.

Rowan gave a cry and teetered forwards. There was a sensation of tree bark and space and twigs giving way, then she felt herself grabbed from behind and Charli's strong arm was around her waist.

Dogs were barking. Men were shouting.

"Quick, let's go! They've seen us!" Charli cried.

The girls slithered and scrambled down the tree and ran as hard as they could, back over the icy stream, weaving between the close-growing trunks. They could hear the frustrated yelps and cries of the dogs behind them.

"They'll unlock that bloody door," Charli gasped.

Rowan was too breathless to respond, but fixed her eyes on Charli, who seemed to spring and swerve and twist through the wood like a young deer.

Suddenly, there was a terrible volley of barks.

"They're loose!" Charli cried.

26

MULO

———◆———

THE GIRLS FLEW ALONG BETWEEN THE matted branches, regardless of cuts and scratches, torn coats or snagged hair. Rowan wished only to be free of the entangling trees. She had a stitch in her side and a crick in her back from running doubled up.

"Look, Rowan: the bridge," Charli cried.

Rowan pressed her fingers to her waist and staggered on.

Charli, reaching the bank below the bridge, sprang to the top in one supple movement.

"Rowan, quick!"

The barking was close. Rowan gasped for breath, forcing her legs to move.

Charli, supporting herself on an overhanging branch, reached out a hand.

"Here!"

Dogs were at Rowan's ankles, snapping, slavering.

She made a desperate lunge forward and grasped the gypsy girl's strong brown fingers. With a frantic scramble, she was up the bank and through the gap in the bridge wall. One black hound made a snarling leap, but was met by Charli's heel smashing down onto its muzzle. She then scooped up a sharp stone and let it fly, striking a second dog full in the face. The yelps of pain threw the oncoming hounds into confusion. Charli grabbed Rowan's hand and they ran down the lane. Ducking low, Charli squeezed through a hole in the hedge on the opposite side of the road and pulled Rowan after her.

"Oh... Cha... Char... I can't..."

"It's okay. Look, we're in the orchard."

And there, on the far side, was the gypsy encampment, with its smoking fires.

"Hi, hi!" Charli called out, waving frantically. Gypsy dogs leapt up, barking; people appeared on the caravan steps.

Rowan stumbled on, the pain in her side driving down into the pit of her belly. She could feel herself being half supported, half dragged through the snow.

"Come on, we're almost there."

Rowan struggled on. Her arm had turned ice-cold.

"I can... feel... their... teeth."

The ground began to lurch, the sky to spin. People were running towards them, through the apple trees. Behind came the savage baying of hounds.

Charli cried out to the oncomers. "They set their dogs on us!"

Far off were the cries of men, the barking of dogs.

"It's all... going... strange..."

Rowan sank down, but not to meet the cold snow; she felt herself gathered up in strong, warm arms.

"Aunt Sonja! Aunt Sonja!" Charli called.

"In the Vardo," commanded a hoarse voice.

Rowan was aware of being carried up some steps and laid on a soft bed, fringed with lace. She could see a blur of bright colours, which, after a moment, resolved themselves into patterned curtains, painted flowers and embroidered shawls. The raw ache in her side was easing, her head clearing.

"Get the child some chuti."

"I'm all right… really," Rowan said, trying to sit up.

"Hush, hush, child. Lie yourself down."

"It's okay, Rowan," Charli grinned, perching herself on the bunk. "Aunt Sonja is a drabengra – a healing woman. She'll work wonders."

"Where are the Foul Folk?" Rowan whispered.

"The what? You mean the *dogs*, oh don't worry about them," said Charli. "Our mutts will see them off. They ain't so big, but they're as tough as a tinker's boot." Her smile revealed a row of pearly teeth.

An old, old woman, face leather-brown, waved Charli away and held a tin mug to Rowan's lips.

"Drink this, little shey. It will calm your spirit."

Rowan sipped the warm, milky drink, fragrant with the scent of caraway and cinnamon, and sank back onto the pillows.

"So what kind of trouble you got into now, Charli?" the old woman growled. "What with dogs and –" she pushed back the tangle of dark hair from the girl's forehead, "– nasty gashes." But there was a twinkle in her wrinkled, black eyes.

"Not *my* trouble, Aunti, I swear. Them Mints is crazy, setting their dogs on us. You know how it is with them."

"Mulo, that's how it is! I told you before to keep well away. Hai shala?"

"Yes, Aunti, I understand, it's just…"

"Just nothing! Mulo they are. You keep away – dragging this poor child into your wild schemes."

The old woman stroked Rowan's head.

"You drink up, now, child, and you'll be bright as a silver button." She was about to turn away when something at Rowan's throat seemed to catch her attention. Before Rowan could resist, brown fingers reached forwards and drew out the leather pouch hidden there. The gypsy's ancient fingers felt it over and for a moment she closed her eyes, then, giving Rowan a crooked smile, she patted her cheek.

"Ah, little shey. Courage it is, ah yes."

Turning to Charli, the old lady spoke in a language that Rowan did not understand. Charli, hanging her head, nodded solemnly. The old woman pressed her tongue behind her teeth, making a sound of sharp disapproval, and hobbling out of the caravan she closed the door firmly behind her.

Charli's eyes were wide with admiration.

"You got a… a talisman."

Rowan blushed and slipped the pouch beneath her jumper.

"Aunti said I got to look out for you. I said o'course. Te'sorthene, that's what we are now – heart-friends."

"She said something else," Rowan said, "about the Mints. She called them *Mulo*. What does it mean?"

"Mulo? Oh, it's…" Charli looked down at her boots.

"It's what?"

"It's like, a dead person, a vampire."

"Oh."

"But you don't want to hear that sort of stuff. Aunti says you gotta take it easy." Charli nodded eagerly towards the concealed pouch. "So what's that for?"

"Oh, it's…" Rowan's cheeks felt as if they were burning. "It's, for luck, I suppose." And then, in a rush, "I need to know, Charli. Does she really think they're Mulo?"

Charli shrugged. "It's a Rom thing, you know. Sometimes it just means a really bad person."

Rowan gazed at Charli. "And sometimes…?"

Charli raised an eyebrow. "*You* think the Mints are vampires?"

Rowan shook her head, then sighing, turned her face away. "I don't know."

"You okay?"

"Charli," she began in a half whisper, "there's something wrong with Luke."

"Yeah, don't I know it," said Charli, rubbing the bruise on her head.

"No, I mean something really, really wrong. I don't know what to do!" Her throat was a stony lump and she could feel hot tears at the corners of her eyes. Charli drew close and took Rowan's hand.

"You think that he's…?"

"How do you become a Mulo?"

Charli's face had turned pale. "There are stories, they take people, in the night. They got these sharp, sharp teeth…"

"Like vampires…"

"They suck out, Oh Del – Aunti will kill me; you should rest."

"That woman, she kissed him."

"An' did you see how white she was?"

"Like ice or snow."

"Or something not living."

"Oh, Charli."

"You think he could be...?

"I don't know. Oh, I don't know! But they've got Luke. On the inside, I mean, Charli. He's gone. He's just not there anymore!"

Charli raised her hand, warm and brown, to Rowan's cheek.

"Hush, s'okay, s'okay. Don't cry. We'll find a way to get him back."

"I can't tell him, Charli."

"Tell him what?"

"About Finn. That's why I was there in the wood, when he hurt you. I was following him, to tell him..." Fresh tears ran down her cheeks.

"Hush, hush."

"To tell him about Dad coming. But..."

There was a rattle at the door and it swung open. Aunt Sonja's face appeared at the top of the steps.

"Will you be staying to share a bowl of something, little shey?"

Rowan sat up quickly and wiped the tears away with the back of her hand.

"You not been talking nonsense, I hope, Charli, and upsetting this poor child."

Charli made frantic faces at Rowan.

"I'm okay, really, Mrs, erh, Aunti. But I'm afraid I've got to get back to the house. There'll be lunch waiting there. But thank you."

"As you will, but, Charli, walk with her, eh? She's still pale as milk."

Coming down the wagon steps, Rowan was aware of curious glances and half-veiled stares. Two men, chopping wood, paused briefly to nod; girls grooming an old grey horse looked up and stared; women feeding their babies turned to watch. There were faces at caravan windows and kids with ragged hair and grubby faces crouched behind trailer wheels. Aunt Sonja, all smoky from the camp fire, put her hands on Rowan's shoulders and bent down to kiss her on both cheeks, then she pressed her thumb against Rowan's forehead, muttering unfamiliar words.

As Rowan walked off, arm in arm with Charli, she whispered.

"Was Aunt Sonja casting a spell?"

"Kind of."

"Kind of? What do you mean, kind of?"

"Well, if your skin turns green and you grow a long fish's tail."

"Charli, I'm serious."

Charli laughed and looked her straight in the eye. "It was a gypsy blessing, to protect you from the evil eye."

"From Mulo?"

Serious now, Charli stared straight ahead of her and nodded.

The hall at Sloethorn was a forest of greenery.

Mr Holly, atop a tall wooden ladder, was dressing the walls with his namesake: prickly, dark green boughs. Poppy followed suit with sprays of trailing ivy and May was tying an enormous bunch of mistletoe to the chandelier. "I live in hope!" she chortled. The three spaniels, rushing from room to room in a frenzy of excitement, pushed their noses into every corner.

"They'll regret that when they find the holly sprigs," May chuckled, then, spying the girls through the foliage, cried, "Ah, just in time! We need some help. Get to! Many hands! More the merrier!"

Mrs Croft appeared from the back of the hall with a laden tray.

"First," she said, lips set firm, "it's time f'dinner. An' all this messing abaht wi' bushes will have to wait."

There was a frivolous, good-humoured, end-of-termish air to the meal, encouraged by two pitchers of Gillkirk Gold. Green leaves, twigs and shiny berries spilt over onto the white table cloth, adorning the cheese on toast, baked potatoes and warm cinnamon buns. Charli, cheeks bulging with food, grinned at everyone and smuggled titbits to the three eager spaniels, who had abandoned their mistress for this generous gypsy girl who smelt of horses and smoke and fresh air. No one seemed to question her presence there. Luke, absent for the first part of the meal, slipped into the room halfway through. Seeing Charli, he frowned, but thereafter kept his head low and mouth full. Even he, after a glass of cider, seemed to make an effort to be civil; listening to the conversation, attempting to smile at Poppy's jokes.

"So," said May at last, leaning back in her chair and unbuttoning her waist band. "Dressing the tree. It'll have to be all hands on deck, you know. We've baked gingerbread men and iced the biscuits. We've got clove oranges and the paper chains from last year. But we'll need new decorations and there are the candles, of course. Are you girls happy to make paper stars and fairies? Yes? Jolly good. And you, Luke, how about putting the candles on the tree – bit messy with all that dripping wax and stuff, but I'm sure you'll do a grand job."

After dinner was cleared away, Rowan and Charli settled down in the living room, in front of the crackling fire, with sheets of silver paper, glitter, scissors and glue. It was good to be doing something so simple and ordinary again; snipping away with the scissors, watching the glitter sparkle in the firelight. Soon, the girls had created a row of dancing fairies and shiny stars.

The door opened. It was Luke. He looked nervous.

"Erh, May said there might be some matches in here."

Rowan stood up, heart pounding and gazed at him. Should she tell him? Should she?

"Luke," she began then paused.

Charli raised one eyebrow.

"Luke, I... I've got something to tell you."

"What?" Luke smiled, but his eyes were arctic cold. She remembered the way Mrs Mint had draped her slender white arms around his neck.

"I've got some news, from Finn."

For a moment he looked at her in the old way, like an ember flaring bright. Rowan dug the crumpled Christmas card out of her pocket and held it out.

"He... he's coming. He'll be here tonight."

A dark shadow seemed to pass over Luke's face, then, taking the card, his expression softened.

"Tonight?"

"Yes."

With a heavy sigh, Luke sat down. He stared and stared at Finn's handwriting, struggling to keep his expression under control. Then he smiled, a real smile, and a slight flush warmed his lips.

"God, I can't believe…"

"I tried to tell you before."

"Is it really tonight?" He turned the card over in his hands.

"That's why I followed you, into the woods."

"I suppose it'll be late, I mean when he gets here."

"I wish I'd caught up with you earlier."

Luke shrugged. "It doesn't matter."

"But I wish you…"

He looked at her.

"I wish you hadn't…" Rowan could feel herself blushing. "I mean…"

"She wishes you hadn't gone and clonked me one," said Charli.

Luke frowned, grabbed a box of matches from the mantelpiece and glared at Charli.

"Haven't you got a home to go to?" he hissed and strode out of the room.

Rowan stared after him, open-mouthed.

Charli laughed. "Don't worry about it."

"But it's a terrible thing to say!"

"Get it all the time."

Rowan sighed and flopped down onto the floor.

"But the *old* Luke wouldn't have said it. I thought, with Finn, I honestly thought…"

Charli reached over and put her hand on Rowan's arm. "You know, he looks okay when he smiles. Nice, almost."

Rowan nodded. He's still there, inside, somewhere, she thought. Perhaps when Finn comes, perhaps…

But she didn't dare speak her hope out loud.

By the time the afternoon had faded, the hearth rug was scattered with a hundred silver decorations.

"Look how they gleam," Rowan sighed.

"I guess it's enough even for *that* 'normous tree.'"

"Shall we take them through?"

With care, the girls gathered up the decorations and rejoined the others in the hall.

Mr Holly was putting a last sprig of mistletoe above the front door and the great tree looked magnificent, decked with red ribbons, fragrant gingerbread, golden pomanders and thin, white tapers.

"Ah," said May. "The fairies are here."

Poppy giggled and gave Luke a friendly shove.

"Well," said Mr Holly, climbing down the ladder, "'tis Midwinter, after all."

"They are *quite* perfect," said May, taking one in her hand. "I expect it to fly up on gauzy wings and startle us all. Well, come on, everyone, let's add them to the ensemble!"

As she tied the delicate shapes to the branches, Rowan was aware of Luke edging his way towards her. Every so often, he would turn his ghostly, pale face in her direction and smile. Charli he ignored, even when Poppy began to twine ivy into the girl's wild, black hair, declaring she was a maenad dancing in the moonlight.

"Rowan."

Luke's breath was moist on her ear.

She turned sharply.

"What?"

That same horrible smile leered down at her.

"D'you fancy a bit of a laugh?"

"What do you mean?" She wished she could shrug him away.

"A bit of fun."

He was trying very hard to make his voice sound casual.

"Well, what… exactly?"

"It's just…" He pretended to concentrate on tying the piece of silver twine. "I was wondering if you, wanted to do a bit of, ghost hunting?"

"Ghost hunting?"

"Yeah, Poppy gave me the idea. You know how she was going on yesterday about spooks and stuff. Well, there are these books in the library and they say, you know, *according to tradition*, that those kinds of things appear at Midwinter."

"What kind of things?"

"Ghosts and stuff. I thought we could go to, say, Hag's Knoll."

"Hag's Knoll? In the wood?"

"Yeah. Yeah, why not?"

"You want to go to Freya's Wood? But it…" She looked out of the tall, hall windows. "It'll be dark soon, Luke."

"And?" His eyes looked wild, desperate in his white face, the smile ragged, like a tear in a sheet.

"I don't think…" She glanced over her shoulder. "I don't think we'd be allowed."

Luke grabbed her wrist, making her wince.

"Come on, Rowan. It's the sort of thing Finn would do. Come on, *ghost hunting*, it'll be fun!"

Suddenly, Mr Holly's shiny red face was thrust between them, grinning, his breath hot and cidery.

"Ghost hunting, hey?" he roared, cheeks like bobbing apples. "On Midwinter's Eve? There'll be sprites, an' ghouls, an' goblins, an' wild magic abroad tonight!"

Poppy was laughing, swirling Charli round and round the hall.

"Dancing and magic and fairies and ghosts!" she chanted.

Luke stood, grinding his teeth, and, tearing down a piece of ivy, cried, "Why all the bloody green stuff? What's wrong with tinsel? This isn't the flippin' Middle Ages!"

He barged past the two dancing girls, marched into the library and banged the door shut.

"It's the mistletoe," winked Poppy. "He's getting nervous."

But Rowan couldn't bring herself to smile. She stooped down to retrieve the spray of leaves.

"Never mind," said May, coming forward and patting Rowan on the shoulder. "No harm done. You two run along now and play. You've worked jolly hard. Most grateful, don't y'know."

"What would you like to do?" Rowan asked as they trailed up the grand staircase.

"I don't know," said Charli. "Have you got any picture books or toys?"

"No, I didn't pack much…"

She stopped and put her hand on Charli's arm. "There's the old nursery, though, if you don't mind cobwebs."

They took candles from Rowan's bedroom and held each other's hand tight as they groped their way along the passage, up the twisting staircase and into the chilly attic corridor. The nursery door was ajar, as Rowan had left it, yet in the fading afternoon light how different the room felt: gloomy, the walls dancing with shadows.

"Urgh, it's a bit spooky. I don't think I like it," Rowan whispered. She was trying not to look at the stag's head in the corner, with its glassy eyes.

"Hey," said Charli and moved to the mantelpiece. She reached for an old-fashioned lamp. "My Aunti's got one of these. I wonder if there's any oil left?"

She removed the opaque glass shade and fiddled with a little brass knob.

"Smells all right, and, listen, you can hear the oil swishing around."

Lowering her candle to the wick, a ring of bluish flame caught hold. Charli replaced the rose-coloured shade and turned the brass knob. At once, the room was filled with a soft and steady light.

"Wow," Charli said, gazing around the room. "This is kushti."

She went up to the rocking horse and gave it a gentle push. It rocked back and forth, creaking slightly on its runners.

"This stuff must be a hundred years old. Look at this." She sat down on the window seat and picked up one of the dolls. "S'made of wax. An' all these petticoats; pretty. What d'you think she was called?"

The pale wax face stared up at them with its glazed blue eyes. Rowan turned away with a shudder. It reminded her of Luke.

"Come and see this, Charli," she said, moving towards the wooden chest. "I found it last time." She lifted the trophy head onto the floor.

"Blimey!" Charli exclaimed as she knelt down next to Rowan. "That old stag thing, creepy or what? I swear its eyes are followin' me."

Rowan raised the lid.

"What do you think of this, though?"

She took out the heavy, leather-bound book.

Charli drew breath and ran her fingers over the fine metal bands. "That's silver, handsome."

"The padlock must be silver too."

Charli put her head on one side. "What do the words say?"

Rowan turned and gazed at her.

Charli grinned. "My reading's not so good, an' the letters are fancy. I know it says 'The... B... Book...' but that's all."

"It says *The Book of Green Magick*."

Charli raised her eyebrows, impressed. "An' what's that little picture, in the circle? There's some words too, ain't there?"

Rowan bent her head low to peer at the strange device.

"Oh, it's so small. Bring the lamp and let's go over to the window. There's still a bit of daylight left."

She placed the book on the window seat and inspected the small circular crest.

"I think it's a man's face, with... with leaves growing out of his mouth and in his hair. There are some letters but..."

"Oh!" Charli cried.

"What is it?"

"Look!" She was pointing out of the window, to the garden far below.

They both pressed their faces against the glass. The setting sun threw long, bluish shadows over the white lawn, and there was Luke, shoulders hunched, striding through the snow towards the yew walk.

"What's he going off for? At this time?"

"Freya's Wood," croaked Rowan, her voice tight with fear. She jumped up. "Something's wrong. Oh, Charli, I've got to stop him."

"Stop him?"

"Yes, I have to. I have to!"

"What's he going to do?"

"I don't know. Ghost hunting, he *said*. He tried to get me to go, but I... Oh, I've *got* to go after him."

The gypsy girl sprang to her feet and caught hold of Rowan's hands. "What if it's a trap?"

"A trap?"

"Yeah, what if the dogs an' the Mul... Mints are waiting for you, out there?" She gestured towards the window with her head. "In the dark."

"But Luke's in danger, Charli. I've got to help him, don't you see?"

Charli sighed and nodded. "Yeah, I suppose; he's one of your own, ain't he? Come on, then, best get our coats an' stuff."

"Charli, thank you." Rowan gave the bright-eyed girl a tight hug.

"Oh Del! Aunti will kill me; she told me to look after you. An' we'll have to be dead quiet getting out the 'ouse. Grown-ups is so nosy."

The air was bitterly cold as they hurried across the garden, but they were warm beneath the extra layers of clothing that Charli had made them put on. "It'll be freezin' up there, believe me!"

They paused only to take an odd-looking lantern that hung in the stable yard. "It's got this shutter, see," said Charli. "It shields the light. Luke won't be able to see us following on the hill, but in the wood we'll need it, I tell you."

They ran swiftly below the tall hedges, crossed the upper pasture and began the climb. In the distance Freya's Wood loomed black and ominous against an orange sky, but they could see no movement on the bare snowy hillside, or hear any sound.

On they pressed and reached the line of trees.

The two of them stood, staring into the darkness.

"Come on, then," Charli murmured and slid back the metal plate, shielding the lantern. It threw out a circle of yellow light. Rowan had the odd feeling that within the circle they were safe.

"Where to?" whispered Charli.

"Hag's Knoll."

Rowan thought she saw the gypsy girl shudder but before she could say anything Charli had grabbed her hand.

"Stay close. Got it?"

Rowan could feel the girl's gloved hand around hers, strong and reassuring. In the dense, woody tangle it became all that mattered. She stumbled on, branches scratching her face, roots catching at her feet, knees aching as they climbed upwards. How could Charli see her way? Beyond the circle of light, there was a wall of darkness, of silence, pressing in around them. Were *they* out there: the men, the Foul Folk, those uncanny faces? Would they hear boots crashing through the undergrowth, menacing shouts, savage voices and frenzied barks? Would they find Luke and the Mints waiting for them at the Knoll, laughing?

An owl hooted.

27

HAG'S KNOLL

⸺◆⸺

THE OWL HOOTED AGAIN AND ROWAN CLUNG
to the gypsy girl.

"Wait!" Charli hissed, dragging her arm away.
There was a sliding click, followed by utter blackness.

"Charli?"

"Shhh!"

Charli's hand was groping for hers and then she
felt herself pulled forwards.

As they moved onwards, Rowan could discern
a change from pitch-black to gloom. The trees were
thinning and a huge pale form loomed up ahead.
They had come to a clearing at the crown of the hill:
Hag's Knoll. The great snow-covered mound rose up
towards the night sky.

Rowan let out a sigh: how beautiful it was. It
sparkled softly in the darkness as if reflecting the last
vestiges of evening light. Yet surely the gleam came
from within, a silver blush beneath the snow?

"That's so strange," she began. "Why...?"

Charli held up a warning hand. "Shhh!"

A figure was walking along the base of the mound.
Rowan gasped. Luke!

She felt Charli pulling her to the ground. "Just
watch."

Luke stopped and took something from his coat pocket. It was something that made sparks of blue light dance in his hands. He gazed at the object as if transfixed, then turned and faced the hill. He stood so still, Rowan thought, he might be made of ice.

Suddenly, Luke threw the object high into the air. There was a searing crackle of light that made the girls start and cling to each other. It seemed to lick the hillside, leaving little sparkling trails in the snow. The trails convened, defining a clear rectangular shape. A deep sound, like the cracking of thick ice, thundered beneath the ground and, inch by inch, a doorway opened in the barrow-side.

Rowan wanted to cry out, but her throat was whisper-dry.

Brilliance flooded from the opening.

Luke took a step forward, then another, his gait mechanical, uncanny, as if driven by clockwork. Rowan leapt up and, dragging herself from Charli's grasp, ran towards him. But Luke passed beneath the lintel of the doorway and the light streamed about him like a net of gold. She caught a strange scent on the air and briefly heard the faint murmur of unearthly voices.

"Luke!"

For a moment he half turned, hair flaming, but Rowan stumbled in the snow and fell. By the time she had scrambled up it was too late. His dark silhouette had passed into the brightness. The door was closing.

"Luke!" she screamed. "Luke, come back!"

She made one last leap forward, arms outstretched. But it was hopeless. She landed on the cold, white hillside.

The door had gone.

Doubled over on hands and knees, she was no longer aware of her surroundings.

"Rowan?"

Sobs wrenched their way up from her stomach.

"Rowan!"

A hand stroked her head. The bright lantern and Charli's anxious face swam into view.

"You okay?"

Rowan sat up and tried to steady her breath.

"Rowan, we got to get help…"

Rowan shook her head.

"We got to," said Charli.

With a grunt, Rowan heaved herself up and began searching the place in the hillside where the door had been. She thrust her hands deep into the snow, digging hard.

"Rowan, come on!" said Charli pulling at her friend's coat.

Rowan stopped, turned and glared at Charli.

"No, Charli. People will think we're lying, or crazy, or worse. Even the nice ones like Aunt May. For goodness' sake, Charli, they're grown-ups; we're kids. What do you think they're going to say?"

Charli brushed her wild hair out of her eyes. "P'raps we are flippin crazy."

"No!" Rowan said, thrusting the snow away. "They've got him. But I'm going to get him back!"

"They? You mean the Mulo, don't you?"

Rowan said nothing, but her efforts redoubled.

"So, you're gonna go in *there*?"

"Yes." She was panting hard with the exertion. "*If* I can find a door."

"But…"

"There has to be a door, under here, somewhere."

Charli sighed, put the lantern down and began to scrape the snow with her hands.

They dug for a long time in the circle of light, scraping the snow away where the door had been. Beneath there was nothing but dead grass and frozen earth.

"There's not even the tiniest crack. It's just solid ground."

"D'you think we imagined it?" said Charli, rubbing her forehead. "Like when Uncle Yacob has too much potato vodka?"

Rowan shook her head.

"I wish I had imagined it, Charli. But I've seen other things. Really strange things. Oh God!" She covered her face with her hands.

Charli held her. "It's okay, Ro. If only we could find out how Luke opened the door. He used that thing, didn't he?"

"The blue light."

"T'was like a firework or summat. He must have got it from them Mints."

"Oh goodness!" Rowan leapt to her feet. "The library!"

"What?" Charli raised the lantern high.

"Luke was in the library all morning." Rowan gazed at Charli, eyes wide. "There were these big, *big* books all over the table!"

"So what's brother Luke been reading?" said Charli, jumping up. "Bet y'a hundred to one it wasn't *How to Bake Mince Pies*!"

"Quick!" cried Rowan, grabbing the gypsy girl's hand. "We've only got a couple of hours before the grown-ups start asking questions!"

The moon was bright by the time they reached Sloethorn House. It cast long, eerie shadows across the white lawn. The girls hid behind a tall hedge, catching their breath and rubbing cold, aching legs.

"If only we could get in through the French doors," Rowan panted.

Charli nodded, "I bet that's the way Luke went."

"Only one way to find out. Come on."

They crept past the stable buildings, keeping to the shadows, and edged their way along the back wall of the great house. Except for the soft chugging of Mr Holly's steam engine, all was quiet. Lights shone from the kitchens, but the library windows were dark. Drawing close, Rowan clasped her fingers around the ornate brass handle of the French doors and pulled down. The mechanism flexed beneath the pressure and there was a pronounced click. The large glass door swung gently towards them. Both girls let out a sigh of relief and, slipping through, closed the door behind them.

A low fire was burning in the grate, casting only the faintest gleam, yet by its light they could see an assortment of leather-bound books covering the long library table. Some were stacked in piles; some lay open. Charli drew back the shutter on the hooded lantern and set it down on the table.

"That's more like it," she whispered. "We can see what we're doing now. What are all these books about, then?"

Both girls leant forward over an open manuscript.

"The print is so old-fashioned, it's not that easy to read," said Rowan, frowning. She lifted the book carefully and read the spine. "It's called *Secrets of the Druids*."

"An' what about this one?" asked Charli, pulling another volume towards them.

"It's all weird and gothic. That's *Ancient Isle: Lord*, no, *Land*, *Land of the Gods*. And this one here is *Celtic Britain: Myth and Magic*. They all seem to be about ancient Britain. Why would Luke be interested in…?"

"Look!" said Charli. "This page has bin scribbled on."

A passage of text had been underlined with a fluorescent yellow marker.

"That's Luke's marker pen. Goodness knows what May will think. Her poor books."

"But what's it say?" Charli urged.

Rowan leant over the text, tracing it with her finger. "*More… moreover it was believed that ba-barrow mounds were doorways into the Otherworld; a shifting, twilight place some called 'The Land of the Dead' and others the 'Kingdom of the Fairies'*. Oh, Charli! *Access to this el-el-elusive domain could be gained only on certain magical days of the year: Midsummer, Midwinter and during the four great pagan festivals*."

"It's Midwinter tonight!"

The girls stared at each other.

"There's this one too. He's been busy with that old pen of his." Charli drew forward another volume.

"How could he do it to these beautiful old books? Aunt May will be heartbroken."

"That picture's a bit creepy."

It was an illustration of a wizened old woman with a long cloak and plaited hair standing in a magic circle, beyond which danced a host of uncanny creatures.

"Looks like she's definitely had too much potato vodka!" said Charli. "So what's the story?"

"Okay, it says: '*The Celts* –' they were people that lived here a long time ago, Charli, '– *The Celts believed that certain spells or amulets gave one the power to see ghosts or fairy folk, and enter their world.*'

"Aunt Sonja always used to say that Hag's Hill was a dangerous place and that we should stay away. She said the Puka would come and get us."

"Are Puka like Mulo?"

"No, they're not bad and not good, they're sort of… spirits, I s'pose, who live in the woods and the water."

"Like fairies?"

"Not so little and shiny. More scary, but not really bad. Us kids thought it was just stories. Least 'til it got dark."

Rowan gazed at Charli.

"Sometimes I think stories have more truth in them than… well, I mean, people think stories are just for kids, but, in one way, they're real." She sighed. "Listen, I should have told you before, Charli. But the people who are after me. It's not just the Mints. I mean, they're part of it, but there are others who are much, much worse. That's why I've got to get Luke back. They're using him to get at me. If they have to, they will hurt him. They'll do anything." Rowan hunched forward. "I've got to find a way through that door."

She felt Charli's hand on her shoulder.

"Don't worry. We'll find it. You said before, didn't you," said Charli, looking at the bookcases lining the library walls, "about a spell or an al-almu… something. You know, it was in that book: '*The Celts believed*'…"

"Of course! 'The Celts believed that certain spells or amulets gave one the power to see ghosts or fairy folk, and enter their world.'"

"That's what we need, a spell or an amulet. But where do we start looking?" Charli mused. "A book o' spells would be quite handy, wouldn't it?"

Rowan gave a sudden gasp. "Oh, Charli!"

"What? Look at you: you're shaking."

"The book! The book in the attic. *The Book of Green Magick!*"

No one saw them creep silently across the dimly lit hall and pass by the great Christmas tree. No one heard as they tiptoed up the staircase and down the long, long corridor of bedrooms. Swiftly, they made their way up the spiral staircase, through the attic, to the old nursery and there on the window seat, as they had left it, was the book. Charli placed the lantern on the windowsill and the two girls sat on the seat studying the banded volume and its silver padlock.

"If we got a knife we could force it open," suggested Charli.

"Force open a book of spells?"

"You're right; we'd end up as toads or something. Stupid idea."

They stared at the book.

"I know!" said Charli, "Perhaps the key is hid somewhere in this room." She jumped to her feet and lifted the lid of an old wooden school desk. "Pencils, rulers, ink bottles, dead beetle – urgh! Oh, but what's this? Ha!"

Charli held up a small silvery object.

"What is it?"

"Hair-grip. My uncle taught me to pick locks."

"Not Uncle Yacob, I hope."

"No. Uncle Bela. 'There's no lock,' he would say, 'that can defeat your Uncle Bela, me hedgehog!' I liked Uncle Bela."

"Okay, then, we might as well try."

Charli crouched down by the window seat and inserted the slender steel wire into the silver keyhole.

"Hold it steady."

She gave the hairpin a gentle twist.

"Ow!" Charli dropped the grip, fingers flying to her mouth. "That hurt! Felt like fireworks all up my arm!"

"Like an electric shock?"

"Dunno, but it was horrible."

"Has it made any difference?"

They bowed their heads to study the lock.

"No, it ain't. But I'm not trying that again."

The girls stared at each other in dismay.

"I suppose dropping it out of the winder wouldn't do any good? No, I know. Probably blow the house up."

"Not very subtle; everyone would hear. What we need is the key. It must be in this house somewhere, but there are so many places it could be hidden, so many rooms and they're all filled with a hundred ornaments..."

"All them fancy boxes and china bowls."

"And ornate vases and pots and marble urns."

"I still think it's hidden up here. What about in that old stag's head?"

They both gazed at the moth-eaten trophy head and it gazed back, eyes glinting green. It really did remind Rowan of Mother Meg.

"I'm not sure. I really don't want to…" Rowan began, and then she clasped her hand to her mouth.

"What is it?"

"Oh my goodness!"

"What!"

"Charli, I've got the key!"

"What?"

"I've got the…" Rowan fumbled for the leather pouch and drew it out from under her jumper. Opening it she took out the small dull key, Mother Meg's gift.

"It's what she said, '*to unlock many secrets*'. She must have meant the book. She must have known!"

28

THE BOOK OF GREEN MAGICK

"WHO KNEW?"

"Mother Meg, this strange old woman down in London. She was the one who first warned me. She told me I was in danger and gave me this."

Rowan held up the key.

Charli raised an eyebrow. "It's a bit rusty, innit?"

Rowan nodded, "Doesn't look much."

They stared at the silver-bound book.

"Go on," Charli urged.

Rowan inserted the key into the ornate lock. Though drab and caked with rust, the key turned smoothly. A white fizz of flames, like a sparkler, burst from the keyhole, showering the floorboards with white stars and suddenly the key was gone. The silver padlock fell open.

"Flippin 'eck!" said Charli.

Rowan opened the silver bands and turned back the heavy front cover of the book. On the fly leaf was a larger, more detailed illustration of the Green Man. Leafy stems grew out of his mouth, twined upwards and framed his eyes, giving him a shrewd, uncanny air. She turned more pages, each thick and yellowed, written in a fine old-fashioned script and illustrated with a curving pattern of leaves and fruit. Odd little faces peeped out from the foliage.

"It's a book of charms," said Rowan. "Listen to this. *'How to Bring forth Rain'*, or there's *'To Charm a Fox'*, or even *'To Fly Like a Sparrowhawk'*."

"To fly!" Charli exclaimed. "Now that *would* be handy."

"What about this one? *'To Growe Magick Beans'*."

Charli knitted her brows. "I ain't climbing no beanstalk!"

"Oh," Rowan gasped. "This is it! She pulled Charli closer. The page was illustrated with a variety of strange-looking imps and winged creatures.

"What's it say?"

"*'If Thou –'* Oh, Charli, *'– If Thou Wouldst see Fairies'*."

Charli breathed out between her teeth. "Go on."

Rowan traced the words with her finger. "It's like a recipe.

'Heat water in the pot. Put thereto the leaves of wild thyme and apple mint, yarrow, wyrmwood, the flowers of elder and Sweete Cecily. Take also a mushroom plucked from a fairy ring and a spoonful of honey. Simmer, cool and keep for thy use. When ready, sip the potion and singest thou this rhyme:

"Honey sweete, wasp gall,
Hunter's moon, flowers fall,
Ivy decks the Fairies Hall.
Out, out, out go I".'"

Charli sat back on her heels. "Where on earth are we going to get all these herbs an' things from? It's winter: everything's dead!"

Rowan frowned, staring at the outlandish figures in the book. They grimaced back at her, sticking out their tongues. She seemed to hear the dry rustle of mocking voices, "*Where, where, in the dead of winter?*" Then suddenly, she knew.

"May's larder! There's loads of weird things stored in jars. I bet she's got some of this stuff. We could start there, at least."

Charli grinned. "Well, if May puts '*mushrooms plucked from fairy rings*' on her pizza, it'd explain a hell of a lot."

The main house was hushed as the two girls made their way back down the stairs. The great Christmas tree with its strong, earthy scent shimmered and sparkled in the dimness of the hall. They passed into the rear corridor and through the green baize door that led to the kitchens.

Mrs Croft, all covered in flour, was rolling out pastry.

"What are you two wanting?" she asked sharply.

Charli put on her sunniest smile.

"Are you making your lovely pies, Missus Croft?"

"Never you mind about pies. What do you want?" But Rowan could see the housekeeper was softening. Charli, with her big brown eyes and cheeky grin, could have charmed a marble statue.

"We're having a doll's tea party, see, and we wondered if we could have some biscuits and stuff, to make it more real."

"Very well," Mrs Croft sniffed. But I'm up to my elbows. You'll have to get the things tha'sen. They'll be in the larder. Don't tek nowt you shouldn't!"

The girls entered the long, narrow storeroom with its well-stocked shelves.

"Have you got the list?" Charli hissed as she pulled the door to.

"Yes," said Rowan. "So what do we need?" She scanned the neat rows of jars. "Look, there's apple mint, up there! And down here is sweet cicely, oh and yarrow right at the bottom. Looks like they're in alphabetical order."

"Urgh!" said Charli, pulling a face. "What's this? Looks like old bogies."

"It's labelled '*Dried Mushrooms – Gillkirk Beck*'. Brilliant! We'll just have to trust they were grown in a fairy ring."

"This *is* May we're talkin' about," Charli grinned, then picking up a large glass jar, "an' this is honey, innit?"

"It say's 'Holly's Honey' on the label. I suppose Mr Holly must look after the beehives. And there's 'Moorland Thyme': that'll be wild, and here's wormwood. Oh, it's marked poisonous!"

"You're joking."

"We better take it anyway."

"Are you crazy? I wasn't planning on copping it."

"Look, we can hardly discuss it now. We'll just have to take some."

"Yeah, and think about our toenails falling out later."

The girls measured out small quantities of each ingredient. Charli stored them in twists of greaseproof paper and hid them up her sleeve.

"Look here," she said, pointing to a shelf of empty corked bottles. "That'd be handy to carry water in, an' then we can use it after for the potion."

"Okay," Rowan said. "I suppose we'd better ask Mrs Croft if we can pour some of the honey into a jug."

"Then if we take some biscuits and mince pies we can pretend they're for the dolls."

Back in the attic nursery Rowan and Charli laid out all the ingredients on the floorboards.

"So, we need a fire," said Charli, poking around the empty grate of the unused fireplace. "We'll have to get some kindling an' wood."

"Hey, what about...?" Looking thoughtful Rowan got up and went over to the window seat.

"Look."

She removed the glass shade from the oil lamp exposing the flaming wick.

"Clever," said Charli. "So all we need now is... wait a minute." She searched the dusty shelves and gave a cry of delight.

"Oh yes!" She held up a small copper saucepan. "The dolly's cooking set. Perfect."

Pinch by pinch, the girls added herbs to the pan of simmering water. Clouds of aromatic steam filled the room.

"So what about this wormy-whatsit stuff?" Charli asked, unfurling the paper.

"The wormwood? We can't leave it out."

"Can't we?"

"It's in the recipe. Probably won't work if we leave it out."

"An' we'll probably drop down stone dead if we put it in."

Rowan stared at the dusty grey herb cupped in Charli's hand.

"Okay. How about we use just the tiniest bit?"

Charli scratched her head. "Hmmm."

"It's in the recipe, Char, and it's not just any old recipe, is it?"

"Well, okay then. Just a nip."

Charli sprinkled a few flakes of the dry herb into the pan. "Smells weird," she said, "like Aunt Sonja's medicine."

"I guess that's a good sign," Rowan observed, pouring in a trickle of golden honey.

Charli stirred the mixture with a small spoon. "Makes me feel happier about drinking it, if that's what you mean."

After a few moments, they removed the pan from the flame and set it on the sill to cool. Rowan gazed through the window. Outside, the gardens were bathed in a cold, silvery light. She shivered.

"It won't be long now until supper. We'll have to go before then, slip away before anyone sees us."

Charli put her hand on Rowan's shoulder. "Best tidy this stuff away, in case they come lookin'."

Rowan nodded, and with a sigh closed the *Book of Green Magick*. With a shiver, the silver padlock clicked itself back into position.

"Oh!" Rowan exclaimed.

"Suppose it's ready for another key," said Charli. "Pity, I really fancied being able to fly."

Rowan placed the book back into the wooden chest, covered it with old clothes, closed the lid and rested the stag's head on top. Then the girls carefully collected together the scraps of paper and the left-over herbs and burnt them in the grate.

"This should be ready now," said Charli, dipping her finger into the potion. "S'cool enough."

With great care, they decanted the strong-smelling, clear green liquid into the glass bottle and replaced the cork.

"Okay then," said Rowan, looking directly at Charli. "We'd better go. We'll slip out through the library again. Less chance of being seen."

It was dark and silent as the girls crept through the upper floor, past the main bedrooms.

They were drawing close to the top of the staircase that led down to the hall when the front door bell sounded. A great clanging toll echoed through the building. Rowan and Charli dropped to their knees crouching down behind the ornate railings. They heard the tread of feet. May appeared from the back of the house and crossed the hall, muttering, "What's this? Tonight of all nights."

She opened the huge front door. A man, well wrapped up against the cold, entered and began to unwind the scarves that muffled his face and neck.

"Goodness, is that you, Harry?" May said. "Come in, come in. What brings you here? It's an odd night for a visit."

"Aye, t'is that."

"You've come all the way from the village, on foot?"

"Aye. An' I'd like nothing better than to wish thee a good evening, May, but tonight is living up to its reputation, I'm afraid."

"Why, Harry? What on earth is the matter?"

"I've brought a message from Betty Beckthwaite for young Luke and the little lass. Betty were in no state to come her sen'. She's had a terrible shock. Our Audrey's sitting in wi' her."

"What's happened?"

"Betty got a phone call, not long since, from the hospital. It's the children's feyther; he's been in an accident, a car crash."

"Oh, bless me, Harry. Is it serious?"

"Aye, he's in a coma."

Rowan heard no more. There was a rushing, pounding noise in her head; a receding, falling numbness. Then Charli's face looming over her.

"Rowan."

"Oh God, oh God, they've got him!" Her words were panting gasps, like when Luke pressed his hand down hard upon her chest. "They've killed my dad! Oh God, Finn! We can't stop them. It's no use."

She felt Charli grasp her shoulders, pull her upright and shake her roughly. The shock of it cleared her head.

"Look," hissed Charli, eyes sparking. "May's taken that 'Arry fella off to the kitchen for a hot drink. Then they're going to look for us. We got about two minutes to scarper!"

Rowan felt herself being dragged to her feet. She moaned. "No, Charli, there's no point."

Charli was fierce. "Yes there is. You got to get Luke back, that's obvious. You found that book, an' the spell, an' that old lady give you the key, didn't she? You can't give up now, just cos you feel like it. You gotta have guts. Don't you see? You gotta put a stop to it. That's your job, Rowan. Your job, no one else's!" Charli grasped hold of Rowan's hand. "Come on, Rowan, for your dad's sake!"

Rowan let out a dry sob.

"Oh, oh, Charli." But she held tight onto the gypsy girl's hand.

"It's time to run f'rit, Ro. Like a bleedin' hare!"

And, following Charli's lead, she fled down the stairs, across the hall, into the library and out into the deep winter's night.

Hag's Knoll rose up against the night sky like a slumbering giant, its summit crowned with a grove of nine twisted hawthorn trees.

"They look like people," murmured Rowan, staring upwards. "Strange people, dancing in a circle."

"Well, that's put me in the mood," said Charli. "You got the spell?"

Rowan nodded, and took a crumpled piece of paper from her pocket.

"Okay then."

Charli uncorked the glass bottle and paused. "D'you wanna go first, or shall I?"

Rowan reached for the potion. She felt as cold and dead as ice. "I'll go."

She tipped the bottle to her lips. The liquid tasted bittersweet, like the green herb-tea that Finn used to drink.

"What's it like?"

"Not brilliant," she said and passed the bottle back to Charli.

"Right," said Charli, looking doubtful. "Here goes." With one swift tilt of the head, Charli swigged the remaining potion then clamped her hand to her mouth.

"Don't spit it out; it might not work!" said Rowan.

Charli pulled a face and struggled to swallow.

"Flippin' 'ell," she said at last. "That was worse than Aunt Sonja's medicine, an' that's saying somethin'."

"Here," said Rowan. "Hold my hand, just in case."

They were quiet. The woods around them seemed as still and silent as the sleeping mound. Rowan cleared her throat and began to recite in a wavering voice, "Honey sweete, Wasp gall, Hunter's Moon, Flower's fall, Ivy decks the Fairies' Hall. Out, out, out go I."

Nothing. Just the deep silence of a Midwinter's night.

"Oh God, Char, I feel stupid," Rowan whispered.

"Say it again."

"But…"

"Say it, Ro. Like you mean it!"

Rowan took a deep breath. She thought of Luke. She thought of Finn. She thought of Mum. "Honey sweete, Wasp gall, Hunter's Moon, Flower's fall, Ivy decks the Fairies' Hall. Out, out, out go I!"

It was as if the air gave a shiver. Somewhere far, far away a bell sounded: a silvery, musical tone. The snow on the mound sparkled and the softest tremor seemed to pass through the ground beneath their feet.

Rowan repeated the charm.

Suddenly, a crack appeared in the mound and a colossal arc of diamond light burst forth. Rowan's head was full of angel voices, the voices that had been with her for so long. Her chest ached with joy. She could feel the tears streaming down her face. "Oh, oh, oh!" she wept.

She heard Charli cry out. "Look, Rowan, look!"

She wiped her eyes and looked.

The door in the hillside was open.

PART THREE

Undiscovered Country

29

THE GREENWOOD

CLUTCHING CHARLI'S HAND, ROWAN entered the tunnel.

The light was blinding, as brilliant as a comet's tail. It seemed to Rowan that her eyes, her hair, her very breath was filled with stars. How long it lasted, she had no notion. Space, time, thought had turned to dazzling light.

When at last the radiance grew soft, the girls were in a chamber, walls glittering with crystal. Standing before them were three tall, beautiful women wearing loose white robes. The first had hair like gold, the second hair like ebony and the third hair the colour of flaming autumn leaves.

"Welcome Dur'ae," they said and bowed their heads.

The one with flaming hair stepped forward and took Rowan's hand.

"Child, my dear child, long have I waited."

"Waited?" echoed Rowan.

The woman put her hand to Rowan's neck and drew out the leather pouch. Charli moved forward with a cry of protest.

"Peace," said the woman, holding up her hand. "The Dur'ae need fear no harm here."

With a movement, light and deft as wind rippling the surface of a pond, the woman removed the Fàinne Duilleoga. It lay on her white palm, gleaming. "It was my gift to you."

Rowan gasped, "Glas Sidhe!"

"So they called me."

"But that was years and years ago."

"Ah yes. It broke my heart to watch the others grow old and die."

"You're still…"

The woman smiled. "Time flows differently here." She placed the Ring of Leaves, suspended on its fine silver chain, about Rowan's neck.

"Wear this, child. It is the emblem of our kinship. It marks you as a daughter of the Fair Folk. Now, you must go on. You are expected."

"P-please," Rowan stuttered. "Did Luke, my b-brother, come this way? I have to find him."

Glas Sidhe shook her head. "None have passed this way. But there are many gateways, many paths to many worlds. Your path may be different from your brother's."

"But he needs my help! That's why I've come!" She felt ashamed as hot tears pricked her eyes.

"Your path lies through the Green Forest, Rowan, the realm of our Lord."

"But I… I can't just…" Rowan began.

Glas Sidhe put her hand on Rowan's cheek. "Your heart burns like a falling star. Good. But trust me, granddaughter. You must journey through the forest to find your way. Come."

The girls were led through a second tunnel. At last, they emerged from a cave mouth, an opening at the foot of a sheer cliff face, hung with lush ferns and emerald mosses. Above and behind them, precipitous tree-clad slopes rose up; before them stretched a vast forest of the largest trees Rowan had ever seen. Gulping, she gazed up at the green-gold light filtering down through the canopy.

Glas Sidhe bent to kiss both girls on the forehead, her lips cool as water. "Fare you well, Dur'ae, fare well daughter. Give greetings to my Lord."

She turned and her pale form melted away into the cave's gloom.

Charli looked at Rowan. "Got to admit, this is weird. I don't suppose we're dreaming? You know, that mad potion stuff?"

"It's not like a dream, though, is it? It's too real. You know, more real than..."

"The *real* world. Our world?"

"Yes."

Charli gave a wry smile.

"Tell you what. I'm roasting."

"Yes, the snow's gone. It's not winter here."

"It's not night, neither."

"Glas Sidhe said something about time being different."

Charli sat down. "Well, I'll tell you what. I'm gonna take off some of my clothes, so's I don't boil."

Rowan laughed, and both girls began to fling off their layers: overcoats, jumpers, hats, boots, woolly tights and thick socks, until they stood there, in bare feet, light and cool, Rowan in a plaid skirt and white top, Charli in some old patched trousers and a red T-shirt. Rowan loved the feel of the rich, spongy soil beneath her feet. She breathed deeply.

"Oh it smells like summer, all green and fresh. Isn't it amazing to have bare feet? Feels like forever since I've been able to do this."

Charli grinned. "I guess you *can* have too much snow. So, anyway, what do we do now?"

Rowan gazed ahead, thoughtfully. "Start walking, I suppose. Isn't that some kind of path over there?"

"What about our clothes? Don't fancy carrying them around."

"Let's leave them inside the cave. They don't really belong, anyway."

The two girls folded the garments as best they could and left them in the narrow opening. Then they turned to face the great forest.

There was something cathedral-like about the deep silence beneath the trees and yet the place seemed to thrill with life. There was a sweetness in the air which made Rowan think of roses or cherries, and yet was neither of these.

"Can't see a path, exactly," said Charli.

"Well, as long as we avoid those enormous roots, it should be quite easy. There's hardly any undergrowth, just this lovely soft earth."

The girls travelled deeper into the woods. On they went, past the never-ending trees whose vast trunks, trailing ivy and lichen, reminded Rowan of ancient castle towers; on and on through the tangled network of roots, some as high as their shoulders; on for what seemed like hours, until they felt hot and hungry and thirsty.

They sat down on a tree root.

"Goodness," said Rowan. "What I wouldn't give for a handful of snow right now."

"Don't suppose any of these trees have fruit?" said Charli gazing upwards.

"They're oaks, aren't they?"

Charli groaned. "What we need is apple trees, like in the orchard at home, full of big, juicy pippins."

"Wait a minute," said Rowan, jumping up. "What's that?"

"Where?" said Charli, craning her neck.

"Over there. Look! That flash, like silver."

"Bloomin 'eck," said Charli jumping up. "I reckon it's a stream."

She bounded forwards, leaping over tree roots, scrambling down a gentle slope. Half laughing, Rowan followed. They reached a fast-flowing brook that wound its way over rocks and stones, through the peaty soil. The girls flung themselves to the ground and plunged their heads into the water, drinking long draughts straight from the stream. It seemed to Rowan she had never before tasted anything so clear and cool.

Charli hooted with delight. "I bet this is what champagne tastes like!"

"Oh no, it's much nicer than champagne." Rowan had tried Finn's champagne one Christmas, and been thoroughly disappointed.

"No, it's more like…" She thought of freshly picked strawberries, iced lemonade, new-fallen snowflakes melting on the tongue, but nothing came close to the delicious, teeth-tingling sensation. Rowan splashed her face again, then stood up and waded into the shallows.

"Oh, Charli, do this, it feels…" but the words died on her lips.

For there on the other side of the water, amongst the trees, stood a great stag, watching them.

"What's up...?" Charli got to her feet and, following the direction of Rowan's gaze, froze.

The power of the creature was palpable; huge and muscular, it bore an immense pair of antlers on its fine head.

Rowan tried to swallow, but her throat had gone dry. It was like being at the zoo, standing feet away from something very large and dangerous: a rhino or a tiger, but without the comfort of a strong, steel fence in-between. Rowan could smell the hot, musky scent of the stag's flanks, could hear the snorting breath in its nostrils. If it charged they wouldn't stand a chance.

"Ro," Charli hissed out in uneven gasps. "Just back away. Slowly."

But Rowan couldn't make her body move. Something in the creature's gaze was so stern, so commanding, she was transfixed. It wasn't simply fear. The overwhelming feeling rising up from the pit of her belly was a sense of awe, a sense of the animal's rightness, its belonging. It *belonged* to the forest. No, more than that, it *was* the forest, body, heart and soul. This was the source of its power. It was real, more real than anything Rowan had ever known. And she and Charli were less than pieces of dry straw on the breeze.

"More real than anything?"

Where had the voice come from? Had the stag spoken? Something pressed against her heart.

"Ro," whispered Charli. "Just move."

Rowan gulped and tried to control the trembling in her limbs. The eyes of the stag were darker than the earth of the forest.

"More real than anything?"

Her throat was tight with pain. "Finn!" she cried. "Luke! Mum!" Tears wet her face and with a desperate effort she took a step forwards.

"Dur'ae!" The voice boomed out deep and low.

The girls gave a start and scrambled towards each other, clinging together in their fear.

"Dur'ae!"

The voice had come from the creature. Its eyes were compelling, untamed, yet something kindled in their depths.

Rowan let go of Charli and took another step towards the stag.

"Rowan?" Charli squeaked.

Another step forward, heart hammering, throat dry, closer, closer and at last she could feel the hot, earthy scent of his breath on her face.

Rowan tried to speak, but her voice was as dry as dead leaves.

"I have come for you." The stag's voice rumbled like distant thunder.

Rowan felt sick with fear. She wanted to avoid his gaze, back away, but she forced herself to meet his eye. And, oh, his eyes were full of leaves, of creatures running in the shadows of a great forest; figures, faces, a woman's face, vivid green eyes gazing back at her.

"Oh, it's her. Mother Meg!"

The stag took one great step towards Rowan.

"What do you see?"

Rowan swallowed hard; she could barely breathe.

"I see, I see…" The creature's eyes were now as dark as night. All she could see in the depths was her own tiny, terrified reflection.

"I see... a... a friend."

There seemed to be the warmth of laughter in his voice. "You are one of the Dur'ae, ally and friend to my Lady and the Forest Realm. You have nothing to fear, child."

"You know Mother Meg?"

"I am my Lady's servant in all things."

"I think she wanted me to come here."

"Yes, you are called."

"Did she call my brother too? He came here, I think."

"The trees of the Greenwood are more numerous than stars. Your brother was foolish if he ventured this way."

The stag raised his muzzle and scented the air.

"I cannot feel his presence. The forest whispers many secrets, but not of a boy. You must ask the Lady; she is very wise. And now we must go. Climb up on my back. I can bear you both with ease. Up now, make haste. We must fly."

The ride through the Greenwood, seated on the stag's back, was more than a dream. It seemed to Rowan as if they were tiny figures in a great tapestry, woven from the richest hues of emerald, viridian, bronze, jade. And yet the sense of reality was profound: the air fresher, the pungent scents of moss and bark sharper, the colours brighter than anything she had known before. At times she could hear the beat of cloven hooves upon the ground; at times it seemed as if they must be flying. On they journeyed, ever on, past the never-ending trees, until Rowan thought the whole world was a forest without end. At times she seemed to sleep, and yet in her dreams still they flew through the air, her fingers clutching the stag's thick red mane. And then it seemed she knew of a secret that lay hidden at the very heart of the Greenwood, a centre around which the worlds revolved and upon which all things depended.

"I must leave you now." In her dream she was gazing deep into the stag's eyes, fearful at what she saw.

With a start, Rowan woke.

The stag had brought them to the edge of the wood. They looked out over rolling hills which swept down to a green valley filled with orchards and gardens.

"This is Summerland, our Lady's realm."

Rowan and Charli slipped down from the creature's back and gazed at the land below. It was beautiful. The light was as clear and golden as the first flush of sunlight at dawn, or the soft-rose glimmer of a midsummer sunset.

"Farewell, Dur'ae and companion. Tell my Lady that the Lord of the Forest is at her command."

"You're the Lord of the Greenwood?" Rowan bowed her head clumsily, feeling tongue-tied. "I should have... Glas Sidhe... she sent her greetings... Th-thank you, sir."

He returned the bow. "The Dur'ae may always expect help in the Greenwood."

Turning lightly on his cloven hooves, he took several steps towards the trees, then looked back and held Rowan's gaze. In the strange light his eyes appeared to glint like jewels.

"Remember, Rowan, there is much courage in your heart. It is courage, above everything, that will lead you to your heart's desire."

Then, with a mighty bound, he leapt away into the darkness of the forest.

Rowan reached for Charli's hand, and they looked down at the golden valley.

"It's like a picture in a storybook," Charli sighed. "All them colours."

Rowan looked at the grass beneath her feet. It was an impossible shade of green.

"Char, can you hear music?"

Charli didn't answer, but gazed at the scene below, a distracted smile upon her lips.

"No, it's not like music; it's more like singing. It's like the voices… the ones I used to…"

The silvery harmonies shivered on the air.

"And Char –" she was whispering now, "– can you see things moving this way?"

She could hear faint laughter. She pulled on Charli's hand, but her friend just sighed.

"Charli, there are people, or something. Look!" She gave the gypsy girl a dig in the ribs. "Charli, wake up!"

Charli blinked and shook her head.

"What's up? Oh crikey!"

Creatures had begun to gather around them. Things that Rowan could barely give a name to: animals, goblins, tiny things with wings, slender, shining people. There was a myriad of forms: the strange, the grotesque, the beautiful; some with flutes, some with bells, some garlanded with flowers, others wreathed in brown nuts and leaves. Some mouse-eared, fox-tailed, hare-pawed, some cat-eyed, berry-lipped, green-gowned, blossom crowned; some hairy with twitching snouts, some pale and luminous as glow-worms.

The creatures drew the girls into their midst, forming some kind of procession, and they danced down into the valley, past flowering gardens, fruiting orchards and sweet-scented meadows. Here they plucked a rosy apple, there a ruby plum; from this vine a cluster of juicy grapes, from that bough a handful of ripe cherries. They gathered wild roses and bryony as they went, and elder-flower and poppies, and wound them in the children's hair.

"Hold my hand tight," Rowan whispered in Charli's ear, "and, whatever you do, don't eat anything."

As the troop led the girls onwards they sang a strange song,

What do we bring for our Lady fair,
Through meadows of hemlock and roses wild?
We bear a fruit both rich and rare,
The fairy's child, the fairies' child.

Charli threw Rowan a worried glance and hissed, "Fairies steal children, don't they?"

What do we bring to Summerland's Crown
What do we bring to our Fairy Queen?
Some cherries and peaches and nuts so brown
And an apple far sweeter than any seen.

By a winding stream they went and up a steep bank of grass. At the top the slope levelled out into an expanse of emerald lawn and here stood a great castle, long since fallen into ruin. Its floors were soft turf and over its ancient walls clambered a mass of greenery: ivy, grape-vine, jasmine, honeysuckle and clambering roses, heavily laden with sweet-scented flowers.

At the far end of what must once have been a great hall, but which now stood open to the sky, grew two tall trees, white with blossom. The branches had grown together in such a way as to form a roof of starry petals.

Beneath this fragrant bower was a slender throne of pale wood. At the foot of the throne sat a group of fair women laughing and talking and weaving daisy chains. They looked young and light-hearted, yet there was something sombre in their mien as if, at a stroke, they could be called upon to lead armies or make grave judgements. In their midst was a woman of startling beauty, her skin as pale as a snowdrop, hair like gold, eyes the colour of newly unfurled leaves.

Suddenly, a creature ran forward. Rowan couldn't decide if it was a tall, upright hedgehog or a little boy with exceptionally wild and spiky hair.

"My Lady, my Lady," he cried. "See, see what we bring!" And all around the troop chanted,

What do we bring to the Queen of the May?
A rosebud fresh as the newborn day.

Rowan stumbled and caught her breath, but the fairy throng drew the girls on and, as they approached, the woman rose up, tall and lovely. Her shimmering gown might have been made of moonlight, Rowan thought, and sunlight seemed to ripple through her long, long hair. Rowan felt herself blush and then turn pale. Charli wiped her nose on the back of her wrist and attempted to push her tangled locks out of her eyes. The lady lifted a slender hand and there was a hush, then her ladies-in-waiting stood up, came forward and placed coronets of flowers on the girls' heads.

"Welcome," said the Lady, and her voice was full of sweet, wild music, low and compelling. "Welcome, my children. Long have we looked to your coming."

Rowan felt a flush of confusion rise to her face, as if she were being rebuked. Yet the lady's gaze, though searching, seemed full of a timeless understanding.

Rowan made an awkward bow.

"Please my... my Lady..." she began and then before she knew what she was saying a flood of words burst forth. "Do you know where Luke is? My brother, Luke. He went through the door at Hag's Knoll, you see, but Glas Sidhe said he hadn't passed that way and I... I need to find him, before... before..."

30

SUMMERLAND

———◆———

THE LADY REACHED OUT HER PALE HAND and touched Rowan's cheek. "Hush, daughter, do not think of your brother now. You are tired. You need rest and refreshment. We shall talk later, at the feast."

"But I..."

The Lady smiled and made a subtle sign. "We have prepared a chamber for you. Now is the time for rest."

Two ladies-in-waiting came forward. They led Rowan and Charli away from the Great Hall to an ivy-clad tower. Up the spiral stairs they went, through a door and into a circular room hung with leaves. There was a bed covered with red velvet and a huge white bowl filled with steaming water and scented herbs. The fair ladies bathed the girls and washed and combed their hair (despite Charli's protests) and gave them simple white robes to wear.

"Now drink this," they said, pouring out goblets of some clear liquid. "The Lady herself prepared it." With that the ladies departed. Charli and Rowan sat down on the bed and stared at the goblets, then at each other.

"Smells delicious," Charli said.

"Yes it does," Rowan sighed. "But we can't."

"I know. Aunt Sonja told me enough stories about

'the Little Folk' and what happens if you eat and drink their food."

"I don't suppose we're locked in or anything?" said Rowan. She went over to the heavy wooden door and tried the handle. It clicked open.

"Phew!" said Charli. "Just as well: look how high up we are." She was gazing out of the arched casement.

Rowan gave a gasp as she leant over the ivy-covered sill.

Below, they could see the gilded Vale of Summerland, with the silver ribbon of water winding its way along the valley bottom. A vast forest stretched away to the horizon on three sides, and on the fourth there were rugged hills and beyond that, far, far in the distance, white mountains.

"I wonder what she wants us for," Rowan murmured.

"Wants *you* for," said Charli.

"Well, yeah, okay, wants *me* for."

"Perhaps," Charli said, moving back into the room and flinging herself down on the large bed, "we shouldn't think about it too much, just try and rest."

"Do you feel sleepy?"

"Not really," Charli said and immediately yawned. "Ooh, there's definitely something weird about this place."

Rowan sat on the edge of the bed. "Did you notice her eyes?"

"Yeah: scary, but somehow you can't help looking into them. Green as emeralds."

"Just like Mother Meg's."

Charli yawned, stretched and snuggled down into

a velvet pillow. "Perhaps I'll just have a quick nap. 'Specially if that... thing... later..."

Rowan lay down and stared up at the ornate ceiling. Was Luke here? Was the Lady hiding him? Was it some kind of test? Or perhaps it was all part of some absurd, feverish hallucination. One thing was certain: she wasn't in the least bit tired. She would probably lie here for hours thinking and thinking. She sighed and turned over. Where *was* Luke? Was he in danger? Were they hurting him? She remembered the expression on his face when she told him Finn was on his way. Oh, oh, why had she thought of Finn? Something horrible gnawed at the pit of her stomach. Oh Finn, Finn! She turned onto her stomach and pressed her face into the pillow, but the terrible dull ache was growing. "Dad," she sobbed, her lips cold and numb. She sat bolt upright, snatched the goblet off the chest and put it to her lips. It smelt like spring mornings and summer evenings. "I don't care!" she whispered fiercely, tipped her head back and gulped it down. A stream of golden sunshine seemed to course down her throat and fill her belly. She could hear the Lady's voice saying, *"Rest now, little Rowan, let the pain pass. It is time to sleep."*

And so she slept.

They were woken by fair ladies filling the chamber with candlelight. Dusk had fallen. The ladies bore armfuls of white flowers. "We must dress you for the feast," they said, laughing, drawing Rowan and Charli from the bed. They wove white rose buds into the girls' hair and placed garlands about their necks and wrists. "There, how handsome you look. Come, come. The

Lady is waiting." Rowan stared at Charli, "You look amazing," she said. "Like a princess."

Charli put her head to one side, quizzically. "An' you, you look different. Glowing, somehow."

The ladies led them down to the Great Hall, which glimmered with a thousand fairy lights. The Lady sat on her fine throne and before her stretched a long, low table, covered in white linen and set with an abundance of sweetmeats and dainty dishes. Seated at this feast was the host of Fairyland and, as the girls drew near, all faces, gnomish and earthy, elfish and pale, leaf-like, flower-like, gnarled or nymph-like, turned towards them.

The Lady rose up, very tall and slender, wearing a green gown embroidered with threads of gold, and upon her head she bore a crown of ivy.

"To this feast of Summerland we welcome our most honoured guests, the Dur'ae and her companion." A great cheer burst forth and goblets were raised.

"Let the feasting begin!"

A second, louder cheer erupted, music and laughter filled the air and the Fair Folk set to filling their hands or plates or laps or mouths with sweets, jellies, puddings and fruits.

"Come," said the Lady, beckoning to the girls. "Here are old friends who wish to greet you."

Rowan noticed a tall man with silver hair and sparkling eyes standing by the Lady's throne. Behind him, partially hidden, was a large creature who now stepped forward into the light.

"Oh!" cried Rowan.

She ran and flung her arms around the creature's neck. "Sage, oh, Sage," she half sobbed. "I'm so glad to see you."

"And I you, child."

"Sage was honour bound to guide you safely to Summerland, child, though it cost him dear. We owe him our lives."

Sage bowed his head. "My Lady, I shall follow you and the Dur'ae to the very ends of the Earth."

The Lady looked upon him, her eyes wise and sorrowful. "It may yet come to that, O most faithful of friends."

Sage held his head high. "And when the call comes, I shall be ready!"

"We shall both be ready, you mean," said the silver-haired man, laughing. "You can't get rid of me so easily, Sage." He turned to Rowan. "But, child, do I not deserve a welcome too?"

Rowan stared at the man, perplexed. She was certain she had never seen him before, although there was something oddly familiar about his bright, luminous eyes.

"Ah, she does not recognise me," he said with mock despair.

Rowan felt a strange tingle at the back of her neck and gulped. "Is it... oh my goodness... are you... Ash?"

He laughed again and bent forward to kiss her hand. "I do not blame you if you prefer me in my other guise. As a man I admit I look well, but as a cat I am irresistible."

The Lady laughed and held out her hands. "My daughters, Rowan, Charli, sit with me and let us eat and enjoy the wine and song."

Their plates were piled high with ice-cold melon, fat blackberries, golden wheat cakes and sugared rosebuds. Charli looked at Rowan uneasily. Rowan smiled and nodded. "It's fine, I'm certain we have nothing to fear. Try it, see."

Rowan sipped from a goblet of sweet red wine. Gingerly, Charli raised a berry to her mouth, paused and then took a bite. The red juice ran down over her lips and chin. A slow grin spread across her face. "Oh Dordy, didn't realise how bloomin' starvin' I am. This is amazing."

They feasted long. To Rowan it felt like the best kind of party. Every mouthful of food, every sip of wine was delicious; now the music was wild and thrilling, now soft and full of enchantment. People talked and sang, laughed and cried. A merry fellow in green britches and a yellow jacket pulled out a fiddle and began to play. The Fair Folk whooped and crowed and leapt to their feet with hoots of delight. "'Tis time to make merry!" they cried. "'Tis time to go mad for joy!" Grabbing partners, they threw themselves into a frenzied, uproarious dance.

The Lady leant forward with a grave expression. "Now," she said. "We must talk." Her face seemed more pale and more lovely than ever and her voice was solemn.

"Rowan, you have been called to Summerland for a purpose. Your brother, Luke..."

"You know where Luke is?" Rowan gasped.

"Your brother, Luke, has been taken by the Hunters. They intend to use him as a lure. He is bait in their trap. It is you, Rowan, they want."

"But why," she half whispered. "What use am I to them?"

"Rowan, though you know it not, you are one of the Dur'ae, the Enduring Ones."

"The... the what?"

The Lady touched her cheek. "What I am about to tell you, Rowan, you will barely comprehend. We have been forced to call on you, to bring you here, before your time. You were in grave danger. The Hunters made their move early. You were too young, my child, to know your true nature. The Hunters hoped to take you while you were weak."

"But who are the Hunters? I mean, I know they've been chasing me, but why? And what *are* the Dur'ae?"

"The Enduring Ones, the *Dur'ae*, are guardians of the heart, the essential pulse that resides in all natural forms. The heart is a flow, a sacred energy that binds all things together in mutual indebtedness. Everything in nature is part of this flow, not just the beasts and birds and plants and people but the sun, the rain, the soil, the rocks. We are all part of a finely balanced whole, where the greatest often depend on the least. The Dur'ae are duty-bound to preserve that balance. And you, you will have sworn yourself to the service of this energy in an earlier time, even though, as yet, you do not remember these things.

"Now, child, the Hunters, who have been close on your heels for many days, are known as the Hungry Ones, the Arak-nus. They feed on the dark energies of hatred, fear, pain and misery. You must understand this, Rowan: such things are their sustenance. They enter into your world to breed conflict and confusion. In seemly form they present themselves as advisors and counsellors to the powerful and mighty, but their intention is to spawn greed, suspicion, division and destruction. Where nations war, where thousands thirst, where millions hunger, they feast, for all miseries delight them, all suffering is their rapture. How silken and reasonable such voices seem in the ears of those with authority and wealth, in the ears of kings or merchants, of statesmen or clerics, of those whose actions could shape the world for good or evil. In every age the Hungry Ones rise up to feed. In this age they have done their work well. They feed, they glut, they grow strong, and the Earth, oh, the Earth, she is crying out for her protectors, for her Dur'ae; she fears for all her children."

Rowan was pale. "But what can *I do*, my Lady?"

The Lady looked deep into her eyes.

"Your task, my child, is to defeat the Hungry Ones, to send them back, for a time, to their infernal realm, so that the Earth may regain her potency and blossom anew."

Rowan gulped and her voice was a squeak of fear.

"But how… how can I do that?"

"The stronghold of the Hungry Ones lies at the farthest reaches of Midwinter, on the shores of the Black Sea. It is a great ice fortress, hewn from the White Mountains. There you must travel to meet an adversary of old. You will not recognise him at first but, Rowan, you *know* him and have defeated him once before. He is Atr'ax, Lord of the Arak-nus, Sovereign of Avarice. In your world you have seen him standing shoulder to shoulder with monarchs and law-makers, giving ill counsel and biding his time."

For a moment, Rowan could hardly think, and then came a sudden shock of realisation.

"Oh!" Rowan cried. "The Grey Man!"

"He wants you dead, child. It is foretold that you are his nemesis. He has hunted you, sent his minions in pursuit and now has taken your brother hostage, a silver lure to draw the golden prey. With courage, and a little help, you have managed to evade him, but now, Rowan, you must willingly enter his lair."

Rowan felt as if icy water was being forced down her throat and into the pit of her stomach. Somewhere in her mind's eye a memory flickered, of a glittering, bloodless form. Her head swam; she felt sick.

"I… I don't know how, but I will… do my best, my Lady."

"I'm going with her!" Charli cried, eyes flashing.

The Lady smiled. "Yes, child. Rowan will be in need of a brave and loyal friend."

"And I too, my Lady, ask your leave to accompany the little Dur'ae on her journey," said the white wolf.

"Indeed, Sage, how could I deny you this? The land of Midwinter is your home. Your knowledge will be invaluable and, of all of us, *you* have sacrificed the most."

Ash leant forward. "Where Sage and the child go, I shall follow," he declared.

The Lady nodded.

"I would have chosen thus, for the bonds between you are strong. You will travel to the high plateau beyond the Vale of Summerland and there be met by the Fair Folk of Midwinter. They will take you to the very edge of their icy realm. Then in stealth and secrecy you must journey to the Fortress of Ice and attempt to gain access. At its heart lurks Atr'ax the Insatiable and all his foul spawn. And, Rowan, this you must know: when the Hungry Ones enter the world, *your world*, they do so in a kind of shadow-form, a projection of their terrible will. In this state, in a wretched 'consuming' sleep, they are vulnerable. Child, you must find Atr'ax thus and destroy his power."

Rowan had grown paler than ever.

"My Lady, h… how do I do this?"

"Sweet child, alas, although I will do everything in my power to aid you, this one thing I cannot tell you. But draw strength from the knowledge that you have cast out Atr'ax before. You must rely on the deep wisdom of the Dur'ae."

Rowan stared blankly ahead. The music still played and the folk of Summerland danced and rejoiced, but her heart felt like stone. How could she do such a thing? How could she?

The Lady made a gesture and a silver cup was brought to the table. She made a sign over it and held it up to Rowan's lips.

"Drink," she said. "It will help."

The drink was hot, sweet and strong. Rowan gulped it down and felt a warmth spreading throughout her body.

The Lady rose and took Rowan by the hand. "Come," she said in a low voice. "I have something to show you."

The Lady led her out of the fairy hall, beyond the walls of the castle and into the orchards and fields. The twilight air was sweet with the scents of evening and above the dusky sky was peppered with stars.

"This is such a strange place," Rowan murmured, half to herself. "It must be past midnight and yet it's not really dark yet. I wonder what time it is?"

"Ah," said the Lady with a low laugh. "It is all time and no time. Here time sleeps and dreams, and dreams have no boundaries. Consider this acorn." The queen held a shiny brown seed in her pale hand. "Lo!" The seed had, at once, sprung into a tiny sapling, inches high. Her hand closed, opened, "And there!" With a sweeping gesture she stepped back, and before them stood a great oak, heavy with acorns. "Each moment we are all and one. The seed is in the tree; the tree is in the seed. The child is of the mother; the mother is of the child."

The Lady continued along a path that wound its way up a hill and entered a dense wood. The canopy clustered so thickly overhead that, beneath the trees, it was as dark as midnight. The only light was the pale gleam that came from the Lady herself. Rowan followed, heart pounding. They walked for what seemed like a long time through the endless darkness, and Rowan no longer knew if she was awake or dreaming. She knew only that she would have been content to follow the Lady forever.

Rowan became aware of a glimmer ahead. The glimmer became a glow. The Lady stopped and uttered a few words, soft yet compelling, and a silvery brightness dazzled Rowan's eyes, as if morning had come in an instant.

Stepping out into a wide clearing, there grew the tallest, loveliest tree that Rowan had ever seen or imagined. It shone with an incandescent light and its branches were laden with an abundance of white flowers and golden fruit. Rowan caught her breath.

"It stands at the centre of all things," murmured the Lady. "It reaches up into the firmament and down into the underworlds. It is the axis upon which all worlds turn. It gives birth to the great cycles of matter and nature and spirit."

Rowan could feel tears rising and gulped. "It's the Tree of Life." Her voice was wobbling and she struggled to get it under control. "Finn used to tell me stories about it. I didn't know it was real."

The Lady smiled, and in the extraordinary light her lips were as red as rowan berries.

"Yes, the Tree of Life. It is strong and beautiful and real beyond imagining. Yet, Rowan, it is not invulnerable. Scars grow inwardly each time one of its daughters is felled or burned. Its very roots sense the taint and destruction of the Earth. If the wounds are not healed, then the tree will die."

Rowan turned in dismay and gazed up at the Lady whose face seemed as white and still as death. "And then all the worlds, Summerland, Midwinterland, the world of men, all will come to ruin and the Hungry Ones will feast 'til they are sick with gluttony."

Rowan felt a crushing sensation in her chest. "Is there no hope?"

The Lady bent down and kissed Rowan on the forehead.

"You, little Dur'ae, you are our hope." Her long white fingers touched the Fàinne Duilleoga. "You, child of Glas Sidhe, are the light in our darkness. You, who already bear such a burden of sorrow in your heart. But grace shall be given you. Go, take the fruit from the tree; it is yours by right."

Rowan gaped at the Fairy Queen. "I... I don't understand."

"As one of the Dur'ae, one of the Guardians, it is your right to eat of the Tree of Life."

Rowan swallowed and looked from the Lady to the shimmering tree and back again. How could such fruit be meant for her?

"Should I send you on such a long, hard road without sustenance, my daughter? A mother's greatest duty is to nurture and protect her child."

And it seemed to Rowan that the Lady spoke with the voice of Mother Meg and also the voice of her own mother.

Rowan moved forward timidly and reached up for a golden berry. The fruit glimmered and sparkled in her hand. For a moment she hesitated, breathing in the sweet perfume, and then she put it to her lips.

Afterwards, Rowan found it difficult to remember, and almost impossible to describe, how it had felt to eat the fruit. It was simply the loveliest thing she had ever tasted. It had filled her; filled her with something so pure, so brimming with joy, that her body seemed to overflow with light.

31

THE JOURNEY BEGINS

———◆———

PERHAPS IT WAS THE FOLLOWING MORNING or many mornings later when the girls were roused from their sleep. They were dressed in travelling clothes: tunic, cloak, britches and a slender belt, which bore a thorn-sharp fairy dagger. Sage led them to the eastern rise of Summerland Vale, where Ash, leading a fine horse and two fat ponies, grinned and waved a welcome. Out of the silver morning mist appeared the Queen of Summerland and her ladies, astride elegant fairy horses and veiled in shimmering grey. Once Rowan and Charli were mounted on their ponies, the Lady rode forward.

"Rowan," she said, throwing back the fine gauze veil. "Listen well, I have three things to tell you. First, you must seek the eagle who nests in the White Mountains, for she alone can tell you how to gain entrance to the Impenetrable Fortress. Second, let me see the Earthstone."

Rowan hesitated for a moment, then tipped the black pebble from the pouch. It was unbearably hot, like a burning coal. "Take care it doesn't burn you, my Lady."

The Lady reached over and took the stone as if it were an ordinary pebble. It did not mark her white skin.

"Use this wisely, child," she said, staring deep into Rowan's eyes. "For it can heal but *once* more. Remember, only when your need is greatest."

Rowan nodded and the Lady placed the stone back into its leather pouch.

"And third, my daughter, noble Dur'ae, know this: courage is your surest guide, but love is your greatest strength."

The Lady seemed then to grow in stature and her hair glowed like a mountaintop gilded with the morning sun.

"Fare well, companions. The blessings and the hopes of all Summerland go with you. Remember us."

She leant forward and into each girl's hair slipped a single rosebud, white for Rowan and red for Charli.

Sage bowed his head low and uttered a single phrase, "My Lady". Then he bounded away and the two ponies, startled into action, trotted after on their sturdy legs, with Ash bringing up the rear. Rowan clung on, breathless and shaken. Out of the valley they climbed, up the steep hillside, higher and higher.

Behind them they could hear a melody, low and sweet. The queen and her ladies were singing. Rowan couldn't understand how something so beautiful could make her want to cry, or how a sound that filled one with such hope could appear so wistful.

"They are singing of the Great Tree," murmured Ash. "And of their love for Summerland."

Rowan bowed her head. She could not help thinking of Luke and Finn and Mum, and for a long time afterwards she could not speak and her eyes were wet with tears.

They travelled through gentle, rolling hill-lands. Eventually, the turf, coarse and springy under hoof, gave way to patches of heather and gorse. Rowan had never ridden a pony before and at first the saddle felt strange and bumpy beneath her. Once or twice she made a grab for the pony's mane. Charli stayed close and offered advice.

"It's all about balance really, Ro. Sit up straight and use your legs; that's it."

"I feel like I'm going to slide off any minute, Char. You must've been born in the saddle."

"Well, I was, pretty much. The Rom grow up with horses, don't they? They're like family. Don't hang on the reins, though; these ponies are a dream, they'll take the lightest touch."

And indeed at times it was as if the animals could read their minds, for they seemed to know exactly what was required of them.

Is it because they are fairy horses or because we have become slightly fairyish ourselves? Rowan wondered.

The higher they climbed, the wilder the landscape grew. Heather covered the hills now and in places the ground grew boggy with tufts of sedge, or hare's tail, sprouting up out of the oozing rust-red earth. A cool wind was blowing from the east and Rowan pulled her cloak more securely about her.

"It will get colder yet, little Dur'ae," said Ash, leaning towards her, smiling. "We're heading for the Midwinter plateau."

Rowan looked up at Ash. She could not help feeling shy of this tall handsome man with golden eyes. Was he really the same cat who had chased away the Rat

Folk, who had eaten peach pie with Sophia, who had climbed purring into her lap? She blushed and looked away. There in the distance on a rocky outcrop stood Sage, ears pricked, head held high.

"What is he doing?" she asked in a low voice.

"Being vigilant, making sure the way is safe," said Ash.

"Are we in danger then?"

"The heart of the danger lies far to the east, child. But the Hungry Ones, the Arak-nus, have long sent their forces west to plague the Fair Folk of Midwinter. It may be that, having laid a trap, they are waiting and watching for a sign. It may be that spies are travelling beyond the snows of Midwinter itself."

Rowan shivered and pulled the cloak closer about her shoulders.

"Ash, do they know I'm here?"

For a moment he said nothing, just scanned the distant hills. A small bird circled overhead and they could hear its plaintive cry: "Pee-wit. Pee-wit. Pee-wit."

Ash turned and looked down at Rowan, his eyes a muted ochre.

"Dur'ae, to them Summerland is a puzzle, a secret, a mystery they cannot penetrate. It shifts, always beyond their vision, beyond their power, and at its heart lies the Tree of Life, all-protecting. My guess is that they hoped, they *planned*, to take you in *your* world. But we foiled them, Sage and I. We shadowed you closely and many times drove them off. Yet once you had passed into Summerland you became invisible to them."

"And now?"

"Now they bide their time. The snare is set; poor Luke is the bait. They know you will come."

"Then, if they're waiting for me, there's not much hope."

"There's always hope, Rowan. What they cannot see is the nature of your coming. They understand only force and might, the brute strength of arms, the hubris of authority. They will expect to confront the dazzling legions of Fairy, the wild creatures of the Greenwood, the valiant warriors of Midwinter, the dreadful powers of the Dur'ae. They cannot comprehend a different kind of power, that which is age-long, deep-rooted, evergreen and, like an aged yew, sends forth fresh shoots from timber gnarled and ancient, a power that endures and protects. They cannot conceive that a small, weak child should possess such power."

Rowan sighed. If she was honest, it was very difficult for *her* to believe that she possessed such power. It seemed, rather, that it must all be a terrible mistake and that some other child, clever, brave and fearless, should be here in her place.

All day they travelled, with the briefest stop for food, and at nightfall they camped beneath a clump of twisted thorn trees. Ash made a fire, over which they roasted apples and chestnuts and brewed a strong honey-flavoured drink called mead. It seemed full of the scent and warmth of Summerland and Rowan found herself relaxing at last, laughing at Ash's jokes and the clownish antics of Charli, who, it turned out, could perform somersaults and walk on her hands.

Later, Sage told them stories about Midwinterland: the endless frozen stretches of ice and snow, of musk ox and reindeer and white wolves; tales of giants and trows, of shades, ghouls and Lych Folk; of the legend of Sain Foin, prince of the Eastern Fair Folk, who fell in love with an ice maiden (those elementals, pure and cold and beautiful as new-fallen snow). In an impossible attempt to win her love (for ice maidens give their love to no thing), he went to fight the Great Kraken who dwelt in the bottomless depths of the Black Sea and was lost, never to be seen again.

Rowan slept, and when she woke with the first light of dawn the wind had grown cold and pale clouds were scudding in from the east.

It continued cold all day, the wind freshening as they went. The hills grew steep and rocky; in places great cascades of loose stone and shale darkened the hillside. By midday the girls were shivering. Sage brought the party to a halt and a fire was lit. Sweet mead was heated and they crouched by the flames sipping the steaming liquid.

"There are woollen mantles and leather gloves in the saddlebags," said Sage. "It is time to put them on, for by late afternoon we will have reached the plateau and there will be snow."

Wrapped in the soft-wool garments and with the hood of her cloak pulled close, Rowan felt almost cosy, but she soon appreciated how necessary the extra clothing was. Leaving the shelter of their hollow, they were suddenly exposed to bitter winds that swept down the hillside and laid back the ponies' ears.

"Oh Del," Charli gasped. "It's freezing!"

Rowan, breathless with cold, could only nod and brace herself against the next blast.

This stretch of the journey seemed to last forever. Step by tentative step, the horses climbed towards the summit of a rocky ridge on a narrow, exposed path. The sky was so overcast it felt like twilight, and great patches of snow were appearing across the landscape. Sage often disappeared into the gloom ahead. Ash stayed close to the girls, riding to the windward side in an attempt to protect his charges from the icy blast.

"It is not far now," he would call out in a cheery tone. "The Fair Folk of Midwinter will give us such a welcome."

"A-a-as l-l-long as there's a f-f-fire I'll be s-s-sorted," Charli stammered through chattering teeth.

Eventually, they passed through a steep, narrow cleft in the cliff. Emerging at the top, they saw the landscape had altered completely. They stared out across a vast, flat plane of snow. Far to the north-east mountains loomed, but all else seemed featureless and white. Then, as Sage had predicted, snow began to fall.

"Should we set up camp?" Ash asked, jumping down from his horse. "Mercifully the wind has dropped, but," and he added in a low voice, "the children can go no further tonight."

"Yes," Sage answered. "The Dur'ae and her companion are exhausted; they need fire and warmth. But listen: do you hear?"

Ash paused and drew down his hood. "Aye, I sense something moving fast over the ice, and it comes this way." He shielded his eyes from the snow and scanned the horizon. "Yet, I see nothing. Should we take cover?"

"There is nowhere to hide on the plateau, beyond crouching in a snow hollow. We must retrace our steps

and shelter amidst the rocks," said Sage. "But wait."
He pricked his ears high. "I believe… is it harness?"

"Then it must be Fair Folk."

Rowan and Charli slipped down from their ponies
and held each other, shivering. Though the wind had
died, the air was bitterly cold.

"I can't feel my fingers or toes," said Charli under
her breath.

"Come here, children." Sage commanded. "Crouch
down by me."

They did so and he warmed them with his body.
Rowan thought it was like cuddling up to an enormous
furry hot-water bottle, so deep and soft and warm was
his thick, white coat.

Ash gave a sudden cry of joy. "Here they come!"

Soon, even Rowan could hear the silver jangle
of harness. The girls jumped up and saw a sleigh
approaching, pulled by reindeer. Alongside ran two
light sledges, each drawn by a pair of white wolves.
With a cry of joy, Sage sprang forward to meet them.

"They are his pups," Ash murmured. "He has not
seen them since…" He fell silent. Rowan remembered
the Lady's gentle words to Sage, "You have sacrificed
the most."

"It will be a bittersweet reunion," Ash sighed.

Three tall, grey-cloaked figures steered the sleighs.
Coming to a swift, practised halt which threw up a
spray of snow, they jumped down, laughing, and
released the cubs from their harness.

"Go to your father."

The young wolves surged forward and there was
much tail wagging, rolling, tumbling and licking of
faces.

Arms wide, the three cloaked figures gave cries of welcome.

"Ash, you old rat-catcher."

"It is good to see thee again."

"Sage, honoured friend!"

Ash bowed gracefully.

"Nightshade, Rough Hawk, Meliot! Let me introduce the noble Dur'ae and her wild companion."

Charli laughed out loud at that. The tall figures strode forward and threw back their hoods.

Rowan gave a gasp. The folk of Summerland she had thought breathtakingly fair, but those of Winterland were beautiful beyond words: a strange, untamed beauty, not the bright gold of summer days but the silver grace of moonlight and snow. Their skin was winter-white, their long, wild hair the diamond-starred black of midnight and their eyes glacier-blue. They bowed low and the one called Nightshade, a woman with braided tresses, spoke.

"Dur'ae, we are honoured by your gracious presence and that of your companion. And, child," she gave Rowan a warm hug, "it is *good* to see you again."

Rowan gazed up at her.

"Again?"

"You do not remember?" She pulled a scarf up over her nose and mouth."

"It was you!" Rowan cried.

"Yes, deep in the roots of the Fortress."

"How can this be?" exclaimed Rough Hawk, moving forward. "The Dur'ae in Midwinterland? In the Impenetrable Fortress?"

"I was on a seeking mission, many moons ago. At first I thought you were one of the Lost Children. It was only when Ash appeared that I understood who you were."

The Fair Folk gazed down at Rowan. She blushed, stepped back awkwardly.

"Come," said Nightshade, with a kind smile, "I can see you are shivering. We have brought wild-wool cloaks and honoured furs to wrap you in. The Midwinter plateau is as beautiful and as merciless as any ice maiden. Without suitable raiment you will not long survive."

The Winterlanders led the girls to the sleigh and bundled them into soft lined boots and gloves, fur hoods and thick wrappings. They brought out silver flasks of hot mulled wine and warm parcels of fragrant honey cakes.

"Oh my goodness, I can feel me toes at last," Charli sighed, cramming a cake into her mouth.

Rowan smiled. "I know what you mean. I didn't think I'd ever be warm again."

Wet noses pushed their way into the sleigh, sniffing into blankets and coverings. Rowan squealed in delight as several large wolf cubs tried to squeeze into the seat. "Oh, aren't they adorable."

"Bet they want cake," said Charli, grinning.

"Children, children," a deep voice rebuked. Sage stepped forward. "Do not dishonour the Dur'ae."

"Father," cried one panting eagerly. "We meant no disrespect."

"We wished to greet the Dur'ae."

"And honour the cake."

Rowan and Charli laughed and fed sticky morsels to wet, pink tongues.

"Sage, don't scold them," Rowan begged. "Tell me their names."

Sage, standing tall and proud, said, "I hardly know them, they have grown so big."

"Father, of course you know us!"

"He'd never forget your smell!"

"Or your ugly mush!"

"She called me ugly."

"Too right!"

"Remember your manners, children. Be still; the Dur'ae wishes to greet you." The cubs quietened down and gazed up at Rowan. "Well now," Sage continued. "This rascal with the ragged ear is Rush; that handsome fellow with silver fur is Moon; this clever cub, who wins twice as much honey cake as her brothers and misses nothing, is Flint, and the one who sits back watching so thoughtfully is Grey Paw."

The wolf cubs wagged their tails.

"Greetings, Dur'ae."

"Welcome to Midwinter."

"Is there more cake?"

"Rush!"

"Sorry, Father."

"Attend, now!" said Sage. "We are ready to travel. Back to the sledges."

The Fair Folk hitched the wolves into their harness.

Ash leapt into the driving seat of the sleigh and flung a rug over his knees.

"What about the ponies?" asked Rowan, turning to look.

"Poor creatures," said Ash. "They do not travel well over deep snow and ice. Meliot bears gifts from Lord Medick to the Summer Folk; he will lead them back to our Lady's realm."

Rowan watched as a Winterlander, with hair down to his waist, mounted the fairy horse and led the ponies back towards the rocky cleft.

"We didn't say goodbye," said Charli, looking after them sadly.

There was a jangle of harness as Ash took up the reins, the bellow of reindeer, an excited volley of barks from Rush, whoops from Nightshade and Rough Hawk, then with a swooping sensation the sleigh surged forward, flanked by the sledges, and at once the party was flying over the snow.

The gentle rocking of the sleigh lulled Rowan and, tired out, she slept. By the time she awoke the sky was full of stars.

"I've never seen so many," she murmured.

"Do you speak, little Dur'ae?" asked Ash, from beneath his hood.

"There must be more stars in Midwinterland than in our world," she said.

"Ah, yes," Ash sighed. "Your nights are full of electric lights. How sad it made me to see the stars so dimmed."

"It seems there are a lot of sad things in my world," said Rowan.

"Yes, child."

Rowan gazed out at the snowy landscape, silvery-pale beneath the stars.

"And the people there seem to be good at making things, well, ugly, somehow."

"Often, Dur'ae."

But for the jangling of the traces and the soft swish of runners on snow, all was silent.

"Ash, do you…" Rowan began, then bit her lip.

"Speak, child."

"Do you think I can, really do, what I have to do?"

"I don't know."

"But I have to try, right?"

It seemed many minutes later before he spoke again. "Yes, Rowan, you have to try."

They saw the Hall of Light long before they arrived. The Winterlanders' great dwelling shone, in the distance, pale and mysterious, like a moonlit tor, lit from within by a soft radiance. It was encircled by what, at first, looked like a silver forest, intertwined branches and glittering needles reaching up to the sky. But, when they drew close, Rowan saw that the trees were carved from ice and functioned as a defence.

Ornate, curving gates opened to admit the party, and they entered a wide avenue which made its way, between the shimmering trees, to the foot of the barrow. Close up, Rowan understood just how big the structure was, like a great hill. A broad flight of ice-hewn steps rose towards a grand entrance and, as Nightshade and Rough Hawk escorted their guests down from the sleigh and up the staircase, the doors opened.

The party passed through the entrance into a vast garden, lit by a thousand flickering tapers. Rowan gasped. It must be open to the sky, for she could see the star-flecked night above, but then she realised that the arching roof was topped by a great dome of clear ice. The chamber was verdant with trees and plants. Rowan could hear the sound of running water, smell the perfume of flowers, feel the warmth of a summer's night. At the very centre stood a huge sculpture: a glimmering, silver-gold tree, so delicately rendered, one could see each twig, each fruit, each leaf, each vein.

It was the Tree of Life.

"It's warm here," said Charli, pulling off her coat.

"Yes," agreed Rowan, following suit. Two young men stepped forward and bore away the thick wrappings.

"Noble Dur'ae, you are tired," said Nightshade. "But Lord Medick has asked to see you, if you are willing."

Rowan nodded. The two Fair Folk bowed and led the party to the far side of the hall. Here they paused before another set of fine wood-carved doors.

Hawk made a gesture, uttered some words and slowly the doors opened.

Rowan gulped, but Sage was at her side.

"Walk with me, child," he murmured.

Rowan moved forwards into a second smaller hall. It was hung with tapestries and greenery and lit with many tall candles. Harp music played and there was dancing, far more stately than the raucous ceilidh of Summerland. The Midwinter Folk were dressed in elegant robes of silver tissue and pale blue silk.

A ripple of sound passed through the room and all eyes turned in Rowan's direction. The music ceased. The dancers parted before the newcomers. Rowan swallowed hard, feeling very small.

Nightshade led the way forward to a raised dais. Sitting on a simple wooden throne was a man clad in a silver-green robe, his long iron-grey hair crowned with a circlet of holly.

Nightshade bowed her head.

"Lord, we have brought the child."

The man rose to his feet. His face shone like moonlight, and to Rowan he seemed young and old all at the same time.

"A child in form, but at heart one of the ancient ones." He bowed down low. "Welcome, Dur'ae, guardian of the Tree, last hope of the Fair Folk. Welcome to the Hall of Light."

"Thank you," Rowan whispered.

"You bear the light of hope in these dark and difficult times. Your task is not an easy one, but you carry the faith and trust of many hearts."

Blushing furiously, Rowan bowed in return. "I will do my b-best," she stammered.

Lord Medick smiled.

"Dur'ae, we will do all we can to help you. Come, you and your companions, whom I know and love well, shall share some supper with me and then you must rest in preparation for the journey ahead."

How long she dwelt in the Halls of Light Rowan could not tell. As in Summerland, time had an uncanny, fluid quality. She remembered days where she and Charli romped with Sage and the wolf cubs, and other days where they learned how to steer a sledge and to kindle a fire on the ice. She was taken, by Nightshade and Rough Hawk, to collect warm reindeer milk and musk ox fleece from the companion herds. Nightshade, and a very handsome green-eyed Winterlander called Larch, taught her how to use a sling and throw a dagger. There were nights of music and song and story-telling, when fires blazed high and goblets overflowed with sweet white wine. There were solemn starlit evenings spent wandering through the fairy-lit halls with Ash, marvelling at the spiralling sculptures of snow wolves, ice bears, narwhals and mermaids. She would stop before the ice figures and wonder at the changing light flickering in their depths.

Once, Lord Medick and Nightshade took Rowan and Charli to a great room filled with scrolls and papers where white-robed Winter Folk sat poring over their books. Unrolling a piece of parchment, he showed the girls an illustration of the Impenetrable Fortress, a huge structure that boasted many jagged towers, spires and turrets.

"Nightshade has told me, child, how she first encountered you in the shifting maze beneath this fortress."

"Yes," said Rowan. "We can get in the same way, can't we, the way Nightshade showed me?"

"Alas, no," said Nightshade. "Some of the tunnels to the maze have been destroyed. They are no longer passable."

Then how?

But she didn't say it out loud.

Lord Medick placed his hand on her shoulder. "Dur'ae, do not doubt yourself. You have been inside the Fortress of Ice and survived. Few can make that claim."

At last, everything was prepared. Two sledges, pulled by Sage and the wolf cubs, had been packed with necessary equipment: one to carry Nightshade and the children, the other for Ash, Larch and Rough Hawk. Rowan and Charli had each been presented with a set of clothes comprising tunic, trousers, boots, gloves and a hooded jacket. "Your own Honoured Furs, tailored by our most skilful needlewrights. These will protect you from the very worst that our beautiful, merciless motherland might throw at us.

"They're lovely," said Rowan, stroking the fur-lined hood.

"Why d'you call 'em Honoured Furs, though?" Charli asked, trying on the jacket.

"Ah, my wild friend," Nightshade laughed. "The folk of Midwinterland do not kill any living creature. It would be like slaying kin. It is against our deepest nature. Beautiful as she is, Midwinter is a perilous mistress. We depend on the wool of the companion herds and animal furs for protection and warmth, but we take only the pelts of those who die a natural death. We honour them indeed, for their death enables our life."

"I like it better that way," said Rowan.

"You bet," said Charli. "Wouldn't do it to our cats 'n' dogs, would we?"

"I should hope not," exclaimed Ash, who had just come in through the door. "The very thought makes me shudder!"

32

FOG

————◆————

A S THE MIDWINTER PLATEAU FLUSHED WITH
the light of dawn, two wolf-drawn sledges
emerged from the silver forest encircling the Fairy
Hall. They were followed by a sombre party, with
Lord Medick at its head.

Rowan and Charli, wrapped in furs, sat in the lead
sledge, driven by Nightshade. Lord Medick spoke,
his voice deep and gentle. "You know your task, my
children: to travel to the Fortress of Ice that lies beyond
the eastern reaches of our land. The companions,
Sage and his cubs, Ash and Nightshade, Larch and
Rough Hawk, shall carry you as far as they are able,
but then you may have to proceed alone. My gift to
you is this: the Arak-nus are waiting and watching,
but in their pride they are watching for might. This
is their weakness. They will be blind to that which,
in their eyes, appears small and insignificant. This
knowledge is your power, a power beyond that of
lords, or monarchs, or kingdoms. Use it well."

He stepped back and bowed low, as did his cohort.

"Farewell, Rowan of the Dur'ae and Charli of the
Wandering Folk. Our debt to you is limitless and our
fate, the fate of all the worlds, lies in your hands. May
you be blessed."

Larch and Nightshade gave wild haloos, and the sledges set off into the rising sun.

Looking back, Rowan could see the Lord of Midwinter and his attendants standing tall and proud, their hands raised in sorrowful farewell.

That first day Rowan felt light-hearted, almost dazzled by the excitement of travel and adventure. The snowy plateau glittered in the sunlight, and as the morning advanced the sky became a deep azure blue. To the far north-east the White Mountains gleamed, and to the south-east she could see the outlines of hills fringed with pines. Occasionally, the girls saw herds of deer, far off in the distance, or snow geese flying overhead, and once she glimpsed a white fox loping up a steep snowy bank. She loved the jangle of the harness and the effortless grace and strength of the wolves: Sage, huge and powerful, and Grey Paw, slender and resolute, bearing their load so courteously.

She liked Nightshade too, loved her bright eyes and her warm voice, full of humour. She pointed out things in the white landscape that Rowan would never have noticed: a snow plover nesting amongst a cluster of rocks, lichen growing beneath the snow crust, a silver hare crouching in a hollow, the paw print of a winter leopard. She told them folk stories: some silly, of Old Treeth, the thick-headed trow, who gobbled up a pile of boulders thinking it was a herd of wild pigs; some scary, such as the tale of the ice ghouls who sucked out your heart while you slept; and others, like the legend of the mermaid who fell in love with a fisherman, were simply sad, for the maid got entangled in an abandoned net and starved to death. When the fisherman found her body washed up on the shore, it was as light and husky as a dried starfish, but the hair shone like spun gold.

On they went, the blades of the sledge whisking, smooth and steady, over the hard snow. Rowan marvelled at the staying power of the white wolves, the easy sinuous motion as they raced ever-onwards towards their goal.

The south-eastern hills were drawing near now. Features became discernible: the size and shape of trees, clefts and gullies in the snow, ice caves and overhangs. The sun rose to its highest point, then began its slow descent towards the horizon.

Sometime later, Nightshade passed the girls parcels of food and drink: hot sweet milk and dried-fruit cakes. As they ate, they watched the sky and the snow turn silver, then pink, then gold.

"It's so beautiful," Rowan whispered.

Charli smiled and laid her dark head on Rowan's shoulder.

It wasn't until the sun had dipped below the horizon, and the first stars were appearing in the indigo sky, that the sledges came to a halt.

"We'll make a brief camp," Nightshade explained, "cook up some broth, let the wolves feed and rest a while, then continue our journey."

"We're travelling in the dark?" said Rowan. Nightshade nodded, her expression firm.

"We must make haste to give you every advantage, allow you to slip in under the noses of the Arak-nus, before they turn their bloated, hungry gaze to the Fair Realms."

The party camped in a copse of resin-scented firs which grew atop a low hill. The Winterlanders raised a sturdy half-shelter of birch poles and scraped hide and kindled a cheering fire. The wolves crept close and the girls found themselves nestled between breathing coverlets of warm white fur.

"Won't you get tired, Sage, running through the night?" Rowan murmured, resting her head upon his broad neck.

"Ah no, child," Sage answered, his voice a soft rumble. "We are used to travelling great distances and, besides, this is Midwinter, our home. The very air here gives us strength."

"It's breathtaking. I didn't think it would be so lovely," sighed Rowan.

"There is a Winter Folk song," said Ash, his yellow eyes dancing in the firelight, "about the uncanny beauty of Midwinterland."

"Only one?" laughed Nightshade. "I swear there are one hundred."

"Or one thousand!" said Larch with a grin.

"I meant," Ash continued, "the one that begins 'O, Lady of Winter, so pale and so fair'…"

"Ah yes," said Larch, pulling out a wooden flute, "I will gladly play if Nightshade will honour us with her voice."

"Beware the croaking of frogs," cried Rough Hawk, slapping Nightshade on the back.

Nightshade bowed low. "Well, 'tis either the frog's croak, the hawk's shriek or the cat's meow, and I would spare my friend's blushes."

"Let the Dur'ae choose," pronounced Larch.

"Well," Rowan began, shyly, "I would like to hear Nightshade sing, and anyway I… I quite like frogs."

The company laughed out loud at that. "Ah," cried Ash. "The frog it shall be then!"

But, when Nightshade sang, her voice was clear and rich with emotion.

Oh silver breast of virgin snow,
Oh maid and mother, O winter crone,
Your frost white arms
Shall call me home,
To where the snow is falling, falling.

When Nightshade came to the end of her song, Rowan had tears in her eyes and even Charli was brushing something hurriedly away from her cheek. The rest of the company were deep in thought, staring into the flames of the fire.

The moon was high in the sky by the time they recommenced their journey.

"We will skirt the edge of the southern hill-lands under the cover of night," said Nightshade. "You must try to sleep, for we will not stop again 'til morning."

At first, Rowan thought she would never be able to sleep. The velvet sky was dusted with stars, and the two girls gazed up at them in wonder. They spent a long time making shapes and patterns from the constellations.

"That one's like a horse," said Charli. "See, there's its head, with the flowing mane, and those nine stars are its tail."

"Oh yes," nodded Rowan. "And over there, look, that is like a hare with two bright ears sticking straight up."

"That one's a fish with silver scales."

"There's a tree with branches of white fire."

"And look, oh, Ro! Those stars are falling."

Away, near to the horizon, streaks of lights were arcing downwards to the Earth, one or two descending slowly, then a sudden, glorious shower.

"Why do stars fall?" Charli asked in awe.

"They're meteors, not stars; at least in our world that's what they'd be."

"Meteors?"

"Pieces of rock and dust from space, falling through the Earth's atmosphere."

"In our world," said Nightshade, "they are omens of great change."

Rowan swallowed. "Change? For good or bad?"

Nightshade fixed her eyes on the far horizon and shook her head. "It would take someone of great skill and understanding, perhaps Lord Medick himself, to interpret such a phenomenon. But, whether for good or ill, we can be certain change will come."

After that, the girls fell silent, each thinking their own private thoughts, and not long after, lulled by the gentle motion of the sledge, they fell asleep.

Rowan remembered waking briefly to see the sun rise, red and livid above the eastern horizon. The fiery glow was reflected by lowering clouds coming in fast from the north and, far, far in the distance, she could see snaking ripples of light. The wolf-drawn sledges made their way into a narrow, high-sided valley and passed under an overhang of ice into a cave.

A fire was lit and Sage and his cubs settled down beside it. The Midwinter Folk prepared themselves beds of fir-branches covered with hide. Ash came and tucked the furs more closely about Rowan and Charli.

"Go back to sleep. We are to rise when the sun is well past the meridian. Now that we have turned north it is wise not to travel in the broad daylight hours."

Rowan slept once more, and dreamt that she was chasing a silver hare through a labyrinth of green ice, tunnel after tunnel, branching and twisting, flickering with strange light.

"Where are you taking me? Where?" and the hare gave a cry that sounded like "Finn, Finn!" And Rowan was sure that a magical fire was burning at the heart of the maze, casting its iridescent glow upon the walls.

Rowan awoke to the sound of voices and the spitting crackle of new pine branches on the fire. The cave was filled with flickering light and shadows and the oily scent of resin. She sat up and stretched. Beside her, Charli stirred, turned over and settled down again amongst the soft furs.

"Ah, the Dur'ae is awake," said Nightshade, tending to the fire. "Are you ready to break your fast?" Next to her squatted Rough Hawk, turning golden drop cakes on a hot griddle-stone. Two wolf cubs watched eagerly, licking their lips. Rowan flung the covers aside, stepped down from the sledge and moved close to the fire, feeling the smarting heat against her face.

"Here," said Nightshade, handing her a cup and bowl. "Hot spiced milk and griddle-cakes with honey."

Rowan began to eat, savouring the warm fragrance of the scones. The cubs, Rush and Moon, crept close, eyes following her every move; cup to lips, hand to bowl, food to mouth. At Sage's rumble of displeasure they backed away, but still their yellow eyes gazed longingly.

"Don't be angry with them, Sage. I don't mind, really."

"You are kind, child, but they have eaten well and as wolves of Midwinter they must learn to master their bellies. This is a serious task, given by the Lord and Lady of the Fair Lands. Much responsibility has been placed on their shoulders; they must carry the Dur'ae to the appointed place. Now is not the time to dwell on their appetites; they would do better to meditate on the urgency of their task."

The wolf cubs hung their heads.

"Sorry, Father," they murmured. "We shall do as you bid."

Rowan smiled gently at the cubs, and to draw Sage's attention from them asked, "So, how much further do we have to travel?"

"If we leave here by mid-afternoon we should pass the Dragon's Throat by sunset and reach the Black Sea before morning. However, the weather is closing in. Snow storms are threatening. In such conditions it is difficult to judge."

"What is the Dragon's Throat?" Rowan asked apprehensively. "It doesn't exactly sound fun."

"It is a broad pass marking the eastern border of Midwinterland, where the southern uplands come within a league of the northern foothills. It has long been protected by Lord Medick's power, and the Dark Folk who serve the Arak-nus dare not penetrate. Yet, beyond the Dragon's Throat, many unearthly things walk, and then we must beware."

When Rowan peered out of the cave mouth she saw that the weather had indeed changed. The clouds were low and heavy, tinged with yellow and the distances were obscured by a greyish mist.

"We must not tarry," said Larch. "The north sends snow."

"Indeed," nodded Rough Hawk, gravely. "A gift we could have done without."

The Winterlanders packed up camp quickly, dousing the fire, buckling the wolves into their harness, strapping packs onto sledges.

Rowan and Charli once more snuggled down between layers of warm fur, and Nightshade gave the call to depart.

As they set off Rowan noticed that the sledges were drawing sharply away from the southern hills.

"Are we changing direction?" she asked.

"Yes," said Nightshade with a grim smile. "We are travelling north."

"Into the bad weather?"

"Alas, yes. We felt it was safer to cut across the Dragon's Throat and stay this side of the divide. Only then shall we head north-east into the Hungry Lands."

Despite being warm in her cocoon of rugs and blankets, Rowan felt a chill around her heart.

Almost at once, the weather turned treacherous. Dark, sickly clouds sent down a blizzard of snow which filled eyes, nose and mouth and obscured the landscape ahead. How did Nightshade and the wolves know where they were going? All Rowan could see were shifting curtains of grey snow. Yet the sledges kept pressing on, two dark smudges on an endless plane of white.

"It's like nothin' else exists," Charli said.

"Oh, what a horrible idea," cried Rowan, shivering.

On and on the sledges went, wolves ploughing through the new snow, runners sending up a shower of flakes. Ahead, they could see the other sledge and occasionally heard the sound of a horn being blown. Nightshade responded with a small silver-tipped instrument of her own, which hung on a belt at her waist.

"What're you doing?" asked Charli.

"Signalling," Nightshade replied. "Larch is telling me what direction he intends to take or what he can see ahead."

"Well, I could tell you that," said Charli. "Snow, snow, and more snow."

Nightshade laughed. "I can see you are a winter warrior in the making."

The journey seemed endless. There was something unnerving, almost hypnotic, about plunging ever forward into nothingness. Rowan had to close her eyes every now and then just to escape from the relentless wall of grey.

Eventually, the snow seemed to ease and yet visibility did not improve, for a heavy mist was descending fast. It clung to them, icy and suffocating.

"I do not like this fog," said Nightshade, frowning and shaking her head.

They heard Larch sound the horn. There was a sudden violent jolt and the sledge was thrown onto its side. Rowan felt herself rolling over and over in the snow. She heard the wolves yelp and scramble, heard Charli cry out, then Nightshade was calling, "Dur'ae, where are you?"

Rowan sat up, her head spinning. She had been thrown clear of the sledge and thankfully the snow had cushioned her fall. She wriggled free of the coverings and looked around. Over to the left, there was a long bundle in the snow. It groaned. Somewhere in the swirling mist Nightshade called, "Dur'ae, Dur'ae, are you there?" Yet her voice seemed faint and far away. The mist was so thick now that Rowan could see no more than a few paces ahead.

"I'm here!" Rowan shouted.

She crawled to the groaning shape. It was Charli, face down in the snow, fur hood covering her eyes.

"Charli, are you okay?" Rowan gasped, rolling the gypsy girl onto her back.

Charli groaned again, "These bleedin' blankets, I can't move. Me arms are totally pinned."

Rowan tugged at the woollen wrappings. "Are you in pain?"

Charli gave a lop-sided smile, "Nah, I just feel like a jam roly-poly, an' I don't mean I'm hungry!"

At last, Rowan managed to pull the blankets loose.

"So what happened?" Charli asked, sitting up.

Rowan shook her head, "We hit something, a rock, I suppose. Are you sure you're okay, Char?"

"Yeah, course."

They heard the far-off sound of a horn.

"That must be Nightshade and the others looking for us."

"This mist is dead creepy," said Charli. "I can't see a thing."

"Nightshade!" Rowan cried. "Over here!"

They listened hard, but could hear no response.

"That's so weird. They can't be that far away. Why can't they find us?"

"Well, let's find the sledge; they're bound to make for that," Charli suggested.

"Okay, but we better take the rugs and furs. We'd probably never find them again."

"Good idea," said Charli, crawling out of her wrappings. The girls rolled the covers into two neat bundles and tucked them under their arms.

"So, which way?" said Rowan.

Wherever they turned, they were confronted with an oppressive curtain of fog.

"We'll follow the markings in the snow, where we rolled. The sledge turned right over; it should be pretty close."

They pursued the tracks their bodies had made but these soon petered out to nothing. They looked out over a blanket of virgin whiteness, unmarked by feet, or runners, or paw prints.

"This just isn't right," said Rowan. "There should be something, some sign that the sledge was here."

"An' it's so quiet."

"And so cold," said Rowan, shuddering.

The mist was swirling around them, growing thicker. Rowan had a sudden sense of dread. They were lost; two insignificant dots in the middle of a vast landscape of ice and snow. They had nothing: no shelter, no fire, no food, no compass, not even a sense of direction. How long could they hope to last? A night, a day? And if they had been lost so easily in this terrible mist, how could they ever hope to be found again? Ash, Nightshade, Larch and Rough Hawk might, at this very moment, be roaming the icy wastes, drawing further away with every step.

Rowan gulped. There was a sharp lump at the base of her throat. "Charli," she whispered, "I think we're lost."

A voice in the mist echoed her words: "Lost... lost... lost... lost..."

"What was that?" Charli hissed.

"Was that... that... that...?" The voice picked up the sibilant urgency of Charli's tone.

Rowan stared hard into the formless, drifting clouds of fog.

"Perhaps just an echo," she said, trying to be brave.

"Echo... echo... echo..." The word was uttered with a sighing, sinister intent.

The girls stepped back, dropping their bundles, grasping each other tightly. But from behind them another voice sighed, "Lost... lost... lost..."

"What do you want?" Charli demanded through chattering teeth.

"Want... want... want..."

This voice came from their left, and from their right a fourth took up the cry, "Lost... lost... lost..."

Charli scrabbled at her belt. "The daggers," she hissed. "From Summerland!"

Rowan followed her example. The belt was tucked deep under her Midwinter jacket, but eventually she pulled the ornate dagger from its sheath. It glinted in her hand like summer sunlight on water and for a brief moment there was the scent of meadowsweet and roses in the air.

She heard a low, fearful hiss and then silence.

The girls circled back to back, golden daggers held ready. Rowan stared into the dense, murky greyness, searching for movement, for shape. She felt blind, suffocated. The whole world was reduced to this pale, shifting void. Only Charli was real, with her snarling lips and fierce black eyes.

The laughter was soft and cold. At first it sounded like a sighing wind, a constant note low and eerie, but soon took on a mocking tone.

"Lost," it breathed. "Lost... Lost..."

And in the mist Rowan could see faces; pale women with long white hair streaming out behind them. "We want... we want... we want..."

Small white hands reached out towards her, beseeching. "So cold... so cold... so cold..."

The eyes were large and shadowy in their ice-blue faces, full of sadness and despair. Rowan felt a pang of pity.

"What do you want?" she gasped.

"Want... want... want..." The hollow mouths echoed back.

"Rowan, don't!" Charli cried.

"But they seem so..."

"Don't trust 'em. Look at their feet!"

Rowan glanced down and flinched in horror. Beneath the ragged hems of misty gowns were thin, skeletal toes.

There was a chilling cry. The faces began to alter, grew sunken, hollow, mask-like. The jaws dropped down, black and yawning.

"Lost..." they wailed. "Lost... lost..." And their voices were pitiless.

"Oh God, Charli," Rowan cried.

"Keep your dagger high. They don't like 'em."

Rowan waved the glinting blade before her and the creatures drew back, baring sharp teeth. But soon they were advancing, their black mouths exhaling a foul stench.

"Lost…" they hissed. "We hunger… how we hunger."

The foul things drew near, and their eyes were black pits drawing all light into their depths. Rowan couldn't look away. Something compelled her to gaze into the gaping sockets. She shuddered and put her hand to her face. A dreadful thought struck her; she could feel the skull beneath her skin. Their mocking voices were at her ear: "As we are, so shall you become." Her hands began to shake uncontrollably. "Your death lies within."

"Rowan!" She could hear Charli's voice, but the world was spinning. "Rowan, use the dagger!"

But it was useless. Her hands were numb. She felt the blade fall from her fingers and yawning death loomed over her, its thin, icy claws at her throat.

"We want… we want…"

So cold, so cold. Fingers like ice, freezing the breath in her lungs. She gasped for air. The cold had reached deep inside. She felt a searing pain in her chest, struggled to breathe, then swirling horror as she tumbled down into darkness.

Far away, a horn sounded.

33

THE BLACK SEA

A BITTER TASTE EXPLODED ON ROWAN'S
tongue. She coughed and gulped and opened her
eyes. Nightshade was leaning over her with a cup, and
just behind she could see Ash and Charli and the other
Winterlanders, their faces pale with worry.

"She's all right, oh my God!" cried Charli. Rowan
tried to sit up, but the world was spinning and she fell
back heavily.

"Steady, Dur'ae," said Nightshade. "You will be
weak for some time."

"What happened?" asked Rowan.

"There was an attack," Nightshade said. "They
drew power from you."

"What are those things?" she whispered,
shuddering.

Without expression, Nightshade answered, "Lych
Folk. Undead spirits. They guard the approaches to the
White Mountains, where the Impenetrable Fortress lies."

"Yet," put in Rough Hawk, frowning, "I have
never known them to cross the Dragon's Throat into
Midwinterland."

"Can you be so sure that we have not crossed over
into the east lands?" asked Larch. "That was a fell
mist."

"Indeed," said Sage. "We lost all scent in that foul fog. It corrupts the senses."

"Aye," agreed Ash. "There was something unnatural about it. It seemed to swallow up your sledge in a moment. We could neither see nor hear you, nor find any trace."

"If it had not been for the glint of that dagger," said Rough Hawk, nodding at Charli's blade, "like a dim flame in the gloom, we should not have..." He stopped at a stern look from Nightshade. Rowan turned her gaze from one face to the other.

"Should not have what?" she asked, shivering.

Nightshade shook her head gravely. "It is not the time to speak of such things. No doubt we have been led astray, but there is a change coming, a fresh wind blows. See, the mist is dispersing and the clouds overhead break. Soon we shall be able to navigate by the stars. We must turn to the east and hope to reach the shores of the Black Sea by morning."

⸻

In the clear, cold night the sledges flew over the snow. There was a real sense of urgency now. Rowan could see it in the cast of Nightshade's face: the set mouth, the determined brow, the glimmer in her eye, cold as moonlight. The girls did not try to talk to her. They pulled the covers close and spoke in whispers.

"What did happen, Char, when that thing... touched me?"

Charli shuddered. "D'you really want to know?"

"Yes."

"It weren't... pretty."

"But no one else will tell me. They all want to protect me, I suppose. But not knowing is worse."

Charli sighed. "Well, that makes sense."

"So?"

"I tell you, Ro..." she shivered again. "D'you remember me telling you to use the dagger?"

"Yes."

"They really didn't like those fairy blades. I couldn't hurt them, exactly; the dagger just went through, but it made them draw away, like they was afraid. But you, you began to listen... to the horrible voices; you kind of wilted and the dagger dropped. They was all over you and it was like something was being sucked from your body, or, like they was feeding on you. Your face went, went..." Charli closed her eyes for a moment. "You looked like them, all pale and hollow and awful. I'm not sure what happened next; there was this incredible bright light at your throat and they screamed, something dreadful to hear, and suddenly pulled back. Then I heard the horn, and those things began wailing and shrieking like they were going mad. I had to cover my ears 'cause it made me feel sick to the stomach. Then the others were there with swords and fire and the creatures just fled."

Rowan stared out into the darkness, her body feeling as light and frail as an empty shell. There was a dull cold ache beneath her ribs; her thoughts were like tattered ribbons.

"Are you all right, Ro?"

For a long time Rowan said nothing. Thoughts shivered, snagged, were snatched away by the wind. She made a strenuous effort to focus her mind.

"I… I just… don't know… if I can do this."

Charli took her hand. "Well, for a start it's 'we'; *we* don't know if *we* can do this, okay?"

And in spite of herself Rowan smiled.

The first thing Rowan was aware of when she opened her eyes was the sight of two tiny dots circling high up in the pale, dawn sky. Pulling herself up into a sitting position she saw, towering to the north, great mountains of ice, brooding like ancient gods, clouds of mist drifting about their summit. Directly ahead, stretching away to the eastern horizon, was a vast, dark sea over which a silver sun was rising. The waters, flat as a mirror, were an oily, menacing black, a stark contrast to the frozen landscape.

There was no identifiable shoreline. The roots of the mountain formed treacherous sea-cliffs lapped by water. But where the sledges passed, southwards, the ice levelled off into a flat and featureless plane, creating a steep shelf which plunged down vertically, some twenty or thirty feet, into the murky depths.

"It is the Black Sea," said Nightshade, gazing solemnly out to where the sun, ascending by degrees, cast a glistening, mercury path over the water's surface. "And it is deep, dark and dangerous."

"Does anything live in there?" Rowan half whispered. "It looks dead."

"Aye, many creatures live in its depths. Some fair, some foul – and far, far out, the foulest of them all, the dread Kraken."

Rowan, staring at the mirrored horizon, shuddered, half expecting to see something coiling and snake-like break the surface, but the water remained as smooth as glass.

The sledges came to a halt. Larch and Ash were discussing something with great urgency. Rough Hawk glanced skyward, his lips a hard line.

"Crow Folk," Nightshade muttered under her breath, following his gaze. Then, out loud, "Come, make haste. We must set to work."

Suddenly, everyone was busy. The wolves were unhitched; large, white leather hides were drawn over the sledges. The Winterlanders took out broad-bladed tools and set about cutting and sawing blocks of compacted snow. Rowan marvelled at the skill and speed with which they shaped the natural materials. Just moments of chiselling and they had produced a perfect snow brick. They positioned the blocks next to one another in a rising spiral, each fitting seamlessly in place, until a small sturdy dome was formed, rather like an elongated igloo.

"So who's it for?" Charli asked, her face pink with admiration. "Bit of a squeeze for all of us, innit?"

Larch looked down at the gypsy girl and smiled sadly. "Just so, brave one. It is time for us to leave you."

"Leave! Now?" Rowan felt the breath catch in her throat.

The tall winter warrior laid a hand on Rowan's shoulder and looked at her with steady, ice-green eyes. "It is time. You will be safer alone. There are Crow Folk abroad."

"Crow Folk?" Looking up, Rowan saw the dark specks moving off north, towards the mountains.

"Spies of the Hungry Ones."

"D'you think they saw us?" Charli asked.

Larch's bright eyes watched the black flecks disappear into the mists.

"Perhaps, although they are very high and we are well camouflaged, but, for your sake, we cannot risk it. A traveller on foot can conceal herself far more easily than a sledge-rider."

"So the igloo is for us?"

"Iggle-oo? Oh, you mean the ice sidhe? No, no, the snow barrow is for my sister Nightshade. She will wait here, with Flint, for your return."

Rowan gulped. And what if we don't return? The unsaid words echoed in her head. Nightshade, who had been shaping the top of the shelter, put down her blade and knelt so that her eyes were level with Rowan's.

"The Lady would not send you alone into such peril."

The warrior maid fixed her gaze on something just beyond Rowan's left shoulder, and when Rowan turned she saw Sage standing there with a handsome silver cat at his side.

"Sage! Oh, my goodness, Ash!"

"Well, I hope you didn't intend to leave us behind," Ash mewed, "just when the adventure is about to begin."

Breakfast was brief and warming: spiced wine and sweet chestnut cakes, eaten within the close confines of the ice barrow. Rowan felt safe and protected beneath the dome of bright snow, hidden from unfriendly eyes. She wished with all her heart that she could stay with Nightshade and the wolf cubs. But soon Larch was preparing a sledge for travel and repacking the girls' backpacks with extra food, flints and kindling.

Finally, the last bundle was thrown onto the toboggan, the last strap adjusted on the harness and everyone was making their farewells. Larch and Rough Hawk bowed low to the girls.

"Farewell, Dur'ae; farewell, Charli. What we owe you cannot be fashioned in words. Your gift to us is unique; simply, it is hope itself."

They jumped up onto the sledge and at once the team of harnessed wolves sprang forward, heading west. Rowan watched as they flew over the snow, the sun at their backs, and found that she was trembling.

"Come," said Sage, his voice as gentle as if he were talking to a newborn cub, as if he understood the pain in her heart.

"We, too, must say our goodbyes."

Nightshade came forward and dropped to her knees, throwing her arms around the two girls.

"I shall be on seeking duty for seven days. Lord Medick has asked me to search for another way into the Fortress. Sometimes fissures open up in the roots of the mountain."

"So, you won't be far away."

Nightshade smiled, "I'll be here," she said and pressed her palm over Rowan's heart.

They had been walking north for half a day and already Rowan felt numb with cold. Sage led them along age-old paths used by his kindred since time out of mind, long before the coming of the Arak-nus.

At first, they had journeyed over the broad, flat ice shelf that edged the waters of the Black Sea. Rowan had tried to avoid gazing at the dark, looking-glass surface, imagining all kinds of grotesque and malevolent creatures, with powerful jaws and many teeth, lurking within its depths. She had sighed with relief when they veered inland and began to climb the northern foothills. From a high vantage point the sea seemed melancholy rather than threatening, and often its view was obscured altogether by the white hilltops.

They had travelled on, climbing snowbound hill after snowbound hill, scrambling down into frozen valley after frozen valley.

Sage knew the safest routes to tread, where the snow was firm under foot and didn't plunge you waist high, or worse, into unseen hollows and crevices. Still, it was hard-going. Rowan was soon out of breath and Charli's cheeks glowed red as holly berries. Yet, on they went, another hill, another clump of stunted thorn bushes, another outcrop of ice and rock. Rowan's hands and feet began to ache with cold; the skin of her face grew raw. She tried to pull the thick cloak more securely around her shoulders, but found she needed her hands to balance and climb.

"Sage, my good friend, should we not stop and rest for a short time at least? The child is still weak from the attack," implored Ash, his eyes uncharacteristically dim.

"It is not far now," said Sage, pressing onwards.

Ash dropped back to Rowan's side. His silver paws barely broke the snow crust. He leapt from mound to mound with ease. Rowan, puffing and wheezing as she struggled up another incline, sighed. "I feel like an elephant compared to you, Ash."

He mewed, "A fitting comparison, my friend, if the elephant were particularly unfit and cumbrous."

"I'd throw a snowball at your head," Rowan said with a faint smile. "But I'm too tired."

"And, of course, you'd miss. I'm so exceedingly nimble."

At last, Sage came to a halt.

"It is here," he said.

Drawing level with the wolf, Rowan and Charli stared at a hole in the hillside.

"Oh," said Charli.

Ash padded forward. "Ah, I sense glamour."

"A simple protection rune. The Midwinter Folk have used this dwelling since the ancient days."

Ash sniffed the mouth of the cave. "Slightly musty, but serviceable," he pronounced and disappeared into the gloom. "You follow, Dur'ae."

Stooping down and moving forward Rowan found herself in darkness, but slowly her eyes adjusted and she emerged into a small comfortable cave with a dry stone floor and a shaft of light coming from above.

"S'nice an' cosy," said Charli, behind.

"And relatively clean," Ash purred.

Sage was last through the tunnel mouth. "Alas, we cannot stay here long. But at least you can light a fire and prepare hot food without fear of being seen."

There was a large pile of dry sticks and thorn branches stored at the back of the cave. The girls carried wood to the sunny patch of floor and carefully laid a fire, then sparked flints into the kindling. Soon there was a healthy blaze and the smoke rose, escaping via the opening in the roof. They scraped snow into a billycan and added some of the grains, herbs and roots provided by the Winterlanders. It cooked down into a thick warming broth, which the girls sipped from small wooden bowls clutched between their hands, sharing the last drop with Ash, who wiped it from his whiskers with a dainty silver paw.

"Tell you what," said Charli, stretching out and yawning, "I could stay here right now."

"Oh yes, and sleep," nodded Rowan resting her head on her rucksack.

Sage, keeping watch at the cave entrance, turned and padded back towards the fire.

"Yet, Dur'ae, we must go on if we mean to reach the eagle's peak before sunset."

Why was it, Rowan wondered, that warm, fed and rested, the second half of the day's journey seemed so much harder than the first? Her legs protested at every step. She gritted her teeth and forced her knees and feet to wade through patches of deep snow, to clamber up rock faces, to slip and slide along vast sheets of ice. Sometimes, Sage was there at her side. "Lean on me," he said in his deep, tender voice, and he would steady her on treacherous paths, bear her weight on arduous ascents. It seemed to go on forever, this impossible task of forcing one foot in front of the other and battling onwards against the searing cold. Cold, she thought, not like that of the north wind blowing poor robin redbreast off his perch, but like the very breath of Winter herself, a frozen exhalation, turning the pulse of all living things to ice.

Sunset was approaching when Sage altered course and led the party to the top of a hill crowned with rocks.

"Keep low," he warned. "Stay hidden in the shadows."

Peering over the craggy edge, both girls gasped. Far, far below, where titanic cliffs of ice – the very skirts of the White Mountains – plunged down into the deathly waters of the Black Sea, a fortress had been built. Its outer walls rose up sheer and featureless for hundreds of feet, before suddenly becoming an over-elaborate display of gigantic towers, crenellated turrets and teeth-sharp spires. The structure was carved from the ice yet, oddly, assumed a skeletal hue – all light consumed by the bone-white surface. There was only one entrance: a vast, studded, iron-black door set into the great ice wall.

Rowan and Charli drew back, shivering. "How on earth are we gonna get in there?" Charli whispered.

Rowan shook her head dumbly.

"Come," said Sage. "We must climb up to the eagle's eyrie. She nests on yonder peak."

Rowan didn't see how she could walk another step, but somehow her feet obeyed her and on the party went, following Sage up the mountain.

The way was becoming increasingly steep and perilous. The paths had dwindled into narrow goat runs and sometimes the track disappeared altogether. They had to scramble up high slopes, edge their way along narrow ledges, climb precipitous rock faces. Sage pressed on and the moon rose, silver-green, throwing deep shadows onto the frozen ground, but where the snow caught the light it sparkled, emerald and pearl. They were crossing a level area, a tiny plateau, surrounded on all sides by sheer cliff faces and sharp peaks, when Sage froze. Something was travelling fast towards them over the snow, a dark shape, clearly visible against the white background. Its size and form altered as it approached.

"What is it?" Rowan cried breathlessly.

"It makes no noise!" hissed Ash.

But, as if in answer, there came a chilling shriek from above.

"Crow Folk!" Sage howled to the skies.

Rowan's head jerked up. A black shape covered the moon, wings vast, claws glittering.

Charli grabbed her hand. "Run!"

Yet, suddenly, the world did not make sense. Rowan's legs had turned to ice, rooted to the frozen mountain.

"Rowan, come on!" Charli was tugging at her arm, but all Rowan could see were black, ragged feathers edged with silver.

"Rowan!"

There was a howl, a sharp hiss, a shattering croak. Sage leapt, Ash sprang forward; sharp claws flashed, needle teeth sank into a black, feathered throat, something dark gushed out onto the snow.

A second cry rang out, echoing amongst the peaks, a razor-scream of malice. Rowan's head was filled with the beating of wings.

"Dur'ae, take cover! It has a mate!"

"Rowan! Run! It's coming!" Charli shrieked.

The clack of a sharp beak, the stench of rotten meat.

Suddenly, she was running, running, running; through the snow towards a steep bank of ice fissured with narrow clefts. The adrenalin surged through her exhausted limbs, ears thrumming, heart pounding, lungs burning. A great shadow fell upon them, bearing down.

Rowan stumbled, felt Charli pull her upright. "Run!"

A word torn from her throat. "Can't!"

"You can!"

Charli gripped her wrist, dragging her forward. Rowan summoned up the last bit of energy and forced her legs to keep up.

But the great beating wings were all around. She slipped and crashed down to the ground, dragging Charli with her. Screeching, the creature tore at her back and head, piercing leather and fur. Blades of pain ripped along her spine.

Charli cursed and rolled over, the fairy dagger flashing in her hand, and suddenly the shadow lifted.

"It's getting away," warned Ash.

Dragging her head to one side, Rowan saw Sage make a monstrous leap into the air. For a moment he caught the black tail feathers between his jaws. But, with a harsh cry, the huge bird broke free and soared up into the sky.

34

GORG

━━━━◆━━━━

THE COMPANIONS WATCHED THE FOUL creature rise up towards the peaks.

"We gotta do something!" Charli cried.

"There is nothing we can do," said Sage.

"Nuffin? But it's seen us!"

"If Nightshade were here," said Ash, "she could bring it down with a single arrow."

"They'll know we're here," Charli said helplessly.

"Yes."

"So it's all for nothing."

"It is my fault," said Sage, bowing his head. "I should have warned you to keep to the shadows."

Rowan sat up, wincing with pain. "We can still go on with the plan, can't we?"

Sage looked old and grave.

"To send you into such peril…"

"Look!" cried Charli.

Rising up from the mountain summit, flickering like a bronze flame in the moonlight, came a huge winged creature. It circled above the spy-bird, making a slow, menacing arc against the evening sky. Sensing danger, the crow gave a croak of terror. It changed direction, swerved this way and that and, in a flurry of panic, dipped low, but the creature marked it skilfully, shadowing its every move.

"It is *she*," gasped Sage.

"She's toying with it," said Ash.

"Yes, and it knows."

Suddenly, the great bird swooped like a fiery comet from the heavens and, in a ragged explosion of black feathers, sank its talons into the crow.

Rowan and Charli stared up into the sky, awestruck. Feathers were falling, like soot. The enormous bird of prey circled once more, its kill clutched in a great claw, and, with broad sweeping motions, began to descend. Dropping the dead crow next to its fallen mate, the eagle landed on the plateau and folded its great golden wings.

"So," it began, in a voice as cold and brilliant as the diamond snow. "Who are you, to make such enemies of these tattered jackdaws?"

Sage bowed his head. "Lady of the White Mountains, we are travellers from Summerland."

"Summerland? Yet *you* are one of the white wolves of Midwinterland, are you not? And your companions –" she turned her glass-bead eyes on the two girls, "– seem a scrawny, changeling pair to me. Is the power of the Fair Lands fading?"

"Lady, the children are from the Other World, but one, who wears the talisman of leaves, is of the Dur'ae."

"Dur'ae?" The great eagle gave a harsh laugh and stared hard at Rowan. "This cub, this... this mouse?"

"Yes, Lady, we came here to call upon your help."

The eagle turned her head away, displaying the sharp, scimitar curve of her beak. "Take care what you ask for, wolf. It is gracious enough that I let you pass, unchallenged, through my domain.

"Lady," Ash exclaimed, impatiently, "the Dur'ae need your help. This surely you must do!"

The eagle snapped her head back, eyes blazing, her soft voice dangerous. "I know not this command '*must*', cat."

Ash arched his back. "Then you would stand by whilst Summerland, Winterland and all the worlds perish?"

The eagle viewed the silver cat with an eager glint in her eye.

"Oh, there has been talk of worlds ending and skies falling since the beginning of time, yet my mountains have ever stood."

"And while *your* mountains stand, the entire universe might perish, is that it?" Ash spat out.

The eagle rose up, wings arching in fury.

"Insolent rat!" she shrieked.

"Dare you call me a rat?" hissed Ash, showing his claws.

"Oh, don't," cried Rowan, hobbling forward. "Don't argue, please." She stood there pale, trembling.

The eagle settled back down on the ground, eyeing Rowan with curiosity.

"So, what has this little rabbit to say on the matter?"

"How dare you speak in that manner to—"

"Ash, please, hush," said Rowan. She drew herself up to her full height and faced the eagle. "All I need to know is how to get into the F-fortress of Ice."

"Hah! That is all?" There was a glint of steel in the creature's eye.

"Yes."

"And when you are there, *what* do you mean to do?"

"I mean to keep my promise, to fulfil my duty as a Dur'ae."

"To do your duty, though the Hungry Ones will snap you in half like a puny hatchling?"

"Yes." Rowan held the eagle's gaze.

"Do you wonder at the wisdom of those who set such weakness against such might?"

"The Lady of Summerland said there is a different kind of strength."

"And you believe that?"

"I believe what she said is right."

"Oh, something may be *right*, but it does not mean that it is *so*. After all it is right that a king and a pauper have an equal claim to justice, but in your world it is not so."

"Well, even if it's not p-possible, I... I still believe it's right, and... and," Rowan gulped, "that's what matters... to me."

"Well, then, Rowan of the Dur'ae." The eagle's voice was suddenly different and the glint in her eye had turned to a soft fire. "I shall grant your request, for never has so courageous a spirit been clad in such a modest form. 'Mouse' I may call you, but not without esteem, for a mouse may creep unseen into secret spaces and hidden corners; a mouse may succeed where a lion, or indeed an eagle, would fail. Now listen, and listen well. To enter the Impenetrable Fortress you must offer your services as a kitchen maid."

Rowan stared up at the great eagle open-mouthed. "But I... is that all? How do I...?"

"Hush. You have wounds that need tending, and you all need food and fire. Aye, even you, noble cat. We will talk tomorrow, but tonight you must rest. Come, I will escort you to my eyrie."

The nest was high in the mountains, far beyond the towers and turrets of the Ice Fortress. The journey there was extraordinary. The eagle had taken Rowan and Charli, one in each of her great talons, and carried them up, up, over the moonlit peaks, to a huge nest where two downy chicks squawked a welcome. In the same way she conveyed Sage and Ash, and neither girl could help laughing at the look of indignity on the silver cat's face as he was deposited next to them.

"Like eaglet supper!"

Behind the eyrie there was a sheltered cave where the girls lit a fire, cooked food and, with Sage's guidance, prepared a remedy to treat the gashes on Rowan's back.

As the night grew bitter, Rowan and Charli were invited by the eagle to share the chick's nest whilst she brooded them, and the two girls slept soundly beneath a living quilt of warm, soft feathers.

———————

Flurries of snow fell from a leaden sky as, early the following morning, Rowan and Charli crouched beneath a frozen mound. The base of the Fortress towered above them, a solid wall of ice which rose up, many hundreds of feet, from the roots of the mountain. Atop this, numerous skull-white towers thrust upwards into the sky, diminishing in a blizzard of white flakes.

The only entrance was the great iron-black gateway, into which was set a small door with a shuttered grille.

It was just before dawn. The eagle had flown the girls down the mountain, to the Fortress edge, then returned for their companions.

"How long d'you think Sage 'n' Ash are gonna be?" Charli whispered.

"Not long. Half an hour, maybe."

"But they can't come with us, can they?"

"No," said Rowan.

"So, we just gotta get on with it. Right?"

"Yes," Rowan sighed. "You're right. But maybe…"

"Maybe what?"

"… we should say goodbye."

Charli shook her head. "It'd be easier if—"

"Oh!" Rowan grabbed Charli's arm. "Look!"

The barred door opened and out trooped half a dozen small figures dressed in hooded, grey robes. They carried a wooden boat, about eight feet in length, which they set down with a thump and proceeded to drag over the snow. Their goal was an ice-encrusted jetty, thrusting out from a desolate rocky shelf into the inky waters of the Black Sea. Here they launched the vessel and leapt in. Four took up oars and began to row towards the rising sun; two sorted through a box of fishing rods, checking reels and preparing hooks with bait.

When the boat was some way out, the hooded figures took up the rods and started to fish. It was not long before the first catch was made; the rod bowed, the line tightened. Slowly but surely the fishing line was reeled in and, after a struggle, the catch broke the surface of the water. Rowan shuddered. It was a fat, pale worm, the size of a cucumber. No doubt it would be thrown back for something more appetising. But the squirming creature was unhooked and tossed into the bottom of the boat. Soon, more catches were made and the writhing heap grew in size.

Despite what Nightshade had said about the abundance of life, the waters of the Black Sea seemed to support nothing but these horrible white leeches. The odd cowled figures in the boat sat in silence; every so often their lines would jerk and were reeled in, the fat maggots plucked from the hook and flung onto the squirming pile. Even from this distance Rowan could see that the hooded figures were shaking with cold. Eventually, a signal was given by the tallest member of the group, rods were collected, oars taken up and the boat rowed back to shore. Throughout this entire procedure not a word was spoken. The boat was dragged back up the ramp and onto the snow.

The catch was tipped out onto the ground, and four of the figures lifted the boat and tramped back to the Fortress, where they were readmitted through the small iron door. The two remaining robed creatures squatted down and proceeded to gut the worms with small, sharp knives, flinging the entrails into the sea, where the waters at once churned with a mass of coiling bodies.

"Urgh," Charli could not help exclaiming. "Them things is eating their own dead."

"Hush," whispered Rowan.

One of the hooded figures looked up, knife poised in mid-air. It stared straight at them, the dark hood tilted to one side as if straining to hear. Then it dropped its head and slit the worm from top to bottom with one deft stroke. When all the catch had been cleaned, one of the figures took a folded sack out from under their robe and proceeded to fill it with the wet lumps of pale flesh. Carrying the sack between them, the two small figures started back towards the Fortress.

Suddenly, they stopped, put the sack down and one of the cowled figures moved towards the snow bank where Rowan and Charli were hiding.

"Don't move," Rowan hissed.

The figure came closer, and when it was a mere twenty or thirty feet away stopped, gathered up the lower half of its sacking robe, unbuttoned the trousers beneath and, with a strange half shiver, proceeded to pee into the snow. The deep hood fell back and Rowan saw its face.

It was a boy, a boy about her age, with cropped hair and a pale, defeated expression on his pinched face.

Before she could think, Rowan jumped up and scrambled forward.

"Whatcha doing?" Charli hissed, grabbing at Rowan's sleeve.

But it was too late: the boy had seen her. His eyes grew large with fear; his mouth gaped. He grasped the top of his trousers and turned to run.

"Wait," said Rowan. "Please."

The boy hesitated, glanced back.

"H-have you got any food?" Rowan said. "I'm hungry."

The boy shook his head, face ice-white.

"Would there be any food at that castle?"

Trembling, he whispered, "Go away."

"But I need food and shelter. I'm lost."

"Don't go there," he said. His eyes were desperate.

"Why?"

"Go away," he stuttered, shuffling backwards.

"Why shouldn't I go there?"

"Cos you won't get out." His eyes darted upwards nervously, scanning the skies.

Rowan placed a gentle hand on his shoulder. "Do they need a kitchen maid?" she asked. The boy gaped at her. "Don't," he hissed. "Leave!"

"But out here I'll die."

A strange look of longing came into the boy's eyes. He backed away, then stopped and in a hoarse, stilted voice said, "Wait 'til after we have entered. Knock on the door seven times."

He fled, pulling up his hood in a pitiful, defensive gesture. Moments later, the two robed children had been swallowed by the vast iron door.

"I'm going with you," Charli stated, looking mutinous. "Even though it was a bloomin' stupid thing to do."

Rowan smiled. "You did say we should just get on with it."

"Yeah, well, next time don't bleedin' listen to me."

Rowan gazed up at the gigantic ice-hewn castle. "I suppose this is it, then? It's time."

"Yes," said Charli, grasping her hand. "We might not feel brave enough if we wait for Sage and Ash to come back. It's time."

The two girls walked towards the towering entrance. Blind and faceless as the Fortress wall appeared, Rowan could not help feeling as if they were being watched by a thousand piercing eyes. The terrible black gates loomed over them. Rowan raised her hand, clasped the heavy iron ring and, as the poor, frightened boy had directed, knocked seven times.

The shutter on the grille was slammed open by an ugly, misshapen creature with a green, toadish face.

"It's no good; the doors are closed," it grunted at them. "You know the rules. You can't come in. It's your own fault. You'll have to stay out all day, and night, and –" it rasped with glee, "– there's a blizzard coming."

"Do you need a kitchen maid?" Rowan's voice was like a feather in the snow.

"Eh, what's this, now?" The creature gazed out at them with its bulbous, watery eye. "New, is it? Well, that's a different matter. Lost, are you? A likely story; that's what they all say. You're starving, no doubt, and cold too?"

It rattled chains and bolts and locks and the small door opened.

"Come in, then. Look sharp!"

The girls entered a great courtyard surrounded by immense walls of ice. Opposite the iron gateway three vast archways gaped darkly. The grotesque creature, slouching and hunchbacked, towered above them. It peered down with myopic, frog-like eyes.

"Have to work, that's the thing. Can't expect something for nothing, oh no. Work hard. Fingers to the bone. Let's see these hands." Rowan removed her gloves and the frog man prodded her palms with a stodgy digit.

"Soft as dough. Pah! Soon get them hardened up. But this is better, now." He turned Charli's hand over in his own and the gypsy girl shuddered at his touch.

"Rough, well-worn; you could be handy with a pick axe, but, then again, no. I need someone to feed my birdies, don't I? That stupid boy fell, broke his neck, the second in a fortnight. They're such clodhopping oafs. But you look nimble. Legs thin." He grabbed Charli's calf, squeezing hard. "But strong, yes! My black beauties need their savouries and titbits, reliable, regular."

The creature pulled an iron chain hanging against a wall and, from somewhere beyond the dark arches, a great bell clanged. "Stand here 'til they come for you, and remember this." It thrust its bloated, stinking muzzle into their faces. "I'm Gorg the Controller – understand?" Gorg flexed his fat fingers. "What? Swallowed your tongue? Do you understand?" he roared.

"Y-y-yes," stuttered the girls.

Gorg eyed them, suspicious of insolence, then grunted and passed through a side door into a room beyond. Rowan could see a sparsely furnished room. The furniture – a table, chairs, chest, bed – seemed to be rough-hewn from ice. On the table stood a large bowl of phlegm-green jelly. Gorg eased his massive frame into a chair, lifted the bowl to his lips and slurped down the meal. Rowan felt her stomach heave, but Charli stood there defiantly, pulling faces and pretending to vomit.

Not until the last mouthful was swallowed, succeeded by a thunderous belch, did anyone answer the summons. A crop-headed child, dressed in thick hessian robes and heavy boots, rushed out of the central archway, breathless and gasping. It scuttled past Rowan and Charli, stealing brief, timid glances, and entered the gate-keeper's room, making a nervous bow of deference.

Gorg clouted the child around the head, "That's for taking so long!" he growled, lumbering to his feet. He pushed the child before him out of the door.

"Now." He grasped Charli's shoulder. "Take this *piece* to the towers. It can be fed after a full shift. This one –" he placed his massive, fleshy hand on Rowan's head, "– this one is to go to the kitchens." He began to laugh and his breath smelt like rotting fish. "Cook will know." He bent over, roaring with mirth. "Cook will know what to do with it."

The servant-child, its eyes wide and full of fear, dared a quick look at Rowan.

Gorg straightened up. "What are you waiting for?" he bellowed. "Go!"

The child motioned that the girls should follow and scampered ahead across the courtyard and back through the central archway. Rowan and Charli almost had to run to keep pace. Rowan stared at the shaven, patchy head of the robed figure. She could not tell if it was a boy or a girl. Its face seemed so pinched and raw and the eyes would not meet her own.

"This way," it gasped, leading them through a large cavern, dimly lit by spluttering waxy stumps that gave off a fatty, acrid stench. Several passageways led from here, and the child scurried down a right-hand tunnel. It wound on and on, seemingly into the heart of the mountain, passing countless doorways and tunnels.

"Where are we going?" Rowan asked gently.

But the child shook its head and did not speak.

At last, they reached a room where several children, dressed in sackcloth robes, were seated at a long wooden table, polishing immense silver platters with sand and oil.

They looked up at the newcomers, faces pale and drawn but eyes gleaming with curiosity.

"It's a new intake for the kitchens," said the child. "Any offers?"

The others drew back, busying themselves with their work.

"Come on," the child persisted. "Gorg's cut a new whip. I've seen it in the rack."

"I'd prefer Gorg's whip to Cook's fist," said one of the children.

"Well, like as not, we'll get both. Come on, kitchen's not so bad. I've got to take t'other to the towers."

The children shuddered. A tall, thin girl with a long dark plait stood up. "I'll take her."

The child nodded. "Okay, Kira. Be quick though, or there'll be trouble."

Charli flashed Rowan a quick wink of encouragement and whispered, "S'okay, I'll find you," before they were hurried off in different directions by their strange, silent escorts.

Rowan tried to make conversation with Kira but, as before, the girl shook her head and turned away. "Hush. We'll be beaten."

Rowan felt that she would never remember the maze of corridors through which she was led. Occasionally, Kira would point out rooms, giving the briefest description, "That's the mess. The dormitories. This is the wash room. The reformatory."

They came to a flight of steps leading downwards. And down they went, until the ice became solid rock. There was a choking smell of burning fat; the air began to grow hot. Strange lights and shadows flickered on the wall ahead. Rowan could feel her face glowing and the sweat trickling down the inside of her clothes. She shrugged off the thick, fur jacket.

Suddenly, the stairway emerged onto a high stone ledge which overlooked a large cavern.

Steam and smoke billowed up from the huge coal-fired ovens below. A dozen solid tables groaned under the weight of butchered carcasses and raw meat. Small half-naked figures scurried about shovelling coal, basting joints, stirring cauldrons, kneading dough, slicing meat and grinding bones. In the middle of the chaos stood a big, fat man with an eyepatch and a close-shaven head. He wielded a steel cleaver. The great blade, loud as a hammer, made a dreadful noise as it chop-chop-chopped through a bloody rib-cage.

"Don't say a thing," Kira warned, leading Rowan down a rough-hewn stairway that hugged the cavern wall.

35

KITCHEN

⸻◆⸻

THE FAT MAN PAUSED, MID-STRIKE, BLADE gleaming in the dullish light. His eyes narrowed as the two girls approached.

Kira bowed low.

"Master Cook, Gorg sends a new girl."

"Girl!" the cook roared, slamming the cleaver down into the table top with such force it stuck fast.

Kira started back. "Please, I mean p-p-piece. Gorg sends a new piece."

"Is she strong or just another puny scrap of offal?" the cook growled, his belly wobbling beneath a blood-stained vest.

Gulping, Rowan edged forward and the cook drew his lip back in disgust.

"Offal!" he cursed through broken teeth and spat on the floor. "Come 'ere, Offal."

Rowan moved nearer. The stink of stale sweat and dried blood was so strong she could barely breathe. He grabbed her tunic and pulled her close. She could feel flecks of warm spittle on her cheek.

"You might be puny, oh yes, a flea, a mite, a tic, indeed, but you will work, see?" His voice was dangerously low. "You will work like a mountain trow.

You will work 'til these small pale digits are cracked and broken, snapped right through."

He took hold of one slender finger.

"D'y'see? An' if you *don't*? Well, my sweet, puny scrap –" he bent her finger back until it hurt, "– I'm sure you'd rather not know what'll happen if you *don't*, eh?"

The cook pushed her aside.

"Rabbit's Piss!" he roared. "Come and tell her what to do! An' tell Vee I want her! And you," he bellowed, aiming a rib bone at Kira's head. "Next time bring me something tasty, something with more meat on its bones!"

Amid a hail of scraps and giblets Kira fled back up the stairs.

Cook wrenched the steel cleaver from the tabletop and proceeded to direct his fury at the bloody carcass, hacking off great chunks of raw meat.

A skinny figure wearing a grubby bandana darted forward, grabbed Rowan's hand and pulled her to the far end of the cave, a shadowy area away from the flickering light of the ovens.

A large wooden spoon was thrust into Rowan's hand.

"Stir the stew," the child whispered urgently, pointing at a great cauldron filled with a bubbling, grey gloop.

"S-stir...?" Rowan stammered in confusion.

"By Atr'ax!" exclaimed a cold, haughty voice. "She doesn't know how to stir soup. Master will have such fun with this one!"

Out of the shadows a tall girl appeared, dressed in a light blue shift and a crisp white apron. Her eyes and hair were as pale as ice and, though she should have been pretty, there was something hard and unrelenting in her stare.

Rowan shivered and thought of Luke.

"Let her alone, Vee," said the thin child. The girl sneered. "There's no point being noble, Sol. If she's useless he'll simply beat *you* twice as hard."

Sol shrugged. "Isn't that my problem?"

"No. You're too useful to me, boy. What good would you be with a broken spine? I'd lose one of my most productive workers. Do you think I want to go back to gutting fish and mopping floors? I like being underchef."

Sol said nothing, but there was an uncomfortable silence.

The tall girl tossed her head, stepped forward and gave Rowan's cheek a spiteful pinch. "It's very simple," she hissed. "You put the spoon in the soup." She grabbed Rowan's hand, forcing it down towards the simmering liquid. "And you go round and round." With an iron grip she wrenched Rowan's arm into a circular motion, careless of the splash of scalding-hot stew.

Rowan gasped with pain.

"Get used to it," the girl said through gritted teeth. "It gets worse."

"Vee," Sol said urgently, "Cook wants you."

She stared at him through slitted eyes and turned away sharply.

The boy took hold of Rowan's sleeve. "Come," he said and led her to a stone sink. Lifting a jug, he poured icy water over her burns. Rowan studied his face, half hidden beneath the dirty scarf.

"It's you," she said, recognising the pale, dark-haired fisherboy.

Their eyes met briefly.

"Does it hurt?" he asked, inspecting the red weals on the back of her hand.

"A bit."

"Keep it covered with this." He handed her a wet rag.

Rowan smiled, but again Sol avoided her gaze.

"Thanks for your—" she began.

Sol put a finger to his lips. "We must work."

He returned to the rough table where he was grinding something in a huge pestle and mortar. Rowan stared at the gooey mess bubbling away in the iron pot.

"What is this stuff anyway?" she whispered, wrinkling her nose. "It smells like drains."

"We call it worm stew," Sol answered in a low voice. "It's made from Black Sea krull – the catch we brought in earlier."

"Those maggots?" Rowan said in disbelief. "How can you eat it?"

Sol looked at her, "What else is there?"

"But what about all that meat?"

"That's… for them."

"Them?"

Sol shook his head. "Cook!" he hissed.

Rowan realised that the sound of chopping had stopped. She felt the hairs on the back of her head prickle. Suddenly, a fat, red hand gripped her shoulder, crushing bones.

"I hope you've informed the wee lass of her duties, Rabbit's Piss!" the cook snarled.

Sol nodded but kept his eyes low.

"*And* warned her what happens to lazy, bone-idle scum?"

Sol jerked his head.

"We'll see, hah?" he chuckled and pinched Rowan under the chin. "Maybe you should come with me, wee scrap. There's polar bears to skin."

<hr />

By the time Rowan collapsed onto the pile of old straw that functioned as a bed, every muscle and bone in her body was aching with exhaustion.

She had worked for hour after hour without break, helping Cook to rip the skins from a pile of full-grown polar bears, carrying platter after platter of raw chopped meat to the ice-rooms, tending the ovens, basting several small whales in their own melted blubber, scrubbing clean the butcher's blocks, sweeping the gizzards into bait buckets, mopping pools of blood from the floor, fetching coal from the store, shovelling fuel into the great fires, lugging the stew cauldron to the mess, where rows of thin-faced, hessian-clad children waited in silence for their meagre bowl of slop and hunk of hard black bread.

The slave-children breathed in deeply as the kitchen workers passed by.

"Why do they do that?" Rowan asked Sol as they hurried back along the corridor.

"It's the smell."

"What do you mean?"

"The smell of roasting meat clings to our clothes and hair. It torments them."

Rowan washed iron pots and pans, and cleaned grills and spits and toasting forks. She swept up ashes and cinders. She carried great pies and pâtés and spiced meats to the pantries.

All day long her work was punctuated by cuffs and blows and kicks from Cook, each delivered with a cunning cruelty.

As Rowan curled up on the straw she whimpered, not so much with pain as with exhaustion and loneliness.

"It's okay," said Sol, placing his hand on her shoulder and offering her a steaming cup. "It will get better."

"That's not what Vee said," replied Rowan, sitting up, wincing with pain. Her bruised limbs ached and the wound on her back was stinging. "She said it would get worse."

Sol sighed and handed her the hot drink.

"For Vee that's probably true."

"But why do you say that?" Rowan demanded. "She has it better than the rest of you."

"Does she?"

"Yes, with her pretty dress and fine apron. She's not wearing sackcloth or sweeping ashes or eating worm stew."

"There's more than one way of being miserable," said Sol.

Rowan stared at him. How could this kind boy feel sympathy for such a cold and spiteful girl? She sipped her drink; there was a hint of chamomile and meadowsweet in the concoction. It brought to mind the rich meadows of Summerland.

"Mmmm, that tastes good," she murmured.

"I took it from Cook's store cupboard." It was the first time she had seen Sol smile. "Cook is no fool, but he's wasteful. He has far too much of everything, so a handful of spices here, a few herbs there aren't missed."

Rowan returned his smile.

"And what do you do with it?"

"Oh, I try and help the others mostly, when they're sick or..."

"Or...?"

"Hungry, I was going to say, but they're always hungry. Mostly they get ill because they don't have enough to eat. I put herbs in the stew, for goodness, but I can give them teas and infusions to take the edge off their hunger or give them courage."

"How did you learn all this?"

"My grandmother knew about herbs."

"Your grandmother? Sol, how did you get here? Where do you come from?"

Sol was very still for a moment then he put his head in his hands. When he looked up, his eyes were dark.

"I don't know," he said in a hollow voice. "I was lost and... I found myself here."

"But surely..."

Sol shook his head vehemently.

"We're all lost," he croaked.

With a hopeless gesture he lay down – his back to her.

Rowan finished her drink and, with a slight whimper, lay down, trying to find a comfortable position on the prickly straw. The kitchens were quiet, dark and lit only by the glow from the banked ovens. She heard a coal hiss and settle and the soft snores of the kitchen waifs. She doubted she would be able to get to sleep, not without Charli's comforting presence. Her friend's cheeky smile swam before her eyes and suddenly they were running through a field of summer flowers, honey and camomile-scented.

Exhausted, she slept.

36

THE MESS

IN THE DISTANCE ROWAN COULD HEAR THE sound of barking.

She turned over, wincing with pain, and felt something rough and scratchy beneath her cheek. Had the barking been in her dreams? The smell of musty straw, flattened and damp with sweat, filled her nostrils. The way her limbs and back ached, she might as well have been sleeping on the stone floor.

Rowan sat up, and at once became aware of a flickering light, casting shifting shadows across the ceiling. A white figure, carrying a candle, emerged from a doorway in the far wall; it advanced quickly, silently, past the glowing ovens and sleeping children. Its long pale hair glimmered in the darkness.

It was Vee. She was crying. Rowan ducked down, close to the straw, but the tall girl, miserable and distracted, hurried on towards her private room.

Rowan remembered what Sol had said. Perhaps it was true then that, despite the nice clothes and good food and special privileges, Vee had troubles of her own.

A terrible clanging sound woke Rowan and she leapt to her feet, befuddled.

"What is it?"

"It's the bell," said Sol. "Morning shift. Come on."

Two kitchen workers, still wiping the sleep from their eyes, were busy lighting the large oil lamps that hung from ceiling chains. The rest, lined up in rows, stood stiff and silent. Sol and Rowan joined them.

They waited.

"Where's Vee?" someone whispered.

Rowan was about to turn to Sol and ask what was happening when Vee appeared, looking paler than ever. There were bluish shadows under her eyes and in her hand she carried a long, thin birch rod.

"Silence!" she hissed.

The children stood as still as gravestones.

"How dare you speak during roll call? Penalty! Bread cut from rations."

There was no response to this statement, no low groan, no intake of breath, but Rowan could sense the despair.

Vee smiled, running her fingers along the pointed top of the cane.

"Today I have a special announcement. We are to give thanks. The most wonderful news! The Arak-nus have woken from their Consuming Sleep!"

She raised the cane high above her head.

"Hurrah! Hurrah! Hurrah!"

The cheers from the kitchen workers were loud and well-rehearsed, but soulless.

Rowan joined in reluctantly, feeling the razor-scan of Vee's sharp eyes, but her mind was racing. The Lady had spoken of the Consuming Sleep. It was the only time the Arak-nus were vulnerable.

"Tonight," Vee proclaimed, "there shall be a great feast to celebrate the Waking and to mark the Midwinter Darkness!"

More cheers. Rowan wondered if all of this was for Master Cook's benefit. There was something of the grand performance in Vee's manner.

"But that's not all," Vee cried. "The Arak-nus have an honoured guest. The Winter Knight has come!"

The expected cheers were delivered, but Rowan's vocal chords seemed to have seized up. A guest? An honoured guest – could it be Luke? The Hungry Ones had lured him into their confidence and then into their world. Was Luke the focus of this entire spectacle?

Vee brought her whip down hard upon the floor. Rowan jumped.

"We have much work to do! Back row: fetch coal, fire ovens, man the bellows! Middle row: bring the carcasses from cold store, prepare the chopping tables. Gil, Yoki: breakfast duties. Sol and..."

Vee paused and brought her cane up to Rowan's chin. "And *what is* your name?"

Her eyes were glacial.

"Erh, A-A-Anne," Rowan stuttered.

"Anne?" Vee raised an eyebrow. "Not that it matters. The master calls you 'Offal', but I think Stew-girl rather suits you." She jabbed the cane into Rowan's throat. "Sol, Stew-girl, slops!"

'Slops' consisted of carrying the buckets of night soil – urine and excrement – from the kitchen urinals to a waste pit at the end of a long sloping tunnel. The cook's night pot was the worst, filled to the brim with a foul-stinking concoction.

They collected it from outside his sleeping chamber, one of a suite of rooms, accessed by a door at the far end of the kitchen.

Rowan stared in awe at the luxurious red furnishings and thick carpets.

"I saw Vee coming out of here last night," she said.

Sol shook his head, a warning not to talk. Together, the two children hauled the heavy chamber pot, shuddering in disgust as the slops splashed against their skin. Sol did not speak until they had reached the cesspit.

"Even Vee has to survive."

Rowan stared at him as they tipped the slops into a deep hole that smoked with malodourous fumes.

"What do you mean?"

Sol looked into her eyes. "Vee isn't underchef for nothing."

Rowan wasn't sure she understood, and then something clicked.

"*There's more than one way of being miserable*; that's what you meant!"

Sol nodded.

"Vee was crying, Sol."

"Yes. She cries a lot." Sol's eyes were full of pity.

With a sudden impulse, Rowan leant over and grabbed his arm.

"Listen, Sol, I need your help. I know you'll understand. I wasn't lost. I came here on purpose to find my brother. I have to save him."

"You *came* here?"

"Yes. I came here to find my brother, Luke."

"You weren't lost?" Sol look perplexed.

"No."

"But... we're all lost."

"Not me, Sol."

"You remember your home?"

"Yes, I do."

"You remember your father and your *mother*?"

"Yes, Sol, of course. I came here to save Luke and I'm going to save you too, all of you."

Sol shook his head. "You're crazy. You can't escape from here. No one ever escapes from here."

"Has anyone tried?"

"Yes."

"And?"

"The crows go up, then the dogs are let loose."

Rowan remembered the sounds she had heard in the night. The sound of barking, echoing up through deep tunnels."

"They don't come back, the ones that try. But the dogs don't need feeding that night."

Rowan shivered and her arm felt icy cold.

Sol picked up the empty pot.

"We must get back to the kitchen."

Rowan stared at the dark, stinking hole for a moment and felt something rise up through the mood of despair and horror. With an air of defiance, she clenched her fists.

"I don't care, Sol," she said. "I don't care if they send a thousand Foul Folk: crows, dogs, trows or Atr'ax himself after me. I'm going to put a stop to them."

Sol gazed at her in astonishment, as if he half believed her.

"You're mad," he whispered.

"Will you help me?"

He paused and stared, his eyes searching.

"Yes," he said, at last. "I will."

"Then you have to tell me everything you know about this place. Anything that you think would help."

"Not now. They'll beat us if we're late back."

"Okay, but tell me one thing?"

"What?" His face was white with anxiety.

"Have you heard of a child called Luke? He's older, like Vee."

"Luke? No, there's no one called Luke."

"Are you *sure*?" She was vehement.

"Yes, I'm sure. No one in the castle. Perhaps he's in the mines, or the dungeons. They keep prisoners in the dungeons."

"So, what about this guest, the Winter Knight?"

"No one ever sees his face. But he's…"

"He's what?"

Sol grabbed her hand. "Look, we can't talk now. Believe me, you do not want to feel Cook's fists on the back of your head. Come!"

"Where have you been?" Vee hissed at them as they returned to the kitchen. "He's in a foul mood. Help Yoki take the cauldrons up to the mess. Quick!"

They could hear Cook bellowing at the other end of the cavern, the walls echoing with his fury.

"If I wanted piglet I would'a asked for piglet. But I wanted seal pups. When I ask for seal pups, *what* d'ye bring me?"

Rowan, Sol and Yoki lugged the heavy pans of warm stew around the perimeter of the kitchen and up the stone steps.

"What d'ye bring me?" Cook demanded.

The answer, if indeed it ever came, was lost in a roar of rage and the smashing of crockery. The three children hurried, as quickly as their burdens would allow, to the top of the flight of stairs, fearful that at any moment a grenade of sharp pottery fragments would explode overhead.

———◆———

The mess seemed far more crowded than on the previous day. Hessian-robed children milled around, collecting tin plates and cups from a sideboard, and formed a straggling line at the top end of the hall. The kitchen staff deposited the cauldrons onto a platform and the low murmur of voices rose to a feverish hum.

Heavy footsteps in the corridor brought a sudden hush. Into the mess strode two squat creatures, who could have been Gorg but for the fact that their skin was a sickly yellow rather than a putrid green.

"Silence!" they croaked. "Anyone caught – hourrgh – breaking the rules…"

"Anyone at all…"

"Will be – hourrgh – what *shall* we do with them Gar?"

"Put them on hunting duty, Gut."

"Yes, indeed, on hunting duty, with us."

"And what'll they be, Gut…?"

"Hourrgh – bait!"

The repulsive pair walked up and down the line, brandishing short leather truncheons and stopping every now and then to stroke the weapon against a child's temple or throat.

Two more kitchen waifs appeared, one carrying a wooden tray of black bread, the other a huge platter covered with a silver lid.

Gar raised his nose and sniffed. "Ah, I think breakfast has arrived, Gut."

Gut, likewise, scented the air. "Most perspicacious, Gar. Seal pup – hourrgh – if I'm not mistaken."

"Acute, indeed, Gut."

They licked their fat lips.

"Ladlers, servers, get to your positions."

The kitchen waifs removed the lids from the steaming cauldrons and fished long-handled ladles from the grey gloop.

"Ready!... Wait for it, you vile lot... Serve!"

The first child in the queue, a crop-headed, thin lad, moved forward proffering his bowl. He received a slop of stew and a crust of bread and hurried to a long table, where he sat down. One by one, the other sackclothed figures followed.

As she doled out their meagre portion, Rowan could see the hunger in their eyes: so hungry, she thought, they would eat anything, even the foul mess in front of them.

Gar and Gut, meanwhile, had seated themselves at an elegantly set table at the far end of the hall. They removed the silver dishcover, revealing large chunks of sizzling meat and a bowl of spicy red sauce. For the briefest moment, every child's head turned in their direction, eyes dark with longing. The two lumpy creatures were oblivious. They grabbed the meat with grubbing fingers and slobbered, grunted and slurped their way through the meal.

"Bleedin' pigs, ain't they?" someone hissed in Rowan's ear. The child pulled back its hessian hood.

"Charli!" Rowan exclaimed. Several voices hushed her. But the odious brothers were utterly absorbed in cramming the savoury chunks into their wide, wet mouths.

"Don't worry about them," said Charli. "Too busy troughing."

"She's right," whispered Sol. "While they're eating they don't pay any attention, but keep your voice down."

A sound like the soft rustle of paper swept through the benches; children were whispering.

"Oh, Charli, I've missed you."

Charli gave her a big grin. "You coulda cooked up something a bit more appetising though." She pulled a face at the greyish slime in the bottom of her bowl. "Come on, Tolly." Charli pulled a small, skinny child forward. "Give this one a double portion. She's the 'ungriest little beggar I've ever seen."

Two great eyes stared out of a pitiful bruised face. The short hair was as matted and tufty as a drowned kitten's. The child's wrists were twig thin. She looked ill, Rowan thought. No wonder Charli had taken pity on her.

"They beat her something rotten," Charli whispered.

Rowan shuddered, and ladled a double-serving into the tin receptacle. The poor child gazed open-mouthed, unable to move, until Charli dragged her to a table.

"You shouldn't have done that," said Sol in a low voice.

"Done what?"

"It's one ladle of stew per worker. If we break the rules they'll withdraw rations for everyone. Some of the others have noticed; they're not happy."

A few of the older children were glaring at Rowan, frowning and muttering amongst themselves.

"But she was sick."

"Yes," said Sol. "All the children here are sick or starving, but if we take pity they'll punish us all. Look, I'll talk to them. Just keep your head down."

He was frightened for her. She could see that and for a fleeting moment she put her hand on his arm.

Eventually, the line of children came to an end. Sol filled their own bowls with the scrapings from the pot, and the three kitchen waifs joined Charli and Tolly at one of the long wooden tables.

Rowan felt too excited to eat. Seeing Charli was better than a feast, but Sol pushed the bowl of stew in front of her.

"Eat, you'll need it."

"I don't think I can."

"Eat or *you'll* get ill," he insisted.

Rowan picked up the spoon and forced herself to swallow a mouthful. It was like eating lukewarm sick.

She swallowed again, forcing down the rising gobbet of food, and smiled wanly at Charli. "Where have they sent you? Is it okay?"

"Not so bad," said Charli. "I'm a 'keeper'. That's what Gorg calls me. I look after his scabby, black birds. You know, like the crow that went for you. They roost up in the castle turrets. I have to take 'em their food, huge hunks of bloody meat, and clean out their nests – doesn't 'alf stink!"

"Up in the turrets, Charli, but that's hundreds and hundreds of feet…?"

"Yeah, it's a pretty hairy climb, all narrow pathways and steps and arches and bridges. Like a knife edge, some of them. But I'm not the niece of Auntie Tullah the Flying Fox (most celebrated trapeze artist in Budapest) for nothing. It'd be a dordy job if it weren't for those birds, evil bleedin' creatures. I can't stand 'em, always trying to peck lumps out of me. Can't think what that disgusting oaf sees in them."

Rowan shuddered, remembering the attack. "Aren't you afraid?"

"Just have to keep your head. I kind of like it. Gorg leaves me to it, doesn't interfere. He's too fat to get up there for a start. So I've had time to look around, find things out.

"What?" Rowan's spoon was suspended halfway to her mouth.

"Well, I found out about the tunnels, miles of 'em under the castle, like you said. Tolly, poor kid, was locked up in the dungeons once. She begged me not to go down there, said I'd be gobbled up by the monster dogs. The children are forced to work in the mines, some for coal but others, well, they don't know what for. They just dig tunnel after tunnel."

Rowan nodded, remembering the maze of passageways where Jaz had been imprisoned.

"Do you know anything about this, Sol?" Rowan asked.

Sol, his expression tense, had one eye on Gut and Gar, who were still burping and belching their way through breakfast.

"Not much. Once, when I was serving in the Great Hall, one of the Arak-nus got very angry. It was Taran'tar, first in command under Atr'ax. He said they were wasting time with all the digging and that they should act. But Atr'ax, in his cold way, insisted they must find the Source."

"The Source?"

"He said something else, about a final… it was a word I didn't understand, a final *Consumption*."

"What's that mean?" said Charli, looking at Rowan.

Rowan shook her head. "Did you hear anything else?"

"Didn't get a chance. One of the council, Aran, said something about discretion and the servers were ordered from the hall."

"It's weird," said Rowan, frowning. "I mean, people usually mine for minerals or precious stones or something, but it sounds like they're looking for a *place*. Like the source of a river."

"This 'final con-sum-shun': don't like the sound of it at all," said Charli, puffing out her cheeks.

"Atr'ax had that look in his eyes," Sol said, shuddering. "I've seen it before when he's about to… dispose of one of his victims." Suddenly, Sol sat up very straight, a gleam in his eye.

"Wait. Perhaps that thing, *Consumption*, is something to do with Consuming Sleep!"

"Didn't the Lady say…" Charli began, turning to Rowan.

"Hush," said Rowan. "Sol, what do you know about Consuming Sleep?"

"Not much. Cook makes this sleeping potion for the Arak-nus; it's from some kind of mushroom. Once, when I was helping Vee to strain the fungi, I told her I was glad *they* spent so much time asleep and she said, 'Don't be; it makes them stronger.'"

"What fungi?" Charli asked.

"It grows under the castle, in the tunnels and mines."

"Interesting," said Charli. "An' where does Cook keep his amazing Mickey Finn?"

"His what?"

"The knock-out drops, the brew."

"Oh, in his private larder."

Charli chuckled, her eyes as bright as lanterns.

A bellow ripped through the chatter.

"Silence!"

The roar of fury made all the children start. Gar and Gut were on their feet, leather batons in hand.

"Silence, you scabby crew! Or we'll feed you to the Kraken. Now, Diggers and Shovellers, up!"

The majority of the children scrambled to their feet.

"Form a line, to the left."

The children began to file out from in-between the benches towards the left-hand side of the hall, leaving the tables cluttered with discarded cups and bowls.

"Servers, start clearing!"

"That's us," Sol hissed, tugging on Rowan's sleeve. Rowan grabbed Charli's hand under the table.

"S'okay," the gypsy girl whispered, winking. "Just remember to find out where Cook's bleedin' larder is."

37

THE MIDWINTER FEAST

———◆———

THE CENTREPIECE OF THE GREAT WINTER Feast was a full-size female polar bear. The complete carcass, skinned and roasted, was presented on a bed of snow, her two cubs cradled in her paws. Cook, screaming for cranberries and working against time, before the snow melted, was adding the finishing touches to his creation. He inserted a fat red plum into each socket of the bear's skull and sucked at his fingers greedily.

"Where are those bloody cranberries?"

The child delivering the bowl received a severe clout across the head. "An' be thankful I wasn't holding my meat cleaver," Cook growled.

The kitchen felt like the boiler room of some great steamship, with the engines going full pelt. Heat and noise and steam drifted upwards until the stairway was lost in a swirling fog. Every oven glowed bright red; every cauldron and pot bubbled like a volcano.

Rowan and Sol were spit-roasting dolphins, turning the huge mechanism and running from one contraption to the next, basting the carcasses with the melted fat which dripped down into large metal troughs. Every few seconds a drop of searing oil would splash onto their bare skin, causing them to wince with pain. Sol had provided a jug of cold water and a rag and when the children dared take a break, they doused their sweating, stinging limbs with a cooling rinse.

There was no chance to talk. Cook's single eye was as sharp as a razor and Vee prowled the floor with her long, thin rod. Every child, head and back bent with effort, dreaded the sharp cut of Vee's stick, or the iron hammer blow of Cook's fist.

The tables nearest the stairs bowed under the weight of prepared food: rich pâtés and cold meats, consommés and jellies, cocktails and canapés. Cook had just given the order for the servers to deliver the first course to the Great Hall. Black-robed waifs appeared and, one by one, they collected a dish and bore it upstairs.

Cook was roaring for platters.

"Get those dishes ready, you pieces of dung! We're plating up!"

"That's us," hissed Sol.

Sol disappeared and came back moments later with two huge metal serving dishes.

"Lay them on that bench, quick," he gasped. "Dress them with seaweed and red coral."

As Sol sprinkled on a last handful of spices Cook arrived. He pushed Sol out of the way and seized the first spit with his gloved hand. The roast dolphin, skin crispy as pork crackling, was slipped onto the prepared platter. He grabbed another.

"Go an' change, yous two. You're serving."

Sol pulled Rowan to a nearby cupboard where the robes were stored. He threw one to her. "They're ceremonial, for serving the Arak-nus," he explained.

"What are they like, the Arak-nus?" Rowan asked. But Sol just shook his head.

Rowan and Sol heaved the platter of roast dolphin between them. Up the steep kitchen stairs they went, along the winding passages and then higher and higher, through ice-hewn corridors and wide glassy stairways to the state rooms. These chambers were extraordinary, adorned with rich blue velvets and fine silver ornaments. Glittering mirrors lined the walls and in several alcoves stood pale, marble statues. Rowan searched for some clue that would reveal the terrible nature of Atr'ax and the Arak-nus. But, far from being sinister, it looked like a fairy-tale castle full of sparkling and priceless things.

"Do they like looking at themselves?" she asked, gazing at the countless mirrors.

"*They* never come here," said Sol. "Their chambers are higher up, but hardly anyone ever gets to go *there*. These rooms are for guests."

"They have guests? Who would come?"

"I don't know. There were some ladies once, in fine dresses and men in uniforms. But they didn't stay long. Quiet now. Raise your hood."

The children mounted one last set of stairs – wide and grand – and suddenly there before them was the entrance to the Great Feasting Hall. Two huge iron-studded doors were flung open and Gar and Gut, dressed in black and silver liveries and holding silver bugles, stood sentry.

With a condescending sneer they waved the kitchen waifs through.

Rowan caught her breath.

They entered a vast, echoing space of carved ice. Immense pillars twisted upwards towards the ceiling and, through great ice windows, a dramatic sunset flooded the hall with crimson light. Rowan could see the snow plains of Midwinter stretching all the way to the western horizon, where a dazzling, bronze sun slipped away. Beyond that, she knew, was Summerland. She could not help but gaze with longing.

"Come," Sol whispered urgently. He led the way, over a red carpet, to a long table which ran down the centre of the hall.

Black-hooded servers were laying out the Winter Feast: polishing glasses, arranging cutlery, repositioning dishes. The two children placed their heavy platter between trays of turtle steaks and bowls of crispy seahorse.

At the head of the feast, perpendicular to the table, Rowan noticed five tall chairs. They were severe, hard-edged, made of some dark, unrelenting material: slate or granite, perhaps. Rowan shivered as she passed by. It was as if they absorbed all warmth and light.

A single harsh note was blown.

The servers drew back at once from the table and began to retreat to a dark corner of the hall. Sol followed, pulling Rowan after him.

The bugle was sounded again.

Through a tall, curtained archway to the right a procession of Foul Folk entered. Gorg was at the head, his bloated limbs squeezed into a tight black uniform. Lumbering behind came granite-skinned trows, snickering rat-men and slavering hounds. They took their places at the table.

The light from the sun was dying. A cold bluish shadow descended on the hall. After the heat of the kitchens Rowan couldn't stop shivering. The temperature was plummeting.

A third bugle call, and a pale iridescence began to gather over the tall chairs, flaming, insubstantial.

Forms appeared in the haze. Pale faces wavering, melting and re-forming, like a lightbulb flickering in and out before it fails.

Suddenly, five dark figures materialised, seated in the stone chairs. They were gaunt-faced, with arctic, impenetrable eyes. Rowan gave a gasp and the ground seemed to shift. The figure at the centre was the Grey Man: Atr'ax. To his left sat the Mint woman, Nyche, and her husband, Aran, and on his far right the burly form of the dog handler. The other man, muscular, handsome and dressed in a black and red uniform, she did not recognise.

A fanfare sounded and into the hall came several kitchen staff. They carried Cook's grotesque masterpiece: the flayed polar bear and her cubs. It was placed at the very centre of the table amidst grunts of delight.

Atr'ax stood, tall and imposing, a cloak of silver-grey fur draped over his black robes, and with a dreadful, articulated precision stepped forward.

"Tonight we celebrate the great Darkness of Midwinter." His voice was soft, a hiss of menace which, like a corrosive gas, seemed to eat through to the heart's core. All the children felt it, for, like Rowan, they shrank back.

"Even as I speak, the last rays of light are slipping away and the gloriously long, bitter night of winter will begin."

An image of Luke came into Rowan's mind, his face stony and mask-like. She thought of Finn too, pale and bleeding in the wreckage of a car. She felt sick.

"We will feast and, when we have sated our appetites, we shall initiate our ritual of renewal. We shall greet the Winter Knight."

There were more howls and cries, and a horrible gnashing of teeth.

Unconsciously, Rowan grabbed Sol's wrist. The Winter Knight: she was sure it was Luke!

"Servants, withdraw!" bellowed Gorg.

With obvious relief, the children began to file out of the hall. Sol pulled Rowan into the line, but something grabbed her shoulder, wrenched her back. Gorg's fat hand gripped her tight and the other hand was around Sol's neck.

"Not you two!" He threw a tinder box at Sol. "Light the torches and tapers!"

Rowan, pulling her hood further forwards, followed Sol to a far corner of the hall. Sol sparked the tinderbox, ignited a thin taper and handed it to Rowan.

"You light the torches around the walls. I'll do the candles on the table. Don't worry, you'll be fine."

Rowan's hands were shaking so much she didn't think she would be able to perform even this simple task, but the torches, oozing with whale oil, flared up at once. They cast a strange flickering light over the chamber, a light reflected, disconcertingly, in the dark, searching eyes of the Arak-nus. Rowan forced herself not to look. They might look stiff, almost robotic, but she could sense the intelligence and malice behind those eyes, like searchlights, capable of penetrating the most secret places of her mind. She tried to focus on the smoking flame in her hand. Soon, she told herself, all the lights would be lit and they would be able to leave. But, as the last torch was fired, Gorg grabbed the two children and pushed them into a corner.

"Wait 'til you're called for," he growled.

Rowan and Sol huddled together, half hidden in the shadows, and watched the hideous party consume their feast.

The trows, the dogs, the Rat Folk and the three brothers, Gorg, Gut and Gar, devoured everything in front of them, not waiting to fill their plates, but tearing lumps of meat from the presentation dishes, with fingers, claws and teeth. Two dogs had actually mounted the table to rip open the belly of the polar bear.

The Arak-nus did not eat at all. They simply sat there watching the proceedings with their strange, dead eyes.

Rowan gulped and looked away.

"Sol," she whispered, staring at the floor. "I think Luke is the Winter Knight."

She felt Sol go rigid. "What?"

"They brought him here. Tricked him. I'm sure he's their guest."

Sol shook his head. "He's probably a prisoner, in the dungeons."

"But, he's worth something to them. He's the lure."

"For you, you mean?"

"Yes."

"Then they wouldn't make him the Winter Knight."

"Why?"

"Because..." Sol paused and lowered his head. "Because the Winter Knight is a sacrifice."

"What?" Rowan felt the floor lurch.

"He is sacrificed three days after the Midwinter Feast. The spilling of his blood brings great power to the Arak-nus."

Rowan rested her forehead on Sol's shoulder. The room wouldn't stop spinning. Sol held her close and whispered into her hair, "It isn't Luke."

But she didn't believe him; she couldn't believe him. The fear in her heart told her it was Luke.

Soon all that was left of the feast were scraps of skin, gristle and bone. Atr'ax rose up. Again a fanfare echoed through the hall and he cast his emotionless gaze over the assembly.

"Now we are feasted on all the delicacies, let us pay homage to Master Cook, who serves us so well."

The doors opened to admit the cook, dressed in a flamboyant scarlet suit and waistcoat which strained across the bulk of his belly. In one hand he carried a lace handkerchief and in the other a pistol, a large, ornate flintlock. Behind Cook, two kitchen waifs were struggling with a large serving dish. It bore a translucent, ruby-coloured sculpture.

"My Lord Atr'ax. Thanking ye for your kind words. They're most gratefully received. Now, let me present you with this gift made from the finest frozen narwhal blood and commissioned by Captain Taran'tar himself."

The statue was carried to the top of the table. Atr'ax cast his eyes over it, briefly.

"Very handsome," he hissed.

The figure to his right, the tall, powerfully built man with an orange streak in his black hair, stood and in a deep tone said, "It is a representation of you, Lord."

"Oh no, Taran'tar. You flatter me," Atr'ax responded. "It is far too handsome. It must be a statue of yourself. Is that so, Master Cook?"

Cook glanced at the captain, uncertainly, "Ah, ah, well, perhaps so, your Magnificence."

"And I must show my appreciation for your long and loyal service, Taran'tar. Is this not so?"

The captain stood proud and defiant.

Atr'ax raised his arm. Rowan felt something deep inside, like a soundless thunderclap. The statue crashed to the floor. It lay there, a large pile of red slush.

Taran'tar gave a terrible, inhuman shriek. The dreadful noise went on.

Rowan gripped her head with her hands. Something hammer-like was pounding against her skull. The dinner guests had collapsed onto the table writhing and whimpering. Cook staggered forward, raised his gun and aimed it at Taran'tar.

"Hauld yer blether!"

Atr'ax smiled. "Shall I give the command to fire?" he mused.

The Mint woman, sleek and black, with silvery eyes, moved forward and placed her hand on Taran'tar. The terrible sound stopped at once.

"A misunderstanding." A voice as soft as cobwebs. "This is Atr'ax's celebrated humour, nothing more." She knelt down and licked at the thawing pool of iced-blood with her tongue. "Taran'tar tastes... as good as he looks."

The table, frozen into silence, suddenly roared with laughter: too loud, too emphatic, an oily outpouring of relief. Taran'tar backed away and Atr'ax, magnanimous in victory, raised a glass of wine. "Ah, fair Nyche, as always your diplomacy is exercised with much wit and charm. A toast to the female, and her would-be mate."

Nyche, eyes flicking nervously towards her husband, made a slight bow.

"And now, my friends, it is time to honour the Winter Knight."

38

MASK

———◆———

AN ORNATE TAPESTRY BEHIND THE STONE chairs was swept aside and a figure, dressed in black armour, emerged. There were soft hisses of approval. Rowan craned forward to look but the Knight's face was concealed by a visor.

The Knight, moving with a stiff, clanking motion, stopped before Atr'ax and knelt. Atr'ax reached out with his long, white fingers and touched the Knight's helm.

"I anoint you, Masked One, servant of my will. Now, rise up and entertain me."

The Winter Knight got to his feet and faced the assembly. With slow, blind movements he turned his head to the left, to the right and back again, as if seeking something out.

Then, locking on to a single object, he drew the great sword from its sheath and strode stiffly across the floor.

He paused in front of the captain.

Taran'tar rose up in disbelief. "This is a challenge? You dare challenge me?"

Nyche cried out, "My Lord, no!"

Atr'ax gave a hiss, soft and dangerous. "Destroy or be destroyed, Taran'tar. Your hunger for power is admirable, but a little premature. Which is unfortunate… for you."

Again Taran'tar gave a hideous scream. His white face grew purple with rage and seemed to bloat. Indeed, his entire body appeared to swell and grow – bigger, bigger – until, with a terrible ripping sound, his form split like a carapace. Several hairy protuberances unfolded, reared up and, in an instant, a great black and orange bulk, with many legs, lunged forward, scattering plates, bones and tankards. The party guests shrank back against the wall.

Rowan clutched at Sol's arm, barely able to breathe.

For a moment it looked as if the armoured figure would be crushed beneath the swollen hairy form but, animated into action, the Knight suddenly displayed the agility and grace of a stag. In a single fluid movement he leapt back and, swinging his sword upwards, he cut off one of the creature's sensitive palps.

The thing that had been Taran'tar screeched and, blind with pain, delivered a venomous strike. There was the deadening clang of fang against steel; the Knight's shoulder plate crumpled, but his sword found its mark. With a gush of dark blood, the sharp blade sliced through the monstrous foreleg.

The Knight's left arm now hung limply, but Taran'tar did not move. A soft sigh trembled through the creature's body. Blood was pumping, forming sticky pools. The fight seemed to be over. The creature's cephalothorax was bowed almost to the floor. The Knight backed away and lowered his sword.

Atr'ax began to rise, jubilant, reaching out to the Winter Knight, when suddenly Taran'tar sprang. He snatched up the Knight in his huge clawed legs and, drawing the armoured figure under his body, began to roll him around and around. Rowan could see the Knight struggling to get his sword arm free, but the monster's movements were deft. A strand of silk was being excreted from its huge abdomen.

The spider creature was beginning to spin.

Rowan could not bear to look anymore. She pressed her face into Sol's shoulder. "Oh, Luke, oh, Luke," she said with a whimper. She had failed Luke. She had failed everyone. Why had she even tried? It had always been hopeless.

"But look," Sol whispered urgently. Rowan glanced up.

The spider had cocooned the Knight from feet to waist but, hampered by the missing leg, had dropped him. In the frantic moment it took for Taran'tar to scrabble for his prey, the Knight knelt up and drove his long steel sword into the fleshy abdomen. Steaming gore spurted out. The armoured figure rolled to one side, away from the stinking ooze, and cut through the silken cords binding him.

Leaping up, he faced his enemy.

A hiss of despair escaped from Taran'tar.

"I was faithful."

The vast bulk stood there, shuddering for a brief moment, then crashed to the floor and with a dreadful spasm the legs clawed inwards.

Atr'ax stepped delicately down from the dais and over to the reeking body. Lowering his head, he licked at the seeping blood.

"Irresistible," he sighed.

All the Arak-nus, including Nyche, moved forward and began to feed on the corpse of their fallen captain.

———◆———

"I can't do it, Sol, can I? It's impossible."

It was much later. Rowan was lying on the straw in the corner of the kitchen, shivering. She couldn't forget how those 'things' had consumed the body, sucking the flesh, until all that remained was a crumbling translucent husk.

The children had been forced by Gorg and his brothers to clear away the remains of the Winter Feast as the grisly cannibalisation progressed.

"I can't do it, Sol!"

Sol stroked her hair.

Somewhere, a clock struck ten. Everyone, exhausted from the long day, had gone to sleep. But every time she closed her eyes Rowan saw the Arak-nus, their dark, hypnotic eyes watching her.

"How can I fight them? How?"

"Hush," said Sol.

"She said I would know, Sol. When the time came she said I would remember." There was a long pause. Had Sol gone to sleep? But then he spoke.

"Perhaps the time hasn't come yet."

Rowan rolled over and looked at him, her eyes wide. "Oh, Sol." She sat up and took hold of his hand. "I'm so glad you're here."

He smiled and held out a piece of crumpled paper. "Kira stuffed this in my hand after the feast. I'll get a candle."

Rowan took the scrap of paper and smoothed it out on her knee. It was a note from Charli, untidy words scrawled in charcoal.

Mete me
In
Mess -
Midnite
Bowt Luuk

Rowan turned pale.

"Luke! Perhaps she's seen him. Or spoken to him."

"Maybe."

"Perhaps if Luke can kill one Arak-nus, he can kill them all."

"Possibly."

"Oh, Sol, it's true. We just have to wait for the right time."

Sol put his hand on her arm. "Yes, but right now, Anne, we need to..."

"It's not Anne," she interrupted. "I lied to Vee. I thought she would tell *them*. My name's Rowan."

Sol smiled. "Rowan. That's beautiful, like the tree. Lie down, Rowan, we need to sleep. I'll wake you at midnight."

───◇───

Once they had left the kitchens behind, with its low murmur of sleeping children, the soft snores, the tearful snuffling, the settling and hiss of burning coal, all was silent. It was the silence of deep winter – stark and empty. Rowan and Sol scurried along the sparsely lit passageways, the torchlight making shadows leap and flicker on the walls.

"I feel as if we're being watched," Rowan whispered.

"Don't worry. They're all asleep," said Sol. "Even *them*. They always drink too much wine at the Winter Feast."

"Even Atr'ax?"

"Hush. Of all nights this is the safest."

They crossed the cold, empty expanse of the entrance chamber and then through an archway that led to the servant's quarters. Rowan strained her ears but could hear nothing, not even the distant bark of a dog. As the two children reached the mess a clock struck twelve.

Raising his fingers to his lips Sol pushed the door open and looked inside. After a moment, he smiled and beckoned Rowan through. Sitting there cross-legged under a table, her face illuminated by a candle, was Charli.

Rowan rushed forwards, fell to her knees and hugged her. "Oh, Charli," she said, her face wet with tears.

Charli held on to her, stroking her hair.

"Is this about that fight and what they did after? There was gossip flying around. You poor darlin'."

"Oh Charli, I think it was Luke. The Winter Knight, I think it's him. He killed that... that thing!"

"Bloody overgrown spider!"

"He's killed one, so perhaps he could kill Atr'ax, like the Lady said."

Charli stared at her.

"If the Winter Knight, if *Luke* kills Atr'ax," Rowan went on, "then we've done what the Lady asked us to."

"But, Rowan," Charli said softly. "I *found* Luke. He's in the dungeon, chained up and, from the way he looks, well, he couldn't hurt a fly, let alone a spider."

"What?" Rowan felt as if she had been punched in the stomach. Charli grabbed hold of Rowan's hand and pulled her up. "Come on. I'm going to show you."

Charli led the two children through what seemed to Rowan a baffling series of tunnels, steps and passageways, all leading downwards into the dark bowels of the Ice Fortress. Charli pulled candles from her pocket, lit them from the last flaming torch and handed them to the others. "It's pitch-black from here on."

Many of the openings they passed were, Charli explained, entrances to the mineworkings. She pointed out iron trackways and the occasional abandoned tool rusting on the floor. They followed her down a winding stairway, cut into the bare, dripping rock.

"Look," said Charli. She held the candle high and Rowan could see long, thin mushrooms growing up the walls, emitting a soft luminescence.

"They're grandmother's fingers," said Sol. "That's what Master Cook calls them."

"An' it makes those 'orrible 'airy 'ouse spiders go bye-byes, don't it?" Charli grinned.

"It's creepy," said Rowan. "Let's go."

Down the steps they went, and into another twisting passageway, which eventually divided into three.

"It's the one to the right," said Charli. "I don't know what's down those other two tunnels, not yet anyhow."

"Shhh!" said Rowan suddenly. "What's that?" At once they fell silent.

There was a low murmuring sound, like the humming of many bees, and then a distinct tap-tapping. The children snuffed out the candles.

"It's coming from the middle passage," Rowan whispered.

The tapping was succeeded by tentative footsteps and a wavering nervous voice attempting to sing.

"*Show me the way to go home. I'm tired and I want to go to...* Blow me, if this ain't flippin' weird. Good God, I could do with a pint. I really could. Or a nice, hot cup of..."

A light appeared, an electric torch.

Charli and Sol drew back into the right-hand tunnel.

But Rowan found herself caught in the brilliant white beam.

39

PRISONER

"**W**ELL, I BLEEDIN' NEVER! A LITTLE KID!"
A man appeared, dressed in a hard hat, bright yellow overalls with reflective strips and big black safety boots.

"You all right, love? How on earth did you get down here? Did you fall?"

"I... I'm fine," Rowan stammered. The man looked so normal, like a policeman. She almost felt glad to see him.

"Don't worry, we'll get you out in no time." He unhooked a walkie-talkie from his belt, put it to his mouth and pressed a button.

"This is Juliet Romeo calling Tango. Juliet Romeo calling Tango, come in." But the only response was a hiss of white noise. He tried again.

"Juliet Romeo calling Tango. Come on, Tommy, come in. Over."

Again nothing. He shook the radio, then tapped it three or four times on his helmet. All it emitted was a crackle of static. He sighed. "Still not working. Bloomin' technology, hey? But there's bound to be a manhole somewhere round here." He looked above his head.

"So, what's your name, then?"

Rowan stared at him open-mouthed and he smiled at her.

"You can remember your name?"

"It's R-R-Rowan."

"That's a lovely name. I'm Jim."

"Are you a policeman?"

"Me? Oh goodness no. I'm maintenance. I inspect the sewers, to see if they need fixing. Mind you, I've never seen this part of the system. It's not on my map." He took out a tablet and prodded the screen, shaking his head. "These tunnels must be medieval, or even Roman. We're right down in the ground rock here." He knocked his knuckles against a wall. "It's very odd."

"Where did you come down?" Rowan asked.

"Eh?" The man was still staring at the flat screen frowning. "What's that?"

"What street did you come from?"

"Erm, Gallows Yard, yes, that was it, Gallows Yard."

Rowan stepped back a pace so that Charli and Sol could hear her whisper. "We've got to show him the way back."

The two children emerged from the shadows of the tunnel.

"What the...?" Jim began. "More kids? Bloomin' Nora." He tried the radio again, clamping it to his ear.

"He's from London," Rowan murmured in a low voice.

"What?" said Charli, "but that's... I mean, how could...?"

"I've been here before, remember?" said Rowan. "I came the same way as him, through the sewers, to rescue Jaz, my friend. Only I didn't realise, back then, it was under the Ice Fortress. I didn't know I was in Midwinterland."

"So that means we could go home," Charli exclaimed.

"Except we made a promise."

"I mean *after*. We could all escape this way, the lost kids, too."

"Maybe. It's not that easy. It's like a maze; things shift and change. And anyway…"

"What?"

"Sage and Ash are waiting for us."

"True, but we might not have much choice, Ro. We might just have to leg it. Anyway, how do you know you can even get Mr Sunny Jim here back?"

"I don't."

"But we gotta try, right?"

"Right."

Jim was still prodding the buttons on his radio.

"Calling Tommy. Come in, Tommy, for goodness' sake…!" There was an edge of desperation to his voice.

Rowan put her hand on Jim's arm. "I remember now. There are some iron steps back the way you came. I can show you."

Jim looked bewildered. "Are you sure? I've checked those tunnels, been going round in circles for, my goodness, it seems like hours."

Rowan made a show of shivering. "Please, we're getting so cold."

She slipped her hand into Jim's and, with Jim's torch illuminating the way ahead, led him back down the dank passage, the others following. Rowan tried to remember what it had been like before, when she had been with Nightshade and Ash. Had there been some definite sign? A point where she could say for certain that they must turn either this way or that way? A mark in the rock? The height of the tunnel? A scent in the air? But no, she knew when it came, if it came, it would be a feeling. An uncanny sense of stilling; of walking into, or out of, a dream.

On and on they went, into the darkness; the only sound was the constant drip, drip of water and the echoing clunk of Jim's boots.

At times the air seemed misty, but when Rowan blinked all was clear again. And with every step they went deeper into the tunnel, away from the dungeons, away from Luke.

Suddenly, they could all hear it: low harmonies of sound, deep and choral, like the chanting of monks or the electric hum of a powerful computer. A shimmering mist swirled around them.

"Must be gases from the sewer," Jim murmured, as if thinking aloud. Jim's light flickered and went out, but the mist was full of a bluish luminescence.

"Hold hands!" cried Rowan.

The children grasped each other and Rowan led them on into the light.

For a moment, they could see nothing but swirling, iridescent fog and then there was the tunnel again, but this time the walls were built of brick and below their feet a shallow, sludgy stream of water flowed sluggishly through banks of dirty ice.

"There it is, look," said Rowan, pointing.

Up ahead was a shaft of sunlight shining down through a hole, and a metal ladder led upwards.

"Gallows Street!" cried Jim, in disbelief, striding past Rowan. He reached the bottom of the steps. "Here, let me try my radio." He clicked the button and brought it to his mouth.

"Tommy, Tommy, are you there? You'll never believe what I found!"

Through the crackle of white noise they heard another voice.

"I'm receiving you, Juliet Romeo. Bloody hell, where have you been, Jim? We've had teams searching the whole network. Over."

"I found some kids down here, poor mites, stuck, they were, and those tunnels, I've never seen the like before, must be Roman, went on for miles, didn't know if I was coming or going, there was no…"

"We better get back," Sol hissed.

Rowan looked at the sunlight shining down from Gallows Street. Up there was London, and normality. Up there was *home*. She ached to follow Jim, but what about Luke? She *had* to go back for Luke, and she had made a promise… she gulped, turned and, with one last glance over her shoulder, followed the others back into the mist.

Rowan closed her eyes and thought of the Lady. The Lady seemed to be standing on a hill, watching, her green eyes reflecting a distant horizon; she raised a hand – in salute, or farewell? Rowan could not tell. The Lady seemed to speak, but her voice was as indistinct as the sighing wind.

When Rowan opened her eyes they were emerging from the mist once more, but into pitch-blackness.

"Wait a minute," said Charli.

They heard a rustle. A strike flickered into a spark, then, with a little breath, into a flame. Charli lit her candle. "I nicked Gorg's tinder box," she grinned, relighting the candles.

They inspected the tunnel. Its stone walls ran with damp, and patches of grandmother's fingers sprouted.

"We're back," said Rowan.

"What *was* that other place?" Sol asked in a low voice.

"It was London, my home," said Rowan.

"Your home," Sol echoed, a faraway look in his eye. "You could have gone home, Rowan, and you came back."

She looked down at her feet and Sol put his hand on her cheek.

"Oh, Rowan," he whispered.

"Come on, you two," said Charli. "Dungeons ain't far now, and we gotta shift."

The children retraced their steps.

Charli led the way into what had now become the left-hand passage. It wound like knotted string, growing so narrow they were forced to walk in single file.

"I remember now," said Rowan. "I came this way with Nightshade. It gets really narrow and comes out into the dungeons, through a crack in the rock, doesn't it? You'd hardly know the opening was there."

Charli put her finger to her lips, "We're really close. The guards are probably all dead drunk after that feast, even them dogs, but we don't want to risk it."

The gap at the end of the path was barely a foot wide. It emerged onto another passageway, sparsely lit, with flaming torches. Rowan sniffed the air; she remembered that smell: damp, foetid, like something had crawled away to die. Charli turned right and they passed several empty cells with open doors, heavily studded, with iron grilles. Then they came to one which was locked, occupied by two stick-thin children, lying asleep on a bundle of rags and straw. Rowan shuddered.

Charli made a sign and Rowan felt her stomach knot. She knew what was coming. The next cell held Luke.

Rowan pressed her face against the grille. Luke was squatting on a dirty pile of straw, wrapped in an old blanket. He looked ill, his eyes wide and unblinking, like two ragged holes in his paper-white face.

"Luke," she whispered.

He didn't move, just sat there, staring at nothing. Could he not hear her?

"Luke," she tried again.

He stirred and wiped something from his nose.

"It's me, Rowan."

He gave a brief sigh, but did not move.

"Can he even hear me?" Rowan asked. She could feel herself shaking.

"Here, let's try this," said Charli, moving to the grille. She took a lump of raw meat from her pocket and offered it through the bars. "Hey, Luke, look. Something to eat."

Luke sniffed the air and then on all fours scuttled over to the door. He was whimpering. Rowan couldn't bear it.

"Luke, Rowan is here. Your sister. Remember."

Luke licked his lips and grabbed for the meat. As soon as it was in his hand he retreated to a corner of the cell and began to tear at it with his teeth.

Rowan felt her eyes and nose fill. Hot tears began to fall.

"I want to go," she said.

Rowan was silent for a long time as they made their way back. The sickness in her stomach felt like a tumour pushing up into her chest. She had thought that finding Luke would solve everything. He would become her champion, kill Atr'ax, fulfil the quest; but it had all turned to ashes. She could taste dust in her mouth.

"What's happened to him?" she said at last, her tongue sticking to the roof of her mouth. "He didn't even know me."

"It's this place," said Sol. "It makes you forget. None of us remember."

"Pah!" exclaimed Charli. "It's something they put in the food, more like. I've always thought that worm stew was weird!"

"But *we* haven't forgotten," Rowan said.

Sol stopped and looked at her. "You're different. Both of you. It's like, like a light shining. The rest of us, we've been snuffed out."

There was something like hope flickering in his eyes.

Rowan swallowed away the lump in her throat, but she couldn't stop her voice shaking.

"If we're going to k-kill Atr'ax, we need to find him when he's alone."

"What?" Sol cried. "You've seen them. You've seen what they are, Rowan!" His mouth was an ugly gape of fear.

"He's right," Charli said, shaking her head. "How d'you kill something like that?"

"If we can get to his chamber and catch him when he's sleeping, then perhaps, perhaps we could..."

"Run him through, like a dolphin on a spit? Could you do that, Rowan?" Sol asked in a flat voice. "Even if you had the chance?"

"Look," said Charli, "if you're going into that overgrown spider's lair, then I'm coming with you. Even if it is bleedin' crazy. I made a promise. But why don't we just slip him some of that mushroom juice. Send our eight-legged friend to the Land of Nod? Then slit his gizzard or whatever?"

She looked at the others eagerly.

Sol shook his head. "The Arak-nus need to drink huge amounts of the potion before it works. They perform a kind of ceremony before they enter Consuming Sleep."

"Okay," said Rowan. "When's the next ceremony?"

"The night of the sacrifice," Sol answered. "The night they kill the Winter Knight."

"So that's the day after tomorrow?"

"Yes," said Sol. "But, Rowan, you won't be able to get near them. Only Gorg the Controller and two servers ever go up above, to the chambers. And when the Arak-nus are in Consuming Sleep the way is guarded by dogs.

"Which servers go?"

"At the moment it's Yoki and Hal. Vee uses it as a punishment, because... because there's always the chance that someone won't come back."

"Then perhaps I can get Vee to punish me. Shouldn't be too difficult," Rowan said with a grim smile.

"What about after, though?" Charli raised her candle to Rowan's face.

"After?" Rowan felt dazed.

"You know, escaping. We gotta get Luke and Sol and Tolly and the other kids out of here."

"Yes, you're right." Rowan rubbed her eyes. Her head seemed to be full of snow: cold, white spaces where her thoughts should be.

"Maybe there should be an extra special sacrificial supper that night," Charli suggested.

"What?"

"Oh, you know, a little mushroom sauce on the side. If you, or Sol, can get into Cook's private larder, we'll souse the lot of them!"

40

THE SLEEPING CHAMBERS

W HAT WAS THAT GREAT CLANGING, EARTH-shaking sound?

"Rowan, come on. Come on!"

An engine was approaching. Clang! Grind! Clang! She stood on the platform watching it draw near through billowing steam. Grind! Clang! Grind!

"Ro, Vee's coming. You've got to get up. Please!" Sol's plaintive voice.

"Out of the way, Shrimp!"

Rowan struggled for breath and woke. Someone had grabbed her by the collar, pulling the material so tight around her throat it cut into her windpipe.

Vee's face loomed.

"You lazy little slug!"

Spittle flew from those spiteful red lips into Rowan's eyes.

"Wake up, Stew-girl!"

Rowan was fully awake now, gasping for breath. She tried to sit up, but Vee's grip forced her down upon the straw.

"Slopping out's too good for you, runt."

Rowan's instinct was to keep quiet, but some half-formed memory was urging her to protest. There was a good reason to fight back, to stay on the wrong side of this icy, pitiless girl.

She looked Vee straight in the eye and with a rasping cry said, "Perhaps you should make me Cook's little pet?"

Vee leapt back as if she had been bitten, her face bloodless. For a moment she couldn't speak. Sol stood there, open-mouthed, shaking in disbelief. Rowan got to her feet, rubbing her neck and waited. The killing blow fell with a hiss.

"You little bitch. How dare you! For that you can serve the sleeping chambers, and I hope you rot there!" Vee turned on her heel and left.

Sol was white with shock.

"That was unforgivable, Ro."

"I had to get to the chambers, Sol. How else could I do it?"

Sol shook his head and turned away.

"Sol, please."

But Sol would not look at her. Even after roll call, when the two of them were sent to wash ironware, Sol would not speak. He picked up a grey brush, dipped it into a bowl of soapy water, and began to scrub out a large cauldron. Moments later, Yoki appeared, gazing at Rowan, trembling.

"We've been ordered to f-fetch a fresh seal c-carcass from the meat store," she stuttered.

Rowan gave Sol one last look, but his head was buried inside the iron pot. She shrugged and followed the kitchen waif.

Dressed in serving robes, the two slight girls lugged the clammy dead weight of a fully grown seal onto a creaking trolley and wheeled it through the kitchen.

For the briefest moment, the other waifs watched them pass: a shovel held mid-scoop, a knife frozen in the air, eyes hollow with dread.

Yoki tugged the trolley towards an opening which Rowan hadn't noticed before. It led into a long corridor that ended in a pair of folding doors constructed of thin metal struts and leather flaps. Yoki opened them to reveal a large hollow box suspended on a chain and pulley mechanism.

"It's a lift," said Rowan, surprised.

"Hush," warned Yoki.

The girls pulled the squeaking trolley onto the box and Yoki rang a bell. The lift began to ascend, swaying precariously.

"Do they eat it like this? Raw?" Rowan asked, trying to keep her mind from the disconcerting motion.

"They prefer it raw. And alive," Yoki added, almost as an afterthought.

"What's it like up there?"

Yoki closed her eyes and shuddered.

"Is it true about servers not coming back?"

Yoki stared at the floor, rigid, but said nothing and the lift came to a sudden jolting stop. The doors were flung open with a metallic screech and there was Gorg, his bloated face creased into a scowl.

"What took you scummy pieces so long? Their Magnificences will be looking for titbits, I'm thinking."

He pulled them and their trolley out of the lift. "Get on with it!" he growled. "His Lordship first!"

Gorg stalked down the ice-carved passageway in front of them, jangling a big bunch of keys. It gave on to a wide corridor dimly lit by torches. Off this led five sets of huge double doors, studded with iron. At the central, largest doorway Gorg stopped, selected a hefty iron key, inserted it into the lock and turned.

The door opened and from within came the stench of something rotten. Gorg gave Yoki a shove. "Be quick about it, my pretty one. You know he can't resist a tasty morsel."

Yoki motioned to Rowan and together they attempted to lift the huge, limp carcass. It was like lugging an enormous sack of concrete. Rowan's joints felt as if they would snap apart. Struggling, the girls entered the dim chamber. Rowan blinked, her eyes adjusting to the gloom. What had she expected: some kind of luxury, extravagance, the gleam of jewels?

But not this dank, gloomy space.

She tried to swallow. Something dry and hard had lodged in her throat.

Vast cobwebs stretched from ceiling to floor. In some of them, cocooned shapes could be seen, one of which twitched intermittently. The stink grew overpowering. In the far corner of the chamber webs clustered in thick spirals to form a kind of cone-shaped nest and from its mouth protruded two huge, silvery, segmented legs and a glitter of black eyes.

The girls moved to the centre of the room and Yoki indicated they should drop the carcass. It slapped against the hard ice floor, quivering slightly.

"P-p-please, your Lordship. B-b-breakfast is served," said Yoki, her voice swallowed up by the vast enshrouded chamber.

Atr'ax neither spoke nor moved, but continued to watch them with lidless eyes.

"P-p-permission to clean," Yoki stuttered.

The great creature gave no sign, but from her pocket Yoki pulled a sack.

"Follow," she whispered. "Move slowly."

Inching forward Yoki approached the nest. Beneath it was a pile of foul-smelling, black droppings and the odd bits of bone or hair or skull. Yoki knelt down and began to scrape the sticky mess into the sack. Rowan helped her, but all the while she could feel the scalpel sight of those many eyes.

"Retreat," hissed Yoki and, still on their knees, the girls shuffled backwards. They had reached the seal carcass when Atr'ax moved. The motion was no more than a flash of silver, a blur of legs, and he was on them. The great, palpating body arched overhead, bristling with thick hairs and the sweet, suffocating stench of death.

Rowan could see fangs glinting.

Yoki gave a cry and cowered down. Rowan's hand grabbed for the leather pouch, but it was too late, Atr'ax struck.

She waited for the horror, the searing stab of venom, the freezing death, then in an instant realised it must have been Yoki. But Yoki was scrabbling towards the exit.

With one last look, she saw the Lord of the Araknus crouched over the seal carcass, sucking out its innards.

He had been toying with them. To him, it had been nothing more than a game.

Feeding and cleaning the sleeping chambers took the two girls all morning. They had missed the midday meal and although Rowan didn't feel hungry there was a yawning ache in her gut and her legs shook alarmingly. She was desperate to collapse on her pallet of dank straw, but no doubt Vee would have some nasty job lined up.

But, when they returned, a strange peace had descended on the kitchen. Although the waifs were still working, there was a sleepy after-dinner feel to their efforts. Vee and Master Cook were nowhere to be seen.

Sol came to meet the girls.

"You look exhausted," he said. "I've saved you some food."

Rowan felt tears rise to her throat and tried to swallow them away, but still they fell, dripping down onto the hot, fragrant pie that Sol offered.

He put his arms around her and kissed her cheek. "You know I was frightened for you?"

She nodded.

"Come and sit down. We can rest."

"What's happening?" Rowan asked, looking around. "Where's Cook and... and..."

"Where do you think?" said Yoki.

"Hush," Sol said sharply. "Do you think she has a choice?" Then, turning back to Rowan, "Eat. You'll feel better. And I've got some news." Rowan gazed up at him, her mouth stuffed with the delicious pastry.

"I saw Charli in the mess hall. She says she can drug the Crow Folk and the dungeon guard if we deal with Gorg and his brothers. The ceremony takes place after moonrise tomorrow. The Arak-nus will fast before they sleep, but everyone still gathers in the Great Hall for what they call the Dark Supper. We'll use the potion then."

"But how do we get into Cook's larder? He's always got the keys with him."

"Ah, well…" Sol looked past Rowan.

She turned, and there, coming towards them and wearing a silky red dress that swept the floor, was Vee. Against the bright scarlet material her skin looked whiter than snow. There were dark circles under her eyes.

Rowan gave a start, but Sol put his hand on her shoulder.

"It's okay."

Vee came close. Her expression was strained and sulky. From a fold in her dress she drew a bunch of keys and tossed them on the floor.

"Just be quick," she hissed. "I don't know how long he'll sleep."

Sol grabbed the keys and hurried away in the direction of the larder. Vee stared straight ahead, her eyes stony.

"Vee…" Rowan began.

"Don't talk to me, you bitch," Vee spat out.

"I'm sorry, Vee, about what I said. I didn't…"

"Do you think I care?"

"Y-yes, I do. You're helping us, aren't you?"

Vee was silent for a long time, so still and white. At last, she smiled, a curve of red, bitter as yew berries, and turned her freezing gaze on Rowan.

"Are you so sure?"

They heard Sol, out of breath, scampering back past the ovens. Each of his pockets bulged with a corked bottle, full of bright green liquid. He handed the keys to Vee.

"Thanks. There's no way he'll miss them; there must be hund—"

Vee turned abruptly, cutting Sol off mid-sentence, her lips pressed together in a thin, tight line.

They watched her go, across the kitchen and through the door that led to the cook's quarters.

"How do you know we can trust her?" asked Rowan.

"Because," said Sol, "she's desperate."

<hr />

The following day a mood of restlessness rippled through the kitchen. Whispered messages had been sent to the Shovellers and Diggers at breakfast to assemble in the mess after the Dark Supper. Rowan saw Vee turn a blind eye when she caught two workers lingering by the coal store. Cook seemed to sense something. His unpatched eye, bloodshot and rheumy as it was, was everywhere, keen as a fishhook. Every child who went within a few feet of him risked the wrath of his hairy fists or hobnail boots.

"What is wrong wi' everyone today?" he roared.

Only Vee could pacify him. In-between the flash of butcher's knives, she would roll him cigarettes, feed him caviar and pour his favourite wine.

As sunset approached, Cook bellowed for workers.

"Hey you, Rabbit's Piss, an' Hal, an' you, Offal, come here!"

With a heavy clink of keys, he unlocked his private larder and opened the door wide.

"Don't touch anything, or I'll skin yi alive."

Rowan stared in amazement. The shelves were stocked with all sorts of precious items: silverware, golden platters, goblets, huge jars of honey, sugar crystals, slabs of chocolate, wine, whisky, rum and many flasks of green liquid. Rowan stared, her mouth watering at the thought of a square of rich, dark chocolate or a spoonful of golden honey.

"Here!"

Cook thrust two huge silver pitchers into her arms. The other children were made to carry out eight large bottles of the sleeping potion.

"Vee, take these." He handed her a silver tray, which bore a flagon of blood-red wine and an ornate goblet. "Be careful, now, Hinny. If we break that, we're cocoons!"

Master Cook brought out four massive silver bowls, then, yawning, relocked the door and buckled the keyring back onto his thick leather belt.

"Right," he said. "Let's get this lot sorted." He yawned again, exposing the broken stumps of many teeth. "Ye know, Hinny, I feel as weak as milk-water."

Rowan couldn't help catching Sol's eye. She was sure that Vee had kept her promise to drug the cook's wine, yet when she glanced at Vee the fair-haired girl stood there, still and pale as a nun, her face expressionless.

"Oi, you! Offal!"

Rowan jumped. Cook was addressing her. She stared at him with a rising sense of panic.

"You're to serve the sacrificial wine." He threw something at her. She flinched but, soft and light, it looped around her neck. It was a silver sash, embroidered with odd rune-like symbols.

"You'll take this tray up. Reet? Then wait for Atr'ax to gi' the command."

He uncorked the bottle and filled the silver goblet. "No one else is to touch this, d'ye ken?"

Rowan nodded.

Still yawning, Cook unstoppered one of the large flasks. "Two bottles of my finest emerald nectar for each of their Magnificences." The brilliant green liquid seemed to shimmer as it poured from the lip of the bottle into a small cup, and a sweet, musty odour filled the air – the earthy smell of damp cellars. For a moment, Rowan felt slightly dizzy.

Cook raised the vessel to his nose, to sample the aroma.

"By all the wraiths of Wreaken, this stuff is makin' my head swim!" Cook cursed and crashed the flask down onto the table.

At once, Vee was by his side.

"Master," she said, soft, compelling. "The potion is excellent, fresh and potent as always. Perhaps you should lie down, for a short while? Everything's prepared. There's plenty of time. I'll call you when you're needed."

The cook, grey-faced, seemed to sink down into himself.

"Aye, aye, perhaps you're right, Hinny. Forty winks would do me the…" His sentence ended in an enormous yawn. "Here, gi' me your arm, girl. I can barely stand."

Leaning heavily on Vee's shoulder, Cook staggered to his chambers.

The tension poured out of Rowan in a deep, prolonged sigh. She could tell from the white, expectant faces of the other kitchen workers that they felt the same. Almost at once, the children began to gather around her.

"What's happening?" they whispered.

"What can we do?"

"We want to help."

Sol appeared with the stolen potion bottles and handed one to Rowan. She held it up and said, "Okay, you've seen what this can do. Vee managed to get just a few drops into Cook's wine."

There was a murmur of surprise, of doubt.

"Vee?"

"The cook's wine?"

"Vee did it? Are you sure?"

"We're going to add it to all the sauces and gravies, to every bottle of wine, cask of ale, or bowl of water that goes up to the Dark Supper."

"Drug the food?"

"Why?"

"What will happen?"

"What if we're caught?"

"If we're caught we'll have our insides sucked out." Vee had re-emerged from the cook's chambers, her voice as sharp and clear as one of her master's knives. Her face inscrutable, she moved across the kitchen, towards them. "If we're not caught, we escape."

"Escape?" The kitchen waifs spoke with one voice, a faint sigh of hope and fear and doubt.

"Where will we go?" It was Hal, a tough, pragmatic boy.

"We'll go..." Rowan paused. She hadn't thought much beyond finding Ash and Sage, or fleeing into the tunnels. "I've got friends, waiting, they'll—"

"We'll get away from here," said Vee, slamming her hand down on table top. "Isn't that enough? Now, shut up, we've got work to do. But first we'll eat – for energy. Yoki, Sol, cut up a couple of the hare pies and share it out. After that, everyone into their robes and then we'll drug the food. A half hour before moonrise we go up to the Great Hall. And you –" she turned her gaze on Rowan, "– as sash bearer, you'll take the sacrificial wine. Sol, Hal, Jamie and Mo, you're responsible for the silver pitchers. Watch out: they're heavy. Yoki and Lou, help Li-Li and me carry the bowls. The rest of you bring the food. Understood?"

Rowan half smiled. She would never warm to Vee, but she had to admit the girl had a ruthless ability to get things done.

She turned to Sol but he was gazing at Vee, and Rowan could see that he was lost.

41

SACRIFICE

<hr/>

TORCHES SMOKED AND GUTTERED, CASTING
grotesque shadows over the Great Hall. Under
Vee's uncompromising eye, the children laid out the
feast. The immense silver bowls and the silver pitchers
full of potion were placed at the top of the table, near
the four remaining stone chairs; the roasted meats,
sauces and ales were set out at the lower end.

Rowan, in her long, black, hooded robe and
embroidered sash, stood in front of a plinth that
bore the ceremonial tray and goblet. She wished she
could stop shaking. Her fingers, cramped and white,
had clenched into fists. She must focus on her task
as bearer of the sacrificial wine. When the command
came, she must take the goblet to the Winter Knight, in
his antechamber, and tend to him whilst the assembly
feasted.

Through the window she could see the first cold
rays of moonlight silvering the sky.

"I hope everything is as it should be," growled Gorg,
striding in through the great entrance doors, flanked
by Gut and Gar. Two huge crows flapped noisily above
Gorg's head, settling, finally, on his shoulders.

"Ah, my black beauties. I hope there are meatballs
on Cook's menu. My dark pets love their meatballs."

"Yes, Controller," said Vee, coming forward and curtseying.

Gorg reached out one of his fat, warty hands and stroked Vee's cheek. "Good girl. Good girl, but..." He looked around. "Where is Master Cook? He usually oversees these preparations."

"Regrettably, Master Cook is... unwell." She looked up at Gorg with her astonishing blue eyes. Rowan had seen them glint like icicles, but now they melted into warm, azure pools.

"Ah, ah, I see, off his food, is he?" said Gorg, distracted. "Unfortunate. Perhaps, girl, you can do me the honour of..." He caught hold of her wrist. "I would appreciate, truly appreciate, being served by these fair hands."

Vee's response was a demure lowering of the eyes.

She was clever, Rowan thought. So clever there was no way of knowing where her loyalties lay. Sol had chosen to trust Vee, but then he had his reasons.

"Shall we give the signal, brother?"

Gorg swung around and gripped Gar by the throat. "It's 'Shall we give the signal, *sir*!'. Understand?"

Gar staggered backwards and Gut let loose a screeching fanfare.

Rowan jumped and tried to rest her shaking hands on the plinth.

Concentrate! she told herself. She couldn't afford to make a mistake. She watched as the feasting party made its entrance, through the western alcove, and sat down at the table.

A hush descended and all focused their eyes on the four stone seats. The hall turned deathly cold and after a long pause the whitish mist began to hover and glisten above the chairs. Rowan couldn't bear the way faces formed in the vapour. It reminded her of the Lych Folk: the hollow eyes and gaping mouths. The forms flickered, translucent and ghostly and then, suddenly, they were there, seated, the four Arak-nus, stiff and pale as automata.

Atr'ax spoke, his breath a hiss of poison.

"It is the third night after Midwinter and the moon rises, its rays silver, the darkness like a shimmering web. We sacrifice, we sleep."

In unison the Arak-nus chanted a response: "We sacrifice, we sleep."

"Pour the consuming potion!"

Struggling with the heavy pitchers, Vee and Sol filled the silver bowls with the iridescent green fluid.

This is our Dark Supper.

The dying powers are renewed through sacrifice.

Darkness over light, void over matter, death over life.

"Death over life," came the repetition.

We spin and spin and our web grows thick
Catches stars in their courses.
This final sleep will consume our prey.
The Tree of Life falls to divine decay.
Drink of Death!

The great silver bowls were carried closer to the chairs and the Arak-nus lowered their heads and began to drink.

Vee directed the kitchen waifs to start serving at table. She herself paid special attention to the controller, filling his glass several times with wine and ladling fat meatballs and generous amounts of thick gravy onto his plate.

Gorg, leering at her, shovelled food into his mouth, pausing only to feed the two evil-looking birds perched on the back of his chair.

Rowan wondered how long it would take for the potion to work. Vee, from her experiments oh Cook, had said about an hour, but then Cook was a big, fat man. It was possible that some at the feast might succumb sooner.

When the Arak-nus had drained their bowls, another fanfare sounded.

Atr'ax rose up and turned towards Rowan.

"Serve the sacrificial wine."

With a start, Rowan realised that all eyes were on her. She shrank back, hoping the hood concealed her face. She grasped the tray, fingers rigid, and began the journey, a mere twenty steps or so, towards the arras. It seemed to take forever. The heavy cloth hung down in folds and, as she gazed at it, a wave of dizziness hit her. The embroidery depicted a stag being hunted by hounds. It was so familiar. It could be the tapestry at Sloethorn House!

Swallowing hard she pushed the corner of the arras aside and stepped into an antechamber. As the curtain swung back behind her, all sound from the Great Hall was deadened.

She was in a small space, lit by candles, bare but for a single door in the back wall and a large tomb-shaped block of ice. Upon the block lay the Winter Knight. He looked like a medieval statue, the kind you'd find in a church: horizontal, rigid, hands folded in repose across his chest.

Was he really alive?

Or was it some kind of machine? Perhaps, beneath

the visor, there was a series of cogs and springs, ready to whir into action, a macabre clockwork toy. Yet how could you sacrifice a machine? Maybe it was Luke, after all, or maybe it was all a charade.

Rowan gulped. The urge to find out was overwhelming. The Knight lay so still. Carefully, she placed the tray on the floor and drew close to the ice block. Hardly daring to breathe, Rowan leant over and stretched out her hand towards the visor. Were there eyes moving beneath that mask? A glint behind the dark slit? Breath coming from a concealed mouth? She leant in, close.

A wrenching pain!

Steel-plated fingers grabbed her wrist. She gasped. The Knight jolted upwards, swung his legs round to a sitting position. His other hand gripped the sword hilt.

"Please," she whimpered. "You're hurting me."

For a moment, the Knight looked at her and then dropped her wrist. She staggered back, heart pounding. He stood up, his movements slow, stiff, deliberate, and took a step towards her. He could kill her, she thought. There was nothing to stop him. She shrank back against the wall. But the Knight just stood there. Was he studying her? Eventually, he motioned towards the goblet of wine. She scrambled towards it, afraid to turn her back, and, hands shaking, held it up to him. The Knight lifted the visor just enough to reveal his mouth, a human mouth at least and, grabbing the vessel, tipped back his head and gulped down the ruby-coloured drink.

But, no, he had not quite finished; he was offering the last few sips to her, thrusting the goblet under her nose. Rowan caught the scent of the wine, heady, unsettling. Her heart ached with longing and despair. How strong, how sweet it smelt! She lowered her head, lips touching the rim of the cup, eyes closing in anticipation. She knew that this was wrong, but how she wanted to taste that wine. Her hands cupped his fingers as she tilted the goblet upwards.

"No!" cried the Knight.

With a sudden movement he knocked the cup from her grasp and flung his arm across his face.

A brilliant silver light flashed at her throat. The leather pouch had come loose and the Fàinne Duilleoga, partly revealed, glinted brightly.

"No!" He staggered away, but something in his voice, some echo from another time and place, made her heart race with fear and confusion.

"Who are you?" she cried, trying to grab his arm. "Luke, Luke, it's you!"

He flung her back. "Go! Leave!"

"But, Luke!"

He drew his sword, holding it at throat height

She turned and fled through the door. Suddenly, she knew what to do. She must find out. She must! A need drove her on, through corridors, down stairways, along tunnels. She couldn't think, couldn't reason. All plans were abandoned. Down, down she went, into the dripping regions beneath the Fortress. The Leaf Ring had long since faded and a tallow stub wrenched from the wall was her only light. Down into the dungeons she flew, down to Luke's cell. She must know the truth.

Was Luke the sacrifice?

In the deep places beneath the Fortress she peered through the bars of a door, into the black hole beyond and gave a groan. Her brother was there, hunched up on the filthy straw.

"Oh, Luke," she sighed. "Oh, Luke."

She didn't know if she was glad or not. She stretched her hand through the bars. "I'll get you out, Luke, I promise."

Perhaps the candlelight caught his interest. He shuffled over to the door.

"Out," he echoed, his voice empty as a broken shell.

"I'm going to take you away."

"Away."

He put his hand in hers. It felt thin and cold. "*They*... won't... come?" His voice was a whisper of terror.

"No, no. They won't come. Oh, Luke."

If she had a key she would free him now and take him through the fog to the sewers, to London or anywhere, anywhere but here. She didn't care anymore about the quest, about anything. She felt sick. She just wanted them to stop hurting Luke.

Suddenly, her shoulder was grabbed from behind. Rowan gave a yell and thrust the candle wildly at her attacker's face.

Someone leapt back.

"Flippin' ell, you almost had me with that bleedin' flame, Ro! What on earth are you doing down 'ere?"

"Charli!" she cried, grabbing her friend in a bear hug.

"Shush! There's a bleedin' rat-face and his hell hound about here somewhere."

Rowan's heart pounded against her ribs and she steadied herself against the cell door. "You gave me such a fright. Aren't you meant to be feeding the Crow Folk?"

"Done that. And drugged most of the guards, the ones that weren't at the ceremony, that is. All except one. He's on the prowl. But look what I got!" She shook a large bunch of keys.

"They're Gorg's. His master set. They open everything. I've come to free the prisoners."

"Luke!"

"Yeah, Luke, and the other poor mites. Listen, though. Something weird has been happening down in the mines. I went to get the Diggers and Shovellers, and found the place abandoned, tools lying around everywhere. Then I meets little Tolly; she's wandering around all dazed, an' white as milk (even though I bin trying to feed her up with bits of meat: them scraggy crows won't miss a few steaks here and there!). But, anyway, I asked her what happened to the other kids and she said they'd all gone. 'Where?' I goes and she said, 'Into the light.' She said this beautiful light appeared in the cavern where they were digging and all the children ran towards it. Somethin' like a Christmas tree, she says, all glowin' and sparklin', though where that poor shrimp ever got to see a... but never mind that. So, they all drops their picks 'n' shovels, she says, and runs towards it. Tolly tried to follow but she wasn't fast enough. By the time she got there the light had gone and there was no sign of the other kids."

"Oh, Charli, another gateway!"

"That's what I thought."

"Perhaps that's what they've been digging for. Perhaps the 'Source' is a kind of gateway to all the gateways. If the Arak-nus have that, then they can go anywhere!"

Charli shuddered. "God, I hope you're wrong, Ro. Poor little Toll couldn't get through, after all."

"So what happened to Tolly? Where is she now?"

"I sent her to the mess. I'm taking Luke and the other prisoners there too."

"And I've got to get back to the feast."

"Yeah, that's a point. What *are* you doing here, Ro? Nuffin's up, is it?"

"I had to make sure that Luke wasn't the Winter Knight... the sacrifice. But I've got to get back... there's still something I..." she paused. "Charli?"

"Yeah?"

"You'll take care of Luke, won't you? Get him back home, I mean."

Charli said nothing for a moment, but put her hand against Rowan's cheek.

"I'm not leaving you."

"But..."

"Luke'll be okay. Now go."

Ripping off the silver sash, Rowan ran through tunnels and up countless steps towards the Great Hall. The uproar above echoed eerily along the corridors of ice: a cacophony of drunken voices, howling and snorting with mirth. She dare not go back into the antechamber. It would be better to slip into the hall, she thought, and try to mingle with the other servers. Panting, she crept up the ice-hewn staircase, towards the great open doors. No one was on duty. Through the entrance she could see guards swarming, like rats, over the feasting table, guzzling dish after dish, slurping at bowls and tipping wine over their comrades' heads. The dogs, growling possessively, cracked meat bones with their huge teeth and licked at the soft, oozing marrow. Gorg, warding off rat-men with a hefty copper candlestick, fed his squawking crows with the choicest cuts of meat. Gar and Gut had upended a guard and were dunking him head first into a barrel of ale. It was utter chaos. The mushroom potion seemed to have sent everyone wild.

The Arak-nus, by contrast, were frozen into some kind of trance, their eyes milky-blind.

Keeping to the shadows, Rowan slunk into the hall, merging with the black-robed servers. They all, with the exception of Vee, stood to one side, adopting a familiar submissive posture: head bowed, eyes fixed on the floor. Vee, of course, was aware of everything. With a keen sidelong glance she watched Rowan take her place.

Atr'ax stirred, his eyes regaining their oil-black sheen.

He did not need to command attention. At the first chill indrawing of breath a hush descended on the gathering.

"Soon," he said, "we will withdraw to our sleeping chambers. We have felt stirrings in the roots of the mountain. The Fountain Head, the Source, is close; all ways exposed. We spin and spin, trap all things. Darkness over light, void over matter, death over life."

"Death over life," the Arak-nus sighed, like long-dead things turning to dust.

"Now is the moment of our renewal. I summon the Lord of Midwinter."

Rowan watched closely. The knowledge that Luke was safe made her almost dizzy with relief. Yet still she felt an odd mixture of guilt and sorrow, for the strange figure facing this cruel execution.

From behind the heavy arras the Knight emerged, as stiff and awkward as an automaton. Yet this was no robot, Rowan had seen his mouth – *flesh and blood*. What was he? The figure bowed low before Atr'ax.

"You have fulfilled your function, servant. You are the rule of Midwinter, the great victory of darkness over light. In death *your power*, the nullifying energy of the void, is reborn within us, the Arak-nus, bringing an everlasting night to all – a feast of despair."

The Winter Knight unsheathed his sword and, kneeling, laid it at Atr'ax's feet. The Lord of the Arak-nus stroked the Knight's head, as a master might pet his dog. But Rowan could see that the long white fingers were reaching for a clasp, as if to remove the helmet.

She could not stop herself. She leant forward, eager to see the Knight's face.

Suddenly, someone screamed, a thin pitiful sound. A ferocious volley of barks followed and cries of "Shut it, scum!"

In through the main doorway came a rat-man; it was Rafe! He was dragging Tolly by the scruff of the neck, and, shadowing them, was a snarling black hound. Rafe threw Tolly to the floor and bowed down low, his twitching snout touching the ground.

"Forgive me, your Magnificence, but…"

The sound that came from the Arak-nus was like the crackle of warm flesh plunged into dry ice:

a dreadful, venomous hiss that seared through to the bone. As a body they turned, their corpse-like mouths gaping.

Everyone in the hall flinched and cowered; even Gorg stumbled backwards drunkenly.

Only the Knight, Rowan noticed, seemed unaffected. Grabbing his sword, he jumped to his feet, ready to defend his masters.

Rafe was grovelling, covering his head with both arms. "Please, your Magnificence," he squeaked. "There is d-d-danger, please."

The female, Nyche, moved swiftly, snatching up Rafe in her hook-like fingers. "How dare you contaminate the Rite of Sacrifice, vermin!"

"No," Rafe squealed. "The Diggers have gone. The mines are empty. Please, please, mistress. Ask that dirty piece. I found it skulking in the corridors, and for a scrap of dog meat it betrayed its friends. There are spies everywhere. The foul Dur'ae are amongst us!"

A hiss of hatred flooded the chamber. Nyche lowered her mouth towards Rafe's throat, sharp teeth glistening.

"Wait, Nyche." Atr'ax's voice was silk soft. "Question the girl."

The woman tossed Rafe aside and grasped Tolly, dragging her to her feet. The child stood swaying, dull-eyed, slack-jawed. Rowan doubted the poor girl even knew where she was.

"Are you one of the Dur'ae?"

The child shivered.

"Are you Dur'ae, scum?" A glacial screech, grinding all to dust.

Tolly gave a whimper.

The woman's fist, powerful as a steel spring, slammed into the side of the child's head. There was a sudden crack, and Tolly crumpled to the floor.

"No! Don't hurt her!" The cry came from the open doorway. Charli ran forward, tears streaking down her face, and behind, slumped against the doorjamb, was Luke.

Rowan, a cry stuck in her throat, tried to take a step towards them. But, in that split second, something, someone, pulled her back – clutching her robe.

It was Vee.

Rowan, stomach contracting, watched as the gypsy girl fell to her knees and took the scrawny child in her arms.

"Oh, Tolly, Tolly, I woulda fed you. I woulda given you anything, cake, chocolate, anything…"

But Tolly's head flopped down at an unnatural angle and her eyes were empty as ash.

"She's dead," sobbed Charli and hugged the frail body close, stroking the moth-eaten hair.

Atr'ax stood and stepped forwards, moving with sinister grace. A wave of bitter cold rippled through the hall, its epicentre his tall, pale, glittering form.

"Bring the girl-child to me," he said.

Nyche plucked Charli from the floor, leaving Tolly's corpse collapsed in a heap. She gripped Charli, forcing the girl's head towards the gaunt, white face of Atr'ax.

Rowan gasped, reached out.

"Don't be insane," Vee hissed in her ear.

Rowan could see blood running down Charli's face, where the woman's nails had cut flesh. The gypsy girl struggled, screwing her eyes tight.

"Look at me," the Grey Man commanded, the sound a seeping poison.

Charli's eyes opened, wide with terror.

No one, thought Rowan, could resist that voice, or the black, kaleidoscopic glitter of his stare. Charli's face turned grey. Rowan understood now what Sol had meant about the children being snuffed out. Some light – whatever spark went into creating that wild, rebel spirit – began to drain from Charli's eyes, leaving them sunken and old, as if the creature was feeding from her soul.

"She is not the Dur'ae," Atr'ax said at last. "But the Dur'ae is here."

He turned his gaze upon the children and Rowan could see countless, horror-stricken faces mirrored in his black eyes.

"Servant!"

With a metallic ring of armour, the Winter Knight was at his master's side.

The Grey Man chuckled, the creak of rusting metal in the north wind.

"Let's use a little midge to catch a fat golden fish. Seize her!"

With sudden agility, the Knight grabbed Charli by the arm and brought the blade to her throat.

"Ah, just one little cut and it is done," murmured Atr'ax. "Or shall it be slow and sure? A tender morsel for my web?"

And he turned, his terrible gaze strafing the fear-stricken children.

They stood. Heads bowed, shaking, barely able to breathe, dreading the inevitable.

Charli gave the slightest cry as the steel pressed deeper into her flesh.

"Kill her, then," said Atr'ax.

Rowan, making a desperate choking sound, lunged forwards.

"No, no, stop! Let her go. It's me. It's me!"

42

THE WHITE TREE

EVERY HEAD TURNED TO LOOK. ROWAN stood, feeling numb with fear, knowing she had walked into the trap and that there was no way out.

Atr'ax sighed with a kind of bliss: a desiccating gust rustling through the frozen tundra. "The silk thread winds in," he murmured softly. "We have our sacrifice."

"Let her go," said Rowan, her voice a faint whisper. She could see a line of red at Charli's throat.

Atr'ax made a strange, twittering sound. "You don't quite understand, child. I can't do that."

"But it's me you want."

"Ah, a true sacrifice, is that it? Your life for hers? I'm afraid that's impossible. It's all over, you see. You do see that, don't you?" He paused, slender fingers raised.

"Kill them!"

"No!" screamed Vee. "Get the torches! Go for their eyes!"

And as the children ran and the Knight's sword flashed, Rowan, driven by some deep urge, pulled the Fàinne Duilleoga from its pouch.

An immense and brilliant starburst of light flooded the chamber. The Knight bellowed and staggered back, dropping Charli.

A dreadful ear-splitting wail, like the high-pressured screech of escaping steam, filled the hall. It was Atr'ax: bloating, splitting, enraged. His human form ripped apart and a gigantic, silvery body emerged – numerous legs waving, fangs glinting. But the intense glare and confusion, and the inebriating effects of the potion, must have been too great for Nyche and her cohorts. They seemed to falter, stagger, blinded by the dazzle and suddenly they were gone, fled into the shadows.

Gorg and his guards, befuddled, stumbled about unseeingly. Some cowered, some scrambled under the table, some took flight. In the chaos, a number of children took their chance and ran for it, others grabbed flaming torches and mustered around Vee.

Only Atr'ax stood firm, abdomen shimmering, the light turning his eyes to eight silver moons.

"She is the Dur'ae!" he hissed, groping forward with his great legs. "Be my eyes. Kill her!"

His will, glacial, implacable, seemed to clear all before him.

The Knight hesitated for a moment, as if dazed, then, shielding his eyes, he made a grab for Rowan and caught her by the wrist. His hand, a steel vice, crushed her thin bones. She whimpered with pain, but refused to let go of the amulet. With a roar of rage the Knight raised his sword, its razor edge a fracturing prism of light.

Rowan closed her eyes tight, found herself repeating words over and over: "Oh, Mum, oh, Dad, oh, Luke, I'm so sorry…"

Any moment the blow would come, and it would end.

But death was still and soft as fallen snow. A timeless holding of breath.

Was this death, after all?

She felt the Knight release his grip, heard a clattering ring of steel on ice, and opened her eyes.

The Knight was clawing at his chest. In the streaming dazzle of the Fàinne Duilleoga, his breastplate was glimmering, changing.

Rowan gasped. An iridescent pattern of white light traced its way across the black metal; it was the image of a tree.

Atr'ax raised his silver claws and screamed, and it was the most terrible sound Rowan had ever heard. The Great Ice Fortress shook on its foundations. Everyone, except the Knight, collapsed to the floor, clamping hands to ears. Even so, Rowan found she could not block out the sickening, rock-grinding screech that turned her senses to mush. She groped her way forward, through a blizzard of pain, and curled herself around Charli.

Suddenly, the noise stopped.

"She *will* die," Atr'ax hissed, edging towards the two girls.

The Knight, looking like a toy soldier, stepped in his way.

"Kill her, servant."

The Knight did not move.

Atr'ax crept forward on his huge, segmented legs, fangs lustrous.

"That is an order!" The creature's voice was a scream of rage.

"I am no longer yours to command," said the Knight.

Apart from a distant rumble of thunder, the chamber was silent.

Then came a flash, like lightning.

Icy fang met cold steel in a bolt of power that seared the air. The Winter Knight spun deftly, stabbing one of the glassy eyes. It burst like an egg. But with awful precision, Atr'ax's metallic leg-hooks caught beneath the armoured back plate and lifted his foe off the ground. The Knight aimed a sharp kick and it caught the spider's vulnerable mouth parts. With a screech of disbelief, Atr'ax dropped him, scuttling backwards.

The Knight pursued his advantage, slicing at the great front legs, driving the creature back. Atr'ax, blind and half drugged, was still quick, cunning. He gave a monstrous spring and landed halfway up the high wall of the chamber and, moving fast, scurried upwards to the ceiling. He crouched there like some grotesque, pendulous chandelier.

Craning his neck back, the Knight watched, sword ready.

Atr'ax began to crawl, crossways: slowly at first and not towards the Knight but towards Rowan.

"Move, Rowan!" screamed Sol.

"Move!" cried Vee.

"Run, child!" bellowed the Knight.

Yet, before Rowan had got to her feet, Atr'ax was above her, descending swiftly on a cable of silk, his fangs glinting.

Even then, she could have scrambled away on hands and knees, but Charli lay on the ground, pale and weak. Rowan crouched protectively over her friend, and was aware of the spider's gross form dropping to the floor. His massive legs enclosed the two girls, like a cage. Rowan could feel the soft palps urgently probing their prone bodies.

She saw the Knight running towards them, sword held high. But someone was there already. A flask of oil shattered over the spider's cephalothorax followed by a flaming torch. There was a soft whoosh and suddenly Atr'ax was engulfed in a crown of flames. Droplets of fire rained to the ground; a golden light danced in Vee's eyes.

The spider, a living torch, lurched forwards towards the Great Hall doors, screeching in agony. Pushing Vee to one side, the Knight plunged into the inferno. Rowan could see him, a shadow in the flames, thrusting his sword again and again into the bloated abdomen. The monster reared up, screaming, its legs flailing.

"Get out!" screamed Vee, in warning.

Then all the children took up the cry, "Get out, mister, get out!" Rowan staggered to her feet and understood why.

With an earth-shattering crash, the hideous creature fell to the floor.

An echo seemed to rumble through the ice castle.

The children, stunned and pale, edged towards the grisly sight.

Half crushed by its weight, they could see the Knight, his head and shoulders protruding from beneath the smoking, blackened hulk. Rowan limped forward.

"We have to get him out," said Sol.

"He's dead," said Vee. "No one could survive that."

"But he tried to save us."

Vee shrugged and shook her head. Again, thunder shook the castle.

Rowan knelt down next to the charred remains. "We can't just leave him," she said faintly, her throat dry as dust. She unbuckled the straps, removed the Knight's helmet and gave a barely audible cry.

It was Finn. The Winter Knight was Finn.

She felt her stomach heave, and suddenly wished that the spider had bitten her, had put an end to her.

This is what death is really like, she thought.

This paralysing sickness.

This deadening ache.

This incomprehensible futility.

She brushed her fingertips across Finn's cheeks. His skin was as grey and cold as old snow.

And the flinty coldness she felt inside would be with her for the rest of her life, slicing away at her heart.

There was a sob.

Luke was at her side, reaching out his hand to touch Finn's hair. His face wet with tears.

"Dad, oh God, Dad!"

Rowan put her arm around her brother's shoulders, trying to swallow away the hard lump of misery. At least Luke could cry. He would cry for them both.

A loud rumble shook the Fortress and fragments of ice fell from above.

"That's not thunder," said Vee. "The castle's falling! We have to get out."

Rowan heard the words, but they had no meaning. She wanted to look and look at Finn's beautiful ice-carved face, wanted to stay here with Luke, the three of them together.

Vee was shouting out directions. "Go to the mess, find whoever you can. Tell everyone to head for the courtyard! And watch out for Nyche and the other two; they could be anywhere."

Someone was at Rowan's shoulder. Someone put their hand on her arm.

"Ro?"

She dragged her gaze away and saw Charli's pale, anxious face.

"Rowan, we have to go."

Rowan closed her eyes and gripped Finn's steel-plated shoulder, but it was as hard and unyielding as the pain inside.

"Rowan, we have to help the others to get out."

She bowed her head and knew that Charli was right.

That the world should fall around her seemed natural to Rowan. This was a new story now, where white towers crumbled, cracks yawned blackly beneath her feet and glittering shards of ice rained down from above.

"The turrets are falling," said Vee, staring out of the tall windows. "We'll have to try to get out through the castle gates. Anyone who hasn't got one already, grab a torch."

Rowan, pulling Luke after her, felt numb with pain. She did not much care if the sky fell, but nevertheless she followed Charli and the others, through state rooms, over disintegrating floors, where mirrors and statues crashed to the ground. On they went across newly opened chasms and down collapsing stairways. The thunderous tremors roared in Rowan's ears, almost knocking her off her feet.

As they reached the top of a flight of steps, they saw lights coming from below, heard shouts.

"Go back! This way's blocked."

It was another group of children, breathless and dusty. "The entrance chamber has collapsed on top of Nyche and the others," they said. "We can't get to the main gates."

Vee frowned. "There's no other way."

"What about the service stairs?" Sol suggested.

"That leads down to the kitchens. There's no way out from the kitchens."

"Try the mines," said Charli, eyes bright now in her pale face.

"Mines?" several voices cried. "What good is that?"

"First," said Charli, "the rock is more likely to hold..."

"Yeah, and we'll be buried alive!"

"Second, there's a passage out." She swayed and leant on Rowan's shoulder.

"She's right," said Rowan. "It's how the Diggers escaped. I've seen it."

"So have I," said Sol, stepping forward.

Vee stared at them for a moment, eyes steely, calculating.

"Right," she cried suddenly. "Down to the mines. Sol, you lead the way."

Sol took the back stairs, narrower and sturdier than the wide state corridors. Down, down they went, scurrying like moles into the cold, dark earth. Here the tremors, though still powerful and thrumming through the rock like deep bass notes, did not make the world shift and crumble around them.

Sol led them through tunnels where mine tools lay abandoned, into passages gleaming with the ghostly swellings of grandmother's fingers, and further down towards the dungeons.

"It's here," he cried. "The passageway splits into three. We take the middle one. Look, look, you can see the light ahead!"

A volley of barks exploded out of the tunnel behind them, echoing, rebounding off the walls, and something launched itself through the air, bringing the last child down with a horrible scream.

"Kill, Ripper, kill!" an oily voice squealed.

"Run," cried Vee, waving the others through. The light ahead was growing stronger – a clear, golden glow that made Rowan dream of a summer's dawn. But she wrenched herself back, saw the hound clamp its jaws around Yoki's neck. Without thinking, she ran forward and thrust the flaming torch into the dog's face. Charli was at her left shoulder, Vee at her right, lunging with their torches. The hound gave a snarling yelp and leapt backwards.

"Take Yoki," said Rowan. "I'll hold them off."

Vee and Sol pulled the injured girl to her feet and struggled towards the light.

"Go on. You too, Char," said Rowan. "And take Luke for me."

"I'm not going, remember," said Charli.

"Nor me," said Luke. "That bloody dog's got it coming to him."

As Vee disappeared into the light, there was the sudden, sweet scent of apple blossom, and the softest strains of fairy music.

"Summerland," Rowan murmured, with a choking sigh.

She heard Vee's voice fading. "Quick, Rowan, now, it's now..."

They turned and ran, the hound snapping at their

heels, but as they reached the golden light it vanished.

"No!" cried Rowan.

She spun back to face teeth and claws, the cruel swish of a blade, the snickering laughter of Rafe.

"Thought you'd escaped, missy?"

In desperation, the three children swung their torches from side to side, but Charli, drained, suddenly crumpled to her knees, a knife sliced into Luke's arm, the black hound reared up and with one crunching bite snapped Rowan's torch in two. She tried to reach for the Fàinne Duilleoga, but the hound's teeth were tearing at her sleeve.

"Oh, Lady, good Lady of Summerland, help us, please," she cried.

There came a dazzling flash of blue. Out of a swirling, ice-cold mist, leapt two creatures – shimmering phantoms, moonlight shapes – yet solid enough to slam into the enemy, bowling them backwards, hard against the rock. With howls of terror, Rafe and the slavering dog turned tail and streaked away into the rumbling darkness.

Rowan ran forward and flung her arms around two furry silver necks.

"Oh, Sage! Ash, oh my goodness! How did you get here?"

"Hush, child," said Sage. "We must go. The Fortress is falling and even these deep tunnels are not safe. Pick up your friend and follow."

Sage turned to re-enter the blue mist, but the light had changed again. As if from far away and long ago came the most delicate rose-tinted gleam.

43

THE ICE DOOR

———◆———

WHEN ROWAN WOKE UP, SHE WAS AWARE that her pillow was very white and very cold. Snow! And there was the earthy scent of leaf mould in her nostrils. She raised her head.

Curled up next to her, fast asleep on a coverlet of snow, lay Luke and Charli. Behind them, still and silent, rose Hag's Knoll, a rising sun gilding the trees.

"Ash?" she called softly. "Sage?"

But there was no reply, and no trail of paw prints in the snow. Were they gone for good? Had they returned into the light?

Then the memory of Finn hit her. Finn's face cold and dead as stone.

Nothing really mattered, after all.

She had fulfilled her promise but, in the end, the Hunters had won. They had taken the thing that mattered most.

From somewhere drifted the sweet smell of wood smoke.

For others, life would go on.

Gently, Rowan shook Charli and Luke awake and the three of them, subdued, rubbing sleep out of their eyes, set off in the direction of Sloethorn House.

As the sun climbed higher, the golden light turned pinkish, then silvery blue. Colours were vivid, the holly leaves and berries sparkled and, emerging from the wood, they heard a horse neigh, dogs barking. Charli paused, her face had changed.

"It's the wagons," she said. "That's Rosie neighing an' I can small wood smoke. Bet it's fried eggs for breakfast." She gave Rowan a great bear hug, then Luke. "I gotta go."

They watched her run down to the far edge of the field. She turned, gave one last heartfelt wave and disappeared through a hedge.

<hr/>

In the stable yard Mr Holly emerged from beneath the bonnet of a battered Land Rover, his grey hair stiff with engine oil.

"Aye up," he nodded as they passed by. "You're out early."

There was a sharp, knowing look in his eye. Perhaps it was the odd assortment of clothes they wore: Rowan still in her black robes and Luke's combat jacket ripped to shreds, the arm stained with blood.

"May wants to see thee," said Mr Holly. "She's at breakfast."

In the morning room they were greeted by the delicious aroma of creamy porridge and sizzling bacon, and three exuberant spaniels jumping up, wagging their tails, licking any patch of bare flesh.

"Clove, Mustard, down! Goodness me!" cried May. "The way these rascals carry on, one would think you'd been gone for days! Mace, Clove, heel now! Do help yourself to breakfast, my dears; time for hot baths after."

May did not remark upon their grubby, tattered appearance, nor comment (thought Rowan) when Luke fell upon the warm rolls and bacon like a hungry wolf cub.

May went on, a little awkwardly. "I'm afraid there's some rather bad news. Your father, Finn, is, in hospital..."

Luke glanced up, stopped chewing.

"Some sort of..." May pushed the salt cellar to and fro, "... car accident."

It was Rowan she looked at. May's manner might be blunt and no nonsense, but there was deep compassion in that gaze.

"Betty, your grandmother, has arranged a visit to the hospital. Mr Holly will drive you there in the old Land Rover. Oh, and she's also managed to contact your mother. Your mother is on her way."

At that, Rowan sank down heavily onto a chair and put her head in her hands. She couldn't believe it. Mum would be here. She would be here soon, today maybe. Oh God, after everything!

She ached and ached... but couldn't tell if it was with pain or relief.

<hr />

The echo of the long corridors, the stink of powerful disinfectant and stale, overheated air seemed to choke Rowan. Uniformed figures hurried back and forth, someone was wheeled past urgently on a trolley, and always, in the background, there was the ominous hum and beep of unseen machines.

Grandma, Luke and Rowan were ushered into a room by a smiley nurse.

Rowan caught her breath.

She hadn't been prepared for... for the shock of Finn. Finn stretched out grey and hollow against white sheets, hair shorn to stubble, a row of bloody stitches stapled into his pale skull. There was something clamped into his mouth, tubes coming from his nose, wires taped to chest and temples. Flickering screens and silver-grey machines crowded round the bed like unwelcome visitors.

Finn looked as if he was... Rowan gulped, then clenched her jaw. There was no point hiding from the truth. She had to face up to it; Finn was dead. He was dead. He had died a long time ago.

The nurse spoke to Finn as if he were wide awake, propped up in bed, sipping tea.

"Mr Maloney, there's someone here to see you."

Grandma sat down heavily in a chair. Luke perched on the armrest bedside her and placed his hand on Gran's shoulder. Rowan shifted uneasily from foot to foot.

"Come and sit here, duck," said the nurse, pulling up a plastic stool.

Rowan sat on the edge of the seat, hands perched awkwardly on knees, and stared at her father.

Finn was cold and grey as stone.

The nurse's smile was gentle, well meaning.

"Why not talk to him? Your dad's unconscious, but he might be able to hear. He'd like to hear your voice."

"What's that thing in his mouth?" Luke asked.

"It's a ventilator. It helps him to breathe."

"Why can't he breathe for himself?"

"Well, his brain is trying to make itself better. It's as if he's gone into a really deep sleep and is too tired to do all the important things. So we're just helping, for a while, until his brain decides to wake up."

Will it wake up? But Rowan didn't ask this. She knew the answer.

The kind nurse left, and Luke reached out and stroked the back of Finn's clawed hand. Grandma began to chatter away; inconsequential things: about the dreadful weather, Grandad's bronchitis, the price of gas central heating. But Rowan just sat there, staring and staring at the bloodless skin, faintly blue beneath translucent fingernails.

A dummy's hands.

For half an hour or more they were there, the hospital clock marking each long second with a dull tick. Sometimes, Luke took over from Grandma, keeping up the flow of words. Rowan was surprised to hear him speak about Sloethorn.

"It's great, Dad, you'd love it. It's hundreds of years old and the walls are covered in ivy and there are these winding corridors that seem to go on forever and a huge library. But best of all is the landscape... it's like Brueghel, the snow changes everything. I'm going to get my charcoals out and start doing some sketches... and work on my portfolio, for college."

Luke must know that it's no use, thought Rowan. "Why is he bothering?"

Grandma leant over, lowering her voice. "Why don't you say something, chick? Just a few words to let him know you're here."

What's the point?
WHAT'S THE POINT?

She wanted to shout it out loud. But the swallowing pain defeated her. She looked down at her feet.

The door opened. It was a woman, smartly dressed beneath her official white coat.

"Mrs Beckthwaite? I'm Doctor Earnshaw. Would it be okay to have a word with you, and perhaps Mr Maloney's son?"

Grandma and Luke left the room.

The ventilator sucked and sighed noisily in the sudden quiet. Finn's chest rose and fell.

Through the glass door Rowan could see Doctor Earnshaw listening carefully, head tilted to one side.

The wound on Finn's skull was long and ugly. They had cut off his beautiful hair. Rowan began to reach out towards his head, then stopped and glanced up.

Doctor Earnshaw was speaking now. Rowan could see the worried expression on Luke's face. Grandma was shaking her head.

Rowan touched Finn's hand. It was icy cold.

"Daddy?"

The machine rasped and rattled as if fighting for breath. Rowan stroked his cheek, rough and unshaven.

"Daddy, it's Rowan."

Now Doctor Earnshaw was shaking her head and Luke was frowning, his face crumpling, fighting back tears.

No!

But the cry was inside Rowan's head. She gripped the grubby leather pouch hanging around her neck, loosened it and drew out the black pebble, burning hot in her palm.

"Perhaps it doesn't matter anymore," she hissed. "Perhaps nothing matters."

For a long time she stared at the stone knowing that she would not be able to bear it if... if...

With a sudden, blind movement she pressed the Earthstone into her father's palm.

For a moment, a long moment, nothing happened. Then there came a burst of light so bright she reeled backwards, her stool crashing to the floor. A high-pitched alarm sounded. The door slammed open. The room was full of running footsteps, of uniforms.

"Come away, dear, come away."

Rowan was swept from the room. Craning her head backwards she saw Finn's arm on the sheet. The clenched fist, furling and unfurling... reaching, reaching out.

———◆———

The three of them were taken to a private room and given cups of tea, which none of them drank. They waited and waited, faces grey. Rowan stared at the floor. She couldn't bear to look at the others. Then suddenly, Doctor Earnshaw appeared looking perplexed, yet unable to hide her smile.

"I really don't know how to... this is the most extraordinary thing. I've never seen... Finn's awake. He, he's sitting up. He's asking for you."

"But... you said..." Luke began.

"Yes, yes, it's..." She shook her head in astonishment. "I can't really explain. But he's off the ventilator. He's sitting up in bed, demanding to see you."

"But... is he...? I mean, I thought..." Grandma was staring at the doctor, eyes wide with disbelief.

"We'll run tests, of course, thorough tests to check that everything is fine, fine, yes. But, right now, I think you should see him. He really is being very insistent."

⁘

Finn was sitting up in bed, a wide sheepish grin on his face. "Sorry I took so long."

Grandma gave him a powdery, scented kiss, but she giggled like a schoolgirl when he swept her up in his muscular, tattooed arms. "Looking as bonny as ever, Betty."

"Ho!" she blushed. "I can see you've lost none of your Irish charm."

"And as for you two." Finn grinned at Rowan and Luke. "Come here, right now."

They sat down on the bed, and Finn pulled them close.

"*That's* what I've been wanting! A great big hug! Feels like I've been away forever."

"Are you sure you're all right? Do you remember anything about the accident?" Grandma asked.

"Accident?" Finn looked confused. "I remember turning off the motorway near Thirsk. Borrowed Geezer's old Range Rover. Snow chains, everything. Then there were these dogs, great brutes charging out of the darkness. They dragged me…" He paused and shook his head. "I suppose I must have cracked my head." He touched the scar and winced. You know, for a while I didn't think I'd get out. If it wasn't for you two."

"What was it like?" Luke asked in a quiet voice.

Finn considered. "Cold. Very cold. Not dark. It was light, like glass, or, or ice. Like being trapped below the ice." He was silent for a moment, deep in thought.

Luke and Rowan exchanged looks. Grandma seemed mystified.

"There were tunnels, corridors. I was trying to find a way out, but I always ended up where I started. Couldn't even remember my own name. There was a girl, a child. She reminded me of you, darlin'." He stroked Rowan's head. "She was holding my grandmother's amulet, you know the one I gave you for your birthday. It was so bright. I remembered then. God, I remembered. And I had to... Oh, there was *something*. This great dark, monstrous... *something*. It wanted to hurt..." Beads of sweat had broken out on Finn's forehead. Again, he pulled Rowan and Luke close.

"Perhaps you should rest, dear," Grandma murmured.

"It's okay, Dad,'" said Luke. "It's okay."

But Finn went on.

"An' there was this dark tunnel, leading down, down into... I knew if I passed through I would forget all the terrible cold and sorrow of the place. Oh, I wanted to go. I wanted to go down, to sleep, to forget. But... but I heard this voice. 'Daddy, Daddy,' you were saying. 'Daddy, come on,' just as simple as anything, Rowan. 'Daddy, come on.' Like it was a Sunday morning, and you were wanting to go for a walk in the park." He laughed. "And I reached out... ah, it was a struggle though, like my arm had turned cold an' heavy as solid ice. I reached out, and I felt your hand, soft and warm and tender, reaching out for me."

He looked up then and his face changed. He was staring at something beyond them.

"Oh my God," he whispered, voice failing.

Rowan turned, and there in the doorway was Mum.

"Oh my God, Lucy," he repeated and reached out towards her.

Rowan closed her eyes.

It was melting: the ache inside was melting away and she could feel the tears, at last, warm and sweet, running down her cheeks, and dropping, like soft, spring rain, into her open palms.